Twisted In Obsession

Sins and Obsession Duet

The Marchetti Family
Book 2

kelly Kelsey

Copyright © 2024 By Kelly Kelsey

All rights reserved.

No part of this book may be reproduced in any form or by any electronic or mechanical means, including information storage and retrieval systems, without written permission from the author, except for the use of brief quotations in a book review.

This is a work of fiction. Names, characters, places, and incidents are either the product of the author's imagination or are used fictitiously. Any resemblance to actual persons, living or dead, events, or locales is entirely coincidental.

Cover design by Crowe Abbey Covers

Editing by Ce-ce Cox of Outside Eyes Editing and Proofreading

Proofreading by Mich

❦ Created with Vellum

To all you good girls that just want a morally grey man that will burn down the world and never give up until he has you. Nico Marchetti is all that and more. You're welcome.

Trigger Warnings

Somnophilia
Violence
Dubious Consent
Gun Use
Morally Grey Man
Red Flags Everywhere

Playlist

- The Funeral – Band of Horses
- Poison & Wine – The Civil Wars
- Love The Way You Lie – Eminem, Rhianna
- I See Red – Everybody Loves an Outlaw
- Broken – Lifehouse
- Ordinary World – Aurora, Naimee Coleman
- Demons – Imagine Dragons
- Way down We Go – KALEO
- Play with Fire – Sam Tinnesz feat. Yacht Money
- Mine – Dan x Toxic Love
- Lose Control – Teddy Swims

Prologue

Nico

Two weeks later...

Loud sobbing to my left echoes around the cold, vast space, breaking the otherwise quiet of the church. The noise is so gut wrenching my chest cracks a little more. Tightening my arm around my mamma, I hold on to her grief wracked, trembling body, like my life depends on it. And it does. I will not let my mamma break further than she already has.

Though my papà was a monster of the worst kind, she loved him more than anything. Did he deserve that love? No. But it doesn't change the fact that he was her husband or that she worshipped the ground he walked on despite his many transgressions. Sure, I wanted my papà dead, but not like this. Not by the hands of my enemies.

kelly Kelsey

Two weeks ago, everything turned to shit. Not only did Ocean, my fucking woman, disappear without a trace, but the Bratva escalated their war with us and ruthlessly gunned down my papà and a couple of his men, in cold blood. And of all places, it was on the street, outside the salon I own. *Bellissima*. At the time, I was confused as to why he would be there, but I soon found out those reasons and it had everything to do with Ocean. My jaw clenches just thinking about what I found out.

Gio, the guard I had assigned to Ocean, had been knocked out cold during most of the chaos, but when he came around, he told me what he knew. That led me to Angelo, one of Papà's senior guards. After learning that his *Don* was dead and I would be the new head of the Marchetti *famiglia*, he sang like a fucking canary and told me *everything*.

My breathing picks up, anger shooting through me and my blood turning hot when I think about how *Ocean* deceived me all those months. Nonetheless, and despite her deception, I have to admit I'm somewhat proud of what she achieved in those months I had her. No other before her, and I will damn well make sure that no one after her will ever be able to betray me in that way again. That doesn't mean I don't still want her deceitful ass. That I will stop at nothing until I find my lying little *Tesoro*. I will burn the world to the ground, inch by little inch if that's what it takes. No matter what has happened or what is yet to come, she is mine. And when I finally get my hands back on her delicate little neck, she will realize exactly what being mine means.

"Nic," a soft feminine voice whispers from my right. Glancing down, I meet my sister's glossy, tear-filled eyes. Her lips tremble, worry all over her face as she jerks her head toward our mother. "Is she going to be okay?" she whispers shakily.

Squeezing my mamma closer to me, I inhale when a heartbreaking sob bursts from her. My gaze meets my sister's concerned one and I lean down, pressing a kiss to the top of Allegra's head, trying to comfort her in any way I can. "She will be," I murmur, my gaze dropping to where Dante holds my sister protectively, as if at any minute she could disappear. Guess he decided he has no fucks to give, now that my papà is no longer with us. His passive eyes lock on mine, but I don't miss the flash of relief in them. Dante believes that now my papà has passed and is no longer in charge of my sister's future, he can love her without restraint.

Unfortunately for him, I fear that won't be the case.

Exhaling a breath, I tear my gaze away from him, glancing over my shoulder to where the Romanos sit. All the families are here to pay their respects to the fallen *Don*. Papà was not only the head of the Marchetti *famiglia* but also the commission. I will now take over both positions, making me the most powerful man in the city.

Riccardo Romano stands beside his father, tense in his stance. His jaw clenches, murder burning in his eyes as he stares at something or *someone*. I don't have to follow his gaze to know who he is looking at, but I do anyway, finding exactly what I knew I would. My eyes land on my best friend and where he holds Allegra. My gaze flicks back to Riccardo and I know with everything inside me, he is going to be a big problem. Not just for Dante, but for me too. And I need to be prepared for that.

Father Michaels' voice trails off, signaling the end of the service and drawing my attention back to the front where my papà's coffin sits. If it were anyone else, we would now be heading outside to the cemetery to watch as he is lowered into the ground. That won't be happening today. Only the family and a couple of Papà's closest friends will be heading to a private service at our family crypt, located in the grounds of our

Hamptons estate. He will be laid to rest alongside his papà and mamma. It's the Marchetti family tradition and will also be my final resting place when the time comes.

"The Marchetti family would like to thank you all for coming today and for your understanding in their need to grieve privately. If you would all like to make your way outside, this concludes today's service." Father Michaels recites the words I asked him to say to our guests. We don't need to be stared at or scrutinized like animals in a zoo any longer. Especially Mamma.

Today has been traumatic enough for her as it is. I refuse to let her be put on display in her grief, while these people pass on their fake condolences and faux concern. At a guess, I would say almost everyone here today is glad to see Lorenzo Marchetti gone. He was ruthless in his ways. Had become unhinged, and unpredictable, which is why our men began to turn on us in favor of our enemies. It was time for change and with Papà gone, I can start a new, stronger, better order. They don't know it and I would never admit to it, but the Bratva did me a favor. I wanted him gone. I just assumed at some point I would do it myself.

"Are you ready, Nic?" Dante asks, breaking me from my thoughts.

Glancing around the church, I notice that it's now empty apart from me, Mamma, Allegra, Dante, Papà's consigliere Giuseppe, his wife Giulia, and the many guards I have stationed around the old church. "Yes. I just want to thank Father Michaels and make sure everything is in place to have Papà transported to the crypt. Have the cars brought around. We will leave shortly." Nodding, he releases my sister, making his way to the back of the building where he will pass on my orders to the necessary people.

"What time are you planning on doing the private service?"

Giuseppe asks, looking older than I have ever seen him. The death of Papà has certainly taken a toll on him.

Sliding my free hand in my pants pocket, I meet his eyes. "Around four p.m. You're more than welcome to join us. I know he would want you there," I tell him honestly.

He dips his chin. "I will be there." His voice is weary, thick with emotion.

"I will let the guards know to expect you." He gives me a curt nod before taking his wife's hand and walking down the aisle.

Glancing at Mamma, I frown when I find her staring off into space. Her blue eyes, that are usually so filled with life, are now vacant and lost. I look at my sister as she steps toward Mamma, taking her free hand and squeezing gently. My chest constricts, a lump building in my throat. "Come on. Let's say goodbye to Father Michaels and get you home."

We move toward where the solemn looking priest stands. I ask him the questions I need to, and he gives me the answers I want, confirming that Papà is set to be transported back to our family home within the next thirty minutes. Not trusting the Bratva not to issue another attack, I made sure to have an armed guard surrounding him on his final journey. Not that he deserves it, but my mamma doesn't need further stress, so I did it for her.

With everything arranged, I lead my mamma and sister out to the awaiting vehicles. Determination heats my veins when I notice all the soldiers watching me and waiting for direction from their new leader. Nodding, I slide into the car next to Mamma, my mind going to what comes next.

Taking over as Don.

Finding Ocean.

Or, if I am going by my recent discovery and her real name.

kelly Kelsey

Emilee Ocean Caldwell.
Whoever she is, whatever her fucking name.
She is still mine.
And I won't stop until I find her.

Chapter 1

Ocean

One year later...

"Lyra, I don't want any more money from you. You pay me enough as it is." Patty rolls her eyes, exhaling loudly in exasperation. We have had this conversation a couple times now and it's always the same outcome.

I chuckle, shaking my head. No matter how much I insist on increasing what I pay her for the room I rent in her house, she always shuts me down. I lucked out when I met her six months ago and I know with absolute certainty that I would not have made it this far had Patty not come into my life.

After leaving New York, I ended up in Dale City, just outside Washington – though that only lasted a couple of months. Not only could I not shake the feeling of being watched – though in the end I think it was just my paranoia – but after learning some very unexpected news, Washington was not far enough away from New York, Nico and his father. I only had one option, so I moved on, eventually ending up in Charleston and meeting my saving grace. Patty.

I didn't need to work, what with my savings from dancing at The Executive Club and the substantial amount of money Lorenzo had given me, so I wasn't pinned down by a job and it was easy enough to move on. Though at the time, I felt dirty taking that bastard's money, it has certainly made things easier. Especially when I found out I was pregnant.

Yes, pregnant.

Not three weeks after running from New York, I got sick. I thought it was from the stress of everything that had happened, but when I missed my period, deep down I knew it was more. Within the hour, I was at the closest drug store purchasing a pregnancy test which subsequently came back as I knew it would – Positive.

Those two pink lines stared back at me almost mockingly. Reminding me that I may have run away from Nico, but a part of him was growing inside of me and no matter how far I ran, or where I ended up, I would never get a chance to forget the man that turned my life upside down.

The irony of being pregnant wasn't lost on me. It was cliché really. The side piece, carrying his baby. My head was telling me to find the nearest clinic and have it taken care of. But my heart? My heart whispered words of comfort and that everything would be okay. That my baby was meant to be and no matter what I learned about Nico, or what went down between us, I couldn't get rid of the innocent life growing inside me. I would love this baby more than anything in the world. My little piece of heaven, who I would protect with my life. Even when I wanted to give up, succumb to the darkness, I would survive and live for my baby. There was no other way.

I glance down at the little bundle cradled in my arms, a smile curving my lips as pure adoration bursts inside me.

Romeo, my four-month-old son, my world. I know with everything inside me that I made the right choice. I can't imagine my life without him. His little fingers grip my pinkie and I smile wider. My heart expands with the feelings of absolute love I have for him. It is so profound it smothers me. He is without a doubt my life. And I know that all I have been through led me to this moment. To him. I was made to be his mom.

Glancing up at Patty, I remember I didn't respond to her little outburst. Pinning her with a look, I sigh. "I don't want you to think that I'm taking advantage of you. I am still paying the same rate as when I first got here and that was before I gave birth to Romeo. I am using extra electricity and water now that I have him."

She grumbles something under her breath, waving me off. "Child, I won't take any more money from you. I knew you were pregnant when I offered you a place to stay. Now enough about it, I don't want to hear you mention it again." Her eyes light up when they drop to Romeo. "Now hand me my boy. I haven't had any cuddles today."

I roll my eyes, handing him off to her. Patty is in her late fifties with no children of her own. She lost her husband three years ago and has been on her own ever since. I met her while heavily pregnant, looking for a job. I ended up in Patty's, the diner she owns, and though she was unsure about giving me a job when I was not far off from giving birth, and without me having the proper paperwork, I managed to convince her. She thinks my name is Lyra, pays me in cash, doesn't ask questions. If I am being honest, I know the only reason she took me on is because she took pity on me when I lied and told her that I'm on the run from an abusive ex-boyfriend. And though I wish I could tell her the truth, I can't, so that is how it will stay. It's safer that way. I am not naïve enough to think that Nico wouldn't have the resources to find me if he wanted. Which is why I don't use any of my real documents. I can't leave a paper trail or anything that would risk him finding me... *us*. Panic surges through me just thinking about it, but I shake it away quickly.

I had only been waitressing at the diner for a couple days, when Patty found out that I was living in a nearby motel. It didn't take her long to talk me into renting out her guest room. It was cheaper and safer than where I was staying. I know I won't be with Patty forever, but for right now it works. For both of us.

"Do you want me to cover Tina's shift tonight?" I ask, as I watch her coo over my son.

She shakes her head. "No, I already got it covered. Sheila's gonna stay and lock up."

My eyes narrow in on her. "I've got to go back sometime."

Her head snaps up, gaze landing on me. "And you will. In fact, why don't you start back at your normal shift Saturday." She grins. "Harrison has been asking after you. I know he would like to see you."

I blush at the mention of Harrison. Though I have no interest in men after everything with Nico, the construction worker with the kind and gentle brown eyes is the kind of man I always imagined myself ending up with when I ran from my family. An easy, uncomplicated, salt of the earth, blue collared man. Harrison understands my situation and knows that I'm not ready for anything serious, right now, though it hasn't stopped him patiently pursuing me. Even after I gave birth to Romeo, he came to visit me in the hospital, loaded with gifts for me and my son. He has also visited me here, at home. I would like to believe he did that of his own accord, but something tells me Patty has everything to do with him coming here. I know she is pushing for us to happen. And though he dotes on both me and my son, I just...

"I'm not ready to date." I tell her, shaking my head.

She shoots me a knowing look. "So you keep saying. I don't know the full story, but from what you have told me, Romeo's dad is terrifying enough that you had to run from him. Harrison is just the type of good man you need after being with someone like that. Sweet. Gentle. Patient. Caring. Someone that will take care of both of you. Give him a chance."

I sigh, knowing full well there is no point arguing with her. Patty will not let this go and, I can begrudgingly admit, everything she says about him is exactly who he is. Harrison is all those things and more. And maybe it is time to move on. Make the life I always planned on living before Nico happened.

My stomach twists when I think about the man who stole my heart before breaking it into a million pieces. Shattering it in a way that it will never be whole again, no matter whether it's Harrison or another good man that comes into my life next. I run a hand through my hair, exhaling tiredly.

I know what I should do.

I also know I'm just not ready.

Chapter 2

Nico

"Did you find anything?" I bark at Tony, an FBI agent on my payroll. I am paying him a shit ton of money to find Ocean or Emilee or whatever the fuck name she goes by now. So far, he has come up empty. My jaw clenches, impatience surging through me, because I know he isn't here to give me the answers I want.

Confirming what I already know, he shakes his head. "Not yet. The bus she boarded out of the city took her to Washington and after that... nothing. She is a ghost. She is used to running Nico, knows how to hide. I am doing all that I can, and have several men working on it, but it's like looking for a needle in a haystack. Don't be surprised if you never find her," he says nonchalantly, as if he is talking about some random girl. She isn't. Not even close. And it's about time he realizes it.

My eye twitches, fists flex. Without even thinking about what I am doing, I am up, out of my chair, my hand wrapping around his neck before I can stop myself. I lean in, so close my nose almost touches his. His face turns red, and I watch as beads of sweat form on his forehead. "I don't care if it takes you *years* or if you have to search every inch of this god damn country.

The fucking planet. You will find her. I want her back, so you better fucking find her Tony. You won't like the consequences if you let me down." I growl in his face.

His eyes bulge in shock and I let him go, pushing him away. He sucks in a breath when his hands come up to his neck, rubbing the area I just held. His gaze comes to mine. Though he tries to hide it, I see the fear staring back at me. He knows I'm not playing. "Is that a threat, Nico?" he splutters out.

I drop back down in my chair. "No. It's a fucking promise. Now get your ass out of my office and stay out of my club until you find my girl." I expect him to do just that, but the fucker must have a death wish because he doesn't let it go.

"You can't threaten me, Nico. You may have power in this city, but I am an FBI agent. One that knows about many of the skeletons in your closet. One word from me and I can have you locked up within the hour," he shouts, slamming his meaty fist down on my desk.

My eyes narrow in on the brave – or stupid – asshole. A smirk curves my lips, my brow cocking arrogantly. "And I doubt your bosses would be happy to know that you are taking huge sums of money from a Marchetti, Tony. Or the other *many* transgressions you have against you. I may have skeletons in my closet, but I don't hide who I am. I don't pretend to be a good man. You, though? You play both sides of the coin, pretending to be an upstanding man, who abides by the law, when you are anything but." His face pales and I know I have him. I grin triumphantly. "Now go and do the job I am paying you for. You have had nearly a year to get me something, to find her, and have so far come up with nothing. I am giving you a week to get me the information I want. If you fail, you better pray that I never see your face again."

His mouth drops open, and he stares at me like I've lost my mind. Maybe I have. Ever since Papà's funeral over a year ago, it's been nothing but shit after shit. If it's not the war with the Bratva, it's the Romanos and the pressure they are trying to put on me regarding the arrangement with my sister. Papà went ahead and signed the contract without me knowing. Though he is dead, the Romanos insist that the agreement remain. I have been working around the clock, trying to find a way out of it for Allegra, but keep coming up empty. The Romanos want their wedding, and so far all I have managed to do is convince them to push it back until she is twenty. I will find a way out for her. Of course, I will. I just need more time.

"I can't promise anything, Nico." He stands, his voice solemn as he buttons up his suit jacket.

"You can and you will. Somebody, somewhere, knows something. You are not looking hard enough. Have a man in every state, every town for all I care, with their eyes fucking open. I want the girl back." My tone is threatening, leaving no room for argument.

He huffs out a laugh, shaking his head. He is trying to act brave again. Act being the operative word. "What is it about this one? Surely, you can have any woman you want in this city. Pick one of them. Hell, what about your ex-fiancée. She is fucking hot." He whistles low, making my blood boil. Not because I'm jealous, but because the mention of Gianna makes me see red. She is the reason for Ocean running – well her and my papà.

I was informed about exactly what Papà told Ocean that day and how he had great pleasure in telling her all about my little fiancée. Truth is, I would have gone through with the wedding had Papà still been here. I had a duty to the *famiglia,* one I would have upheld. I also had no plans of letting Ocean go and would have kept her forever. Oblivious and in the dark about everything. It was a shitty thing of me to do, but I never pretended to be a saint. The moment I got in her virgin cunt, she was mine. And she will be mine forever. This little disap-

Chapter 5

Ocean

"Two dates in a week. I must be doing something right." Harrison says, beaming at me from across the table.

He's brought me to a restaurant just outside of town. He said it's his favorite place to eat and wanted me to experience it for myself. He is considerate and thoughtful like that. Though I am still hesitant about this whole dating thing, I like Harrison. I would even go as far as saying that I feel comfortable with him. He doesn't set my pulse racing or set my whole body on fire like Nico used to, but maybe that's a good thing. After all, Nico may have had that effect on me, but look how it ended. Shaking all thoughts of the devil away, I focus on Harrison.

"You are," I agree, a big smile curving my lips. "It must be the nice restaurants you keep bringing me to and all this delicious food."

He laughs, shaking his head. He sobers, his eyes turning serious. My heart flutters in my chest when he reaches across the table, taking my hand in his. He gives me a gentle squeeze, comforting me as if he is afraid I might run when he speaks his next words. "I know you're not ready for anything serious, Lyra, but…" noticing me stiffen, he trails off but doesn't let me go. He sucks in a breath, his kind eyes lock on mine, imploring me just to hear him out. To not bolt. "I know you have your reservations, that you're not ready for anything serious. But I really like you. I think we could be good together." My pulse kicks up a notch and I shift in my seat, growing uncomfortable with where this conversation is going. I know what comes next and I'm not sure whether it's what I want – yet. He said it himself, that I am not ready, so why is he pushing this? Why can't he just let things happen slowly, organically. He must spot my panic because he grimaces, as if he knows he said too much. His next words confirm it. "I'm sorry. I shouldn't have said that. I just couldn't let another minute go by without telling you how I feel."

I relax a little, only to feel guilty when his face falls at my resistance. Gripping his hand, I force a soft smile. I don't want to lead him on, but I should open myself up to him more. Wanting to give him something, *anything,* because he is a good person and has respected my boundaries, I blurt my next words before I can stop myself. "Look Harrison, I may not be one hundred percent ready but, if it helps, I like where this is going. I just want to take it slow. See what happens. Is that okay with you?" I say timidly.

His whole face lights up like a firework at my words and, though I'm hesitant about everything, I know telling him that was the right thing to do. Harrison deserves happiness and if me saying a couple of words gives him that, then so be it. He nods. "That's perfectly okay with me. And I promise not to push you. I am happy with whatever you have to give me right now. Just know that when you are ready for more, I will be waiting. I want to take care of you and Romeo, be the man you need. I want you to know that I cherish you both. A lot," he adds sincerely.

My heart squeezes at the honesty in his voice. He really means everything he says. Now if I could only forget about and get over Nico, that would be fantastic. I know Harrison is everything I need in a man. Dependable. Good. Loyal. *Not* a mafia heir. Though it should be easy to give myself to the man in front of me, it's just not as simple as that. The heart wants what it wants, and currently mine is still stuck on the dark, dangerous, blue-eyed man that is bad for me and my health. I can never regret Nico because then I wouldn't have Romeo, but I wish with everything in me I could erase him from my heart, head and soul. Things would be so much easier that way.

Pushing thoughts of the past aside, I lock eyes with Harrison. He deserves my attention more than Nico ever will. "Oh, I forgot to tell you. I think I found a dance studio. It's around twenty minutes from Patty's," the excitement is evident in my voice. "Martha, the lady who owns it, is a retired ballet dancer. I showed her what I could do and though I was a little rusty, she agreed that in exchange for teaching one of the beginners' classes a week, I could use the studio to practice whenever I want." I grin when I recall my meeting earlier. I've been wanting to get back to dance for a while now. Not only to get back into shape but to help with my mental health. Dancing is my therapy. I need it to survive.

Harrison smiles. "That's great. I will have to come and watch you sometime." I blush, only for my face to fall when memories of how Nico watched me resurface. A shudder runs through my body, the whole scene of how he fucked me on the bar against the mirror at my old studio, assaulting my head on loop. "Everything okay?" My gaze snaps up to a concerned looking Harrison. Frowning, he studies my face. For what, I'm not sure.

I shake my head, ridding myself of the thoughts and forcing a smile. "Yeah. I'm just nervous, I guess. I haven't danced for over a year now."

He squeezes my hand. "I'm sure you will be great. Even if

you think you've forgotten how to do something, I doubt you have. Don't they say that muscle memory kicks in and it all comes back to you?"

"Apparently so," I agree.

He grins. "You're strong Lyra. You can do anything you set your mind to. I know it." His belief in me warms my insides. Sighing, I lean back in my chair. Harrison's confidence in me knows no bounds. Now if I could only believe in him and give him what he deserves.

***

"Do you think Patty will be awake?" Harrison whispers, as we quietly pad down the darkened hallway toward the living room. Harrison ended up taking me to a park, where we sat on the hood of his truck and talked for a couple hours. It is nearly midnight by the time we get back to Patty's. I was going to end our date at the door but after giving myself a pep talk on the ride home, I decided to take the plunge and invite him in for a hot drink and maybe a movie. By the way his face lit up and his eyes twinkled, he was happy with my offer.

"I don't think so. All the lights are off and so is the television. It's late, so I guess she went to bed," I respond quietly.

Moving into the living room, I flick the light switch on the wall. Blinking, I take in my surroundings and freeze. My heart drops, all the air leaving my lungs at the scene playing out in front of me. I blink, then blink again just to make sure this is real and not some sick nightmare, but no matter how much I try to shake the vision, it doesn't disappear. It's real. So fucking real, my body shakes and I think I might pass out.

He stands there like an ominous presence, sucking all the air from the room. The devil himself.

Nico.

Nico Marchetti, leaning casually against the wall of Patty's living room like he owns the place. And not just him.

Dante.

Leo.

And several other men I have never seen before. I swallow, panic flooding my body as I take it all in. Nico smirks, though his eyes are cold, dead and detached. I shift my gaze to Dante, who watches me with indifference and a hint of annoyance. I jerk my head to Leo. Leo, my *friend,* who is hovering over Patty like the Grim Reaper waiting for his orders.

Despite not wanting to look, my eyes drop to Patty. The woman who has been my rock since I met her, has her mouth taped shut and her wrists bound. Guilt heats my veins when I see the look of pure fear in her eyes and, though it's selfish, I can't focus on that right now. There is only one thing going through my mind.

Where is Romeo?

Patty must see the silent question in my eyes because she subtly jerks her head in the direction of the bedroom we occupy. I force my body to relax, though I feel anything but. It's pointless though. Because when my gaze shifts back to Nico, I turn into a terrified statue at the look I find on his face. His eyes flick from me to the man behind me, then down. I didn't think it was possible, but his eyes darken to almost black when they lock on where Harrison is holding my hand. My pulse kicks up and I think I stop breathing altogether.

"What the fuck? Who the hell are you?" Harrison shouts, making me jump, and pulling me in closer to him as if he can protect me. He can't. Not from the predator staring us both down with murderous intent in his now dark orbs.

Nico's eye twitches, his jaw clenching and I know it is taking everything in him to keep his cool right now. Without his gaze leaving mine, he jerks his head. In the next second

Harrison is ripped away from me. He shouts, screams, and then it's muffled. I glance over my shoulder to find a hand slapped over his mouth and his face beet red.

"Don't look at him, *Tesoro*. Eyes on me if you want him to live," Nico hisses. Hearing his voice for the first time in over a year does something to me and my eyes immediately snap to him. From the feral look on his face, he isn't messing around.

"Nico, please," I choke out, finally finding my voice.

He holds a hand up, cutting me off and stopping me from saying anything else. "We have been waiting for you, *Ocean*." I don't miss the way he says my name. Condescendingly. Mockingly. "And I don't like to be kept waiting."

I flinch. By the contempt and derision in his tone, he knows everything. Everything about who I am. His father must have told him. Fuck. Swallowing, my eyes rake over every inch of him. As much as I don't want to be affected by his presence, I can't help it. It's like he has a direct line to my pussy. Like he trained my body to react this way every time I see him. And maybe that was exactly what he did, all those times we had sex. I don't know. I just know my reaction to seeing him again is not normal and it's the only explanation considering I hate him.

"Ocean?" he drawls, and my eyes close at the feelings of unwanted desire running through my body. I don't want to be that girl, the one whose body betrays her, and she succumbs easily to the man that betrayed her. But right now, I understand how it happens. I have no control over my body or the feelings he is eliciting in me. A throb starts between my thighs. I want to rub my legs together; ease the ache inside me. But if I do, he will know exactly what he does to me. Fuck. Who am I kidding. He is a perceptive motherfucker and can read my body like a book. He knows exactly what he is doing to me.

Nico pushes off the wall, closing the distance between us in only a couple of short strides. The manic look in his eyes makes me want to run, but I stay frozen to the spot. He smirks as if he knows exactly what is going through my mind right now.

Reaching up, he runs a finger down my cheek. I want to squirm, push him away, but I stay put. I don't think I even breathe as his finger draws circles on my heated flesh. Toying with me. Playing with me. It's all a mind fuck. I hate it. Nico leans in, my eyes close when his hot breath hits my ear. "Who has been a naughty girl then," he whispers, the threat in his voice making me stiffen. He pulls back to look at me, his next words soft despite the tension radiating from him. "I've missed you, *Tesoro*."

My mouth parts. I stare at him in disbelief, while he just watches me with a manic look in his eyes, but there is also a hint of... relief?

"Don't fucking touch her." Harrison growls out, snapping me out of my stare off. I guess his mouth is no longer covered if he can talk. I cringe, silently begging him to shut up. Though I appreciate his attempts at bravery, he doesn't know who he is provoking.

Nico's cold gaze lands on him. Zoning in like the predator he is. One that has just caught his prey. Panic consumes me, zinging through my body like a live wire. I can't let Harrison get hurt. He doesn't deserve any of Nico's wrath.

"Nico don't," I cry out, but it's no use.

Ignoring me, he steps around me. Discreetly, I shift on my feet so I can have a view of what is about to happen. I watch in horror as Nico circles Harrison - and the man that is restraining him – with murder in his eyes.

"Who the fuck are you?" Nico snarls, his voice low, threatening.

Not wanting to witness anymore of this exchange, I turn away like the coward I am. My eyes stay locked on the wall but when I see movement out of my peripheral, I shift my gaze to

Leo. He stares back at me, concern, pity and apology in his gaze. I almost smile, wanting to ease his worry, but then I remember who he is loyal to. Who he came here with. He is part of this and letting it all happen. In fact, he is top of my shit list as he is the one restraining Patty.

"I'm her date. Who are you?" Harrison finally responds, making me break my gaze from Leo. I focus back on the wall. Harrison is trying to sound confident, but I hear the tremble in his voice.

Nico laughs but there's no humor to it. It's a cruel sound that sends a shiver down my spine. "Me?" he muses, and I can't help but glance at them. Nico still circles him, toying with him. A game of cat and mouse. Predator and prey. It's clear to everyone in this room which one Nico is. "I'm your worst nightmare, *kid*," he sneers. "The man that owns the girl you dared to take on a *date*. You may be with her here now, but make no mistake, she is *mine*," he seethes, and I jolt as fear takes hold of me. "And I swear on every single cent I have, that I will end your miserable life if your cock has been anywhere near *my* pussy." My heart rate spikes to an unnatural speed, spine jerking straight at the threat in Nico's voice. Pure terror slithers in my veins and I wish I could put a stop to this nightmare.

"Wh-what?" Harrison stutters out, his eyes bulging in shock. I feel so guilty that I dragged him into this mess. I knew I shouldn't have gotten into anything with him. Not that I anticipated this outcome, but still.

Nico comes to stand in front of me. Pinching my chin between thumb and forefinger, he lifts until my gaze locks on his. "Did you let him touch what is mine, *Tesoro*?" His voice is soft, a caress at odds with the anger rolling off him. I shake my head as much as I can with him gripping me. It's the truth. We haven't so much as kissed. And when Harrisons lips did touch mine it all happened so fast, I doubt it could even be called a kiss.

Nico's eyes me with something I can't quite decipher. His mouth parts and just when he is about to respond, a cry sounds, breaking the otherwise quiet of the house and shattering my world even more. Of all the things that could happen right now, this is the worst outcome. I don't know how I expected things to go tonight, but this was definitely not it. I would have told Nico about Romeo, of course I would have, but not like this. I was hoping I could at least get Harrison out of danger first and then maybe talk like reasonable, sensible adults. Jesus. Who am I kidding. Nico is the least rational person I know.

Nico's head snaps up, ears straining toward the noise and brows furrowing in confusion. My heart pounds in my chest. I want to cry. I want to take my son and run far away. This can't be happening. Please, no. Not my baby.

His eyes zone in on the hallway and in the direction of the bedroom, where Romeo cries. Turning, his cold, deadly gaze locks on mine. A range of emotions flash in those pale blue orbs, but I don't have time to make sense of them because my body locks up with pure dread.

He tsks. "Does that belong to you, *Tesoro?*" My head lowers. A tear leaks down my cheek. I work to keep my mouth clamped shut as if I can keep all my secrets locked inside. Squeezing my chin almost painfully, he gives me no choice but to look at him. "If I find out you have been hiding my own flesh and blood..." he trails off, jaw clenching and not finishing that sentence. "Dante, go and get the baby."

Chapter 6

Nico

"No," Ocean cries out, shooting forward and trying to grasp at Dante. Grabbing her arms, I pull her into me, restraining her arms and holding her tight as I wait for my best friend to come back. I know, even without seeing the baby, that it's mine. Don't ask me how, I just do. Maybe it was Ocean's reaction when the baby cried. She knew she was fucked. All the blood drained from her face, her eyes turning frantic as she waited for me to react to the crying.

My pulse beats in my ears, so loud, it nearly drowns out the noise of Ocean's sobbing. Muffled screams have my attention shifting to the gray-haired lady tied to a chair. She wriggles from side to side, pulling at her restraints, trying to break free. It's no use. She won't get out of them. My head tilts and I study her. I've got to give the woman credit, she has some fight in her and right now, she is trying to protect Ocean and the child... my child?

Turning away from her, I grip Ocean tighter. My whole body throbs in anticipation, waiting for Dante to return with the baby. Seconds feel like hours but in reality, it's only a couple of minutes before he is striding back into the room with a small bundle in his arms. A blue blanket covers him, but the tight lipped, shocked look on Dante's face confirms what I already know.

"Please, Nico," Ocean sobs, struggling in my arms. Out of my peripheral, I spot the motherfucker who clearly has a death wish, fighting with Marco and trying to move closer to us. With one threatening look in his direction, I smirk when he pales and freezes on the spot. This kid needs to realize he is well out of his league before he gets himself killed over someone - or two people if I am being specific - who doesn't belong to him.

Swallowing, his voice wobbles when he mumbles, "Don't hurt them."

I search his face, biting back a snort. Like the old lady, I've got to give it to the asshole; he is trying to be brave. Though he is fighting a losing battle - and he knows it - he still wants to be the hero. To be *my* girl's hero. Fucker's lucky I haven't slit his throat yet. "I suggest you keep your mouth shut. I'm about three seconds away from making sure you can never say another word again." He turns an unusual shade of white, his mouth clamping shut and stepping closer into Marco as if my soldier will help him. He won't. "Good boy." I mock before turning my attention back to Ocean. Dropping my lips to her ear, I say. "Who has been a naughty girl? Hmm?" Looking at Dante, I jerk my head, signaling him to come closer.

"Please, Nico," Ocean whispers, her voice catching, body shaking in my arms. I like when she begs. But under very different circumstances.

Dante comes to a stop in front of us, his face impassive. He stares down at the child in his arms and shifting closer, I do the same. My breath catches in my throat at what I find. Eyes the same shade as mine stare back at me. My gaze shifts up, landing on the tufts of dark hair on his small head. There is no mistaking who his father is. He is a perfect replica of me. My jaw clenches, agony ripping through me. I have a fucking son and I didn't even know. My lying, deceitful little *Tesoro* ran away from me, taking *my* son with her. She kept him hidden and there is no doubt in my mind that if I had not found her, she would have kept him from me for the rest of my life.

Disdain for what she has done slithers through me and in this moment, I hate her. Don't want to be near her. I shove her away from me. She stumbles, her palms landing on the wall as she steadies herself. My eyes shift back to the baby and without another thought I take him out of Dante's arms. Someone sobs almost hysterically. I know without looking its Ocean. Fuck her. She had my son and never thought to even try to contact me.

"Nico," her choked, raspy voice goes straight to my cock, but I ignore it. Now is not the time. I hate her. *We* hate her. I amend, letting my dick know the deal and wanting him on board.

"Don't," I warn, letting my gaze finally shift to her. "I don't need to ask, but I will anyway. Is he mine?"

A tremor wracks her body, but she nods. "Yes," she responds so quietly, I almost miss it.

I tsk. "Oh, what a tangled web you have woven, *Tesoro*. These people know you as Lyra, I knew you as Ocean. But your real name is Emilee. You lie. To everyone. Can't even be honest about your name." She shakes her head, slapping a palm over her mouth as if that will stop me. It won't. "Then you run, taking my son with you. Not only that, but you also dare to date another man, bring him around *my* son when I never even had the chance to meet my own flesh and blood." I shake my head, venom lacing every word out of my mouth. "Then you bring this pathetic asshole back here to give him what's mine." My anger rises to an unhealthy level. I am fucking raging. I don't know which of her transgressions is the worst. It should probably be hiding my son, but right now I can't get past the fact she went out with the trembling, wide eyed idiot behind me.

"I already told you. Harri—"

I cut her off, shifting my son in my arms. "Don't say his name. If you even look at him right now, you will sign his death warrant." I seethe, making her back up against the wall. "Or maybe he signed it himself? Hmm? I should kill him for touching you. Slit his throat and fuck you in his blood, so the last image he has before he eventually dies is me claiming what's mine? Maybe then wherever he ends up in the afterlife, he will think twice about touching things that don't belong to him." The sound of liquid hitting the wood floor lets me know my words have had their desired effect. The motherfucker has pissed himself. I glance at him, smirking when I see his wet jeans. My lip curls up in disgust. "Get him out of here, Marco.

"Nico, stop." Ocean cries harder, a pleading look in her eyes. "Don't hurt him. If you leave them alone, I will do as you say. I won't fight you. I will come back to New York."

A sardonic chuckle leaves me. "You don't have a choice in what happens or where I take you, *Tesoro*. Fight me if you want. You know your anger and defiance gets my dick hard."

She gasps as if that's the worst thing I have said this evening. "Just let them go. Patty, she hasn't done anything wrong. Neither has..." my good girl has taken note of my warning and stops herself saying his name.

Disturbance to my right has my gaze landing on where Leo holds the restrained older woman. Bless her, and the death looks she is shooting me even though she is terrified. But at least she isn't pissing herself like the fucker behind me. "Dante, go pack Ocean's and..." I trail off, frowning when I remember I don't even know my son's name. Glaring at his mom, I demand. "What is his name?"

She swallows, shifting on her feet and murmuring out a soft, "Romeo."

I cock my head when I hear his name and study her face. Hmm. Though she kept him from me, she chose to give him an Italian name. So, she was thinking about me when she was betraying me? Hmm. Interesting.

"Go pack their things and meet me back at the SUV." I say all this without moving my stare from Ocean. "Marco, Leo, Enzo. Please explain to Patty and *him* what will happen if they say a word about this to anyone." I order. Footsteps sound in the small space as everyone heeds my commands. I glance down at my son, my chest tightening with something I didn't think I was capable of. Love. I run a finger down his soft cheek, smiling when his eyes close shut. Forgetting where I am for a minute, and the situation, I clear my throat, before looking at his mamma. She watches us with a whole range of emotions flickering in her ocean blue eyes. Shock. Disbelief. Awe. Regret. Fear. Guilt. Resignation. Ocean has always been expressive; she could never hide her feelings from me. I may have been away from her for over a year, but I can still read her like an open book. I almost want to soften toward her, go easy on her, but my head demands I punish her for her betrayal. She needs to understand that what she did is unacceptable and going forward I will never tolerate something like this again. Clearing my throat, she snaps from her trance. "Let's go," I growl.

She shakes her head, staying rooted to her spot and angering me further. "I want to say goodbye to them."

I chuckle, almost proud that she thinks she can make demands. "Feel free to say your goodbyes to her." I jerk my head to the woman I now know is called Patty. "But you will not go near him unless you want his blood on your hands. I mean it, Ocean. Try me."

Her flawless skin loses all its color. She sucks in a breath, nodding her acquiesce and I'm almost disappointed that she gave in so easily. Where's that fire she once possessed? It may have disappeared, but I am going to make it my mission to bring it back. After all, it is what drew me to her in the first place.

But first she will be punished for her transgressions. This isn't going to be easy for either of us, but it will be worse for her.

I will punish her for her sins.

Make her pay for hiding my son, for thinking that she could ever run from me.

And I'm going to enjoy every second of it.

Chapter 7

Ocean

I stare down at Romeo bundled securely in my arms. We are on a private jet, and I sit like a statue in the buttery leather seat. Because I don't want to look at Nico, or anyone else for that matter, I keep my attention on my son and can't even appreciate the luxurious interior of the plane.

After saying a very teary goodbye to Patty, Dante loaded up what I assumed were bags of my and Romeo's belongings before we were whisked away from the only life my son had known - one that had been mine for the last year - in a blacked-out SUV. Twenty minutes later we arrived at a private airfield, where we were escorted by Nico and his men onto a flashy jet. It was only then, once boarded with nowhere to run, Nico decided to hand me back Romeo. It was only once he had handed him back that I could release the breath I was holding and some of the tension in my body.

From the moment he held our son in his arms, my emotions have been all over the place. It's a sight I thought I would never see and though it was under less-than-ideal circumstances, there was no feeling to describe what I felt, finally seeing them together.

"Is he going to be okay like that?" I startle at the sound of Nico's voice, glancing up to find him glaring at me from across the aisle.

"What?" I mumble.

"With you holding him? Would it not be better if we strapped him in his car seat?"

Unable to look at his beautiful face any longer, I drop my gaze back to our sleeping son. "He will be fine with me holding him," I insist.

"Hmm," is the response I get, and I want to ask what it is supposed to mean, but I refrain.

"Everything is loaded. Shall I tell Hansen that we are ready for take-off?" The voice I know as Dante's asks from his position in the plane.

"Yes. The sooner we get back the better," Nico replies ominously.

There is something underlying his words, laced with a tone that I don't like. I have a feeling that whatever comes next is not going to be good. No doubt he feels betrayed, and even more so now that he knows about our son.

"Where are we going?" I ask through a tight throat, my body full of anxiety.

"I am taking *my* son home. Where he belongs. But don't worry, you will be dealt with accordingly, *Tesoro*." The threat is clear, making my spine snap straight. My apprehension increases and I wish I had never asked. But fuck this. He doesn't get to do this to me. Not after all he kept from me. His engagement. Him being Mafia.

Lifting my chin, I muster all the strength and confidence I can find in my body right now. It's not a lot, but it will do. Pinning him with a glare, I hiss. "Fuck you Nico. You're engaged. You made me your side piece without me even knowing. If that is not bad enough, you forgot to mention that you're in the Mafia."

He smirks at my outburst, nonchalantly running a thumb across his full bottom lip. I want to hit him in his stupid, arrogant face. "Ah, there's that defiance I love so much. Keep it up baby, you know it gets my cock hard." He reaches down, gripping his long, thick length as if to prove his point. My thighs clench, as I watch him palm himself through his pants. And visions of him fucking me, of just how good he felt inside me filter my brain, but I shake them away before they can fully form. "Hmm, I might take you to the bedroom and show you just what it does to me."

My eyes snap up to his. I glower. "No. You're not touching me."

He laughs but it's humorless. "Again, you have no choice in the matter. I will fucking touch what's mine when and as I please."

"Touching me without my permission? That's called rape, Nico. I didn't take you for a rapist." I know I should stop provoking him, but I can't stop.

His eyes glimmer, a sadistic smirk curving his lips. "Call it what you like, *Tesoro*. I will touch you when I please and you will like it. And what's more, you will fucking thank me for it."

My body shakes with the force of my anger, tears filling my eyes. "I hate you."

He grins. "Good. Your hate is what will get you through this and make you stronger in the process, *Emilee*." The taunting way he says my birth name sends a shiver up my spine.

"Don't call me that," I snap.

"It's your name, yes? I have to give it to you, Tesoro, you did well to hide that from me. Not even my PI found out who you were when I had him look into you. It's impressive really. You covered your tracks well. This time included. It took me a year to find you even with all the resources I had at my disposal."

"How did you find me?" my lips wobble with the question.

He grins triumphantly. "The how doesn't matter. I told you before, I would always find you. Told you that you could never hide from me. I wish you had listened. You would have saved us all this inconvenience and I wouldn't have missed my son being brought into the world." The accusation in his tone makes me recoil. I know I should not engage with him right now, but I can't help but taunt him further. After all, he has uprooted my life.

"I managed to hide for a year." I shoot back, ignoring everything else he is saying.

He watches me for a long beat, his blue eyes flickering with malice. "Yes. You did. But I found you in the end, *Tesoro*. And that's all that matters. I win. I will always win. Remember that when you are burning with so much hate for me, and the thought to run again crosses your mind. Just know that I advise you against doing anything like that again. Because if you do? Next time, I will kill you."

Pure ice sweeps through my bones and I hold Romeo closer to my chest. I believe every word of his threat. I may be the mother of his child, but Nico will not hesitate to kill me if I don't follow his rules.

Swallowing, I search his face for any sign of the man I once knew but come up empty. Turning away from him, I look at my son.

He is my world, the reason I need to stay alive.

And no matter what Nico puts me through, I need to remember, I am doing it for Romeo.

***

Clutching an irritable Romeo to my chest, we disembark the jet. My eyes go wide at the line of black SUV's waiting for us. I pause, my heart pounding in my chest when the reality of the situation hits me. Fuck. Not that I would dare try after what Nico said, but there really is no way out of this. A firm hand hits the small of my back, startling me.

"What is wrong with him?" I glance up at the sound of Nico's voice to find him frowning down at our son.

I blow out a breath, looking down at Romeo. "He's hungry. He is due a bottle."

"So why don't you give him one?" he deadpans, shooting me a droll look.

Irritation surges through me. I have looked after him this long without Nico's help, he does not get to just come in and treat me like I am an idiot that doesn't know what she is doing. Glaring, I snap out, "Because he won't drink the milk that I expressed when it's cold. I have nowhere to heat a bottle. I was going to breastfeed him–"

He cuts me off before I can finish. "No. You will not get your tits out in front of my men." His words are final, but he is delusional if he thinks I'm not going to feed my hungry son.

My jaw drops open, and I can't help the laugh that bursts from me. "If you would let me finish, I was going to say that I was waiting for some privacy. I can't not feed him, Nico. It doesn't work like that. He needs his milk."

His jaw clenches and he jerks his head toward the cars. "Come."

He strides to the SUV in the middle of the convoy, rounding the vehicle and opening the driver's door. Within seconds, I see a man step out of the car and when he turns, I can see it's Christopher. Meeting my gaze, he dips his chin, flashing me a small smile, but doesn't speak to me.

"Ocean?" Nico barks and my head snaps to him. Moving

around the vehicle, he pulls open the passenger door waving his hand for me to get inside. "Car. Now. Feed our son and then we will be on our way." His tone leaves no room for argument and this time I won't. Romeo needs feeding and Nico has made it so that can happen.

Sighing, I move toward the vehicle and slide inside, staring at him when he makes no moves to shut the door. My throat tightens as he watches Romeo and emotion consumes me. Despite the circumstances, I can't regret that Nico has met his son. Had things been different, we could have been a family. But he ruined that by lying. By having a damn fiancée. With the reminder, anger surges through me.

"Can you shut the door?" he doesn't miss the bite in my tone.

His eyes narrow in on me. "Don't push it, *Tesoro*. You are in enough trouble as it is." I go to respond but he shuts the door before I have a chance.

I exhale a calming breath, hoping it brings me the strength I am going to need going forward. Romeo's cry of hunger drags me from my thoughts. I make quick work of releasing my breast and he latches on.

With one look at him, I relax into the seat, knowing with everything inside me, no matter what happens, my son is my strength, and I will do everything in my power to protect him. To protect us both.

There is no other way.

Chapter 8

Nico

"Where are we?" Ocean's soft voice has me looking over at her from my position in the front passenger seat. My eyes shift to Romeo, who is asleep in his car seat, and my throat thickens. I still can't believe I have a son.

"My family's estate. In the Hamptons," I clarify.

Her beautiful face pales, her teeth going to town on that plump bottom lip. She is nervous. Worried about what is going to happen to her. As she should be.

"Why are we here and not going to the city?"

Irritation slithers through me. I am bringing her here because I know she will never be able to escape me. The estate is guarded twenty-four seven by no less than a hundred of my most trusted soldiers. This will be her new cage. One that will keep her with me and Ocean and Romeo safe. And because I am not a complete monster, I have made sure that she will have the company of my mother and sister. After what she has done, I didn't need to give her that luxury, but I want her somewhat happy in her new gilded cage. My intentions aren't exactly pure, but Ocean will have my family to lean on and help with our son.

But also, it will give Mamma something to focus her energy on. It's perfect. For everyone.

"You had your chance in the city, you ruined it. You will live here. Where I can protect you both."

She eyes me, her blue orbs flashing with a hint of anger. "Right. Because you are in the Mafia. Will we be living here along with your fiancée? Or is she your wife now?" Her voice is a growl but I hear the resentment. Her jealousy would be cute had she done it in private and not in front of my men. Well, Christopher, but still. She needs to remember her place. I cannot be seen to be weak in front of anyone.

"Watch your mouth." My voice is threatening but low, so as not to wake Romeo. She glowers at me. I can tell she wants to say more but she thinks better of it, keeping her smart mouth closed and leaning back in the seat.

I watch her for a long beat, searching her face. Christ she is just as beautiful as I remember. Flawless skin, plump lips, high cheekbones, blonde hair. My cock hardens in my pants just thinking about what I am going to do to her. The thought of getting back inside her pussy... my dick throbs, begging me to get inside her and return home. But it will have to wait.

She doesn't know it yet, and I probably will never admit it to her, but I haven't fucked another woman since Ocean. Not even when she ran and was away for all that time. I tried, of course I did. I'm a man with a healthy appetite for sex and am used to fucking on the regular. My dick wouldn't work though. She must have broken it or something. The little witch that she is did some voodoo shit on me, now all my cock wants is her. I grit my teeth in frustration, hating that she has such a hold on me. I knew I should have stayed away from her, but the dick wants what the dick wants, and it wanted her.

But now that I have her back, maybe I should try to fuck another woman just to prove that I can. That the hold she had on me was because I was so determined to find her. That my obsession stemmed from not knowing where she was. Or that she dared to run from someone like me. A king. Yes, now that I know who she really is, and how prominent her family are, she is no longer just some girl who takes her clothes off. A stripper. She is American royalty in her own right, but still, she is batting out of her league with me. I am the fucking Don of the Marchetti *Famiglia*. She needs to know her place, understand that this is her life and that she is never getting away from me again. I crave her like I've never craved anyone in my life, even with all her wrongdoings. It's madness, makes me unhinged in the worst way, but I can't deny the feelings she brings out in me. And now that I know she brought my son, my heir, into this world, the possessiveness I felt before has turned into something more. I can't explain it, and I'm not going to try. I just know that neither of them will ever leave my side ever again.

The vehicle coming to a stop has me turning back to face the windshield. I smirk at the sight of the big metal gates, at all the guards standing to attention, ready and waiting to protect my family. We are home. Finally. My whole body relaxes and I'm fully aware it's because I know that as soon as we enter the estate, I don't have to worry about Ocean being a flight risk. From this point forward, her every move will be watched. There will be no place she can go that she will not be seen. No place she can hide.

Aldo's head pops up in the guardhouse. He smiles, nodding in respect as the gates open. Though he can't see us inside the vehicle, he knows full well it's me inside. He was informed about our imminent arrival by Dante when we left the airfield.

"Nico?" Ocean's panicked voice echoes in the small space of the SUV.

"Yes?" I respond, without looking at her.

"I would prefer to go to the city."

I chuckle under my breath. "I'm sure you would, *Tesoro*. Close to public transport. People. Easier to get away if you wish to do so? Yeah. It's not happening. I already told you this is your new home. Nothing you say will change that, so I suggest you start coming to terms with it."

"But–" she starts, but I cut her off.

"No buts. I don't want to hear another word. *My* son will live here. *You* will live here." A sly smirk curves my lips when a thought like a threat crosses my mind. I turn to show her the sardonic look on my face. "Unless you would like to live in the city or wherever the hell you like on your own?" her eyes widen, faces pales. She isn't going anywhere but my family estate, but she doesn't need to know that. If I have to control her using Romeo, then I will. "It's your choice. But *my* son stays here." I continue and when her mouth snaps closed, I know I have her. "Thought so."

The hurt in her eyes makes my chest tighten. Not sure why, considering she had no trouble keeping my son from me. She swallows, her resigned nod confirming she is accepting her fate. Good. I don't want there to be any misunderstanding between us when it comes to who is in charge here. Not able to look at her or the emotion flashing on her face, I turn away.

Christopher moves us slowly up the long stone paved drive, lined with trees. A quick glance in the mirror confirms Dante and my other men are following behind us in another SUV. Rounding a bend, the circular driveway comes into view. I grimace when I spot Mamma and my sister waiting on the marble steps. I haven't told them about Romeo yet. Not because I wanted to hide it from them, but because I only just found out about my son myself, barely six hours ago.

"You can stop here." I tell my driver when we are in line with the entrance to the house. Doing as I ask, Christopher slows the vehicle to a complete stop before putting it in park.

Opening my door, I step out, making quick work of opening the back passenger door and unbuckling Romeo. "I will take him," Ocean snaps.

Glancing up, I shoot her a look. "I don't think so, *Tesoro*. You've had your time bonding with him, now it's my time." I know I am being deliberately cruel, but I can't help myself. Every time I look at him, all I see is her betrayal.

"Please, Nico. Don't do this," she pleads, her breath hitching with her words.

"Do what? I am simply introducing my son to his family," I rasp, taking him in my arms. "Now get out. My mamma wants to meet you," I tell her honestly. My mother knows all about Ocean and knows I went to get her. She has no idea of the other surprise that is awaiting her.

She looks out the window then back to me. Her lips tremble, along with her voice when she speaks. "Is that your wife?"

I smirk, knowing full well she is talking about my sister. I should tell her the truth about Gianna but for right now, I want her to stew in whatever scenario she has made up in her beautiful little head. "No. It's my sister. Now move. I won't ask again."

Slamming the door, I round the car knowing full well that she will follow. My gaze lands on my mamma. Her eyes drop to my arms. She frowns, shock and disbelief crossing her features before her whole face lights up. She rushes down the steps toward us.

"Oh my God, Nico. Who is this?" The excitement in her voice has me smiling.

"Meet your grandson, Mamma. This is Romeo." Teary eyes come to mine, a silent question in them. "He is mine, Mamma. *She* was pregnant when she ran," I confirm.

She gasps, reaching out and taking him from me. "Oh my.

He is beautiful." Her voice is thick with emotion, and I watch as she runs a finger down his face. "Look at you, Nipotini."

My sister steps up beside us. She glances at me before peering down at my son. "He is adorable, Nic," she murmurs, taking his little finger in her hand.

Pride fills me as they coo over my son. The adoration that flows from my sister and mamma is palpable and I can't help but bask in their excitement. As if my body is attuned to hers and knows exactly where she is, I stiffen when I feel her presence behind me.

"Nico?" her soft, unsure voice hits me straight in the chest. My jaw clenches in frustration and not for the first time do I wonder, how the hell this woman - out of all the women on this damn planet - managed to worm herself under my skin. Mamma and Allegra shift their attention to the little liar behind me, studying her curiously. I turn my head to look at her, noticing how a pink hue graces her cheeks and she shifts on her feet nervously.

"You must be Ocean." Mamma speaks up before I can introduce them.

Ocean flashes her a small smile, nodding. "Yes."

"I'm Nico's mamma, Valentina. Come, let's get you and my grandson settled in."

"Mamma," I growl.

She shoots me her *I dare you to fight me on this* look. "What? You will treat this girl, the mother of your son, with respect. I don't care what happened in the past, I will not allow you to show her anything but love and gratitude for bringing this beautiful bundle of joy into our world."

Irritation surges through me but, no matter what, I will not disrespect my mother. That doesn't mean I will take note of her words. "Take them to the west wing. Have the staff set Ocean and Romeo up in the room next to mine."

Mamma nods. "Of course."

She turns, taking my son with her. Allegra looks to Ocean with a soft, friendly smile. "I'm Allegra, Nico's sister. Come on. Let's get you inside."

Ocean glances at me before her gaze shifts back to my sister. She sucks in a breath as though preparing herself to walk into the lion's den. Little does she know it is far worse than that. Swallowing, she forces a smile, then follows my sister up the steps. I grin, licking my lips as I watch her heart shaped ass move with every step.

"You look like you want to eat her," Dante drawls drily, coming up beside me.

I chuckle. "I do. She doesn't realize what I have in store for her."

Dante laughs. "God help her," he says, shaking his head. Slapping me on the shoulder he makes his way up the stairs and inside.

Blowing out a breath I stare at the entrance my *Tesoro* and son just disappeared through, feeling something a lot like contentment. For the first time since she ran, my whole body relaxes.

Though things aren't good between us, and we have a long way to go, I know with everything in me she is worth it.

By the time I am done with her, she will be a queen worthy of standing by my side. But it won't be easy. I will make her fight for it, earn her place.

She might hate me, but I can deal with that. I would rather have her hate than not have her at all.

I will never let her go. Not now. Not ever.

The sooner she accepts that... the better.

Chapter 9

Ocean

"He really is the most adorable thing I have ever seen." Valentina coos over Romeo. We are in the bedroom – well more like suite - Nico has allocated for us. It has everything you could possibly imagine for a bedroom in a mansion as big as this. Apart from one thing. "There's no crib." I say to no one in particular, my gaze moving around the space to double check I haven't missed where my son will sleep.

"It is on its way. I contacted the owner of a store in town with my requirements. They will be delivering everything we need within the hour. In the meantime, I am sure he will be okay to sleep in his car seat for another couple of hours." Nico's deep voice startles me when he answers my question. The air thickens with his presence, almost choking me as he strolls inside my room without a care in the world.

"Right." My eyes roll of their own accord, because of course he did. It's just like him to take control of everything.

His gaze narrows in on me, assessing me with a hint of irritation. His jaw clenches but instead of indulging me further, he shifts his eyes to Romeo and his mother. "How is my boy?" Ignoring me, he closes the distance between them, taking our son in his arms.

I shift on my feet, feeling uncomfortable. Not because Nico is holding Romeo, but because I don't know what's going to come next. A soft hand lands on my bicep, giving me a gentle squeeze. My eyes snap up landing on Nico's sister.

"Are you hungry?" she asks softly, sincerity radiating from her.

As if on cue, my stomach growls, confirming that I am. I blush, smiling when Allegra grins. I haven't eaten since last night. Since my date with... my heart clenches just thinking about it. With Harrison. Patty. My family for all intents and purposes, for the last year. My hand comes to my heart, rubbing as if I can alleviate some of the pain. I will miss them both. My feelings for Harrison were nowhere near what I feel for Nico but still, he was a good man. Kind. And Patty was the best woman I have ever met. Tears prick my eyes, realization slamming into me. I will never see her again.

"Ocean?" Allegra frowns at me.

Clearing my throat, I speak. "I am actually. Though I need to feed Romeo first."

She smiles with a nod. "I will ask the cook to prepare some breakfast."

"Mia Figlia, why don't we give Ocean and Nico some space. We can prepare breakfast ourselves, yes?"

Allegra chuckles. "I would have suggested it had I thought I could pry you away from your grandson."

Valentina smiles softly down at Romeo in Nico's arms. "He is just so beautiful." Her hand comes to her chest. "I can't believe that I'm a nonna." She shakes her head in disbelief, a dreamy look in her eyes. My chest tightens with comprehension. Not only did I keep Romeo from his father but kept him from Nico's family. "Ocean, is there anything you don't eat?" Valentina asks, snapping me from my inner turmoil.

"I'm not a huge fan of lamb, but everything else is fine."

She claps her hands. "Perfect. I will see you shortly." Taking Allegra's hand, they leave the room.

Sighing, I turn to face Nico. His eyes are already on me, those predatory blue orbs sending a shiver down my spine. I swallow. There is something to be said about the way Nico Marchetti looks at me. But I can't focus on the way he makes me feel right now. I need to remember all that he did. That I hate him.

"Can you leave? I need to feed Romeo," I huff.

He smirks. "No. You had no problem thinking about getting your breasts out in front of my men, you can do it in front of me."

"I didn't do anything of the sort. Now get out," I say through clenched teeth.

"No. It's nothing I have not seen before. In fact, if I recall correctly, you used to love me sucking on your tits."

My cheeks heat at his words but I straighten in defiance. "I don't care what you have or haven't seen before. Things are different now. You have a..." I trail off, the word catching in my throat. Clearing the lump away, I straighten my spine and lift my chin. "You have a fiancée. Or is she your wife now?" And then something hits me. Something that I forgot until now. I frown. "And where is your father? I need to thank him. You know, for setting things straight. Telling me the truth."

His face darkens as he steps into me, so close his hot breath fans my face. With a tight jaw, he grits out four words that I never expected to hear. "My papà is dead."

I recoil. "Wh-what?"

He smirks. "Yeah. The day he confronted you with all my secrets, he was gunned down outside *Bellissima*. Poetic. Karma if you ask me. He took you away from me, and my enemies took him."

Nico's face is impassive, his voice detached as he tells me all this. I can't say that I'm sad Lorenzo isn't here. Spending even twenty minutes with the man made me uncomfortable, so I can't imagine living in the same house as him. But still, it's sad, losing a parent. I would know. Though mine are still alive, I lost them a long time ago. Their need for power exceeded their need to be loving parents and their treatment of me. Though my father's behavior toward me was appalling, now that I am a mother myself, I can see that my mom was just as complicit. I would never treat Romeo, or any future children I have, the way they treated me.

Realizing it's been minutes since anyone has spoken, I clear my throat and whisper out. "I'm sorry for your loss."

He chuckles but it's humorless. "No, you're not, but thank you. My understanding of what went down between my papà and you that day is that he threatened your life several times, to the point that you had no choice but to run. He was a bad man, *Tesoro*, one who would stop at nothing to get what he wanted. And that was you gone."

"He did threaten me. But that doesn't mean I wished him dead," I tell him honestly.

He eyes me for a long beat, then looks down to Romeo. An emotion I can't quite decipher crosses his face before he covers it with that blank mask of his. This is the first deep, meaningful conversation we have had since we reunited, and everything is hitting home at what my actions caused. Though I had no choice but to run, my throat thickens, shame at keeping a father and his son apart consuming me. I have a maelstrom of emotions running through my body and I don't know which is the most dominant or how to feel.

"Now, back to feeding our son," Nico prompts.

I roll my eyes knowing full well that I need to pick my battles. I won't win this round. "Ugh. Give him to me." The asshole grins, knowing he has won and hands him over to me.

Taking him, I move to the Chesterfield chair that overlooks the big bay window. My mouth drops open at the view. Plush gardens, an Olympic sized swimming pool and a stone path that leads to the beach.

"Wow," I gasp, feeling Nico step up beside me.

"Don't tell me that you're impressed by all this? You must have had similar surroundings growing up in a rich family."

I stiffen, my head snapping up to him. I grind my teeth so hard I'm surprised they don't turn to dust. "You don't know anything about *my family*," I spit.

His eyes light up in challenge. "Oh yeah? I know the Caldwell's are a prominent family in Seattle and that they have been looking for you."

My heart picks up speed, panic coursing through me. "You-you didn't tell them where I am, did you?" Right now, I don't care about anything. I am more concerned that my father might know where I am.

He searches my face, for what I'm not sure, before shoving his hands in his pants pockets. His gaze narrows. "No. Not yet. But don't think I won't contact them. You do as I say and don't step out of the lines I draw for you, then I will keep you hidden. Will keep you safe from whatever it is you ran from."

I don't miss the threat in his voice, but I can't bring myself to be scared.

Living with Nico's rules is a far better fate than returning to my family.

"I understand," I say with resignation, my shoulders slumping in defeat.

He watches me with a blank look, no doubt for any trace that I am lying. I'm not. I would rather be a prisoner here for the rest of my life than ever see my father again.

"I am glad we got that cleared up. Now feed our son."

Chapter 10

Nico

"So how is it going with the little Houdini?"

I frown, pinning Dante with a confused glare. "Houdini?"

He chuckles. "Yeah. She is good at disappearing."

"Idiot," I mutter, running a hand through my hair.

He laughs harder before his expression sobers. "Well?"

I sigh. It's been two days since I brought Ocean and my son home. Two days of mixed feelings. One minute I want to fuck her senseless, the next I want to wrap my hand around her pretty little throat and watch as I squeeze the life out of her. Don't get me wrong, it's been amazing having Romeo here, but every time I look at him, I am reminded of Ocean's betrayal. Of how she kept him from me. At missing his birth. At the time I lost with him. I'm just so fucking angry with her.

Children were never in my future plans. I knew I would have to produce an heir one day, but I would have been quite happy not bringing a child into my world. Now that I have a son, I want to keep breeding with Ocean and never stop. It's a paradox of mixed emotions for sure. And then there is my mamma and sister, the happiness that exudes from the both of them just from having Ocean and Romeo here. They are besotted with my son. Especially Mamma. And I see the way she is with my deceitful *Tesoro*. How she has taken her under her wing. Mamma has a new lease on life and after what happened with my papà, it makes me happy to see.

"Honestly?" I ask, and he nods. "I have mixed feelings. Obviously, I am happy about my son, but I am just so angry that she kept him from me. Even if it was only a matter of months. There is a part of me that wants to forget what she did, move forward as a family and make her mine forever. But there is also a small part of me that wants to take Romeo from her, even if only for a couple of days, just so she knows how it feels to be away from him. It's fucked up, but it's the truth," I admit.

He runs a palm down his face. "I get it Nic. I would feel the same. You were denied being there for your son, for the first couple months of his life. It sucks, because I know how much you would have wanted to have been there, even if your papà had still been alive."

My jaw clenches. The anger I have been trying to tamp down the anger surging in my veins. "Exactly. Which is why I want to punish her for it."

"Nic, she has nowhere to run. Her life is in your hands." He smirks, telling me what I already know, his underlying message clear. I grin. Yes, yes, it is. She is mine to do with as I please. Though I don't want to hurt her, I can toy with her. After all, she did it to me for over a year.

"She thinks that I married Gianna," I tell him.

His eyes light up with amusement. "Use that," he frowns. "Just don't tell your sister I said that. She has taken a shine to the girl and will have my balls."

I grimace. "I don't want to hear the words sister and balls in the same sentence."

He barks out a laugh. "Noted. But seriously. Use Gianna.

You know she is desperate to get on your dick. I am sure she will come running if you give her a call..." he trails off, leaving the rest unspoken but I hear exactly what he is alluding to.

I run a finger across my bottom lip, mulling over Dante's words. "That could work. Ocean will lose her shit." I chuckle.

His brows furrow, confusion marring his face. "You're still using Ocean and not her real name?" he asks.

"Yeah. It's what I know her as and it suits her better. She will always be Ocean to me." An unfamiliar feeling tightens my chest, when I remember how she reacted to me calling her by her real name. Some shit must have gone down with her parents and at some point, I want to know exactly what happened. What made her run. "She freaked out when I called her Emilee." I rasp, my throat thick.

"Have you asked her about it? I mean, it must have been bad for her to run from a privileged life like that when she was just seventeen."

I think about his question for a long minute. It rings true and I have every intention of sitting Ocean down so she can tell me everything. The opportunity just hasn't presented itself, yet. What with my mamma or sister not leaving Ocean alone for even a second.

Tonight, that changes though. It's time I know all about the little runaway.

Looking him in the eye, I speak. "I will. Tonight."

***

"Thank you for dinner, Valentina. It was beautiful," Ocean murmurs from her position at the table. Romeo is beside her, fast asleep in his stroller. I asked why she didn't just put him down to bed in his crib, but she said that she didn't feel comfortable leaving him so far away. I don't understand it myself. We have one of those mobile baby monitors that she can check if she feels anxious. I also have cameras set up in their room and with one click of the app on my cell, I can see what our son is doing.

Mamma smiles softly, as entranced by my *Tesoro* as I was when I first met her. I still believe she is a witch, with some sort of magical power. Everyone she meets falls under whatever fucking spell she is casting.

"I am happy that you enjoyed it, honey," Mamma replies.

"I fear that without me doing any exercise, and eating your delicious home cooking, I am going to be a lot bigger by the time I leave." She laughs, but it's cut off when I bark out.

"You are not leaving. In fact, you are not going anywhere." The whole room goes deathly silent. My narrowed gaze shifts to her face and when she looks at me all the blood rushes to my cock. Christ she is beautiful.

Defiance flashes in those ocean-colored orbs. She lifts her head, her chin jutting out as she stares me down. "I am taking Romeo to bed." It's not a question but a statement. Rising to her feet, her lips clamp shut, keeping the words I know she is desperate to spew inside.

"I want to speak with you," I tell her.

"It will have to wait," she hisses, making me bite back a grin. She doesn't realize – or maybe she does - but her smart mouth turns my cock to steel.

"No. It won't. You have thirty minutes. I will come to your room, so you don't have to leave *our* son."

She rolls her eyes. Irritation slithers through me when they soften as she looks at my mamma and sister. A sincere smile curves her lips when she addresses them. "Thank you again. For everything. Goodnight."

She turns on her heel, taking my son with her. Once she gets to the stairs, she will take Romeo out and carry him. I shake my head. Stubborn woman. It's a battle of wills, one she won't win. I just wish she would back down now and know her place.

But you like her fight, that little voice in my head whispers, and by the way my dick thickens it agrees.

"Nico, I already told you that you need to be nicer to that girl." Mamma scolds me like I'm a child and my cock instantly deflates.

"Oh, please. She brought everything on herself." A snort sounds. Without even looking I know it's Dante. I shoot him a scathing look which wipes the smirk clean off his face. "I will treat her as I see fit," I mutter.

Mamma shakes her head, disappointment clear in her eyes. "You're a good man, Nico. Don't let your anger at what happened control how you treat her. She is a good girl, young and scared. Do the right thing. Please."

I sigh, falling back in my chair. Mamma knows damn well I can't deny her anything. That doesn't mean I am going to stop.

Ocean betrayed me.

She needs to pay for that.

Chapter 11
Ocean

The door being shoved open has me yelping in surprise, though I already know who it is. My head snaps up to find who I knew I would find. My own personal devil, Nico, sauntering into my room like he owns the place. Technically he does, but still, that's not the point right now. It may be his mansion, but I don't think wanting a little privacy is too much to ask for. My eyes narrow in on him.

"The door was closed for a reason. Do you have no concept of personal space?" I hiss.

Ignoring my ire, he smirks, closing the distance between us in only a couple of long strides. Reaching out, he grips my chin harshly. Though his touch should repulse me, I can't help the butterflies that erupt in my stomach.

"No. Not when it comes to you. There is no door, no wall, *nothing* you can put in front of me that will stop me from getting to you or *my* son."

My heart jackhammers in my chest at the possession in his words and I know he means every single one. He would get to us no matter what. I don't know why I expected any less. The man never gave up looking for me. It may have taken him a year to find me, but he did. That's perseverance if ever I heard it.

"I was just about to shower." I say, ripping my chin out of his grip. I need to put space between us, remember who he is. That he is *married*.

"No. Sit. We have things we need to discuss." He gestures toward the lounge area where a couch and two Chesterfield chairs sit. Frowning, he glances at where Romeo's crib has been set up. "Our son is asleep?"

I nod. "Yes. He went straight down."

"Good. Now sit."

"I want to shower—"

I am cut off when his palm hits my lower back. Electricity shoots through my veins at the small touch. I know he feels it too when he grimaces. He hates that I affect him, as much as I hate the way he has this hold over me. I almost snort, wanting to tell him that the feeling's mutual. "It wasn't a question, *Tesoro*. Sit."

Like a petulant child, I stomp over to the chair, dropping down in it. Glancing up, my eyes lock on Nico's. My lips part, heart thrumming wildly behind my rib cage. Why does he have to be so beautiful? Full lips. Dark hair. Blue eyes. He is a God. And he damn well knows it.

As if he knows exactly what I'm thinking, a smirk takes over his smug face. I grit my teeth, preventing myself from throwing him an insult as frustration claws at me. His gaze never leaving mine, he takes a seat on the couch opposite me, all the while watching me with a complete look of madness in his eyes. I stare at him with a look of nonchalance - though I feel anything but - waiting for him to say whatever he came here to talk about.

Sighing, he leans back, getting comfortable, then finally speaks. "We have things to discuss. For one, your real name and age." I flinch at the way he spits the last part, his jaw clenching. "Your family and why you ran."

I'm shaking my head before he even finishes. "No. I don't want to talk about my family."

His eyes narrow. "You will talk about them. I want to know everything." A devilish grin curves his lips. Without him even saying anything, I know I am not going to like what he says next. "If you don't tell me, I will go straight to the source. Or even better, I will bring them here."

Nausea churns in my gut, sweat dripping down my back at the thought of that happening. I shoot out of my seat, my chest heaving as I glower down at him. "Stop threatening me with them. You have no idea what I went through growing up in that *family*," I snap.

His face remains a blank mask, but the way his jaw tics and his eye twitches, tells me that he doesn't like my outburst. "Sit down. And if you don't start spilling your secrets from that perfect mouth of yours, then I will search for the information I want in any way I deem necessary. You lied to me, *Emilee*." I recoil at the sound of my real name out of his mouth. I am no longer Emilee Caldwell, haven't been for a long time. Why can't he understand that? "Not only about who you really are, but your fucking age. You were barely legal when I fucked you." he growls, and I blush at the memory of how he took my virginity.

"The legal age to have sex in New York is seventeen. I was eighteen, so therefore, legal." I mumble as I resume my seat.

"Just," he barks, and I glance at Romeo to make sure he hasn't woken him. Thankfully, my baby boy is still fast asleep. "And anyway. That doesn't matter. What matters is that I am a fucking decade older than you. Twenty-eight. Had I known how old you were, I would never have touched you. I would have stayed away."

That thought alone makes me feel hollow inside. Though I hate him right now, I wouldn't change what happened between us.

"Would you?" I shoot back. "I seem to recall it was you that chased me. You who wouldn't take no for an answer." I'm challenging him, poking the beast, but I don't care.

He scowls before clearing his throat. "That's not the fucking point. My whole club could have been shut down. The other girls could have lost their jobs, because of the lies you told."

I swallow, guilt hitting me right in the chest. I didn't even consider that when I started working at The Executive Club, and maybe that was selfish of me. Nonetheless, it never happened so it's a moot point. "Everything worked out." My voice is nonchalant, and he doesn't look impressed by my response.

"Get to your family. I am this close," he moves his thumb and pointer finger millimeters apart, "to wrapping my hands around your delicate little throat and squeezing the life from you."

I gasp at his cold, cruel words. One look at him tells me that he is serious. Not wanting to antagonize him further, and knowing I have no choice in the matter, I give him what he wants. Sucking in a breath, I try to calm myself before I delve into my past. It's no use. Every time I think about it, let alone talk about it, it puts me on edge.

"I ran from home because my father is a monster. When I refused to do the many things he asked of me, he would beat me and keep me locked in my room for days. My mother would never intervene, too scared that he would turn on her. I was watched constantly, told what to eat and wear. When I turned sixteen, he informed me that I would be marrying Xavier Anderson, the mayor's son." I don't miss the way his eyes darken as I tell him that bit of information. "It would happen the day after my eighteenth birthday. I didn't want to marry Xavier. I had heard the rumors about him. What he did to women. My life would have been hell. So, for months, I started saving my allowance. I then spoke with a friend who put me in touch with someone who could make me a really good fake ID. I asked him to put my age as twenty-one because I knew I would have a better chance at getting a job... in a club, whether as a dancer or even a stripper. It didn't matter, I just needed to make as much money as I could." He glowers, making me shrink back but I continue, wanting to get everything off my chest. Every single little detail. Clearing my throat, I continue. "My father progressively got worse with his abuse. He was obsessed about me marrying into the Anderson family and securing himself business deals. He was fanatical, bordering into dictator territory about keeping me away from boys and anyone that he thought could lead me astray. My virginity staying intact was part of the agreement. Anderson would not accept an impure bride for his son, and I heard from several people that Xavier constantly talked about all the sick ways he was going to rip it from me. He was going to take my innocence whether I wanted him to or not and no one cared." A growl rumbles in his chest, startling me out of my reverie. "What?" I snap.

He pushes out of his chair. Not looking at me, he paces the room, running a hand through his hair. "You tell me right fucking now whether you have let anyone else inside my cunt. You said that fucker never touched you, but how can I believe a word you say."

My mouth drops open. Out of everything I just told him, that is what he is focused on? A bitter laugh leaves my mouth before I can stop it. "You're one to talk. You're *married*, Nico. How dare you question me?"

He is in my face, his hand wrapped around my throat before I can blink. I swallow, my pulse kicking up to an unnatural speed. He squeezes. Not hard enough to cut off my air but enough to warn me of my place. "Did. You. Let. Anyone. Touch. You. While. You. Were. Running?" The manic look in his gaze has me scared. Though he always had that ruthless look about him, he hid that side from me before. But there is no hiding it now. No protecting me from who he really is. He wants me to see every ruthless, twisted part of him.

With wide, fearful eyes, I shake my head as much as his grip allows me. His gaze tracks the small movement and his jaw clenches. "No, Nico. You are the only man to touch me in that way." My voice is a soft whisper as I try to placate him. Not that he deserves it.

Satisfaction flashes across his face. Releasing me, he takes a step back. "Good. Finish your story." He moves back to the couch, looking a little calmer.

Sucking in a breath, my hand comes up, rubbing the spot he just held. Though I somehow already knew it, with that one action, it made me realize that within seconds, a mere tightening of his hand, he could take my life. I can only hope that somewhere deep inside him he still has feelings for me and will show me some mercy.

"I wasn't going to accept the fate my father had chosen for me, and I found my out. My mother would usually attend all my ballet classes with me, but fortunately, one day she was too sick to come, so my driver took me. I knew it was my only chance, so I packed some belongings in my ballet duffle, took my fake ID and the money I had saved. I said goodbye to my parents and brother, like I usually would. I was as normal as I could be. When we arrived at the studio, I knew Colin would wait in the car. Before I even made it inside, he was distracted by something on his phone. I used that distraction and ran. I ended up at a bus terminal, and you know the rest. I found myself in New York. The moment I left, I became Ocean and that is who I am. I never want to be Emilee Caldwell again." I finish with conviction.

Understanding passes between us and he nods. Rising, he

closes the distance between us. I recoil slightly, which makes him pause. Confusion flickers in his eyes. I don't know why. He was the one with his hands wrapped around me not even five minutes ago. He moves closer, his hands landing on the arms of the chair. All the air leaves my lungs when he bends toward me. Leaning in, his hot breath caresses my ear, sending a shiver running down my spine. I shudder when his tongue runs a wet hot trail down my neck.

"Hmm, so fucking sweet, *Tesoro*."

"Please don't." I choke out, through the thickness in my throat. He is married. I am not going to do this with him.

He pulls back, his eyes narrowing in on me. "I will touch you when and how I want, baby. And trust me when I say, you will want it. Beg for it even."

Shaking my head, I whisper, "You're married."

He smirks, leaning in so close his lips touch mine. "That won't stop me. You're mine and I intend on reminding you of that fact."

Chapter 12

Nico

"I want you to find out everything you can about Wesley and Xavier Anderson. *Everything*. I want no stone left unturned." I bark the order at Tony. Next, I will be contacting my PI and demanding the same. I want to know about the man my *Tesoro* was promised to. The man that was meant to take her virginity. Just the thought of that fucker's dirty hands on her perfect skin makes me see red.

"As in Wesley Anderson, the Mayor of Seattle?" Tony asks, curiosity lacing his tone.

"Yes, as in him. Find out everything. I want to know about every single skeleton in his closet and, more importantly, his son, Xavier's. I want every single piece of information you can get, right down to their shoe size and their fucking medical records."

An exasperated sigh sounds down the line. I grip my cell tighter, waiting for the inevitable questions. "Nico, what's this all about? And what shit are you getting me into now?"

My jaw clenches, anger heating my blood. "I pay you enough money not to ask me questions, Tony. Now get me what I need." I hang up before he can say more. Fucker doesn't need to know anything. He just needs to get me the information I want. After all, it is what I fucking pay him for.

After my conversation with Ocean last night, I came to my office. I have never felt remorse in my life, it's not an emotion I allow myself to feel. But the fear I saw in her eyes when I wrapped my hand around her throat… guilt hit me square in the chest, making me want to beg her for forgiveness.

Ocean thinks I'm a monster. And I am. But no matter how angry I feel toward her, I don't ever want her to cower or feel unsafe in my presence. Yes, she fucked up with her actions, but I'm no saint. Christ, she thinks I'm married to another woman and I haven't corrected her on the matter. I should tell her the truth. But a part of me wants to torment her, like she tormented me for over a year.

I scrub a frustrated palm down my face. Jesus, my thoughts are so contradictory it would be laughable if the situation wasn't so fucked up. She gets under my skin. So deep, I lose all control. I shake my head, knowing that I need to get my shit together.

Clicking on my emails, I type out the information that I am after and send it over to my PI. Just as I pull up the security cameras I had installed in Ocean's room, Dante strides inside. I glower at him.

"Don't you ever knock?" The memory of Ocean saying the same thing to me not even an hour ago flickers through my mind. I smirk. I love her defiance almost as much as I love her submission. No woman has ever gotten to me like she has, and I thrive on wondering what she will do next.

He glances up from his cell. "I thought you would like to know that the shipment came in. Everything is accounted for and there were no problems."

I nod, satisfaction filling me. "I think changing the location of our warehouse helped. I know full well the Bratva have eyes on our usual sites."

"I agree." He drops down in the seat in front of my desk. "It also helps that our men are now loyal. They respect you, Nico. I think you becoming Don is the exact influence the *famiglia* needed. It solidified loyalty. They have confidence in you and how you are running things."

I watch him, settling back in my seat as I mull over his words. Dante's right. In the year since my papà passed things have progressively improved. Though it's hard for me to trust anyone but Dante, my mamma, and sister, I trust my men more now than I ever did when Papà was Don.

"Yeah," I agree. "I will be happier when this shit with the Bratva is under control though."

He sighs, scrubbing a palm across his mouth. "Nic, I know it's probably the last thing on your mind, what with everything going on with Ocean and Romeo, but are you any further forward with getting Allegra out of the contract with the Romanos?" I frown, looking at him. Like really look at him. The concern in his eyes. The weariness on his face. It has taken a lot for him to come in here and ask me this. I just wish I could give him the answer he so desperately wants to hear.

I shake my head. "Not yet. But I will." I promise him, even if it is a lie. The contract is sealed tight. Iron clad. With no stone left unturned, I've had my lawyers pore over it for hours upon hours and still they can't find a way out. The only way to do so is to go to war. Hmmm, or for Riccardo to have an "accident", and if that can be blamed on the Bratva, even better. I sigh, remembering that it would not only mean a war with the Romanos but with the entire commission. It would be suicide. Still, knowing all that, I won't allow my sister to marry Riccardo. I just need to get everything in order before I plan my next move.

Leaning forward, his arms drop to his knees, his eyes imploring. He lets me see everything he usually hides. All the emotion currently running through him. "I won't be without her, Nic."

My eyes narrow in on him when I remember something. "Dante, you're my best friend and I love you, but if I find out you've..." I trail off, grimacing as I try to find the right word. "Fornicated with my sister out of wedlock, then I will kill you. The Romanos will kill Allegra if they get their hands on her and find out she is impure."

His eyes darken with murderous intent. He shoots out of his seat. "They won't get their dirty Romano hands on her." He barks out a laugh, but it's humorless. "And fornicated? Really, Nic? What era are you living in? You know I wouldn't disrespect your sister like that. I know how this world works."

I relax a little. I know they are in love, but it would be disrespectful of Dante to be intimate with my sister. It's hypocritical of me, considering my relationship with Ocean and us having a child. But Dante and my sister need to wait before they take their relationship to the next level. At least until they are married. I sneer at the thought of them together and bile fills my throat. Yeah, no. That's not something I want to think about.

"Anything else?" I ask, quickly trying to change the subject.

"No. I will leave you to your stalking." He smirks, jerking his head to my laptop.

I growl. Fucker knows exactly what I was doing.

***

The following morning, I am just finishing up breakfast when Ocean, who has been at the table with me for the last hour, decides to speak to me.

"I want to take Romeo down to the beach." It's not a question, but more of a demand.

Glancing up at her, my eyes lock on our son and my chest

constricts, like it does every time I look at him. I still can't believe that I'm a father.

"That will be nice. I would come with you, but I have a yoga class in town at eleven." Mamma responds, beaming at Ocean like she didn't keep my son away from me for the first four months of his life. I try to push the negative thoughts away, but it doesn't work. I need to accept that things will be up and down. That I will have days where I hate her for what she has done, and days when I feel some sort of compassion toward her. That things will not just slot into place like a perfect puzzle piece just because she is back here with me.

"You are not going anywhere without a guard." I snap, breaking whatever mushy shit Mamma and my woman have going on.

Ocean's eyes flash with blue fire and I smirk, daring her to challenge me. Obviously, she realizes it's not worth the fight. Her shoulders slump, gaze dropping to Romeo. "As you wish. Can you arrange that? I would like to go before he has his afternoon nap."

I grit my teeth, trying to rein in my quickly rising temper. Little witch knows just how to push my buttons. "I will. I would also like to spend some time with *my* son on my own today." I don't miss the way she tenses. "You know, since I have missed so much already."

"Asshole," she mumbles under her breath, before forcing a fake smile. "Why can't I be there, too?" Her brows furrow, a mixture of emotions flicker on her beautiful face. "I don't want him around your wife," she grits out.

I smirk, only for it to drop when I hear my mamma's confused voice. "Wif–"

I cut her off before she can say more. "I will do as I damn well please. You know, I have a good mind to take him away from you for a couple months just so you know how it feels."

She gasps, her face paling. Satisfaction unfurls in my chest at her reaction. It's petty of me. Beneath me really. But still, I can't stop. She brings this side out of me. A malicious side that I can't control. "Now go and get ready. I will arrange for a couple of my men to take you down to the beach." My tone leaves no room for argument. She jumps out of her chair, grabs our son, and scurries out of the room before I can say more.

"Nico." Mamma admonishes and reluctantly my gaze shifts to her. "Don't you dare threaten that girl with her child." Her brows cinch. "And what does she mean by wife?"

Throwing down my napkin, I push out of my seat. "She thinks I married Gianna. That is how it will stay for now." I pin her with a look that dares her to argue. "And I will threaten her all I like. Are you forgetting that she kept me from my son?" I point out, hating that my own mamma seems more loyal to the lying little *Tesoro* over her own son.

She scowls, disappointment clear in her eyes, as she shakes her head. "This isn't you, Nico."

My jaw tics in annoyance. I don't want my mamma to be disappointed in me, but fuck. What does she expect after everything Ocean has put me through? I can't back down now. No matter how much I want to. Throwing Mamma one last look, I say. "Maybe it's the new me." Then I quickly leave the room to arrange for a couple of my guards to take Ocean and my son to the beach.

Chapter 13

Ocean

"Asshole," I mumble under my breath, as I stomp down the steps toward the beach. Two guards follow behind me. Close enough that they invade my personal space and a stark reminder that I'm not alone. I know without a doubt, it's a power play. Nico's way of showing me that there is no way out. "Can you step back." I hiss over my shoulder. It's not a question but a demand I want them to follow.

The older of the two grins, pausing briefly. "Sorry miss, boss's orders. We are not to let you out of our sight."

Shaking my head, I continue down the steps. All I wanted was a nice day with Romeo on the beach. Yet I'm being followed by these two idiots, like their lives depend on it. And maybe they do. I wouldn't put it past Nico to kill them should they lose me.

Nico. My jaw clenches. That fucker had the audacity to threaten me with taking my son away? Surely, he knows that I would die before I let that happen. He may think that I am still that weak, scared, girl I was a year ago. But I'm not. I have changed because I had to. Because I had no other choice.

Romeo depends on me and for that, I will be whoever I need to be to keep him with me. To keep him safe.

Glancing down, my heart bursts with intense happiness at the way he is snuggled close into my chest. As long as I have him, I have everything I will ever need. My eyes shift to the wrap he is snuggled up in. Nico really did think of everything, covering every possible base for what our son would need. Even right down to the baby sling currently wrapped around my body.

Stepping onto the sand, I sigh, my lips curving into a smile as I inhale the salty sea air. It instantly relaxes me, and I almost forget about the two men watching my every move. Romeo lets out a little noise of contentment, his hot breath hitting my chest. I run a finger down his soft cheek before moving closer to the water.

Finding a spot, I drop down and exhale a breath. I want to look over my shoulder, see where the goons have positioned themselves, but I refuse to give them the satisfaction. Instead, I focus on my son. On the sound of the water hitting the sand. It's calming. If I had a cellphone, I could picture myself out here, music playing as I practice ballet. Or even better, I could call Patty, and let her know that I am okay. My heart clenches in my chest, hand flying up to the spot and rubbing as if it will alleviate some of the pain. It doesn't. I miss the lady who became my family. The woman who took a chance on me when most people would have left me to struggle.

Tears blur my vision as thoughts of her filter through my mind. I suck in a breath, trying to calm myself. Get it together, Ocean. Crying won't achieve anything. It will not change my situation. That doesn't negate the fact that I need to talk to Patty. Need to put her mind at ease... Nico would understand, right? Understand that she was there for his son, and she deserves this courtesy? I hum to myself, making a mental note to speak to Nico about this. It's the least he can do, and surely he isn't that much of a monster that he would say no? I sigh. After this morning, I know I shouldn't bet on anything. After all, he did threaten to take my son. Nothing is impossible when it comes to him, and I need to remember that.

Glancing around, I spot families laughing and playing in the sand. People in the sea as they enjoy the hot weather. They look happy, carefree. The kind of life that I was looking for and I imagined for myself when I first ran from my family.

Swallowing, I think back to last night and how I told Nico everything. Just recalling the fate my father bestowed upon me, of the many times he put hands on me, hitting me until I was a canvas of bruises. The purple, blue, and yellow hues of my skin. Of how there were times I couldn't dance or go to school because my injuries were so bad. I shudder. He was a monster. Money and power meant more to him than anything else. I dread to think how my life would be had I stayed. I know I would be married to Xavier Anderson by now, no doubt suffering more than I ever did at the hands of my father.

Nico may be the devil, dressed up in his designer suits, with a handsome face that draws you in and a perfectly sculpted body. But my father and the Andersons are the worst kind of monsters. They hide their sins and deviant behavior behind nice smiles and fake façades. At least with Nico he doesn't hide who he is. Before I knew he was a mafia heir, you could tell from one look that he exuded power and a ruthlessness that would scare most people. Even knowing all that, I would rather face off with Nico a million times over, than ever having to see my father or Xavier again.

Loud squealing snaps me from my thoughts, and I smile at the child being chased by who I assume is her mother. What I wouldn't give to be like that. Free to do as I please. My throat tightens. Fucking Nico and his overbearing ways. Glancing over my shoulder, I glower at the two men standing guard not ten feet behind me. Their stance is combative, ready for any threat that may present itself. My eyes drop down their bodies. I smirk at the black dress pants and shirts they wear in this heat. It's karma.

Turning back to look at the sea, my thoughts go to Nico's words at breakfast this morning. The vitriol he spat about me keeping Romeo from him and how he should do the same, just so I know how it feels. I shiver. I can't even imagine life without my son. A question echoes in my mind. One that, if I'm being honest, has been there since the moment I saw Nico again. I give it life, allowing it form in my head.

If Nico had never found me, would I have told him about Romeo?

I think it over for a second, though I know with everything in me what the answer would be. It's selfish of me, and I should go to hell for even thinking it. But no, I wouldn't have told him. What with him being in the Mafia and the fact he has a fiancée – or a wife, or whatever the hell she is to him – those two things would have kept me away indefinitely. It's fucked up and under normal circumstances, I would never condone keeping a child from his father, but this isn't your usual, everyday situation. I only did what I had to do in order to survive. Had Romeo's dad been someone like Harrison, it would have been different. But it's not. I am where I am, and it is what it is. I chuckle humorlessly under my breath. Out of all the people in the world, I had to go and get knocked up by Nico Marchetti.

"Jesus," I mutter quietly.

Even though Nico is a complete asshole, he is right about one thing. The web of lies that I wove are getting so far out of hand, the truth is now blurred with all my dishonesty. I huff, shaking my head. I made my choices and I now have to live with them. Literally. Nico has a lot of anger inside him and from the way he looks at me, it's all aimed in my direction. It's clear in the spiteful, venomous, words he spits at me. I know damn well he is going to use me as his punching bag and it sucks, but like I said, I am no longer the girl he remembers.

He can throw whatever the hell he likes at me. Because one thing that I am certain of.

He won't break me.

***

I don't know how long we spend at the beach, but by the time we get back to the house, Valentina is home from her yoga class. Being the absolute saint she is, she offers to watch Romeo after I feed him, so that I can go and speak with Nico in private.

"Thank you for doing this. I don't want him to pick up on any animosity we have toward each other."

She rolls her eyes, tsking. "Ocean, it's my pleasure. I don't know whether Nico told you, but I lost my husband the day you left..." She frowns, trailing off. Her face turns solemn, eyes apologetic. "I'm sorry for what he did to you."

Shaking my head, I reply softly. "That's okay. It wasn't your fault."

She smiles. "Anyway, this little boy has given me a purpose. I love having you both here."

I nod. "I am happy he got to meet his grandma. Even if it's not under the best of circumstances."

She waves me off, smiling down at Romeo. "Everything will work itself out. You will see," she says, so quietly I almost miss it. Glancing at me, her eyes narrow. "And less of the grandma, you're making me feel old. I'm Nonna." There is no malice to her words. If anything, all I hear is humor.

"Got it, *Nonna*," I tease, grinning.

She chuckles, jerking her head to the door. "Now stop putting it off and go talk to my son."

I groan. It's scary how she knows that I am stalling. How quickly she has picked up on some of my habits. With a peck to Romeo's cheek, I turn and start toward the door. Exhaling a deep breath, I pull it open and step onto the landing.

Determination surges through my body.

I won't leave his office until I get what I want.

Chapter 14

Nico

A soft knock on the door has me pausing my conversation with Tony. By the way the hair on the back of my neck stands on end, I know exactly who it is.

"Tony, I will call you back." I end the call before he can say anything else. Blood thrums through my veins, igniting every nerve ending in my body and I can't wait another second before seeing her. Leaning back in my seat, I steeple my fingers, clearing my throat and locking that blank mask back firmly in place. "Come in."

Not a second later, the door is pushed open and, just as I suspected, my little *Tesoro* steps inside. Worry filled blue orbs lock on me before she breaks the connection, and they shift around the room. She takes in the opulent space with intrigue on her face. I can't say that I blame her. My papà designed his office like he did all things that belonged to him. Over the top. Lavish. Luxurious. I never bothered to put my own stamp on it when he passed. I didn't see the point as I never spent much time here in the Hamptons, anyway. But now that Ocean and my son are here, I don't want to be anywhere else.

"Can we talk?" she says softly, stepping further into the room.

I wave a hand to the chair in front of my desk, my way of asking her to sit. "Sure."

Her cheeks turn that delectable shade of pink, I love. I want to run my tongue up the soft flesh, nibble on it. She averts her gaze as if she knows exactly what I'm thinking. I relish the way I affect her. Take pleasure in her innocence. Even after all the sexual things we have done together, and knowing her body in ways that nobody else does, she still gets shy around me. Its fucking adorable.

Sucking in a breath, she drops down in the seat. Déjà vu hits me. Memories of all the times she did the exact same thing in my office at The Executive Club flashing in my mind. Of the time she crawled to me when I lounged on my couch like a king. My cock hardens at the thought. Fuck. I need back inside her pussy. And it's the least she owes me after the little witch broke my cock, making it only want her, *crave* her. My jaw clenches in anger. I try to tamper down my irritation, but it doesn't seem to work. Christ, she gets under my skin.

Big blue doe eyes come to me, and I drown in them. Her decision to go by her middle name is ironic really. Just like if you were in the middle of the ocean with nothing to save you, I sink into the depths of her. Shaking my head, I grit my teeth. I can't allow myself to get sucked in by her feminine wiles again. She screwed me over once and I have no doubt she would do it again if given half the chance.

"Get to it, *Tesoro*, I don't have all day," the bite of my tone has her reeling back. Despite the way it makes my chest tighten, I can't bring myself to let her relax in my presence. I want her on edge. Unsure. Questioning everything, including, but not limited to, what I might do next. Its fucked up, but I can't forget her betrayal. That doesn't mean I don't want her with everything inside me. I do. And I will have her. Even if I have to slip her one of those melatonin tablets she likes so much. Fucking her while she sleeps opened up a whole new kink for me and I can't wait to do it again. Hmm, I run my finger across my bottom lip. Now there's a thought... one I might put into action later.

She chews her plump bottom lip nervously. My eyes follow the movement like my life depends on it. Fuck, what I wouldn't give to have that plump flesh wrapped around me right now. My cock likes the idea, if the twitching in my pants is anything to go by. Her hot mouth, taking me deep inside. Fucking her throat until tears fill her eyes. Until she makes those cute gagging noises, begging for air, that I won't give her. Coming so hard, I choke her with my seed and then watching as she blacks out. I bite back a smirk as memories of doing just that assault me. Christ, she was the best fuck I ever had. And she had to go and ruin it by running away from me.

"I want a phone so I can call Patty," she blurts, pulling me from my erotic memories.

My narrowed gaze snap to hers. I glower, my blood boiling at her request. "No."

She sighs like she expected that to be my answer. From the determination flickering in her eyes, I know this isn't the end of her argument. "Nico, please. She was my family. I just want to know that she is okay. To let her know that me and Romeo are okay. Please." Her breath catches on the last word.

Something cracks inside me, and I relax slightly as I mull over her words. She is right. The old woman was her family. She took in *my* family. My son. Helped them when most people wouldn't have. Patty isn't a threat to me. Not now. Not ever. Maybe in letting her have this one thing, she will soften toward me... and let me have her. Exhaling, I watch her as she watches me. I already know that I am going to let her contact Patty. But it does come with conditions.

"Okay." Her eyes widen in surprise, no doubt at my acquiesce. "But," I add, and her face falls. "I will be in the room with you. You don't ask about the *boy*. You don't even mention his goddamn name." My eyes narrow. "You won't so much as think about the fucker." It's irrational, and I know there is no way on earth I could monitor whether he crosses her mind or not, but still, she needs to hear this. Know there will be consequences if she disobeys me. The thought that she does think about him makes me want to get back on my jet, hunt him down and slit his throat open. My heart rate kicks up with my anger and my eye twitches. Why did I have to mention him? Now I've probably put the thought of him in her pretty little head. Fuck. I scrub a palm down my face, trying to control my rage. Looking at her, I continue. "If you can't abide by these simple rules, then you can forget about calling her." I finish before I completely lose my shit. It's not even her fault this time. It's my own jealous thoughts and the ones I'm putting in her head.

She swallows, eyeing me cautiously as if I'm going to withdraw my offer. "Okay," her easy agreement has me pausing for a second. Narrowing my gaze, I search her face for any hint of a lie but all I see is the truth. And gratitude. She shifts in her seat, and I know she has more to say.

"Out with it," I demand.

Her lips part on a soft breath. She smiles, a real smile and it's so breathtaking my heart skips a beat. This obsession with her is out of control. A runaway train with no end. I should not allow these emotions toward her to rule me, but right now, with that look on her face, I can't bring myself to care.

"I want to go back to dancing. Are there any local studios I could attend?"

Leaning back in my chair, I smirk. "You're very demanding today, Tesoro. Anything else you want while you are here?"

Her smile fades and she mumbles out, "The only other thing I want you won't allow, so I won't bother asking."

I don't have to ask what she means. I know full well. She wants me to let her go which will never happen. "You're right. I will never allow it. You're mine whether you like it or not Ocean, so you better get on board and start being more accepting toward me." Pushing out of my seat, I round the desk. Coming to stand in front of her, I drop my hands to the arms of her chair, caging her in.

Leaning in, I revel in the way her breath hitches and eyes dilate. "Even after everything you have done, I'm being reasonable toward you, *Tesoro*. I will allow you to have your ballet. You can have your phone calls, but I won't tolerate you even thinking about me letting you go. Get the thought out of your head. It will never happen." My hand drops to her bare thigh; she tenses slightly. Narrowing my eyes, I dance my fingers up to the hem of her dress. Her chest heaves, lust flashing in her eyes. She tries to force herself to relax but she is as stiff as a statue, the only indication she is still breathing is in the quick pants of air leaving her mouth. I smirk. She still wants me. Though she will never admit it, it's written all over her face. "It would be so easy," I trail my fingers higher, and she stops breathing altogether. "To shove my hand under this pretty dress, push your panties aside and thrust my fingers inside your tight little cunt. I bet you're soaking." A small gasp leaves her lips. With that reaction alone, I know that I'm right. "You want me. I see it in your eyes, smell it in the air." I sniff just to prove a point. "Though you hate that you still want me, it doesn't change the fact that you do. And I want you too, baby." My tongue darts out, desperate to touch her skin. Licking a trail up her neck, I grin as she whimpers. "I want to be buried so deep inside *my* pussy, that you will never get me out."

Those words snap her out of her trance. She pulls back,

shaking her head. "No," the one word is an unconvincing whisper.

Straightening, I smile down at her, "Yes."

The fire and defiance that I love so much light up her eyes. She darts out of her seat, pushing me back in the process. "You're fucking married, you asshole. How dare you?" she seethes. I just grin, dropping down on the edge of my desk. Her little finger jerks between us. "We have a son together and I will co-parent for his sake, but as for anything else? We are done." She spins on her heel, walking to the door and pulling it open. Pausing, she glances over her shoulder. "I would rather be celibate for the rest of my life than let you touch me again."

I grin. "That will most definitely be the case, Tesoro. Trust me. The only cock you will ever have is mine, so if you don't have me, then you *will* be celibate for the rest of your life," I tell her honestly.

"You are so full of double standards. Fuck you, Nico." She growls like a little lioness and without another word, she steps into the hall, slamming the door closed behind her.

I chuckle, shaking my head. Though she is pissing me off, I will allow her little tantrum. But only because she really has no choice in the matter. I will be fucking her again and very soon. But first things first, she needs to be punished for her insubordination. Especially as I have been so accommodating toward the requests she has made.

Grabbing my cell from my desk, I open it up and scroll to a number I haven't used in nearly a year. Smirking, I hit dial, my lips curving when she answers on the first ring. It's an asshole move of me, but I never pretended to be a nice man and with this one move, my lying little *Tesoro* will understand just who she is dealing with.

"Gianna? I would like to invite you for dinner tomorrow evening."

Chapter 15
Ocean

I keep my gaze locked on the big floor to ceiling windows, watching with rapt attention as Nico carries our son around the backyard. My heart constricts, emotion tightening my throat. It's a sight to behold and not even a week ago I thought I would never get to see this. I am a mixture of emotion, both loving and hating it in equal measures, though I would never admit to the former to Nico. The hate part comes from what Nico threatened me with. His words about taking Romeo away from me. I can't pretend that he is not capable of doing something like that, because he is. I want to pretend that everything will be okay, but it's a naïve way of thinking, since every time he looks at me it is with a sneer curving his lips and disdain in his eyes. He wants to punish me, but he can bet that I won't go down without a fight. He may be a ruthless mafia Don, but when it comes to me and my son, he will be stepping into a battle that even the devil himself would avoid.

My body stiffens as if preparing itself for a war I'm not yet privy to. My gaze narrows in on them both, breath quickening when I witness how Nico gazes down at Romeo with a softness and awe I have never seen from him before. Tears prick my eyes at the knowledge that I have denied him the privilege of being a father for the first months of our son's life. Though I never had a choice in the matter, I am a paradox of emotion and what ifs. I shake my head, knowing that I need to pull myself together before I completely fall apart. That is one thing I cannot allow, despite how I am feeling.

As if Nico can sense me watching him, his head lifts, cocking to the side when those blue orbs lock on me and pinning me in place. For a split second, I don't see the resentment or betrayal that I've become accustomed to staring back at me and my body relaxes. The tight ball of tension, that has been within me from the moment I saw Nico again, leaves me and before I can stop myself, a timid smile curves my lips.

Nico's eyes narrow in suspicion, and he studies me for a long beat, no doubt looking for any sign that my grin is insincere. When all he finds is sincerity, I think he may return my smile but then, as if he thinks better of it, he turns away, giving me his back. My face falls, shoulders sag. It would make life so much easier for both of us if we can be civil, and me extending a smile toward him was my way of waving a white flag of sorts. This situation is hard enough as it is, it will be better for Romeo if we get along – though Nico seems to have other plans. Figures.

Swallowing, I look away, startling when I find that I am no longer alone. "Jesus, you scared me."

Allegra grins, stepping closer. Her gaze shifts to the window, then back to me. "I never thought I would see the day." My brows furrow in confusion at her words. "Nico as a father," she clarifies.

Snorting a laugh, I stare at her in disbelief. I don't mean to be rude but come on. Surely, he will have children with his wife one day. Though, I do have to wonder why I have never seen her, or why no one mentions her in this house. It's like she is a ghost. Or perhaps Nico has ordered everyone, including his mother and sister, to keep their mouths shut and not talk about her in front of me. For all I know, he could have the woman he loves, the woman he deemed good enough to marry, holed up in another wing of this ridiculously sized mansion. Maybe he visits her for sex when the mood strikes him, while I am oblivious and naïvely think he sleeps in the room next to me every night.

Every time I even bring her up, he just smirks, shutting the conversation down before I can ask him more. My guess is he doesn't want to discuss his wife with his baby mama. Shaking my head, I try to rid it of my errant thoughts as an emotion I don't even want to decipher right now surges in my veins. I shove it down before it takes life in my mind, and I go down another rabbit hole of questions. At this rate, I am going to go crazy by the time the week is out.

Shaking my head, I try to rationalize my thoughts. Of course, everything is subjective. Until I find out the truth, or concrete evidence, I don't know anything for sure. I could ask Allegra, but I don't want to bring her into our mess or put her in an awkward position with her brother.

Plastering on a smile, I murmur. "I'm sure he will have a brood of heirs someday."

A knowing smirk tips her lips before she covers it. "I think we should get to know one another better." Her quick change of subject gives me whiplash, but I need all the allies I can get in this place, so it's a no brainer. And anyway, I want to get to know Allegra and Valentina more. After all, I am living with them, and they have both been so lovely toward me since I have been here.

"That would be nice," I say honestly, before taking a seat on the big plush leather couch.

Her eyes light up with happiness, but it's in that moment I see something else. Loneliness. Sadness. I have no idea what it was like for her growing up in a powerful mafia family, but without her even telling me, I can tell that her life is completely different to Nico's. "You look like you are going stir crazy and it's only been a couple of days," she muses, and I frown. She chuckles, shaking her head. "I know what it's like being kept a prisoner here," she says, confirming my thoughts about her upbringing. She sighs. "It's not much, but I will speak with my brother about allowing us to go shopping in town. We will have a team of guards, of course." She rolls her eyes. "But at least it will get us out of the house, have a change of scenery. Even if only for a couple of hours."

I smile, grateful at her attempts to make me feel better about my situation. "I've never been one to shop, but maybe we could check out some dance studios?"

"You're a dancer?"

I nod. "Ballet." My cheeks heat in embarrassment. Not that I have anything to be embarrassed about, but I do feel a little mortified telling her this. "Though I met Nico when I worked at his club."

Understanding crosses her features, a breathy laugh leaving her lips. "The Executive Club? The high-end gentleman only club?"

"The one and only," I admit.

"So, you were a stripper?" There's no malice or condescension to her question, just curiosity.

I sigh, "I was..." I trail off, thinking about how much I should tell her. I don't have anything to hide, so I continue. "Well, I was until Nico fired me. He then gave me a job at *Bellissima*, which I loved, but dancing is in my veins." I wring my hands together, nibbling my lip as I watch for any judgment, but it doesn't come.

"I know it's something that many look down on, but with stripping I was able to earn enough to afford to live and eat in New York."

Dropping down beside me, she takes my hand, giving it a gentle squeeze. "There's no shame in doing what you need to do in order to survive, Ocean. I would do the same if I had to."

I open my mouth to reply, only to clamp it shut when a deep masculine voice growls. "There is no fucking scenario I can think of in which I would allow you to take your clothes off for a living, *princepessa*."

Both of our heads snap up to find Dante, his gaze fixated on Allegra, as he saunters into the room with so much swagger it should be illegal. I watch him with curiosity as his eyes rake over every inch of her. The love and hunger in his dark orbs have me wanting to turn away. I suddenly feel that I am intruding on something personal. Something that is theirs and theirs alone. I stare, somewhat transfixed by the open display of affection between them. A boulder lodges in my throat and I swallow, emotion slamming into me. I want someone to look at me the way Dante looks at Allegra.

The sound of the glass door sliding open has my attention shifting in that direction. Nico enters the lounge with Romeo securely in his arms. Wanting to move away from the palpable bubble of love radiating from Dante and Allegra, I push off the couch, rushing toward my son.

"Hey, baby," I coo, reaching out to take him. I'm a little shocked when Nico hands him right over to me, until I get a whiff of the diaper that needs changing. I scowl at him, though he can't see it.

"Nic," Allegra calls, and I guess she has finished whatever silent conversation she was having with Dante. "Ocean and I would like to go shopping." She steps up beside us.

Nico stiffens, glancing at me then back to his sister. He is quiet for a minute and I think he will deny her, but then he speaks. "I can arrange for my men to take you, but it might be later in the week. I have some things to take care of first."

Allegra chuckles, shoulder checking her brother. Nico shoves her back playfully. I watch them curiously, fascinated by how Nico seems almost...normal? I don't know what I expected from their relationship, but it wasn't this. He is not a Don right now. He is just a brother. One that I can tell loves his sister dearly... unlike mine. I shake the thought away.

As if remembering who he is and that I am standing here, he clears his throat. "I have business to attend to. Let's go, Dante." His tone leaves no room for argument and without another word, both men leave the room.

***

The next day, I'm told by Nico that we have a formal dinner this evening and to dress accordingly for our guests. I asked him why he was asking me to join him and not his wife, but he completely shut me down, so maybe she will be joining him after all. I feel sick at the thought, and everything inside me screams at me not to go, but Nico assured me there would be consequences if I don't attend, so I don't fight him on it further.

I don't know who is joining us and what the dinner entails, but I do find a long, red silk cocktail dress, with matching red soled pumps, waiting in my bedroom later that afternoon. Just from the outfit laid out for me, I come to the conclusion that it must be someone important if he is going to these lengths. I'm not particularly in the mood for socializing, but I know I have no choice. And like I said, I need to pick my battles.

Sighing, I take a seat in the Chesterfield chair so I can feed

Romeo. Once he has had his milk, he will be due his afternoon nap, which means I will be able to prepare for tonight.

I don't know why, but something tells me I'm going to need every little ounce of strength that I possess.

But that's okay.

Because I will be ready for it and whatever Nico throws at me.

Chapter 16
Nico

The front door being opened by one of the staff has me smirking. I already know who it is. Security alerted me of her arrival not even five minutes ago. I'm an asshole, but this needs to be done. Ocean needs to know her place.

Just as that thought crosses my mind, Gianna sashays inside, a triumphant smile on her face and her guard hot on her heels. She is dressed to kill, in a tight black dress and high heeled black pumps. With perfect make-up and hair, she is the typical spoiled mafia princess; coddled all her life by her papà and given whatever the hell she desired. Her papà has given her too much power and free rein, hence why she is allowed to dine with me this evening, alone, with only one bodyguard to accompany her.

This whole charade is a shit move on my behalf, but I want to get a reaction out of Ocean and using Gianna will do just that. Though she pretends otherwise, she still has feelings for me, and I know she is curious about the woman she thinks is my wife.

"Nico," Gianna purrs, stepping right into my chest. Her

hard nipples brush my white dress shirt, a tactical move on her part. She wants to get a reaction out of me. Little does she know, my dick only seems to work for one woman now.

"Gianna. You look stunning as always," I say honestly, because despite me not wanting to marry the woman, or having a single sexual feeling toward her, I can appreciate that she is beautiful. Unfortunately for her, my cock is already owned and that is how it will stay. Leaning in, I press a kiss to one cheek, then the other, before pulling back.

Her eyes drip with lust, a seductive smile curving her lips. She flutters her thick black lashes up at me, her hand landing on my arm in a possessive grip. "Thank you. I have to say, I was both confused and thrilled at your invitation to dinner. Have you changed your mind?"

Resisting an eye roll, I smirk down at her. "We have much to discuss. Why don't you head on into the dining room? I will be with you shortly."

The sound of heels on the marble floor has me glancing over my shoulder, to find my sister and Dante entering the large foyer. Allegra's face scrunches up in confusion when she spots Gianna. I can't blame her. As far as she knows, the engagement is off. Indefinitely.

"Gianna?" she asks her name as a question, the bewilderment in her voice clear.

"Allegra. How lovely to see you," Gianna's voice drips with fake sincerity. I grit my teeth. It's one thing I always hated about her. Like a snake in the grass, ready to attack at any point, Gianna knows just how to act to get what she wants. And she wants me. Unbeknownst to her, that will never happen, so she can quit the nice act. My sister's lips form a tight line. She looks at me, with clear disappointment in her eyes.

"Dante, can you escort Gianna to the dining room and get her a drink." It's not a question but an expectation.

"Of course," he holds his arm out for her to take, but the viper looks back to me.

"Is there somewhere Carlo can wait?"

"Mis–" her guard starts, but she cuts him off with a single glare.

"Sure. A couple of my senior guards are currently eating in the staff quarters. He can join them if he likes?" She smiles, nodding. As if Gio, one of my senior men, knew I was going to summon him he appears. "Ah, Gio, please take Carlo to the staff quarters while Gianna joins me for dinner."

Gio glances at Carlo, jerking his head and silently telling him to follow him. He does. Poor guy has his orders and will follow them. Though he knows full well that Gianna's papà, Arturo, will have his ass if he ever finds out that she was left alone with me, or any other man for that matter, while she is unmarried. I doubt Gianna is the innocent he thinks her to be, but Arturo would expect Carlo to stand guard, hidden in the shadows of my dining room while we eat. Strange to some, but it's normal in our world.

Latching onto Dante's outstretched arm, Gianna saunters down the hall with my second in command. Allegra watches them with narrowed eyes before she looks to me. Shooting me a glower, she hisses out. "What the hell are you doing bringing her here?"

Irritation slithers through me. She may be my sister, but she doesn't get to interrogate me. Clenching my jaw, I pin her with a glare. "She is our guest. You will treat her with respect, Allegra," I warn.

She shakes her head, concern flickering on her face. "Don't do this to Ocean, Nico." She pleads. "I know full well you don't want that..." she trails off, her face screwing up like she is sucking on lemons. "You don't want Gianna, Nico. I know

Ocean hurt you. I know you want to punish her. But I see it in your eyes, you love her."

A snarl curls my lips. I see red. "You know nothing. Stay out of it, Allegra, I won't tell you again."

My sister flinches, her eyes turning glassy. The sadness in them makes my throat tighten with guilt, but I can't back down. "You want her to hate you?" It's a rhetorical question so she doesn't expect an answer. "This is the way to do it. You want her to start trusting you, loving you? Tell her the truth," she snaps, glowering at me. With one last look of disdain, but without another word, she turns on her heel and heads for the dining room.

Scrubbing a hand down my face, I contemplate my sister's concern. She doesn't understand or know anything. She doesn't know the torture and pain I felt every day for over a year, not knowing what had happened to Ocean or if I would see her again. Or how it feels, knowing that I missed the first couple months of my son's life, Ocean's pregnancy, and the birth, all because of her selfish actions.

Loosening my top button, I exhale a breath. My lying little *Tesoro* deserves to be tormented a little, even if it's just to understand a fraction of how I felt.

With the reminder of what she has done, I push any thought of putting a stop to this aside.

Plastering a smirk on my face, I stride down the hall to where my guest awaits.

Let the games begin.

***

Glancing around the twelve-seat dining table, I smile at a smug, beaming, Gianna with hearts in her eyes. Looking away from her, my gaze lands on my sister. Her face is blank, her lips tight, and I feel the tension radiating from her. I grimace but know full well that no look will make me back down. I'm too far gone now.

Mamma refused to join us for dinner, knowing exactly what I was doing by inviting Gianna here. She played off her refusal by offering to watch Romeo for the evening, but I saw the real reason for her anger and animosity toward me. My jaw clenches. The reason hasn't arrived yet. In fact she is, I glance down at my watch, fifteen minutes late. Little witch has probably done it on purpose. She knows I expect punctuality.

"Nico," Gianna purrs, her hand landing on my arm. I resist the urge to pull away from her touch but hold still so she doesn't suspect anything. "How are things since your papà passed? Rumor has it that you are ruling the *famiglia* with an iron fist." She smirks, a hint of pride in her tone. Bless her little delusional heart. She still thinks that one day she will be my wife. It's clear she wants nothing more than that. To be my wife would give her the power she craves. Though her papà has influence and money, being Mrs. Marchetti will give her even more – and that's exactly what a woman like Gianna wants.

"Of course. That's the only way," I drawl, lifting my scotch with my free hand and taking a sip.

Her eyes light up with even more interest. She rubs small circles on the forearm of my white dress shirt, her face a picture of seduction and lust. Gianna's mouth opens only to snap shut when my sister speaks.

"That's a lovely dress, Gianna. It shows off all your..." Allegra trails, grinning, "all of your assets." It's an insult, one Gianna misses.

"Thank you, Allegra." She beams, completely oblivious to the passive aggressiveness radiating from my sister.

The sound of heels on the tiled floor cuts all conversation. Blood thrums in my veins, everything inside of me sparking to life. She's here. My little *Tesoro* has finally decided to grace us with her presence.

Leaning back in my seat, I lace my fingers with Gianna's. Her eyes snap to me, confusion swimming in them, but I pay her no attention, fixing my gaze on the entrance. I watch as Ocean steps inside the dining room. Her eyes instantly land on me, making my breath catch in my throat. Fuck, she is so beautiful it hurts to look at her. The red dress, that I picked out for her, hugs her body perfectly, accentuating every curve. Her hair is down in long blonde waves, covering her bare shoulders. Her dark lashes are laced with a hint of mascara, and her pouty lips are a shade of red that matches her dress. Christ, I want that lipstick printed all over my cock. She is perfect. Stunning. My cock thickens in my pants as I watch her, and I can no longer deny the effect she has on me when we are in the same room. This need, to throw her over my shoulder, claim her. It. Happens. Every. Fucking. Time.

Without breaking eye contact, I watch as her steps falter when her gaze shifts to Gianna. Her lips purse, eyes bouncing between the two of us before they lock on me. Hurt shines in those blue orbs and I hesitate, only to quickly shove the hesitation away. I have to see this through.

"Who is this, Nico?" The bitchy tone of Gianna's voice irritates me, and I nearly pull my hand from hers.

Glancing from the pawn beside me back to the little witch in front of me, I smirk. "Don't worry about her, darling."

"Jesus," Allegra whispers under her voice. Pushing her chair back, she stands. "I'm not waiting around to watch this." She storms from the room, and it only takes seconds for Dante to follow her.

Ocean stays rooted to the spot, her eyes glistening with unshed tears. Being the defiant little thing she is, she doesn't let them fall. Something a lot like pride blooms in my chest but I tamp it down. Her blue orbs drop to where my hand is laced with Gianna's. Her jaw clenches, lips twisting as something a lot like jealousy flashes in her eyes. I resist the urge to smirk. Mission accomplished. It's exactly the reaction I wanted out of her. I know these games are juvenile and beneath me, but they need playing if only to show Ocean exactly who is in control here.

"Nico?" Gianna prompts, gripping my hand in a vice grip, like she is never going to let go.

Ocean looks at her, a slight tremble in her voice when she speaks. "Don't worry. I'm a nobody and I'm leaving." She glances at me, "You're a fucking asshole, Nico." And without another word, she lifts her dress and rushes from the room.

Pulling my hand from Gianna's, my eye twitches when I stare at the spot she just vacated. I thought I would feel triumphant at getting the reaction I wanted out of her, but all I feel is the emptiness of her absence.

"Nico?" Gianna whines, snapping me from my thoughts.

Pushing out of my chair, I glare down at her, spitting, "Leave."

Chapter 17

Ocean

My feet hit the sand, each step getting heavier, jerkier, and angrier as I run toward the sea. The wind whips through my hair, blowing it all over my face as blind rage, with a hint of jealousy, courses through my body, getting stronger with every moment that passes. I am wound so tight; I feel like I could snap at any second. I want to scream, shout, punch Nico in his perfect face. I want... well, I don't know what I want.

Grains of sand stick to my feet and between my toes, the feel of it freeing somehow. I can only be thankful that I had the foresight to remove the ridiculously high pumps before I made my hasty exit through the glass sliding doors in the lounge.

I don't know what I am doing or where I am going, I just know I need space. A minute to myself, to think, without being watched by Nico or his men. Valentina is watching over Romeo which makes me feel a little better about leaving him at the mansion. I trust Nico's mom with my son, know that she will keep him safe, while I am out here having a complete meltdown.

Hitting the shoreline, I come to a stop when water hits my feet and legs, soaking the bottom of my red dress. My chest heaves from the exertion of my little run, reminding me how unfit I am. I suck in air, trying to catch my breath, but anxiety trickles into my veins, making it difficult. Suddenly the designer dress feels too tight, and I feel like I'm suffocating. Bending at the waist, my hands rest on my thighs. I inhale then exhale, trying to calm the incoming panic attack.

Inhale. Exhale.

Inhale. Exhale.

I repeat the words in my head like a mantra and it seems to work because my breathing evens out. I haven't had an anxiety attack since I lived with my parents, and though I have managed to talk myself down from a full-blown panic attack, I'm still pissed that I have allowed myself to get to this point. I have worked hard to control this part of myself, so why all of a sudden have I allowed Nico to make me feel this way? Why am I giving him so much power over my emotions? I'm stronger and better than all these games he insists on playing. I've survived and overcome many things in my life, yet I fall at Nico's first hurdle. Frustration claws at my skin, making me want to itch it away. Without even thinking about it, I let out an animalistic scream. It's cathartic, much needed, and somehow, I feel much better than I did minutes ago.

Straightening, I wrap my arms around myself, and stare out at the waves. It's tranquil out here, exactly what I need after feeling smothered in that big house. I don't know what just happened in there, and though I hated every second of being in that room, being the butt of Nico's joke, I blow out a breath, setting free all the anger Nico stirred up in me. Calm washes over me, thoughts of my next move flickering in my mind. I could fight the asshole. But I know, without a doubt, that will not get me anywhere. The only other option I have right now is to accept what is and resign myself to the fate Nico has bestowed upon me.

The other woman.

Though Nico never introduced me to her, it was obvious that she was his wife – or whatever the hell she is – from the way she was touching him. The way he held her hand. Their intimacy looked easy, like they had been doing that same thing their whole lives. Nonetheless, it was a shock to see the woman in person, the queen of Nico's castle and the one he deemed worthy of a permanent place in his life. I knew she existed, it's why I left in the first place. I just didn't think Nico would be so cruel as to flaunt her in my face. I get that he is angry about me running and missing Romeo's first couple of months, but to do that without warning was vindictive, callous, and down-right humiliating. No matter what happened between us in the past, he needs to respect that I am his son's mother. Not throw his wife in my face, every chance he gets.

My chest cracks, pain radiating through me as images of them together flash in my mind. His wife. With her long dark hair, blood red lips, big, almond shaped, chocolate eyes surrounded by thick dark lashes, she is beautiful and exactly the kind of woman I always pictured him with. Not only was she gorgeous, but she also exudes power, wealth and confidence, in a way that most could only dream of. Seated next to Nico, she looked like a queen beside her king, while I am just his... I swallow when the words Nico's father said to me that day slam into me.

Whore.

Nico's fucking puttana.

It is all you will ever be.

Tears prick my eyes, the reality of the situation and being confronted by it slamming into me. I fell for that asshole, told him that I loved him and all the while he had the perfect Italian woman waiting to take his name. I fucking hate him. Hate him for what he did and what he continues to do.

"You, okay?" a gentle voice asks, making me yelp in fear. My head snaps around to find a man standing to my right. He watches me with wide, apologetic eyes, hands held up placatingly, as if I am a corned animal getting ready to bolt.

I don't take my attention from him as I wipe the tears from my eyes. My gaze rakes over him, searching for any sign of threat, but I find nothing. All I see is genuine concern and a kind face. From the clothes he is wearing, I am also one hundred percent sure that he isn't one of Nico's men, which puts me at ease further. I don't need that bastard's goons witnessing me like this.

"I'm fine thank you. I was just getting some air." I murmur, throwing him a smile.

He frowns, shoving his hands in his cargo pants pockets. I let my eyes roam his face. My guess is he is in his early twenties, and he is cute, in the boy next door kind of way. With blonde hair, green eyes and perfect white teeth, he looks like a real-life Ken doll.

"You sure? I heard you screaming, and you look like you've been crying," he prods.

My cheeks heat in embarrassment. I hate that he was privy to my meltdown. I nod. "I'm sure. I was just letting out some pent-up frustration," I chuckle softly.

"Next time I'm frustrated I might try it myself," he teases, a big grin curving his lips. Cocking his head, his eyes bounce over every inch of my face. He frowns. "I haven't seen you around here before. Did you just move here?"

I laugh, but it's humorless. "You could say that."

He smirks. "Maybe I could show you around some–"

Before he can finish, he is cut off by a dark, threatening voice. We both jump in surprise, our heads snapping toward the sinister tone. "Finish that sentence, and you won't be able to show yourself around, let alone *my* girl." My eyes widen, but

Nico isn't watching me, no. His predatory gaze is locked on his prey. "Now I suggest you run along, little boy, and forget this conversation happened. Or even better, forget that you ever met her, before I do something that *you* can't come back from." He runs his thumb across his bottom lip, his blue orbs sparking as if he is enjoying every second of this. Twisted bastard probably is. "If there is any confusion, *Rhys*, I will spell it out for you. I will fucking kill you and dump your body in the damn ocean if I catch you sniffing around my woman again."

"Nico–" I hiss, but he holds a hand up, cutting me off.

I glance at the man I now know is called Rhys. His eyes are wide, and he looks an unnatural shade of white. He swallows, his whole body trembling. "I'm sorry Mr. Marchetti, I didn't know she was with you."

"Well, now you do. Now fuck off before your parents find your body washed up somewhere along this beach."

Nico jerks his head and without another word or look in my direction, Rhys turns, taking off down the beach like his ass is on fire. Nico watches after him, his stance threating like he thinks Rhys might turn around and rejoin this shit-show.

"How dare you?" I seethe and he finally looks at me, as if he now deems me worthy of his attention. "You don't get to do this to me. You have a wife. A fucking wife, Nico, and yet you threaten to kill any man that comes near me. You have some nerve." I hiss, shaking my head.

"You are mine," he grits out through clenched teeth.

A disbelieving laugh leaves my mouth before I can stop it, my lip curling in disgust. "Go back to your *wife*, Nico. I won't be your whore."

Shouldering past him, I start back to the house only to stop when he grips my wrist and pulls me into him. "You will be whatever I want you to be, *Tesoro*." His hot breath hitting my ear makes me shiver. "And don't you forget that. You. Are.

Mine." he enunciates. "In every sense of the word. The more you fight it, the more I will enjoy breaking you until you accept what is, before reconstructing you back up to the woman you are meant to be. Mine." he growls, his grip tightening almost painfully.

My lips part, body vibrating with disgust and anger. Pulling out of Nico's hold, I shove him away from me. Shooting him one last glower, I turn, taking off back toward the house as fast as my feet will take me. Heavy footfalls sound behind me and my heart rate kicks up to an unnatural rhythm. I don't look back, not wanting to see the devil chasing me. When I make it to the dunes, I grin to myself, thinking I have outrun him and I'm home free. I should have known better. Known that Nico will always catch me.

Strong arms wrap around me, and I cry out as I'm tackled to the sand. All the air leaves my lungs and I grunt when my body hits the ground with a loud thud. Nico's big body surrounds me, the weight of him on my back pushing me further into the sand. He is only on top of me mere seconds before he is flipping me over onto my back.

"Nico," I gasp out, my hair wild and the feel of sand everywhere. He comes down on top of me, shifting his body until he is settled between my parted thighs. His hard cock rubs against my clit causing a delicious friction. I stifle a moan, not wanting him to hear what he is doing to me. "Get off me," I hiss, pushing at his chest. My attempts at dislodging him are futile. He is just too big. Too strong.

"No," he rumbles, a smirk curving his sinful lips as his blue eyes flare with desire.

Before I can argue further, his head drops to the crook of my neck, tongue darting out as he licks a wet trail up the sensitive flesh. I squirm, my stomach tightening with a need that I try to resist. I don't want to be that girl. The one who accepts being treated like a fool.

"Get off me. Go back to your wife." I snap, my body wriggling in my attempt to get free.

His hand moves under the material of my dress, trailing up my thigh, toward the place I want him most but don't want him at all. It's a complete contradiction, but I am a mixture of emotions right now. He feels so good on top of me, touching me. And I can't deny the way my body lights up with his touch. Though I hate him with a passion, he is a master when it comes to sex. But... I shouldn't let him do this.

Pushing my dress up, he shoves my panties to the side. Within seconds his finger is circling my clit. My back arches as pure desire rips through me. And suddenly I'm torn. On one hand, I want to stop it going any further, but on the other hand, it feels too good. It's been so long since anyone has touched me there and the silly girl that I am, I'm caught up in the sensations running through my body.

"Hmm, there's my dirty *Tesoro*. You are a slut for my fingers and cock." His voice is like a cold bucket of water being thrown over me, and I am reminded of who he is. And that he is *married*.

"I swear to god Nico, you better stop this and get off me."

Lifting his head, he stares down at me. "I already told you once before, *Tesoro*, I am your God. Your fucking religion. And you will pray to me. Bow to me. Even after a year of you being away, that statement still stands. You will submit. You will be everything I want and more. There is no other way for you. There is no life for you without me."

My mouth drops open in shock. This asshole. Who the hell does he think he is? "You're married!" I scream, getting right in his face.

He shakes his head, his mouth dropping to my ear. He still rubs at my clit as his free hand snakes up to wrap around my throat. It's a power move, not just to hold me in place, but to let me know who is in control. Despite the clear anger rolling off him, his thumb circles the erratic pulse in my neck gently. I would like to think it's an affectionate gesture, but I know Nico. He doesn't do affection.

"No. I'm not. Yes, there was an arranged marriage in place last year, but after my papà died, I put a stop to it. I don't want her. I want you. I will have you. You are mine. Nothing and no one will change that." His voice is a dark whisper, and he circles my clit harder. My eyes widen. I want to say something. *Anything*. But I can't while he is playing my body like this. I need a release and I will take every bit this bastard is offering me right now and address his confession when I am done.

Melting into the sand, I submit, letting the pleasure take over. My eyes roll shut, and I roll my hips into his touch, seeking the friction I so desperately need.

"That's my girl." Nico whispers, nibbling on my ear lobe. I want to cry at the satisfaction in his voice. The smugness. And the worst thing is, he has every right to be smug. I've played straight into the devil's hands. He knows it. I know it. But right now, as he shoves a finger inside me, I can't bring myself to care. I cry out at the intrusion, my back arching as I ride his hand. Fuck, this feels good. So good, I am going to…

"Now come all over my finger so I can take you inside. It's been too long since my cock was inside this perfect pussy, and I won't wait any longer," he growls, snapping me from my thoughts.

Adding another finger, he curls them inside me, rubbing at a spot that has me seeing stars. His ministrations are just like him, slow, torturous, calculated. I don't have anyone to compare Nico to, but the way he makes me feel… wanton, out of my mind, fireworks, surely it can't be normal? My stomach tightens, legs tremble, and like a freight train my orgasm barrels through me.

"Oh, God," I whimper, my hands raking through the sand trying to find purchase.

"So fucking beautiful when you come," Nico murmurs, his lips pressing to mine as he finger fucks me through my climax. He kisses me through my orgasm, the move intimate and familiar. I want to push him away, but I don't have the strength. Instead, I break the kiss, as I slump back in the sand. Not wanting to look at Nico or confront what just happened, I squeeze my eyes closed and try to process everything. All that he just confessed.

My eyes shoot open, landing on his arrogant face, and in that moment, I know three things.

Nico. Isn't. Married.

He lied.

And I don't know how to feel about it.

Chapter 18
Nico

Ocean blinks up at me, her bright blue eyes shining with sated lust in the moonlight. Fuck, she is so beautiful when she comes undone. It makes my obsession with her grow further. Deeper. Stronger. Out of control. I'm free falling into her web and no matter how hard I try, I can't stop it. My cock jerks, begging to sink itself into its home and I cannot wait another second to fuck her. Taking her to my bedroom will take five minutes at least, which is at this point unacceptable. I need her now.

Pulling my fingers from her tight cunt, she watches as I bring them to my mouth, sucking them inside. I lick her essence clean, something snapping inside me when her taste hits my tongue. I'm feral, unhinged with a need to stake my claim. Remind her exactly who she belongs to. Releasing her throat, I quickly unbuckle my belt.

"I need to fuck you now," my voice is urgent, as is my need to release my cock and sink inside her. Pulling my pants down, followed by my boxer briefs, I watch as my hard length springs free, slapping against my white dress shirt. Ocean's gaze drops to my thick cock, her eyes dilating with pure desire. I nearly come on the spot, the look of hunger on her face matching my own. For some reason, everything about this woman does it for me, but I'm not stupid enough to believe if she wasn't so boneless from her orgasm, that she wouldn't be fighting me right now, which is why my moves are hurried.

Gripping her panties, I rip them from her body in one swift move, revealing her bare pussy. I salivate at the sight. Wet. Swollen. *Mine.* Palming my shaft, I line myself up with her entrance and without another thought, I thrust inside her tight cunt. Gritting my teeth, I still. Christ, she is even tighter than I remember. Her pussy hugs my cock in a vise grip, fits me like a glove and it's like she never wants me to leave. The feeling is mutual. *I don't want to leave.* If I could stay inside her forever, I would.

Ocean jolts, snapping out of her post orgasmic trance. She pushes at my chest, her eyes wild. "No, Nico. Wait," she cries out, but nothing will stop me from getting what I want. "I'm not on birth control," she adds, her words are a whimper as I bottom out inside of her.

Leaning down, I press my lips to hers, tugging at her full bottom lip and sucking it into my mouth. "I don't fucking care. I will never accept anything between us. Not now. Not ever."

"Nico. No," she gasps. "We can't do this."

"We can and we will," I snarl, covering her mouth with mine so she can't spew anymore stupid words.

But still, she protests, her head shifting from side to side as if that will stop me. Gripping her neck, I hold her in place, keeping her exactly where I want her. Snapping my hips forward, I fuck into her so hard, so deep, I don't know where I begin, and she ends. My eyes roll shut at the pure pleasure coursing through my body. Nothing has ever felt this good. Nothing ever will. I don't know how I lived without feeling her for so long. But it will never happen again. That's a promise.

Though hesitant at first, and knowing she will not get away, she settles into our fucking. Her hips roll forward, meeting me thrust for thrust as she chases her own pleasure. She is close already, her cunt contracting around me, desperate for release and I want it, too. I want to fill her so full of me, that I will be leaking out of her fucking pores for days.

Snaking my free hand down her body, I press down on her plump, wet, clit, circling so hard, she has no choice but to come. It does exactly as I thought it would. She throws her head back in ecstasy, back arching as her cunt nearly swallows me whole. It won't take long to push me over the edge, not with the way her inner walls are clutching me like their life depends on it. Pumping into her harder, faster, I groan when her pussy tightens around me even more, begging me to fill her with my seed.

Ripping my lips from hers, I stare down at her. Her eyes are closed, but pure bliss covers her face. I smirk. "Look at you baby, taking me so well. You are such a good girl, allowing my big cock inside your tight little pussy. You are clenching me so hard, it's like you never want to let me leave. Who owns this cunt? Who, Ocean?" I growl, but the questions are rhetorical. We both know who owns her. "No other man will be inside you but me. Just me. Your pussy fits me like a glove, *Tesoro*. I broke your cunt in. Took your innocence. Molded your pussy to fit only my cock. I claimed you. I. Own. You." I snarl, sounding like a madman. But I don't care. I mean every single word.

"Nico," she cries out, her eyes snapping open when her third orgasm of the night hits. She likes my dirty, possessive words. Likes the praise, even if she won't admit it. Her body thrashes, eyes rolling shut. Small fingers claw at my shirt, trying to find purchase as her climax takes hold. She chants my name, like a goddamn prayer, her pussy contracting as she soaks my cock with more of her juices. She exhales, her body going lax as she slumps back into the sand, a serene, contented, look taking over her face. My gaze drops to her breasts which bounce with the heaving of her chest. Dropping down, I lick a trail across her collar bone, biting the soft flesh and marking her. She stiffens, yelping, but I don't let up. I won't stop until she is covered in my mark.

Once satisfied I have bitten and bruised enough of her flesh, I release her, my gaze moving to her stunning face. Her lips are parted in a silent O, and she is completely lost in me. In her pleasure. I can't help but smirk. She can fight it all she wants, but her body doesn't lie. She wants me.

Bringing her leg up to my hip, I angle my body and pound into her harder. I want to make a home and live inside her cunt. Bury myself so deep she will never get me out. I want my cum leaking out of her for days, want her to feel me every time she moves, while at the same time wanting to punish her for denying me this. For running. For keeping me from my son.

My jaw tightens, I move faster into her. So fast, I'm surprised, I don't punch a hole straight through her. Groaning at the intense feeling of being back inside her, my balls draw up as that familiar tingling sensation zips up and down my spine. I'm going to come. Slowing my thrusts, my balls throb with the need for release. Gripping her neck tighter, I brush my lips against hers, growling out, "Eyes on me, when I come inside you." The good girl that she is, her eyes snap open, locking on mine. My chest tightens. I see my whole life in those blue orbs and the emotion is so strong, I come in thick spurts, filling up her insides. "Christ," I groan, my cock pulsing and filling her with over a year's worth of my seed.

"Nico?" her small voice snaps me from my pleasure filled trance.

Cocking my head, I stare down at her, and not for the first time I ask myself why she has such an effect on me. Yes, she is easily the most beautiful woman I have ever seen and yes, she also has the tightest cunt I've ever been inside. But I have never been a man that has been controlled by sex. I enjoy it, sure. But the feeling Ocean gives me when I'm inside her pussy is addicting. It makes me feral but calm all at the same time. A contradiction, but the truth all the same.

"Yeah?"

She sighs, her eyes glistening with unshed tears. "We shouldn't have done that." Her lip wobbles with her words. I would feel guilty if I was capable of it, but it just irritates me. Something that feels this good has no place for remorse.

Reaching toward her, I run a finger across her soft cheek. "Oh *Tesoro*, it's what our bodies were made to do. And we will do it again and again and a-fucking-gain. I can promise you that much." I pull out of her, frowning when a surge of liquid leaks out down the crease of her thighs. Scooping it up, I shove it back inside her swollen cunt.

She jumps, wriggling beneath me. "Stop. I told you I'm not on birth control. Now you or I am going to have to go a pharmacy to get Plan B."

My hand flies up, wrapping around her delicate neck. I squeeze, not hard but enough that she knows it's a warning. Glaring, I growl out. "You will do no such thing. My seed belongs inside you. If it takes root and you get pregnant, then so be it."

Her eyes widen, head shaking as much as it can in my hold. "No. I will not have another baby with you."

Grinning, I lean down, licking a trail up her neck until my mouth hits her ear. "Oh *Tesoro*. You will have a hundred more of my babies if that's what I want." Obviously, I don't want that many children, but she will be having at least two more. Not that it was my fault, but I missed her pregnancy with Romeo. Missed those first four months of his life and I want to rectify that. Be there through every single moment she is carrying my child. Hold her hair as she throws up with the "morning sickness". Watch her belly swell as she grows my baby inside her womb. Fuck, the thought alone has my cock thickening against her leg.

Leaning back, I glance down at her. She sighs, resignation crossing her features and I'm glad that's settled. I don't want to keep fighting about something that's pointless. She has no choice in the matter.

Pushing to my feet, I tuck myself back inside my pants before grabbing Ocean's hand and pulling her to her bare feet. Sand coats her red dress along with my pants and I briefly wonder where else it has lodged itself. Inside her pussy? I grit my teeth. It better not have. The only thing allowed in her cunt is me.

I shake the irrational thoughts away, my jaw clenching as I realize the extent of my obsession with this woman. It's twisted, maybe a little unhealthy and pushes me to the point of madness. Sighing, I blow out a breath. At this point, I am too far gone so why stop now?

Might as well embrace it.

And I won't be doing this madness alone.

Ocean can resist all she likes, but if I am going down this path, she is coming with me.

"Come on. Let's get cleaned up and then I am going to fuck you again."

Chapter 19

Ocean

My eyes flutter open, a sleepy sigh leaving my parted lips. I blink against the sunlight streaming through the small opening of the drapes, but the sun blinding me is the least of my worries. As if to prove my point, a heavy weight pins me to the bed. Glancing down, I stiffen at the sight of the veiny, muscular, arm wrapped possessively around my naked body. And not just any arm. *Nico's arm.*

After ushering me inside the house last night, he insisted we stay in the same bed. Of course, I refused his demand. Even maintained that just because we had sex, nothing had changed. But of course, being the arrogant bastard that he is, he wouldn't listen. All I managed to achieve with my refusal was to anger him further. By then, I knew my attempts to decline him were futile. The more I pushed, the harder he pulled. By that point, I was too exhausted to fight, so I allowed him to win that round, but not without a compromise. I wouldn't be away from Romeo, even if I was just next door, so we ended up in my room, in my bed, with our son sleeping peacefully next to us, in his crib.

Memories of last night hit me, making me blush when everything comes rushing back. The beach. Rhys. Fighting. Nico chasing me down. Tackling me. Admitting the truth about his *'marriage'* and then fucking me like a wild animal. My body heats, a throb starting between my legs, just thinking about the savage way he took me. I would say I hated it, but then that would make me a liar. The way he dominates me, takes what he wants... my body craves it. Craves his brutality. No doubt it makes me sick, but it's clear Nico is my sickness. I could fight this thing between us, but what's the point? I would only be doing myself a disservice. My head might still be hesitant, but there is no confusion in that my body wants him with a need so fierce it makes me weak.

I know that I gave in way too easily to him, but I can't bring myself to feel shame about it. Not when he played my body like an instrument, giving me three amazing orgasms. It was only a matter of time before it happened anyway. The tension between us has been building since the minute he found me and now that he has fucked me, I feel a little more... relaxed, dare I say?

Sighing, I twist my head to look at him. He looks so peaceful in sleep. Calm. Gentle. A complete contrast to his usual impassive face and blank eyes. I prefer him this way. Nico Marchetti, the human. Not Nico Marchetti, the ruthless Mafia boss. The devil.

Without even thinking about it, I reach up, running a finger down his cheek. As soon as my skin touches the sharp cheekbone, his eyes snap open, making me freeze. His gaze locks on mine, blue orbs trapping me in his web. A knowing smirk curves his lips. Conceited asshole. I scowl, my eyes narrowing in on him threateningly, but he just smiles wider.

"Don't stop on my account, *Tesoro*. You can touch me when and where you like. Though, I would prefer you take care of him first. I'm painfully hard and dying to come inside your cunt." He looks down to where his hard length is straining against the comforter.

Throwing him a dirty look, I move to get out of bed, but he grips my wrist, stopping me in my tracks. "I need to check on Romeo," I hiss, glaring harder at him.

Cocking his head, he glances at our sleeping son. His eyes spark with challenge, his hold on me tightening. "He is still sleeping," he deadpans, pointing out the obvious. And though I am happy my son is peacefully asleep, I wish more than anything he was screaming his little lungs out for me to nurse him and therefore cockblocking his horny father.

Grabbing me by the waist, he flips me onto my back, then hovers over me like a dark presence, daring me to deny him. The man possesses so much strength and power, it's pointless to struggle against him, but that doesn't stop me. I slap at his bare, muscular chest, hissing in a low, whispered voice. "Get off me. Romeo is due for a bottle. He will wake soon."

He smirks, gripping my wrists and pinning them to the bed above my head. He grinds his cock into me, showing me just how hard he is. My eyes roll shut, stifling the whimper begging to leave my lips.

"*My* son is still asleep." He enunciates the words. "You fed him at 11p.m. last night and, from what I have gathered, he doesn't wake until at least seven thirty for his morning feed. Which gives you." He glances at the clock on the nightstand. "Forty minutes to take care of my cock." Leaning down, he runs his tongue up my neck – something I've noticed he likes doing – before nipping at the skin. "Now be a good girl and spread these legs, *Tesoro*. I need *my* pussy."

I roll my eyes. Guess we are back to *his* pussy again. Wriggling, I try to break free from his hold. "I'm not having sex with Romeo in the room."

He chuckles. The sound so raspy and sexy it hits me straight between the legs. "Baby, he doesn't understand what we are doing. And like I said, he is still sleeping. So, stop fighting me on everything and open up that cunt for me. I need to feel you before I start my day."

Nico shifts and I have no choice but to accommodate his big body. My stomach tightens with need when I feel his cock rub against my slit. Reaching down, he grabs his thick length, lines it up to my entrance and thrusts inside of me. My eyes close at the way he fills me. Just like all things he does, it's wholly, fully, leaving no room for anything else. He stretches me wide open only to fill me with all of him. A mix of pain and pleasure surges through me and I've come to realize it's just how I like my sex.

"Hmm, look at you all wet for me, baby. Is it my voice that does it for you? Or is it the way I dominate your body and take what I want?" My eyes fly open, my lips part. He grins. "Hmm, that's it isn't it." He thrusts harder into me. "It turns you on the way I just take your body. Own you. You're so fucking wet, you're dripping down my balls."

"Nico," I gasp, arousal seeping out of me.

A triumphant smirk tips his lips. "I love it, too, *Tesoro*. The thought of taking you, owning you, dominating you? It gets me harder than I have ever been in my life." God, how I wish what he is saying wasn't true, but I can't deny how much it turns me on. The evidence is running down my ass and thighs. "I can feel your pussy tightening and pulsating around my cock, begging for me to release my seed, and paint your insides with me." He continues with his dirty words before latching onto my nipple. He bites down hard on the rosy bud, and I can't take anymore. I cry out, my stomach tightening and every nerve ending lighting up with the force of my orgasm. Covering my mouth with my hand so as not to wake Romeo with my cries. I scream my release into my palm, coming so hard, I see stars.

"Good girl," he murmurs, lapping at my nipple. A shiver runs through me, something I can't quite decipher stirring inside me. "Look at you. So sexy with milk leaking out of your breasts." He pumps into me harder.

My eyes snap open, fear snaking down my spine at the look of utter madness in his gaze. Glancing down, to where he laps at me, I pause, my body heating in embarrassment at what I find. Milk runs in rivulets, down the plump flesh and onto my stomach. What the hell. That has never happened before. Shame courses through me. Turning my head, so I don't have to look at him, I push at Nico's hard chest. "Get off me. I need to get cleaned up."

Gripping my chin, he pulls until I have no choice but to face him. "No. You have nothing to be embarrassed about, *Tesoro*. In fact, it's fucking hot that you leaked all in my mouth." As if to prove his point he drops down, running his tongue up my body and licking up all the liquid. I squirm but he holds me still until he has lapped up every drop. A feral look flashes in his blue orbs as he runs his tongue across his bottom lip. My eyes widen, in shock or arousal I'm not sure. "Fuck, you taste good," he groans, thrusting into me harder.

His speed picks up, eyes never leaving mine. He holds me down, keeping me exactly where he wants me and using me like his own personal sex doll as he pumps into me. Pleasure crosses his features. His forehead drops to mine. Stilling, a deep rumble vibrates in his chest with the force of his groan. Then I feel it. His dick pulsing and warmth coating my insides. My eyes close in resignation. That's twice now. Twice he has come inside me without protection. I really need to get on birth control.

Despite what Nico said last night, I have no intention of having another child with him – at least not yet anyway – I just need someone to help me with getting some form of birth control. I could ask Allegra. Surely, she will understand the need to protect myself. I can only hope, because my only other option is Valentina, and I really don't want to discuss our sex life with his mother. Not that I think she would judge, but she is a last resort if Allegra won't help me.

"I love coming inside you. There is no better feeling in the world." Nico murmurs, pressing a kiss to my lips. For some reason, his words feel like a taunt. His way of telling me I have no choice in the matter.

My gaze locks on his as I force a smile. "I need to get cleaned up before Romeo wakes."

He frowns down at me, searching my face, for what I'm not sure. Sighing, he pulls out, and I grimace at the surge of liquid that follows. "I will shower with you. Then I want to watch when you feed our son." He pauses. "Though I can't promise not to get jealous. Not now I've had a taste of what is in your tits."

Swatting at his chest, I roll my eyes. "You're incorrigible. And anyway, he is mainly on the bottle now."

Chuckling, he says. "Yes, I am when it comes to you." He taps my nose. "And I will never change. So, its best you start accepting it."

Blowing out a breath, I stare at him, shaking my head. "Seems I have a lot of things to 'accept'," I air quote. "When it comes to you."

"Yes, you do," he confirms, pinning me with a glare. "There is no way out of this for you, Ocean. Not even death. It will make things easier if you accept your life and what is because I will never let you go. Not now. Not ever."

Without another word, he climbs off me. His feet hit the floor in the next second and he stands. I stare as he moves toward the crib and glances down at our son with a big smile on his face. Leaning down, he drops a kiss to Romeo's forehead then saunters in the direction of the adjoining bathroom.

I watch after him, swallowing hard as I replay his words. It's

in that moment I know, with everything in me, that he means every single one of them.
    There is no way out.
    Realization hits me.
    I ran from one cage only to run headfirst into another.

Chapter 20

Nico

"Hansen has the chopper ready," Dante drawls, striding into my office.

I sigh, running a palm across my mouth. It's been a week since the night on the beach and the last thing I want to do is leave Ocean and Romeo - especially after the progress we have made – but I have no choice. There is urgent business in the city that needs my attention. I can't put it off for another day.

"I want you, Marco, and Enzo with me. We leave in thirty minutes." I tell him, pushing out of my chair.

He nods. "Will we be staying in the city?"

Rounding my desk, I move past him, throwing over my shoulder. "Not planning on it. But if shit doesn't go according to plan, then we might have to."

I don't hear his response; neither do I care. I have more pressing matters to attend to right now, namely Ocean and my son. If my calculations are right, she will be feeding him right now. Climbing the stairs, I move along the landing toward her bedroom door. I frown. Her bedroom. That doesn't sound right. Now that we are... well, whatever we are, I would prefer we have *our* bedroom. I won't spend a night without her while in our home, not now that we are moving forward with our relationship. With that in mind, I make a mental note to have the staff move their things into my suite. Knowing my little *Tesoro*, she will protest, but she should know by now that she doesn't have a choice in the matter.

Coming to a stop outside her door, I push it open without knocking. As I guessed, she is in the big Chesterfield chair that overlooks the grounds, beach, and ocean. Romeo is in her arms as she feeds him from her breast. My gaze drops to her plump tits, my mouth watering at the hardened nipple my son doesn't have his mouth on. My cock swells in my pants. Its sick really. Getting turned on while she nurses our son, but I have no control over it.

"What are you doing?" she hisses, trying to cover herself.

My jaw clenches that she even dares try to hide herself from me. I thought we were past this. Thought she understood that I am her life now. Kicking the door shut, I close the distance between us. She glowers at me but it's more adorable than anything else. I bite back a laugh at her attempt at being aggressive.

Dropping down in front of her, I stroke a finger down Romeo's soft cheek. My chest constricts. I don't think I will ever get used to the fact that I'm a papà. "If you ever try to hide from me again, I will remove all of your clothes, so you have no choice but to walk around naked." My gaze never leaves my son as I say all this.

She gasps. "You wouldn't."

Glancing up at her, I shoot her a sardonic smile. She is right. I wouldn't, if only for the fact I don't want anyone else seeing her perfect body. She doesn't need to know that though. "Oh, I would, so I suggest you don't test me. Now, I came to tell you that I am heading to the city for business. I should be back later tonight if everything goes to plan. If not, I will be home tomorrow. I trust you will behave in my absence?"

She sighs, covering the nipple Romeo was just latched onto. He is asleep so obviously done with feeding. Lifting him gently, she holds him up to her shoulder. Her hand comes to his small back where she rubs soft circles. Her blue eyes shift back to me. "I'm not a child Nico, so stop treating me like one."

"Your disappearing act last year says otherwise." I deadpan, straightening to my full height. Not that she would get far if she ever tried to run again. I smirk, my mind going to a couple days ago.

"Ow," Ocean whimpers, rubbing at a spot on her neck.

My gaze drops to the movement, but I keep my face blank, not wanting to give anything away. You see, last night I plied her with a sedative. Not for nefarious reasons – depending how you look at it - but because I didn't want her to be awake when I pierced her skin and inserted the tiny tracking chip I had specially made for her. It was so small, I injected it just below her ear, with a syringe the doctor on my payroll provided me. Though it's for my peace of mind, it's also for her safety. If my enemies ever find out about her, then they will do all they can to try and take her from me, to use her as bait. And it's not just Ocean that is at risk. My son is also a target, which is why the doctor injected one into him. It's not something I wanted to do when he is so small, but it is necessary. His little cry pierced my heart, but it only lasted a couple of minutes and then he went back to sleep. The pain I felt from having to do such a thing soon turned to satisfaction at knowing I will always find them if anything ever happens.

"What's wrong?" I ask nonchalantly, even though I already know the answer.

She frowns. Her beautiful face screwing up. "I don't know. I have a really sore spot just below my ear. Maybe I was bitten by an insect or something. Can you check to see if there is a mark?" 'Or something' is right, but she doesn't need to know that.

Closing the distance between us, I run a finger up her neck and over the spot I inserted the tracker. There is no mark and had I not injected her myself, I would question if anything was beneath the skin. "No. Nothing." I press my lips to her temple. "Take an antihistamine and some Tylenol. I'm sure that will get rid of any pain if it is a bite."

"Nico?" Her soft voice brings me back to the present. Ocean rolls her eyes in exasperation then pushes up from the chair. Taking Romeo out of her arms, I pad to his crib, pressing a kiss to his little head before gently placing him down. An unfamiliar emotion slithers through me when I look at him. Worry maybe? Fear of leaving them. Of not having them in my sight. For the first time in my life, I don't want to leave this place. I want to stay cocooned in the little bubble that I have created with my family. Where I can keep them safe.

Though none of my enemies are aware that Ocean or Romeo exist, I know it will only be a matter of time before they find out. They are my weaknesses and I know, without a doubt, anyone out to hurt me will try to do it through them. I can't have that. Which is why I need to keep them here, hidden. Safe. At least until the Bratva and Romanos are dealt with.

"You know why I left," irritation laces her whispered voice.

Turning, I pin her with a look. "That's beside the point. Now, enough about that. My cock is hard and needs attention before I leave."

She reels back, no doubt at my quick change of conversation, her mouth dropping open, in shock. She shakes her head, then spins, moving toward the door. "No. No way. I am not your *whore*, trapped in this bedroom and ready to service you whenever you demand. Just go, Nico."

Grabbing her wrist, I pull her small, soft body into mine.

"I'm not going anywhere until my dick is empty and my cum is inside you." Gripping her hips, she yelps when I lift her into my arms. Striding to the bed, I drop her down, quickly climbing on top of her. She blinks up at me, wriggling her body from side to side. My heavy weight pins her to the bed, stopping any escape she might have planned. Snaking my hand down, I trail my fingers up her thigh to her panty covered pussy, enjoying when I find her wet. "I don't even have to touch you. You're always soaked for me. Willing and ready to go," I murmur.

"Nico, stop," she demands, her words at odds with the desire in her eyes.

"Never," I say, shoving my fingers under the fabric of her panties.

She squirms, trying to free herself from my hold. "I got my period," she blurts, her cheeks turning a bright shade of red. My cock turns to steel at her words. And then I feel it. The string of her tampon. Inside her cunt.

A. Tampon. Inside. *My*. Cunt.

Rage like I have never known, fills me. How dare she have something else shoved in my cunt, even if that something is a damn tampon. Grabbing the offending string I pull it out in one quick move, eyeing the bloodied cotton in my hand with disdain. Her eyes widen in horror.

"Nico. What are you doing." She hisses, bucking underneath me as she tries to shift me off her body. It's no use. I am too big. Too strong.

"You will not have anything in your pussy but me," I growl irrationally. Yes, I'm aware of how crazy I sound, but I can't bear the thought of anything but my cock breaching her tight channel. "If you are menstruating you will use a sanitary towel from now on."

Her mouth gapes, incredulity lacing her tone when she speaks. "You're insane. Get off me."

I smirk, leaning down to brush my lips across hers. "Maybe. But only for you. Now back to why we are in this position. My hard cock needing to blow my seed in one of your holes." She pales, her body stiffening. I know why. It's the mention of all her holes. We have never done ass play. It will come, but she isn't ready for that. I keep forgetting that she is only nineteen. That's her fault though. Her and her little lies. She wanted to play the adult and that is how I will treat her. "Don't worry, I won't take your ass. Not yet anyway. I want to fill your ripe cunt with my cum." I groan.

"I got my period," she repeats, her mouth a tight line.

My head cocks to the side, amusement curving my lips. If she thinks a little period blood will stop this, she is wrong. "I have a lot of blood on my hands *Tesoro*, so trust me, a little of your pussy blood doesn't scare me. In fact, the thought of smearing my cock in your blood sends me feral. It reminds me of the time I claimed your virgin cunt, painting my dick with your innocence." Shoving off her, I grab her hand, pulling her to the bathroom. "Come on, let's take a shower."

"What? Why?" she protests.

"The water will wash away any blood, therefore not tarnishing your pretty white bed sheets." I give her a droll look. I thought that would be obvious.

Stripping her out of her little nightgown, I then make quick work of removing my own clothes and drag her into the spacious shower. Turning on the spray, I watch as the water hits her perfect body. Chest heaving, she stares up at me with those big blue eyes. My heart tightens in my chest. Fuck. She is so beautiful. Ethereal. If I didn't know first-hand that she is real, I would think she is a figment of my imagination. Her beauty is so startling, a living, breathing thing, that sometimes it's hard to look at her face. But it's more than that. Though I would never admit it, because I don't want to sound like a pussy, Ocean is the other half of my soul. I feel it. With every touch. Every word spoken. I know it. I think that's why I never gave up looking for her. She is a part of me. The very air that I breathe. I couldn't live without my air, so I had no choice but to find her and it paid off. I have her back exactly where she belongs.

A soft hand cups my cheek, bringing me back to the now. I smile down at Ocean, a real smile, and revel in the way her breath hitches. Not wanting to wait another second, I lift her up my body. Her long, toned legs wrap around my waist and satisfaction fills me. "Good girl," I murmur, taking her lips with mine.

She moans, grinding against my hard dick. I smirk. No matter how much she protests, and fights me, I know it's all a front. She wants me as much as I want her.

"Nico," she whimpers when I shove a finger in her pussy.

"So fucking wet and tight. Your cunt is gripping my finger," I groan, before pulling out and lining my cock up to her entrance. I shove into her, my eyes rolling shut at the sensation of her wrapped around me.

She cries out, her body stilling. Gaze locked on mine, her small hand comes to rest on my chest. "Can you go slow? I'm a little sensitive and sore." Her cheeks turn pink as if she is embarrassed and she looks away.

Gripping her chin, I pull until her eyes meets mine. "I don't do slow, baby, but I will try," I say honestly, because I don't want to hurt her if she is sore. Glancing down, I pump in and out of her. An animalistic feeling consumes me when I see my cock smeared with her blood and I almost lose control. "Look at you taking me so well. You're such a good girl taking my cock in your tight little cunt. And look at your blood. Marking me. *Owning* me. Just like I marked and owned you." I grit my teeth when I already feel my orgasm building. Fuck. I'm going to embarrass myself and come like a teenager on his first hook-up. Shaking the thought away, I lock down my muscles, pumping into her harder. ocean isn't looking at me, and I follow her gaze to the spot where we are joined. She is watching me take her, her rapt attention on my cock sliding in and out of her with ease. Smirking, I snap my hips forward, hitting that spot deep inside her that I know will have her seeing stars.

"Nico," she moans, rocking her hips faster, riding me like it's what she was born to do.

Grabbing her chin, I pull her mouth to mine and lick across the seam of her lips. She moans, breaking the contact so she can look at me. A possessiveness like I have never known surges through me, heating my veins and begging me to conquer, own, and make her mine in every way possible. Never breaking eye contact, I fuck into her harder. It's as if we are the only two people that exist in the world. Lost in each other as our pleasure builds.

Reaching down, I circle her clit with my finger. Her back arches, allowing me to take her deeper. "This pussy was made for me. So fucking good." I praise through gritted teeth.

It's the push she needs. Her cunt contracts, tightening around me. She cries out my name, her nails clawing at my back when her orgasm takes hold. My balls draw up and I can't hold back any longer. With one last hard, deep, thrust into her, my cock pulses as I release inside her.

Dropping my forehead to hers, I suck in air, trying to calm my racing heart. Jesus, that was intense. Probably the most intense, connected sex I have ever had. Cracking one eye open, I find Ocean's gaze already on me.

"You ruin me," I whisper.

Her breath hitches in her throat as she searches my face. Fuck. I shouldn't have said that. With three words, I am basically handing her all the power. Though what I said is true, I don't want her to know the extent of the hold she has on me.

Suddenly feeling vulnerable, I quickly pull out of her, dropping her to her feet before rinsing off my body. I feel her stare on me, but I don't look at her. Don't want her to see the truth in my eyes.

Stepping out of the shower, I grab a towel and start toward the door. Without another glance in Ocean's direction, I leave her with parting words of, "Get cleaned up. I will see you tomorrow."

Chapter 21
Ocean

My mouth parts in shock, head spinning, as I watch Nico literally run out of the bathroom, his words playing on repeat in my head.

You ruin me.

Something tells me he didn't mean to say them. But he did. He said those words out loud for me to hear, and now I can't forget them.

You ruin me.

You. Ruin. Me.

Yeah, well, feeling's mutual, asshole.

My heart pounds in my chest, and I replay everything that just happened. The way he took what he wanted without abandon or shame. His possessive and, quite frankly, over the top ways. He doesn't want me to use tampons? What the fuck? I snort out a laugh. The man is certifiable and clearly insane. But I already knew that didn't I?

I would never admit it, but I like how he is with me. The possessiveness. The madness. Though it can sometimes be overbearing and suffocating, it makes me feel wanted. Desirable. It's not healthy, but I can no longer deny it. I want Nico as much as he wants me.

Since the night on the beach, things have changed between us. Though we haven't discussed his fake wife further or why he felt the need to torment me with it, I know it's a conversation we need to have. I want everything laid out on the table. I want us to start fresh. Free us from all the lies that once tore us apart. I can only hope it's what Nico wants, too.

The cold water snaps me from my thoughts, and I turn the faucet off. Stepping out of the shower, I grab one of the big fluffy towels, wrapping it around my body only to remember that I have my period and I don't want to get blood on the pristine white fabric.

Spotting the box of tampons on the counter, I smirk. Nico insisted I wear pads going forward but he can go screw himself. I don't have any. And anyway, screw him, it's my body, I will use what I damn well like. Grabbing a tampon from the box, I dry my legs, then grab some toilet paper to wipe up any moisture around my pussy. Pulling it back, blood coats the tissue and I'm thankful I had the foresight to use it instead of messing up the towel.

Dropping to the toilet, I part my legs, open the tampon, and insert it. Though Nico isn't here to see it, it's a big fuck you to him and I smile. It might only be a small win, but it's a win all the same.

A knock sounding startles me. Quickly washing my hands, I move into the bedroom when I hear another knock on my door, followed by a soft voice. "Ocean, breakfast is ready," Allegra calls.

"I'm just getting dressed. I'll be down in a minute," I tell her quietly, so as not to wake Romeo.

"Okay. I will let Mamma know." Footsteps sound down the hallway, until they disappear completely.

Toweling off, I pull on my panties, bra, some yoga pants, and a loose-fitting sweatshirt. I didn't wash my hair, so it's still up in a messy bun and that is how it will stay. Checking on Romeo, I smile at how peaceful he looks in his sleep and decide that instead of moving him to his stroller, I will just take the monitor with me. It's something I haven't been comfortable with since we came here, but I feel it's time to let go of some of my anxiety. It's a big step, but it's not like I'm leaving him. He is just up the stairs if I need to get to him for any reason.

Smiling, I grab the monitor and move to the door. It will be nice to spend some time with Nico's mom and sister without having him hovering over me. My stomach jumps when something hits me. Maybe I can even speak with Allegra about the whole birth control thing. I just hope and pray that she doesn't tell her brother. It's maybe a little hypocritical of me after my thoughts in the shower and wanting a fresh start, only to keep this from him. But he already said he doesn't want me taking the pill. Right now, I don't want another baby and at the rate he is fucking me without protection, I will be pregnant within weeks.

I can't have that. At least not until we are more stable in our relationship... or whatever it is we are doing.

And anyway. What he doesn't know, won't hurt him.

***

"Another delicious meal. Thank you, Valentina." I say honestly, wiping my mouth with a napkin.

She beams at me. "I love cooking for my family. When my husband was alive it didn't happen as much as I would have liked. He was so focused on the business, he sometimes forgot about us at home." She swallows, her eyes glistening. "But the time we did have together, well, I made the most of it and would spend hours in the kitchen cooking up Lorenzo's, Nico's, and Allegra's favorite meals."

"I would help," Allegra adds, a small grin on her face.

Valentina chuckles. "Yes. As you got older, I taught you how to cook our family recipes. It was expected. A good Italian woman in the Mafia, should always know how to prepare home cooked meals for her husband." Allegra stiffens. Valentina's face falls as if she just remembered what she said and she reaches over taking her hand. "I'm sorry."

Allegra shakes her head, her words bitter when she speaks. "Nothing to be sorry for Mamma. You didn't sign that contract."

I watch them, wondering what they are talking about. I could always ask, but I don't want them to think I am prying. But contract? A contract for what exactly? Valentina presses a kiss to her daughter's cheek. "Let me get the dishes cleared up. When Romeo wakes, we could take him for a walk on the beach?"

I nod, smiling. "That will be nice."

"I will tell Mario." She pushes out of her chair and starts collecting the empty dishes. I offer to help but she waves me off.

When she leaves the room, I glance at a now pensive looking Allegra. "Everything okay?" I ask.

Sighing, she shoots me a forced smile. "Yeah. I'm hoping it will be." she says cryptically, waving me off. She clears her throat. "Anyway, enough about me. How are things going with Nico?"

Exhaling a breath, I shake my head, my cheeks heating. After the debacle of that dinner last week, Allegra apologized. Not that she needed to. I know everything that happened that night was because Nico had orchestrated it. Though it hurt seeing that woman, now that I know the truth about her, I feel a little better about the situation.

"I wanted to talk to you about something actually." My gaze

darts around the room, making sure we are still alone. She eyes me curiously. Embarrassment fills me at what I'm about to say, but this will probably be my only chance, so I need to get over my discomfort and just ask. I mean there might be a small chance I'm already pregnant, with the way Nico has been screwing me every chance he gets, but I have to try. Squirming in my seat, I suck in a breath, preparing myself to say the words. "Can you get, or do you have any birth control pills?" I blurt.

Eyes widening, she stares at me in what can only be described as surprise. Shit. Did I read this all wrong? I mean realistically, why would a sheltered mafia princess be on birth control anyway? I've witnessed how controlling Nico is and I can only imagine how hard their father was on them growing up. I can't imagine she would have been allowed boyfriends, let alone sex.

Allegra chuckles softly under her breath and I relax a little. "I do, actually. I started taking them at sixteen due to heavy periods. Not that my papà knew that little bit of information. He would have thought it was for other reasons and locked me away more than he already did. Mamma helped me out and took me to the doctor in town. She didn't trust asking the *famiglia* doctor because he was on Papà's payroll and she knew he would mention it to my papà." She waves her hand. "I'm going off track. The answer to your question is yes, I have *my* pill. I'm sure if you ask Nico, he will arrange for you to get on birth control."

My cheeks burn, mortification surging through me. Swallowing, I admit, "He doesn't want me on birth control."

Her head cocks to the side, face screwing up in confusion. Then she turns about as red as I feel when it hits her. "Christ, he wants you pregnant?" I nod in confirmation. "My brother can be such an asshole. You're nineteen, right? Same age as me?"

"Yeah."

She shakes her head. "Don't get me wrong, I love Romeo, but I wouldn't want a baby right now. Even with..." she trails off sighing, but somehow, I get the feeling she was going to say Dante. "Anyway, because you are still so young and deserve to live your life, I will help you. But if my brother ever finds out, I will deny that I gave it to you. Brother or not, you don't interfere with relationships in the Mafia." The look on her face is stern and I know she means every word.

Worrying at my lip, I nod. "Deal. I'm not saying I don't want more children. I just don't want them right now."

"I get it–" A piercing cry coming from the monitor cuts her off. She laughs. "You better go get him."

Sighing, I stand, an appreciative smile on my face. "Thank you. And I promise, he won't find out."

Obviously when it comes to Nico, I can't say that with certainty, but I will do everything in my power to make sure he doesn't.

Chapter 22

Nico

My jaw clenches when I take in the blood on the floor of my club. The bullet holes that mar the couches, walls and stage, a glaring reminder of what happened here last night. Fucking Bratva.

"Now, how the fuck did this happen?" I bark my question at a weary looking Leo.

Exhaling a sigh, his gaze meets mine. "I asked Carl and Nolan to lock up for the night. Not five minutes later they were dead and five men spewing Russian stormed the building. Fortunately, everyone had gone home, otherwise we would have had a club full of dead people. When I heard the gunshots, I locked myself in your office." He swallows. Lucky for Leo, my office also masks as a panic room should any situation like the one that happened in the early hours of this morning arise. "They left around an hour later. I called you as soon as I knew you would be awake and didn't let myself out until you arrived," he finishes.

"Fuck," Dante mutters.

Fuck is right. I need to end those fuckers once and for all. From the moment Tony called me with the news that he found

Ocean, I have been so caught up in all things her and my son, that I haven't had a chance to deal with any of the other shit I have going on. Time to get my head back in the game. I need my woman and son safe and that means wiping out any potential threats before they escalate their war.

"There's one more thing." Sweat beads dot his forehead, a look of fear in his eyes as he swallows. My body tenses. I don't like that look on his face.

"What?" I growl, urging him to talk.

"I heard them talking about *the girl*. I was confused at first when they mentioned the name Emilee Caldwell, but then I remembered that's…" he trails off, clearing his throat.

My heart rate kicks up, all my senses go on high alert. "Ocean's real name." I finish for him, anger igniting inside me. "And you didn't think to mention this first?" I roar. Before I can stop myself, my fist connects with his face, knocking him backward. I'm taking my anger out on the wrong person but still, he should have mentioned this when he called me.

"Fuck, Nico," he grits out, staggering back. His hand cups his jaw, rubbing at the spot I hit.

Pulling out my cell, I call Mario, my head of security at The Hamptons house. It's a position my papà promoted him to a couple of years ago now and one he excels at. Though he was pulled into the *famiglia* by my father, he has been loyal to me and is one of my most trusted men. He picks up on the second ring. "Boss?"

"Mario. I want you to increase the number of soldiers around the perimeter of the estate. Give them extra weapons. And don't let Mamma, Allegra, Ocean, or my son out of the house or your sight." I snap the orders at him, knowing he will obey.

"As you wish, boss. Mrs. Marchetti, Miss Ocean, and Romeo were just preparing for a walk on the beach. I will inform them that will no longer be happening. If they ask why a walk is not allowed, what reason would you like me to give to them?"

"Don't give them any reason. Just tell them you are under strict instructions from me. I am trusting you, Mario. Don't let them out of your sight and be on alert."

"May I ask what the threat is, boss?"

My jaw tightens, body wound tight, ready to snap at any moment. "No. I will inform you of everything upon my return. Just keep them safe. If anything happens to my family, I will hold you personally responsible. Anything you have witnessed me doing before will pale in comparison to what I will do to you, if you don't protect them with your life," I threaten, meaning every word.

"Got it, boss. I will protect them, Nico." He promises and before he can say anything else, I end the call.

"Did you call it in?" I ask Leo.

"Nah. I was waiting for you to tell me how you want to proceed with it," he responds roughly.

"Call it in. Security footage will back up any questions the Feds might have as to what happened," I mutter. Turning to Marco and Enzo, I say, "Stand guard outside. I don't want anyone coming in unless it's law enforcement." With a nod of their heads, they do as I ask, moving toward the front doors. My gaze shifts to Dante. The concern in his eyes no doubt matches my own. "I want to be back in The Hamptons as soon as this mess is cleaned up." Relief crosses his features. I know he is just as worried as I am about the Bratva attacking my home. Though we have always kept the location secret they clearly have intel on me and I'm not sure how deep that information goes. What do they want with Ocean? Why did they call her by her real name? Did her father send them? Do they know she is with me? These are all questions I want answers to immediately and there is only one way I'm going to get them. I need to set up a meeting with Vadim Mikhailov. It's risky, especially after what they did to my papà, but I want to know what he wants with my woman.

"I will be in my office if anyone needs me," I say to no one in particular.

Time is of the essence.

Those Russian bastards will pay for daring to even say her name.

***

The Feds arrive, and after cordoning off The Executive Club as a crime scene they start their investigations. They requested the security footage, as I knew they would, and Leo handed it straight over. I know full well they are aware of my reputation and will be skeptical about what happened, but the footage doesn't lie. It should be a straightforward open and close case.

During all this, I manage to contact my PI and Tony. I want them to continue looking into Ocean's family. Find out any evidence that leads to their involvement with the Bratva. Hopefully, they will have all the information I require by the end of today. In the meantime, I will be doing my own investigations. I have reached out to a middleman to get in contact with Vadim and am hoping he will have a meet set up in the next couple of weeks. I can be civil if it gets me the answers I want. And though I will never admit it to anyone but Dante, the Bratva did me a favor by taking my papà out. That doesn't mean, I won't kill them all. Eventually.

"You ready?" Dante asks, striding into my office.

"Feds gone?"

"Yeah. Leo has spoken to all the staff and told them we will be closed for a couple of weeks for renovation purposes."

I nod. "Have Leo call in some of our contractors. I want the whole place remodeled." Standing, I eyeball him. "Let's go. I feel on edge being here."

He chuckles. "You and me both." His face sobers. "What do you think they want with Ocean?"

I scrub a palm across my face, tension filling my body at the unknown. I hate not being in control. Though I will protect Ocean and my son with my life, I need to accept that there is only so much I can do. No matter how much I want to, I can't always be there, watching and protecting them. I trust Mario and the soldiers I personally selected to guard my home, but there is only so much I can do. We are prepared for almost anything, but sometimes the unexpected can happen. And that scares me. Nonetheless, I would die trying to protect my family, to keep them safe, and so would my men. I can only hope it never comes to that.

"I don't know, but you can be damn sure I'm going to find out," I mumble through clenched teeth.

Dante nods, clamping a hand down on my shoulder in silent support. He understands. He gets me. And I know, come what may, he will be by my side. Exactly where he is meant to be as we fight to protect our family.

Chapter 23

Ocean

With my son secure in my arms, I carry him down the stairs, excitement bubbling in me that we are going to the beach. Lifting my head, I spot Valentina standing beside Romeo's stroller, the excitement I witnessed earlier on her face now gone and replaced with a look of concern. I stiffen, coming to a stop when my feet hit the marble floor of the foyer. My heart pounds in my chest, worry slithering through my veins. I swallow, trying to wet my now dry mouth and wait for her to speak.

Valentina sighs. "I'm sorry, honey, but we won't be going to the beach today."

Her words only increase my anxiety. "Did something happen?" I ask, cradling Romeo closer to my chest in a protective move.

Valentina eyes me, searching my face for a long moment. I can tell something is on her mind. That she is debating how much she can tell me. "The order came from Nico. There were some...." She trails off before clearing her throat. "Problems in the city, that he is dealing with. He would rather we stay inside. At least until he gets home," she adds.

My face screws up, but the look on Valentina's has my heart pumping faster in my chest. I know Nico is a dangerous man, but how big is this threat? I don't know much about the Mafia, or what it entails. My father used to watch The Sopranos, and I would catch glimpses of it. But to be honest, I never took too much interest. To me, it was a soap opera with everything exaggerated. Or so I thought. Could the real Mafia actually be worse than anything I saw on the TV? Fear hits me in the chest, and I glance down at Romeo. Is my son at risk? Am I at risk? I know Nico would do everything in his power to protect us, but he can't be around us twenty-four seven.

"Should I be worried?"

Her face softens. "No sweetie. We are safe here. Come. Let's go to the den. I have set up some of his toys to keep him occupied."

A little bit of tension leaves my body. I laugh. "I don't think he knows what toys are."

Placing a hand on my lower back, she pushes gently, urging me forward. "I bought him one of those baby playmat gym things. They are good for their cognitive development as well as sensory stimulation, awareness, and a whole list of other things."

"Sounds good," I hum, impressed. Though I shouldn't be. Valentina did bring two children into the world, so I guess she knows what she is talking about.

She exhales. "I know things haven't been ideal since Nico brought you back, and he hasn't treated you in the best way, but I'm happy you're both here. It's made this house feel more like a home."

Emotion clogs my throat, my gaze shooting to hers. I see the truth on her face. Hear the honesty in her words. From the moment I came here, Valentina has been nothing but nice. I thought she might hold some resentment toward me for keeping Romeo away from her son, from her, but it's clear that she doesn't. From my one interaction with her husband, I will never understand how such a kind, empathic, woman was married to someone like him. But then that's me being judgmental. Maybe there was a nice side to him that I never got to witness. Because to Lorenzo Marchetti, I was just the girl that stood in the way of his perfectly made plans. One that he would get rid of, no matter the cost.

Shaking the thought from my head, I step into the den. Stopping on the threshold, I take Valentina's hand with my free one. "Thank you, for everything. If it wasn't for your kindness and hospitality, I don't know what I would have done."

Giving me a gentle squeeze, she shoots me a knowing smile. "Something tells me that you would have been just fine. You're strong and resilient, Ocean. Exactly the kind of woman I imagined for my son."

***

I'm putting Romeo down for his afternoon nap when I hear it.

A helicopter.

Nico is home.

My stomach dips, in excitement or worry, I'm not sure. I hate these confusing feelings. They really mess with my head. All I know is that I have felt empty since he left this morning. It's messed up, but it doesn't change the fact that it's true.

Sighing, I drop a kiss on my son's cheek, grab the baby monitor and decide to head downstairs. I know Nico is busy taking care of business, but it's been over a week since I asked him about calling Patty and it still hasn't happened. I don't want to wait any longer. I could have gone behind his back, called her while he was in the city, but I didn't. I'm sure had I asked Valentina about making a call, she would have allowed it – well, unless Nico said otherwise - but she has been so nice to me, I don't want to use her like that. Or put her in a position that could possibly make her uncomfortable.

Making my way downstairs, I pause when the front door is pushed open. Nico steps inside, followed by Dante and two other men. His cold gaze meets mine. He pauses, shock flashing in his eyes before he covers it. His blue orbs narrow, searching my face. My cheeks heat under his scrutiny, my body burning up with something I don't want to decipher right now. His hungry gaze rakes over me and though I am fully dressed, I feel naked as he takes me in.

"We will wait for you in your office." Dante says, breaking the tension currently suffocating the big foyer.

"Tell Mario to join us," Nico drawls, his eyes never leaving mine.

My heart thumps in my chest. A throb starts between my legs. I loathe my traitorous body for reacting this way to him. It's like I lose all control over myself when he is around and turn into a wanton hussy. As if he knows exactly what he is doing to me, his lips curve into a sexy smirk. Asshole. I roll my eyes.

"Nico, I need to talk to you."

"How is my son?" he asks, completely ignoring me.

"*Our* son is fine. He just went down for a nap. Can I talk to you about what we discussed last week? Patty," I clarify.

He sighs, hand coming up to loosen his tie. "Not right now, *Tesoro*. I have a lot going on and I need to take care of it. Patty can wait."

He steps forward to move past me, but I grab his wrist, stopping him. Electricity zips through me and I know he feels it too by the way his brows scrunch up. "Please, Nico." I beg.

"Not right now, Ocean," he barks, making me flinch. Dejection surges through me at his easy dismissal. Guilt flickers in his eyes before they turn hard, cold. It's a look I have come to expect from him but has been absent this last week. The one I hate. He runs a hand through his hair, sighing. Its only then I notice the weariness on his face. "Look, let me take care of business, then you can call her later. Okay?" It's his way of compromising and I jump on it.

"Okay," I agree, perking up slightly.

He nods, his lips a tight, tense line. With one last look thrown my way, he saunters down the hall toward his office.

I smile, a sense of accomplishment hitting me. It might not be right now, but I will be speaking to Patty at some point today. Excitement bubbles inside me at the thought of hearing her voice. She doesn't know it and would never accept it, but she saved me.

And for that, I will forever be grateful to her.

Chapter 24
Nico

After two hours locked in my office discussing everything from increasing our security, the attack on my club, why Ocean is involved, to meeting with the Bratva, we are finally done. I'm exhausted to say the least, but we got everything covered, which is exactly the outcome I had hoped for.

"I think we could both use a drink," Dante drawls, when it's only the two of us left in the room. Pushing out of his seat, he strides to my bar cart, pouring us both a Macallan.

Sighing, I lean back in my chair, taking the crystal tumbler when he hands it to me. "This shit with the Bratva and Ocean is putting me on edge," I admit.

Taking a sip of his drink, he lowers the glass, eyeing me. "It's a concern, sure. But once we know more about what they want with her, we will have a better idea of what we are dealing with."

My body tenses. What do they want with her? I will kill every last one of the bastards before they put a hand on *my* woman. Staring at the tumbler in my hand, I don't look at Dante when I speak my next words. "The Russians don't know it and never will, but they did me a great service killing Papà. If it wasn't for keeping face in front of the commission, I wouldn't even go after them. I would be buying them drinks and thanking them for taking his life." Lifting my head, my gaze meets his. "You know how bad things had gotten with Papà. He was becoming unpredictable, unhinged. He was blood. But he had to go." Dante knows my feelings about my papà, but it is considered blasphemy saying them out loud. If the commission knew how I really felt, my loyalty would come into question and no doubt they would issue a bounty for my death.

"Nic, we both know he would have only gotten worse. Look at the shit he has got your sister locked into. His own daughter. Selling her off to the highest bidder, knowing full well she will never survive a man like Riccardo. You've heard the stories just like I have. We knew Lorenzo was losing his mind, but to even consider signing an agreement with the Romanos. It's fucked up and scary to think what he would have done next. He already mentioned fucking trafficking women before he died." Disdain laces his voice, his face full of disgust. Revulsion is a living, breathing thing inside me when I think about the direction my papà was taking the *famiglia* in. At what he did to Ocean. At missing her pregnancy and my son's birth. Anger surges through me, but I tamp it down. He is gone. But if he wasn't already dead, I would without a doubt have killed him myself.

"No one can ever know what we just talked about. Especially not my mamma." I pin him with serious eyes.

"I would never say anything," he vows honestly, and to be completely transparent, I don't know why I even said it. I trust Dante. More than I trust anyone else.

Just as I'm about to speak, there is a small, soft knock on my door. "Mio figlio?" Mamma calls, pushing the door open. She smiles. "Dinner will be served in thirty minutes."

I nod, draining the rest of my drink. "I will be there."

"Dante?"

He chuckles. "You don't even need to ask, Valentina. I'm starving."

"Good." She glances over her shoulder, and I don't miss the way her eyes light up. "Ocean wanted to see you." The object of my obsession appears with our son in her arms.

"I will give you some privacy." Dante stands, leaving my office in the next second.

Ocean steps inside, and I hate the way my heart beats faster at the sight of her. Pushing out of my chair, I close the distance between us, taking Romeo from her. The soft click of the door alerts me to the fact that we are now alone. Clearing my throat, I say. "You wanted to see me?" I'm pretty sure I know the reason behind her visit, but I want to hear her say it again.

She wrings her hands together, nibbling on that full bottom lip. I want to bite down on it, suck it into my mouth. Play with her until only pleasure consumes her body. "I know you are busy, but I thought I could call Patty before dinner?" she blurts, snapping me from my Ocean trance.

After the shit show today has been, I want to say no. Tell her that she can call her another day. But I promised her over a week ago and it still hasn't happened. She deserves this. Sighing, I maneuver Romeo to my left arm making sure he is comfortable.

Grabbing my cell from my desk, I hand it to her. Jerking my head to the couch. "Sit. And remember I want it on speakerphone."

She rolls her eyes in exasperation. I shoot her a *don't test me* look as I drop down on the plush leather couch. Deciding not to push me, she sits on the other end. "It's locked," she points out, holding up my cell as if to prove her point.

"Zero, one, one, one, zero, five."

Her brows furrow as she punches in the code, recognition

crossing her features. She gasps, her eyes snapping to me. "That's my birthday. January eleventh, and the year I was born. Two thousand and five," she squeaks, her lips parted in shock, disbelief in her tone.

I nod confirming that she is correct. It is her birthday. I would never tell her, but as soon as I saw her real birth certificate, I wanted to honor it in some way. I don't have tattoos so the code to my cell had to do. Every time I entered it, it reminded me that she was real. That I hadn't made her up in some fucked up part of my brain.

"Get on with it. Mamma has prepared dinner. You have," I glance at my watch. "Twenty-five minutes." She blushes, her eyes dropping to my cell. "Do you know the number?"

"Yeah. I memorized it in case of an emergency."

"An emergency?" I repeat.

She glances at me, nodding. "Yeah. Like if I was out and my cell died, I could use a payphone." Her eyes twinkle. "Or you know, I was ever kidnapped by a mafia boss."

I glare. "I didn't kidnap anything. I just simply took back what's mine."

She shakes her head, mumbling, "Same difference."

Dropping the phone to the couch, the dial tone rings out. On the third ring, Patty answers, her southern twang filling the silence of the room. "Hello?"

"Patty?" Ocean whispers, tears filling her eyes.

"Lyra? Oh my God. Is that really you? Are you okay? Is my boy okay?" She rushes out, her voice borderline hysterical. But I ignore that. All I can think about is the way she said *her boy*. I shouldn't be jealous of a sixty odd year-old woman, but I don't like it.

"It's me," Ocean chuckles before it trails off, and a frown wrinkles up her smooth forehead. "I lied to you Patty. My name is not Lyra. It's Ocean." I hear the shame in her confession.

Patty tsks, laughing softly. "Honey, I don't care what your name is. I'm just happy to hear your voice. I have been so worried about you. About our boy. I thought..." she pauses, before clearing her throat. "I thought that I would never hear your voice again."

Ocean's face falls, her eyes shining with unshed tears. "I'm okay. I promise. And Romeo, he is amazing. I know it has only been a couple of weeks, but he changes every day..." her voice wobbles, gaze coming to me for a quick second before dropping. "We miss you," she chokes out, wiping a tear from her cheek.

It's quiet for a moment. She exhales and though I can't see her, I can imagine this is just as emotional for Patty as it is my woman. "I miss you both, too. But you must tell me. Who was that man? Has he hurt you?" the woman asks, curiosity and disdain evident in her tone.

Oceans head snaps to me. She shakes her head, though the woman can't see her. "No, he hasn't. I'm safe. Romeo is safe. Nico, well he is..." she trails off, her eyes bouncing between me and our son. "He is Romeo's father," she breathes out.

Patty chuckles, "I gathered that, dear." Her laughter dies, voice dropping to a whisper. "I thought they were going to kill me, Ocean."

"I'm sorry you got caught up in that. I never meant for anyone to get hurt." The guilt in her tone is evident, and though Ocean never meant to drag anyone into this, she hates that Patty was a casualty in her lies.

"I didn't get hurt," Patty rushes out, no doubt trying to make her feel better about everything that went down. "Sure, I was scared, but once he got what he wanted - that was you, by the way - they let me go without harm. Even left me a couple thousand dollars to clean up the place."

Ocean's head snaps up. I see the question in her eyes and confirm it with a nod. "Well... that was nice of him. It's the least he could have done after everything." She glowers, no doubt remembering the scene she came home to that night. Yeah, well the feeling's mutual. The image of her with another man is still burned into my brain, begging me to go back to Charleston and kill the fucker.

"Harrison comes in every day to ask about you. We have been so worried." Patty changes the subject.

I freeze at the mention of his name, as does Ocean. Her gaze darts to mine, she swallows. My eyes drop to the pulse in her neck. The way it beats erratically. I know she wants to ask about him, but if she is as smart as I think she is, she won't dare say his fucking name.

"Ocean?" Patty prompts. Ocean startles, her blue orbs dropping to the phone.

She clears her throat. "Sorry, Patty. I have to go. Romeo is due a feed." It's a lie. I know it. Ocean knows it. And Patty probably knows it. But it's her way of ending this conversation, so she doesn't have to discuss that fucker. I knew my girl was smart.

"Oh, okay." I hear the disappointment in Patty's voice and by the way Ocean's face falls she does too.

"I will call you again soon," Ocean promises.

"Okay, sweetheart. Give my boy a kiss from me."

"I will. I love you, Patty. Thank you for everything you did for me. For Romeo. I can't ever repay you for the kindness you showed us both." The emotion in her tone has my heart constricting.

"That sounds like a goodbye," Patty responds suspiciously.

Ocean shakes her head even though she can't see it. "It's not. I will call you soon," she assures, and after a round of goodbyes she ends the call. Picking up my cell, she hands it to me with clear trepidation in her eyes. She bites down on that pouty bottom lip of hers and I know she has more to say. "You will let me call again, won't you? I didn't mention him, Nico. Please don't take this away from me because Patty brought him up," she begs.

Sighing, I take the phone then rise from the couch. Romeo sleeps peacefully in my arms and instead of looking at the worry on Ocean's face, I keep my gaze on my son. "I won't. But next time, you will tell her not to discuss him with you." It's not a question but a demand. An irrational one at that, but still. Deep down, I know there is nothing between them, it's just the principle of the matter. She went on a date with him, so at one point she considered more. My jaw clenches just thinking about it.

"Okay. Yes. I can do that," she agrees easily.

"Good. Now let's go eat."

Chapter 25
Ocean

It's been almost a week since my phone call to Patty and I'm desperate to speak with her again, but I don't know how to broach the subject with Nico. He has been on edge lately, more so than normal, and no matter how much I want to talk to Patty again, I don't want to add to his stress.

Though Nico has now permanently moved Romeo and me into his suite - much to my resistance, I may add - he has been distant. I should welcome the reprieve but, being the stupid woman that seems to lose all brain cells when I'm around Nico, I don't like this distance he has put between us. I hate that he comes to bed when I'm sleeping and is gone before I wake. And I loathe the fact that there are more men around, patrolling the grounds like it's the White House itself. And the icing on the shit cake is that I am still not allowed to leave the estate, not even to go to the beach. It is obvious that something big is going on, but Nico waves me off every time I bring it up. He said all I need to know is that we are safe. I want to believe it, but it's hard when the evidence to suggest otherwise is all around me.

The only good thing with Nico being so distracted is that he isn't watching me like a hawk. The timing of it couldn't have worked out more perfectly since Allegra came through with the birth control. She managed to get me a brand-new package that will last me twenty-one days. I am grateful for what she is doing for me but am hoping that she will be able to figure out something more permanent for when these run out. No matter what Nico's plans are for another pregnancy, I am not in agreement with it. It simply cannot happen. And I will do everything in my power to prevent it from happening.

"Hey," as if I just conjured her, Allegra appears in the den, flopping down on the couch next to me.

"Hey. You okay?" I ask, frowning at the look on her face.

She sighs, her eyes shifting to Romeo who is rolling around on his playmat. "Yeah. Just bored. Whatever is going on is serious enough that we have become prisoners in our own home. I need to get out of this house before I go crazy."

I chuckle softly, shaking my head at her dramatics. It's only been a week and it's not like we can't go out in the backyard. "Do you know what's going on? Nico shuts me down when I ask him."

Her eyes move to mine, a look of worry in them that makes my stomach clench. She shakes her head. "No and Nico won't tell me either. I asked Dante, but his response was the same as my brother's. I knew I wouldn't get anything out of them. It's a mafia thing. Women aren't allowed to be involved in business. It's such sexist bullshit, but it's always been that way. They act like we are back in the nineteen twenties when women were without rights." She huffs. "I just know that if we are on lockdown, its bad."

Fear tightens my throat. I swallow, trying to speak over the ball of anxiety. "Has this ever happened before?"

She purses her lips, thinking over my question. "Umm, I mean we have always had security because of who my family are, but I can't remember it being this heightened."

Nausea swims in my stomach. What the hell has Nico brought us into? "Maybe it's just preventive?" I ask hopefully.

She shrugs. "Maybe. Things just suck right now, and its making my mood plummet even further than it had."

Chewing my lip, I study her. The resignation on her face makes my heart crack. I know that look. And I remember the precise moment *I* wore the same expression. It was the day I was told I would be marrying Xavier Anderson. I felt hopeless. Resigned. Scared.

"Allegra, is everything okay?" I ask tentatively.

Her watery blue orbs, a shade lighter than Nico's, meet mine. She exhales a harsh breath, her shoulders sagging in defeat. Her eyes search mine and I think she is going to shut down, but then she speaks. "My papà signed a contract before he passed. It was a marriage agreement. I am promised to a man called Riccardo Romano." She laughs, but it's humorless. "Riccardo is nearly forty and a complete pig. I've heard the rumors about him and how he treats women. It's bad, Ocean. So horrific, I wouldn't wish him upon my worst enemy, let alone my own daughter. Yet Papà thought it was a good idea to sell me off to him," she spits, disgust lacing her tone. "Nico is trying to get me out of it, but he has been trying for a while now, but the contract is ironclad. Of course, he hasn't told me any of this, but I can tell. I see it in the haunted, guilty, look in his eyes every time he sees me. I know the only way to end the engagement is to break the agreement, but that will start a war. I don't want anyone to get hurt, but I also can't marry *him*. Even if I wasn't in love with Dante," I gasp at her admission, cutting her off. Allegra's lips part as she watches me, her cheeks turning pink.

I smile, grabbing her hand. "I kind of gathered that there was something going on with you two."

She sighs. "I love him. He is everything to me. But my papà would never allow it, not that we asked him, but we know the rules, knew what was expected of me. An arranged marriage. And Papà decided Riccardo was the best fit." She snorts, shaking her head. "Anyway, I don't want anything to do with Riccardo. I would be nothing more than a trophy to parade around when he feels like it. A body to carry his heirs. A punching bag when he is angry. And from what I've heard, he is always angry. He has no shame when it comes to putting his hands on women. In fact, if the tales are true, which I believe they are, he gets off on it. Apparently, his first wife, who just happened to 'disappear'," she forms quote marks in the air. "Held a haunted look in her eyes and was always covered in bruises. He is that egotistical, he didn't even think to cover them up."

I take in all that she just told me, mulling it over. No way will Nico let it happen. It's clear that he loves his sister so I can't imagine him ever just handing her over to a man like that. "I'm sure Nico is doing all he can to get you out of it. Though we have had our ups and downs, I know he is a good man. It's clear he loves you and will do anything to protect you, Allegra. Which is why I know that he won't let you go through with it." I squeeze her hand tighter in a gesture of comfort.

"I hope so. Because if not. I will run. Dante and I will run." Determination crosses her features, telling me she means it.

Wanting to lighten the mood, I shoulder check her. "So, you and Dante, huh?"

She chuckles, a dreamy look crossing her face. "I've been in love with him since before I can remember. Like I said, Papà would have never allowed us to be together so..." she trails off, her eyes dropping as if she is ashamed. "I know this sounds awful, but I was almost relieved when he passed." Releasing my hand, her hand flies up to her mouth. Her eyes widen in disbelief, no doubt at her confession.

I shake my head, understanding exactly how she feels. "You

don't need to be ashamed. Not around me. I would feel the same if my father died. He..." I swallow. "Just like your papà, my dad also set me up for an arranged marriage. The man he sold me to also had a bad reputation. Its why I ran. So never apologize. I know exactly how you feel."

She gasps, gripping my hand again. "I'm sorry."

I smile. "Nothing to be sorry for. It all worked out in the end." My brows furrow and I add with a chuckle. "Well, there were a few speed bumps along the way, but I think it's all finally taken a turn for the better."

Allegra sighs. "You're so strong, Ocean. I know my brother isn't the easiest guy to handle but I see the way he looks at you. He worships the ground you walk on."

I snort, suddenly feeling shy and looking away. "I don't know about that."

"He does. Trust me," she says adamantly.

My lips part, ready to speak, only to snap shut when a presence fills the room. I don't have to look to know who it is. I feel him. Head lifting, my gaze locks on Nico, who is watching us intently. He leans against the door jam, his eyes flicking from Romeo, to where Allegra and I sit on the couch. His brow cocks as his predatory blue orbs narrow. "Am I interrupting something?"

Allegra laughs. "No. We were just talking."

"About?" he prompts.

Allegra wags her finger at him playfully. "Girl stuff."

He shakes his head in exasperation, but I don't miss the twitch of his full lips. "Can you watch Romeo. I need to talk with Ocean."

"Of course," Allegra chirps, dropping to the floor to play with her nephew.

Nico jerks his head. "Come." He demands, turning on his heel and disappearing down the hall.

Knowing that's my cue to follow, I sigh, pushing off the couch.

What the hell does he want now?

Maybe he is allowing me another call to Patty?

Excitement hits me in the chest and with a quick glance at my son and a thank you to Allegra, I follow Nico to his office.

Chapter 26

Nico

"Do you know of any reason as to why your father would be involved with the Bratva?" I get straight to the point. Though I am pretty sure Ocean won't know anything, I needed to ask her the question.

Her brows furrow, face scrunching up, and I see the confusion written all over her features. She knows nothing. "Bratva?"

"Russian mafia. My enemies." I confirm.

She blinks, before her bright blue eyes widen. Panic replaces the confused look and she shakes her head. "No. Do you think he knows where I am?" she whispers the *he* part as if saying the word *father* out loud will make him appear. It won't. And if he did, she doesn't need to worry. I would kill him before he ever got his hands on her.

"Truthfully, I don't know." I decide to go with honesty. I know it will increase her concern but I'm not going to hide it from her. We need to be prepared for everything and anything. She visibly shudders, her face turning a ghostly white. My jaw clenches that she is so frightened of this man. Her own flesh and blood.

Pushing out of my chair, I round my desk, dropping down

beside her on the couch. Wrapping my arms around her shaking body, I pull her onto my lap. "*Tesoro*, you have nothing to be afraid of. I won't let anything happen to you." I tell her, and unable to resist I press a kiss to her neck.

Gripping my bicep, teary blues meet mine. "I should have known he wouldn't stop. I can't go back there, Nico. I *won't* go back. He will kill me." Sheer panic laces every word, making red dot my vision.

"Hey," I growl, grabbing her chin so that she can't look away. "I don't know for sure that it's anything to do with your family." I sigh, debating how much to tell her. Maybe if I tell her everything, it will keep her in line more? She won't fight me on security or even dare to run. It's downright manipulation but I never said I was a good man. Pinning her with a serious look, that I hope conveys the seriousness of the situation, I speak. "The Executive Club got raided the other night. Its why I had to go to the city."

She gasps, her eyes widening further. "Are all the girls okay? Leo?"

My jaw tics at the concern in her voice. Fucking Leo. I still haven't forgiven him for taking her on that 'date'. "Yes, the girls are fine. It was after hours, and security were just locking up. Two of the guards were killed, but Leo managed to get to safety in my office. Fortunately for him, it transforms into a panic room in the event of something like that ever happening."

Ocean stares at me, her forehead scrunching up and frown lines appearing on her beautiful face. "So, what do the Bratva have to do with me or my father?"

I sigh, suddenly exhausted with everything that's going on. Is it too much to ask for a couple of days without drama? "That's the thing. Leo heard them talking about you. Specifically, Emilee Caldwell."

She stiffens in my lap. My eyes drop to her neck, where her pulse beats erratically. I want to bite it. Lick it. Mark it–

"Nico?" she chokes out, bringing my gaze back to hers. "The only people that know my real name are from back home. Which means they are here for me. They know where I am. They found me." Her voice now borders on hysterical. I want to comfort her. Assure her. But I know she won't hear me right now. She is too caught up in her own panic.

Cupping her cheeks, I grip her head in my hands, forcing her shaking head to still and making her focus on me. My jaw clenches at the pure fear staring back at me. "Stop," I grit out. "If it is your father, then I will deal with him. Now, I don't want you to think about it. Concentrate on what matters. Our son. Me."

She blinks. Then blinks again. Long dark lashes, wet from her tears, make her blue eyes appear even bigger somehow. Like big sparkling sapphires. Sucking in a breath, she exhales it then repeats. It's her way of calming herself. I don't know how long I watch her breathing, but eventually she speaks.

"On what matters," she repeats softly.

I nod. "Yes."

Her body relaxes against me. Soft. Pliant. Fuck, she looks beautiful. With watery eyes, pink cheeks and the needy way she clings to me, I've never wanted her more. My cock hardens to steel, punching against my zipper as if it's trying to break free and bury itself in its home, her cunt. Lips parting on a gasp, her gaze drops to my groin. She swallows, her chest heaving as pure lust flashes in her eyes. Burying my face in her neck, I groan.

"Nico?" she whimpers.

Pulling back, I look at her. "I want to fuck you over my desk." It's not a question, but more of what will be a reality in the next couple of minutes. With Ocean in my arms, I rise, taking the couple of steps over to my desk. Dropping her down,

I smirk at the desire on her face. "Bend over. Palms flat on the desk," I order.

I turn her before she can second guess this and fight me. Hand landing on her back, I push until her chest is flush with the wood.

"I still have my period." She squirms against me.

"Don't care. I like your blood coating my cock. Just like my cum is going to coat your insides. It gets me fucking hard just thinking about it." Yanking her cotton dress up her body, my mouth salivates at the sight in front of me. I run a palm down the curve of her ass, squeezing the flawless flesh in my hand. "So fucking perfect," I growl.

She wriggles against my touch and without thought I spank her. "Nico," she squeals out, writhing against my desk.

I tsk. "Stay still, *Tesoro*. And keep your voice down. We don't want my mamma or anyone else coming in to witness what I'm about to do to you." Pushing her panties to the side, I smirk at the pad lining them. I had the housekeeper stock since I don't want her inserting tampons in my pussy and from the small, faint pinkish stain, I would say her period has nearly finished. Blood or not it won't stop me eating what's mine. My eyes lock on her glistening pussy, satisfaction coursing through me. "Look at you. Always dripping for me," I murmur, and I can't wait another second. Leaning down, I swipe my tongue up the length of her wet cunt, a growl vibrating in my chest when her essence with a hint of metallic hits my tongue. "Fuck, you taste like mine."

Running a finger down her slit, I relish the way her arousal coats me. She is fucking soaked. I thrust two digits inside her, stretching her out. With my free hand, I unbuckle my belt and release the zipper, my cock throbbing with the need to be inside her. Pushing down my pants and boxer briefs in one fast move, my cock springs free, rock hard and ready. Pre cum makes the tip glisten and I'm so hard it's painful. Pulling my fingers free, I line my cock up to her entrance and without preamble, push inside in one quick thrust. Her tightness grips me, sucking me and furthering my obsession. In this moment, it hits me. I never stood a chance with this woman. No matter how much I tried to deny myself in the beginning, I was always going to make her mine.

"Oh my–" she starts, but I cut her off when I ram into her with so much force, it takes her breath away.

"*Oh my Nico*, is what you were about to scream, wasn't it, *Tesoro?*"

"Yes," she whines her agreement as I hit her cervix.

I smirk. "You love me owning this pussy, don't you? Love me claiming you. You take every inch of my dick. Open this cunt up to me, so perfectly, just like I taught you to do. You're such a good girl, baby."

Her pussy tightens around me, no doubt at my dirty mouth and the praise. She would never admit it, but I know she loves it. Reaching around her body, I find her clit. Wanting her to come, I circle the little bundle of nerves.

"Nic–," she is cut off by the knock at my door.

"Nic?" Dante's voice sounds strained.

"Give me a minute." I pump into Ocean harder, pressing down on her clit with so much vigor she will have no choice but to come.

Struggling beneath me, she bucks, trying to get away. "Stop. He will hear us," she hisses.

Possession surges through me. My free palm covers her mouth. She is right. Dante will hear. And that is something I won't accept. "Your pleasure belongs to me," I growl into her ear. "You will scream but it will be into my hand. I am the only one allowed to hear you when you come undone." My words push her over the edge. Her cunt spasms around my cock, her muffled cries hitting my palm as her orgasm hits. My eyes roll shut at the sensation of her squeezing my cock. Wetness coats my dick, and she grips me like a damn vise. Pleasure consumes my whole body, and nothing has ever felt this good. Stilling, I groan when my own climax barrels through me. I release inside her, filling her pussy up with all of me. Coating every inch of her. *Claiming* her.

"Nic?" Dante's voice breaks through my sated, lust filled haze.

"What do you want?" I bark.

"We have a problem."

Ocean stiffens, her malleable, soft body now full of tension.

Pressing a kiss to her neck, I pull out of her. "Get cleaned up."

Grabbing some paper tissues from the box on my desk I hand them to her.

"Thank you," she says, dropping her gaze to her pussy. I watch as she wipes up the mess of blood mixed with cum between her legs. If it weren't for Dante calling me, I would be pushing every last drop of me back inside of her.

Tucking my cock back into my pants, I grab her chin, lifting until she has no choice but to look at me. "You have nothing to worry about, so get any bad thoughts that you are currently having out of that pretty little head. I need to speak to Dante. Go to Romeo and I will be there shortly." She nods, turning and starting to the door. Gripping her elbow, I stop her before she can reach it. Spinning her to face me, I capture her lips with mine in a bruising kiss. She melts into me, all the apprehension leaving her body with every second that I'm kissing her. Breaking apart, I smirk. "Now go before I rip your clothes from your body and fuck you again."

Shoving me away, she rushes to the door, pulling it open. Dante stands there, brow raised and a knowing grin on his face.

"Ocean," he greets.

"Hi," she squeaks out, quickly moving past him.

He chuckles, shaking his head as he strides into my office. "Man, if I hadn't heard the sound of your skin slapping together, then the clear embarrassment on her face would tell me exactly what you were up to. Couldn't wait the couple minutes it would have taken you to get to your bedroom?"

I grit my teeth, annoyed that he has seen Ocean post sex.

Dropping down in my chair, I wave my hand, grumbling out. "Just say whatever it is you interrupted me for."

His face turns serious and then he says the words, I have been waiting to hear. "Vadim has agreed to meet with us."

Satisfaction washes over me.

Good.

It's time to find out just what he wants with *my Tesoro*.

Chapter 27

Ocean

The next couple days pass in a blur.

Nico stays home, locked up in his office with Dante and his other men. Though he said he will protect me from any threat, I still feel a little on edge about my father. I know Nico is a powerful man with the right resources, but Samuel Caldwell and the Andersons are not to be underestimated. There is a small chance they have nothing to do with the Bratva but deep down in my heart, I know it's them. No one else would be looking for me. I shudder at the thought. I can't go back there. No way. I would rather be locked in Nico's cage for the rest of my life than have anything to do with my father or his evil plans.

Glancing down, I watch as Romeo feeds from a bottle. My heart clenches in my chest. They would never accept my son. Not my sperm donor or the Andersons. My value and worth were solely placed upon me having my virginity intact. Xavier and his father would never take an impure bride. I dread to think what my dad would do, if he ever got his hands on me and realized I was no longer valuable to him. The whole thing is draconian to say the least, but it is how their world works. And from what Allegra told me, Nico's world is very much the same. How sweet that we have that in common. I would laugh if it wasn't so depressing.

Romeo releases the bottle, his eyes closing in contentment. Lifting him, I bring him over my shoulder, gently rubbing his back to get rid of any potential wind before I put him down for bed.

The door being shoved open startles me. Nico pauses in the doorway, his gaze coming to me. I shift, trying to cover my breast which is half on display where Romeo has pulled my tank top down. Nico's eyes narrow. "Don't hide yourself from me," he growls. Stepping inside, he closes the door and moves further into the room. "You look exhausted. I will draw you a bath."

My brows jump in confusion as he walks past me to the adjoined bathroom. A bath? He hasn't done something like that for me since before I ran. Has he finally forgiven me? Hope blooms in my chest. Maybe we can move past everything that came before and have a fresh start after all. Not five minutes later, he is striding back into the bedroom, heading straight for where I still sit with our son. I watch him closely, but his face gives nothing away. He wears that infuriatingly blank mask, hiding everything I want to see. Reaching down he takes Romeo from me.

"What are you doing?" I ask.

"Go take a bath. Relax. Read your Kindle or whatever it is you do. I will put him down to bed," he drawls, jerking his head to the bathroom.

I bite down on my lip, suppressing the smile that wants to break free and ask. "Why are you being so nice?"

Sighing, he grabs my hand with his free one, pulling me to my feet. Irritation flickers across his features. "I'm not. Stop questioning me and just go bathe. I want to spend some time with my son. Alone." he enunciates.

I blink, my shoulders sagging. Silly me, thinking he would actually forgive me. "Okay," I whisper defeatedly.

Before he can see the disappointment on my face, I turn, making my way to the bathroom and shutting myself inside.

***

Wrapping the towel around me, I hold it together in a death grip. In my confusion of Nico's hot and cold behavior, I forgot to bring fresh clothes into the bathroom. I spent a good thirty minutes relaxing in the lavender scented bubble bath that was waiting for me. It was bliss and exactly what I needed to release all the tension in my body. I even managed to get a little reading done, the smutty book's primal sex scene arousing me in ways I never thought possible from reading words on a page.

Opening the door, I peek into the bedroom. My gaze lands on the chair, where Nico sits with Romeo in his arms. His eyes are closed but I doubt he is asleep. Tip toeing across the plush carpet, I move to the closet where I grab a matching sleep set. Toweling my body dry, I pull the shorts and tank on.

"Much better," I murmur, catching a glimpse of myself in the floor-length mirror.

Picking up the towel, I make my way back to the bathroom where I throw it in the laundry basket. Taking my time, I brush out my long blonde hair, moisturize my face and body, then clean my teeth. I know I'm stalling but I don't want to deal with whatever mood Nico is in when I go back out there. It is giving me whiplash and making me question everything.

Deciding I have wasted as much time as I can, I exhale a breath before stepping back into the bedroom. I frown when I find him in the exact same position. Padding toward him, I hold my breath as I get closer, only to release it when I find that he is, in fact, asleep.

Emotion clogs my throat. Seeing him like this, unguarded, protectively holding our son. It's a sight I thought I would never see and one I never want to forget. I wish I had a cell phone so I could capture this moment. So innocent, natural, and quite possibly the most adorable thing I have ever seen. For once, Nico looks like a normal human, and not the god above men he usually portrays. I sigh, taking them in for a long minute and committing the image to memory.

Reaching down, I try to pry Romeo out of Nico's arms but it's no use. His eyes snap open, confused but defensive when his gaze meets mine. He blinks, relaxing slightly when he sees that it is me.

"I was going to put him to bed." I murmur, suddenly feeling like I am doing something wrong. He glances down at Romeo, his blue orbs softening as he watches our sleeping son.

Blowing out a breath, he runs his free hand down his face. "I'll do it." His tone leaves no room for argument. He pushes out of the chair, moving toward the crib where he gently places Romeo into his sleep bag. It's such a simple, ordinary thing to do but my chest tightens almost painfully as I watch him. Guilt floods me when I think about how Nico would have missed his chance at doing this had he not found me.

"I'm sorry," I whisper past the lump in my throat.

He glances up at me, his brows furrowed in confusion. "What?"

"I'm sorry," I repeat. "If I'd had any other choice, I would never have kept him from you. Your father, he threated to kill me if I ever came back." He knows all this, but I can't help but tell him again.

Nico's eyes narrow. He searches my face, studying me like I'm a puzzle he can't quite solve. And maybe it will always be like that. But going forward, I want to be more transparent. Closing the distance between us, he cups my face in his big hands, his own serious when he speaks. "I don't know if I can ever forgive you for keeping me from my son. I missed so much, but I understand why you did it. You are young and no doubt you were scared and confused. Having a man like Lorenzo Marchetti threaten you would be enough to keep a grown man away, let alone a teenage girl. I just wish you would have come to me. Yes, I made mistakes, did things that I'm not proud of. But you, Ocean, you lied for the entirety of our relationship about who you were."

"You lied, too," I say weakly.

"I did. I had a duty to my family, and I would have gone through with the marriage to Gianna," he tells me honestly, making my stomach drop. "But I also would never have let you go. Its selfish, hypocritical and I'm sure you hate me for admitting that, but it's the truth. You were and always will be mine. If that meant being my side piece, then that's how it would have been. You didn't have a choice in the matter."

I gasp at the conviction and honesty in his words. He really would have kept me as his whore. *La sua puttana*. The phrase Lorenzo used flashes in my mind. Anger bubbles inside of me and if looks could kill, I'm sure he would be dead right now.

"There is always a choice," I grit out through clenched teeth.

He shakes his head. "Not for you, baby. From the moment you stepped into my club your fate was sealed."

"You asshole," I spit, trying to pull my face out of his hold.

He smirks. "Calm down. Fortunately for you, *Tesoro*, my papà is dead. Which means you don't have to be my dirty little secret." He brushes his lips against mine, whispering five words that send a thrill through me. "You can be my queen."

Chapter 28

Nico

"I don't like this." Dante grumbles beside me, as we stride toward the derelict warehouse.

We are surrounded by Marchetti soldiers, and there is no doubt in my mind that Vadim will be just as prepared with his own security. Having our own teams of guards was not only part of our agreement when the meeting was scheduled, but a requirement should anything go wrong. We are on neutral grounds, at a place that was decided by an intermediary at the last minute so neither side could have a chance to set a trap if they had decided to.

I know for a fact Vadim will be just as on edge as we are. This is the first time he will be facing me; the son of the man he had murdered in cold blood and the man who owns the club his men shot up. I am sure that in his mind, he thinks I want his death as vengeance for my father. I do want him to die at my hands, but it is not for the reason he believes it to be...

"It will be fine." I drawl, waving off his concern. "No one is allowed to take any weapons inside." I remind him of the other security measure in place. A metal detector will be set up at the entrance making sure no one is carrying a gun or any other weapon. Not that I couldn't kill a man with my bare hands if I decided to. I could. But with these measures in place, it will hopefully ensure we get out of here alive.

"Mr. Marchetti," Callum, the middleman in all of this and the federal agent that works for both our organizations, greets me as I step inside the warehouse. Whereas Tony is only in *my* pocket, this fucker isn't. Callum Halstead is a greedy fucker – one I don't trust, but he was the only way this meeting was going to happen - and takes money from *The Famiglia* and the Bratva. He toys with both sides of the coin, earning good chunks of money from both organizations. The asshole could easily retire with what I pay him and the fact he is still doing this tells me one thing. He gets off on his double agent shit, loves the danger that comes with being involved with the wrong side of the law.

"Callum." I nod, lip curled in a snarl. He knows full well I don't like him, and I know the feeling is mutual.

He eyes me, before his gaze shifts over my army of men. A look of disdain flickers in his eyes but he covers it quickly. Hmm. Interesting. I make a mental note to look into his hostility when this is over.

"Vadim is already inside. Like him, my men," he jerks his finger to the four men standing by what look like two standard airport metal detectors. I don't miss the guns strapped to their belts. Makes sense. They are getting in the middle of a war between mafia families. "Will take you all through the machines to check for any weapons. Once we are satisfied that you are all clean, we will take you through."

"Let's get on with it then. I don't have all night." I say, clear irritation lacing every word. I knew all this was going to happen, so I don't understand why he feels the need to tell me all this again. I'm beginning to think he just likes the sound of his own voice. Either that or he is stalling. Either way, I just want the information I came here for and to get back to my family as quickly as I can. I shove the thought of them aside, knowing I need to keep a clear head going into this.

Callum's jaw clenches in annoyance. I know he wants to say something, but he won't. Not if he values his life, anyway. "Let's go," he moves toward the machines. One by one we all go through without setting the alarm off. There are twenty of us altogether and within fifteen minutes we are all checked. Once Callum is happy, he gives the nod, and we are escorted through the warehouse by him and his men, the tension radiating from them so thick, I almost choke on it.

We move down a dark, damp hallway, toward double metal doors. Callum pushes them open, revealing a room filled with men. My gaze travels over them, one by one. They all watch us with blank faces, their stances protective as they guard their boss. My gaze shifts to said boss, Vadim, who sits at a large table with who I assume is his underboss, Lev. They don't rise from their chairs - I don't expect them to – it would be a sign of respect and that's something they don't have for me.

"Vadim," I address him by his first name, not missing the way his jaw grinds together.

"Nico. Nice of you to grace us with your presence." His thick Russian accent bounces around the room.

I smirk, pulling out a chair and taking a seat. Dante drops down beside me, with Callum playing Switzerland and sitting just out of the way, at the side of the table with one of his men.

"I wish I could say the same," I drawl, making him glower. "Anyway, enough of the small talk, let's get straight to the point. I have better things to do than sit around with you."

"You requested this meeting, Nico. Say what you came here to say." Vadim shoots back, sitting up in his chair, like he is a king waiting for the peasant to speak.

My jaw clenches at his blatant disrespect but I push it

down. "You shot up my club, Vadim." It's not an accusation but a statement, one which he confirms with two words.

"I did." He grins, no shame for what he did. Anger heats my veins and I want to kill the bastard, but I just about manage to tamp it down. I will kill him, but not before I get the information I need.

"They asked about a girl. Emilee. What do you want with her?" I don't know how I manage to get the words out. My teeth are clenched so hard, I am surprised they haven't turned to dust.

He eyes me, curiosity sparking in his gaze. Leaning back, he gets comfortable. "Ahh, so this meeting is not about your club or your papà. It is about the girl." He chuckles, shaking his head.

"What do you want with her?" I repeat, a red haze dotting my vision.

He smirks. "Her father, Mr. Caldwell, is paying me a substantial amount of money to find her. His PI informed him that she was working at your club. Samuel Caldwell is a smart, resourceful man. He did his research and found out that I was your enemy. Let's just say, he made me a deal I couldn't resist." His gaze narrows. "She wasn't there, though. Any idea where she could be? I would like to fuck her at least a couple of times before I take her back to her father. Have you seen that body?" He licks his lips suggestively and I have to grip the arms of the chair to hold me in place.

He is baiting me. I know this. But it doesn't calm the blood burning in my veins, or the voice in my head, begging me to wrap my hands around his neck and choke the life out of him. "Call the deal off," I growl.

He barks out a laugh. "And why would I do that? Did you know she is promised to a mayor's son? If I bring her back, they have assured me that I will have no problems or questions asked bringing..." he trails off, as if he needs to think about his next words. "My *business* through their ports. It will make things easier for trade on the west coast. I just need the girl, and something tells me you know exactly where she is."

My face is impassive, eyes cold, not giving anything away, but inside I'm seething. With that kind of deal on the table, I know Vadim won't stop until he finds Ocean. But I would die before I let him touch her. Which is why I can't show my hand, or act on impulse. I need to keep my cards close to my chest. Stay calm. Not give anything away. If I show any hint of possessiveness he will know.

"That's where you're wrong, Vadim. The girl left my club over a year ago. I haven't seen her since. Why would I care about some dancer? The only reason I called this meeting was because you shot up my club, and to do that for some girl? Well, she must be important. I wanted to know why." I chuckle condescendingly, leaning back casually as if I really don't give a shit.

His eyes narrow. He searches my face, looking for any hint that I'm lying. He won't find it. I mastered the skill of hiding my emotions before I was a teenager. "So let me get this straight. We kill your papà, and you barely even retaliate. But yet you call a meeting for some *dancer*? Makes sense." He nods mockingly.

My eye twitches before I can stop it. Blinking it away, I lean forward, resting my elbows on the table. "Don't mistake my lack of retaliation for me letting you get away with murdering my papà, Vadim. Your time will come. And as for the girl? She was just a dancer. A nobody. A fucking whore. And now she is gone." Bile fills my mouth with the lies coming from my mouth.

"If that is the case, then we will find her. Mark my words, the girl is as good as mine. They have given me permission to punish her however I see fit. I will break her cunt in. Her ass. Her mouth. By the time I am done with her she will be a broken little submissive doll, just like the Andersons wanted, ready to spread her legs whenever the mayor's son," he cocks a taunting brow, "or maybe the mayor himself, demands."

Fuck acting calm. I am up and out of my seat before I can stop myself, but I don't get far. Dante grabs at my suit jacket, pulling me back as my guards move in closer to me. Vadim's men do the same, ready to protect as soon as the word is given. Rage surges in my veins at the picture he has painted. My *Tesoro*, beaten and broken by this piece of shit.

"I guarantee this won't end well for you, Vadim. You want my retaliation; you're going to get it. And believe me when I say, I won't stop until you are fucking dead. That's a promise."

He smirks as if he just got exactly what he wanted out of me. And maybe he did, but I am past caring. He points at me. "I look forward to whatever comes next, Nico. But just know this. The girl is mine. *That is a promise.*"

I growl, lunging toward him. Again, my asshole friend who I am about two seconds from smacking in the face, pulls me back. "Calm down," he mutters for only me to hear, but I shrug him off. A throat clears.

"I think that's enough. Meeting is over." Callum's strong voice breaks my stare off with the Russian that is going to die.

My glare lands on Callum and the gun he is now waving around in warning. I could tell him to fuck off, beat the shit out of him before he even gets chance to fire the thing. But there is no doubt in my mind he has colleagues who know his exact whereabouts and that in the event of anything happening to him or any of his men, they will know who to come for. I can't risk that. Can't risk going to prison, not now that I'm a father. Not now I have Ocean. Vadim's time will come, just not today.

Without another word to any of them, I turn, striding down the hall and making my way out of the building. Heavy footsteps trudge behind me and I don't have to look back to know it's Dante and my men following me, *protecting* me.

I should have known the meeting with Vadim would turn south as soon as he mentioned Ocean, but nonetheless I got what I came here for and that was finding out who exactly it was after *my* woman.

They can try all they like. But I will kill anyone who is a threat to my family.

That is something Vadim, and anyone else that threatens my woman, can count on.

Chapter 29

Ocean

"I would like to start dancing again. Allegra mentioned that there is a dance school in town." I announce, my voice strong, confident, and I won't leave this office until I get what I want.

Nico's head pops up from where he is watching his laptop. He leans back in his seat, his cold blue eyes narrowing. He has been in a weird mood since he came back last night. It's probably not the best time to demand this from him, but I am going crazy being trapped in this house and need something to do with all my free time.

"No." His response is instant. I frown. He didn't even pretend to humor me and think it over.

Fire ignites in my body. I will not leave until I get this. I am probably being a little bit of a brat, especially because I know he has a lot going on right now, but he has to give me this.

"Nico," I start, stepping further into his space. "I am going stir crazy. I *need* to dance." My voice wobbles with my annoyance.

"What you *need* to do, is to take care of our son. I'm not discussing this with you now. I have other shit to deal with that is more important than you wanting to dance." He looks back to his computer, dismissing me. My fists ball, anger surging through me. I will not accept this. I don't care what he has going on, he cannot do this to me.

"I do take care of Romeo. That is all I do," I grit out, motioning down to the baby monitor in my hand. "But I need something for *me*. Even though I have a baby to look after, I am still me. The Ocean that loves ballet. That loves to dance. You have to give me this Nico. Please." I'm not past getting on my knees and begging at this point. I love Romeo and would not change him for the world, but when you become a mom people stick you in that category, forgetting that you have your own identity. Above all, I am a mom, but I am also a dancer, and I will never give that up.

"You have me," he drawls, not even sparing me a glance.

I scoff. "Do I? Because you are so distracted lately, I haven't really seen you. Plus, your hot and cold attitude toward me gives me whiplash. I want more. I want to dance."

He is up out of his chair, around his desk, and in front of me before I can blink. His hand comes up, wrapping around my throat as he pushes me against the wall. I gasp, my breath stuttering in my chest. He squeezes, not hard enough to stop my breathing, but it's a warning all the same.

"Listen to me, *Tesoro,* and listen well. I'm distracted because I'm trying to protect *my* family. Not only did the Bratva kill my papà, but now your father is working with them to find *you*." My eyes widen at his words, fear turning all the blood in my body to ice. His thumb strokes my erratic pulse point so soft and soothingly, it's in complete contrast to the harsh way he holds me. "Sometimes I think you are more hassle than you are worth. Maybe I should just give you back to your family. Maybe *they* will let you dance. Or maybe they will kill you for your insubordination. For no longer being of use to them because you are not pure." His face is a blank mask as he spews his vitriol. "It would be so easy. I could keep our son and hand you back to them, just like they want. It would put me in your father's good graces, and would no doubt secure me some good business deals," he drawls nonchalantly, like he isn't threatening to take my child and hand me back to a monster worse than him.

I claw at his hand, with my free one, trying to break free of his hold. Though I want to be strong right now, I can't help the tears that leak from my eyes just thinking about that outcome. "No," I choke out.

He smirks. "Now do you see why you are being kept here? It's to keep *you* safe. Not me. *You*. So, if you want to go dance at some studio in town, then do it. But I can't promise that the Bratva or your father won't get their hands on you." He leans in, his tongue darting out as he licks up my tears. "What I can promise you, *Tesoro*, is that I am a far better fate than anything else that awaits you outside these gates."

My breath hitches in my throat. I stare up at him with watery eyes. I need to remember that no matter how many times he shows me the nicer side of him, that underneath the façade of the Nico I like, he is still the devil. He hides it well most of the time, but I can't forget that beneath the sexy smiles and expensive suits, is a monster waiting to reveal himself.

"Okay," I whisper in acquiescence.

His blue orbs light up in satisfaction, he presses into me, his hard cock hitting my stomach. My eyes widen. This is turning him on, the sick bastard.

"Your submission turns me on as much as your defiance," he growls, rolling his hips into me and proving his point.

Gripping the monitor tighter, I hold onto it as if it's my lifeline. My earlier words to Nico, about giving me whiplash, stand truer in this moment than they ever have before. He literally has done a complete one eighty in the last minute. How can he go from being so cruel, to this? Hard and ready to rip the clothes from my body.

"Nico, stop," I grind out, not really in the mood for sex after his threats.

"Never. I want to fuck your little pussy raw, fill you with my cum. I want to put another baby in you, watch your stomach grow with my child." He groans, his hand snaking down my stomach to the top of my yoga pants. "That reminds me. I need to start tracking your cycle."

My head jerks back, lips parting in shock. I laugh but it's humorless. "You are insane if you think I'm going to let you track my period," I bite out.

"No, *Tesoro*. You are insane if you think it won't happen. Romeo needs a sibling," he counters, grinning.

"Oh my God. You are being serious." I shake my head. "No. No way. I'm nineteen, already a teenage mother and not married. Not even close to marriage. Our relationship – if you can even call it that – is so up and down, it gives me anxiety from all the back and forth. And. I. Want. To. Dance." I enunciate.

Nico stares at me with an unreadable look on his face. Contemplative. Calculative... Oh, fuck. What is going on in that head of his? His lips curve into a sexy, triumphant side smirk. My heart pounds in my chest as I wait for him to speak "If it's marriage you want, then that is what we will do. I can have everything arranged and you can be Mrs. Marchetti by tomorrow."

My eyes widen and I think my jaw just hit the floor. I stare at him in disbelief, my head shaking in small movements. What the fuck is happening right now? He leans in, snapping me from my trance. "No. Just no. Did you even hear anything else I said?" I screech.

"No, because none of the other shit matters. You will have

my name and you will have my baby. I don't care if we are up and down, or round and fucking round, it's normal when we are still getting to know each other. Still trying to trust each other after..." he trails off, his blue eyes narrowing in on me. "*Everything.*"

I search his face for any hint that he is just trying to scare me with this marriage talk but come up empty. He is being serious. I don't know why I expected anything else. Nico is nothing if not serious when it comes to the things he says to me. My mouth opens to respond to his ridiculousness only to close. It opens again. Then closes. Quite frankly, I'm shocked and really have no idea what to say. When I came in here, I never expected we would be having this conversation. I should have known better though. It's just like Nico to do something like this. Take my free will and force me.

Nico grins down at me, his brow cocked waiting for me to say something, *anything,* but nothing comes. A cry pierces the room, breaking the silence and making me jump. I glance down at the monitor, relieved for the interruption.

"Romeo needs feeding," I mumble pathetically.

Nico sighs, stepping back and giving me space. "Cock blocker," he grumbles. The words sound so odd coming from his mouth, I can't help the giggle that bursts from mine. He glares, jerking his head to the door. "Go take care of our son. I have some business to take care of, but when I am done, we can maybe see about setting up a dance space in my gym." I blink, thinking I might have heard him wrong, but I heard it clearly. I mean it's not exactly what I asked for but it's something. Hope blooms in my chest at the thought of getting my own dance studio. He looks at me pointedly. "I expect you to follow my rules, Ocean. If you break them, then I will take away your privileges and that includes calling Patty."

Before I can stop myself, I throw my arms around him. The

way his body stiffens tells me he is shocked at my reaction. To be honest, so am I. There is always a condition with everything he does, but all I can think about is the possibility of having a place to dance. Even though the initial conversation went to shit, he clearly heard my desperation and is offering me an alternative.

"Thank you," I whisper.

He relaxes a little, his arms wrapping around me and giving me a gentle squeeze. Pulling back, he clears his throat. "Now go. Our boy is hungry."

With a grateful smile in his direction, I leave the room.

Yes, he may have started out with threats, but in the end, I got what I wanted.

To dance.

Chapter 30
Nico

Pushing Romeo's stroller, Ocean walks beside me as we stroll around the grounds of my estate. The sun shines, the day is warm, and I have never felt more content than I do in this moment. It's a revelation and something I never thought I would experience, but here we are.

I glance at Ocean, who talks animatedly to Patty on my cell phone with a big smile on her face. Despite all the shit that is going on, the things I've done and threatened her with, she takes it all in her stride. She is strong. Probably the strongest woman, beside my mamma, that I have ever met. Sometimes her maturity, the way she isn't afraid to go stand up to me, it makes me forget that she is nineteen - a teenager for Christ's sake - and only a couple months older than my sister.

It also makes me a hypocrite. Because the thought of my sister marrying anyone at that age makes me see red. Yet all I can think about, since I mentioned marriage to Ocean a couple days ago, is getting my ring on her finger and giving her my last name. Not only will it tie her to me in every way possible and assert my ownership over her, but being the wife of Nico Marchetti will ensure a level of protection she doesn't get from only being the mother of my child. Though I doubt Vadim will stop in his pursuit of her, I will have more leverage against him if we are married.

"He is getting so big, Patty. I will have to send you some pictures." Ocean grins bigger as she glances at our son. She is quiet for a long moment, her face falling and a distraught look taking over. "I wish we could visit, too," she whispers so low I almost miss it.

Tension fills my body with those words, my muscles pulling tight and ready to snap. The thought of her going back there, seeing that asshole fucker... a red mist coats my vision just thinking about it. I stop walking altogether. Ocean frowns, her gaze meeting mine when she comes to a halt a few steps in front of me. Worry fills her blue orbs and I know it's because she fears my reaction. Guilt is an emotion I'm not accustomed to, but a slither of it hits me right in my chest. I don't want her to feel this way when she hasn't really done anything wrong, but I also can't have her thinking that I will ever allow her to run back to Charleston. I must assert my power over this woman when I can. Now is one of those occasions.

"Time's up." I grunt, suddenly feeling irritated. I hate that she brings out all these differing emotions in me. I also don't know how to deal with how she makes me feel, so naturally, I revert to my default mode. Asshole.

Disappointment flickers in her gaze but she does as I ask. Saying her goodbyes, she tells Patty that she will talk to her soon then ends the call. Chewing her plump bottom lip, she hands me back my phone. I know she wants to say something, so I give her a *go on* look. Straightening her spine, she juts her chin, hissing out, "Stop treating me like a child, Nico. I am quite capable of deciding when to end a phone call."

"If I don't like the way the conversation is going, then I will end it for you," I state.

Her hands land on her hips, defiance sparking in her big blue eyes. She scoffs. "Oh my God. Just because I said I wished we could visit, you what? Have some childish tantrum. Grow up, Nico. I was saying it in passing. It's not like we are actually going to visit. Though I would like to. There I said it. I would like to see Patty again." She taunts, now acting like the *childish* one as she put it.

"No, you're not," I agree, ignoring everything else she said and making sure she understands that when it comes to this conversation, it is non-negotiable.

"You're incorrigible." She shakes her head in exasperation.

I shrug. "I've been called worse. Now stop with your *childish tantrum.*" I throw her words back in her face. "And let's finish our walk."

"That's the difference, Nico. I'm nineteen, so I get a little leeway when it comes to acting like a child. You're pushing thirty, it's a bit embarrassing when you do it." She spits, storming past me.

Embarrassing?

Nico Marchetti embarrassing? She has some damn nerve.

Grinding my molars together, I want to get the last word in but stop myself. Later she will receive her punishment for her insubordination, and I shall look forward to every minute of what I do to her.

For now, I will allow her tantrum, only because I know what comes next is going to change everything. I smirk as I think of what I have planned.

Though she doesn't know it yet, by the end of the week, Ocean will legally be my wife. That is when she will finally realize that there is no escaping me, no way out of this, but death. And even that's debatable.

Because in this lifetime and every one that comes after? I will find her and make her mine.

***

"Really? You're getting married?" Mamma gushes, her eyes glassy with happy tears.

"I am. Ocean doesn't know yet, so I would appreciate your discretion. I want it to be a surprise," I drawl. It's not technically a lie. I do want it to be a surprise. But I also don't want the annoyance of her fighting with me about it over the next couple of days, which is my main reason for keeping it hushed.

Mamma gasps, her eyes dreamy, hands coming up to rest on her chest in the place where her heart sits. "A surprise? Who knew *mio figlio* could be so romantic."

I resist a snort but don't miss the choked noise Dante makes. I glare at him. Romantic isn't really the word I would use. Ocean is going to lose her shit when she realizes what's happening. I smirk, knowing that I'm going to enjoy every second of her reaction.

"Can you organize a dress and someone to come in to do her hair and make-up? I've spoken with Father Michaels, and he has agreed to officiate the ceremony on Sunday evening. The County Clerk is issuing the marriage license, and will have it ready by no later than Thursday." I tell her. Normally it would take longer to issue the license, but he owed me a favor and I called it in.

"When will you tell her?" Mamma asks.

"I am not going to tell her. Though, I think it will be obvious what's happening when they start pulling out wedding dresses." I frown when I remember something else. "Can you call my tailor? I want a custom all in one suit made for Romeo."

Mamma beams. "Of course. As if *mio nipote* isn't adorable enough, now he is going to have a matching suit with his papà."

My chest tightens at her words. My son and me in matching suits. I mean, I'm never going to be the man that wears cringe-worthy matching holiday pajamas with his family and takes pictures for social media. But me and my son in the same outfit? Yeah, it does shit to me. "Good. Now that's sorted, I need to talk to Dante." Mamma doesn't ask questions, just gets up from her chair with the biggest smile on her face and leaves. A chuckle breaks the silence in my office. My glare lands on Dante.

"Something funny?"

His laugh dies out, though amusement still dances in his eyes. "Man, Ocean is going to fight you every step of the way on this. You will have to drag her down the aisle."

I shrug. "Then I will drag her down the aisle, but this marriage is happening. It's the only way I can fully protect her."

He eyes me for a long beat, then shakes his head. "Don't try to play this off as just some way to protect her. You love her. I see it in the way you look at her."

Irritation surges through me. Though there is truth to his words, I would never admit it. What I feel for Ocean transcends anything I've ever felt for anyone before. I don't know if it's love, but it's something. I know I want her. Need her. Can't imagine going a day without seeing her face. The time she was away, it was torture and I refuse to ever go through it again. Which is why she is safely locked in her cage – my estate. Is all that I am feeling love? I shake my head. It can't be. A man like me doesn't do love.

"Don't make this into something it's not," I grit out.

Dante sighs. "Nico, you can't fool me, so stop fooling yourself. You have been obsessed with that girl from the moment she stepped into your office at The Executive Club. It's not a bad thing being in love. You shouldn't be scared to admit it or allow yourself to feel it." He sucks in a breath. "I love Allegra. And I will not allow a day to go by without me telling her that."

Emotion clogs my throat witnessing his vulnerability. And yet, he is still the same man I've always known. He isn't weak.

Love hasn't made him weak. If anything, it has made him stronger. He is willing to fight for his love and I know without a doubt he would die before he let my sister marry another man.

Nonetheless, I'm still not going to give him what he wants. Clearing my throat, my mask slips back into place. "I don't love her."

Dante rises from his seat, chuckling as he shakes his head. "Keep telling yourself that."

Without another word he leaves my office.

Slumping back in my chair, I mull over his words, realization hitting me.

She is the other half of my soul.

My everything.

Fuck.

I run a palm down my face, knowing that I am officially fucked.

Because what I'm feeling has a name. Is something. Is *everything*.

And it's time I admit it. At least to myself.

I, Nico Marchetti am in love.

I love Ocean, Emilee or whatever the fuck name she wants to go by.

The little liar swept into my life, crawled beneath my skin, and brought me to my knees.

I always knew was a witch and now she has achieved what I thought was the impossible.

She made me fall in love.

Chapter 31

Ocean

I'm just pulling on a pair of yoga pants when someone knocks on Nico's bedroom door. My brows furrow in confusion and I wonder who it could possibly be. Nico would never knock, and as far as I know, Valentina was taking Romeo down to the beach – surrounded by guards per Nico's request – while I took an hour for myself and spent some time dancing in my new studio.

Nico wasn't lying when he promised to have a home studio set up for me. I don't know why I was surprised when he got everything a ballet studio would ever need and had it constructed within a couple of days, but I am. Though I am quickly starting to realize that nothing is out of reach or off limits when it comes to Nico Marchetti. He literally clicks his fingers and shit gets done.

"Ocean?" Valentina calls, snapping me from my thoughts.

Her unsure voice has panic seizing my chest. I thought she was at the beach. Worry floods my veins, my heart picking up to an unnatural speed as I rush to the door. Pulling it open, I pause when I find a smiling Valentina with two other women I don't recognize.

"Where's Romeo? Is he okay?" I blurt, needing to know the answer to my question before I even ask anything else.

Gripping my arm, she gives me a gentle squeeze. "He is fine, sweetie. Nico has him."

A puff of air leaves my lips, my body relaxing. My gaze shifts back to the two women standing behind Valentina. The tension that was leaving my body soon rises again. Who are they? And why are they looking at me with creepy smiles?

"What's going on?" I murmur, my voice small, hesitant.

Valentina's lips curve into the biggest smile I have ever seen, but it doesn't calm me any. Taking my hand, she pulls me into the room, waving at the women to follow. Glancing over my shoulder, only then do I notice the mobile clothes rail being pushed into the room with them. Garment bags hang from it, and I don't know why but my stomach dips, a feeling of unease washing over me. The door is closed behind them, the click of the latch ringing in my ears like a bad omen. I swallow, my eyes bouncing between all three of them, waiting for one of them to tell me what the hell is going on right now.

"Honey, this is Mia and Theresa. They are here to measure you for your wedding dress." Valentina finally speaks, her tone soft, placating.

My stomach sinks, eyes widen, mouth parting.

What did she just say?

Surely, I didn't hear her right?

Wedding dress?

What wedding dress?

A nervous laugh bursts from my mouth before I can stop it. Valentina frowns, which somehow makes *me* feel guilty. Sobering, I clear my throat. "I'm sorry. I don't understand what's going on?" I ask it as a question though really, it's a statement.

Valentina's face softens. Taking a step toward me, she cups my face. "Nico wanted it to be a surprise. I think it is so romantic," she says dreamily. I don't want to burst her bubble, but the reality is it's not romantic. It's Nico asserting even more control over me. His way of showing me that he has all the power. Not that he needs to. I'm already very aware of that fact.

"Where is he?" I try to keep my voice even, but know I haven't succeeded when Valentina's face falls.

Her hands drop from my cheeks, and she takes a step back. "He was in his office. Do you want me to go get him?"

I shake my head, moving past her and the two women who I realize I haven't even said hello to. I am being rude, but all this... this talk of weddings has been thrust upon me and quite frankly, I'm in shock. Surely, they can understand that?

"No. Give me ten minutes. I will be back." It's a lie. At this point I don't know what I will do. It's not like I can run again. And though I am acting brave, I get the feeling there is only one way this conversation is going to go and that is with *me* in a *fucking wedding dress*. Do I want to marry Nico? Maybe. But he hasn't even asked me, presented me with a ring or given me a choice in the matter. He just expects it to be a given. Well, screw him. He is going to get a piece of my mind.

Storming out of the room, I make my way down to his office. Without knocking I push the door open. His head snaps up, eyes narrowing when he spots me. My gaze drops to Romeo, who he rocks in his strong arm. I nearly melt into a puddle at the sight of such a powerful man, gently cradling our son, but I can't let him disarm me so quickly. Shaking my head, I remind myself why I'm here and that I can't let this image distract me. My eyes shift back to Nico, stomach tightening at the smirk curving his lips.

"What can I do for you, *Tesoro*?" his voice is a caress across my skin and has a direct line to my sex. His arrogant smile tells me he knows exactly what he is doing to me and why I am here.

"Why are there two women up in *your* bedroom with a rack of wedding dresses in tow?" I demand.

He glances at our son who makes a little noise before his cold blue orbs come back to me. He pins me with a look. My muscles lock, heart pounds and I know I am going to lose this war before it's even started.

"It is *our* bedroom, Ocean. And because we are getting married. I thought that would have been obvious." His brow arches condescendingly.

I grit my teeth, wanting to go off on him but knowing that it won't get me anywhere. Exhaling, I shake my head. "I can't marry you, Nico, I don't even have a ring. We–"

His hand rises, cutting me off and he glares. "You can and you will. And you don't need a ring to know that you're mine. Nonetheless, I have the family jeweler visiting this evening. We can pick an engagement ring for you and wedding bands for the both of us. Now I don't want to hear another word out of your mouth. Go try on the dresses. On Sunday you will become my wife. So smile, be happy, grateful. I am giving you my name. You are in a position that many women would kill for, so stop acting as if marrying me is beneath you." The arrogance in his tone makes me want to punch him in his beautiful face.

"Nic–"

"Don't say another word, Ocean. If you do, I will have no choice but to stuff your mouth full of my cock and fuck your throat until you can't speak for a week. Is that what you want? Hmm?" His head cocks, challenge sparking in his eyes. It amazes me how he can go from nice to asshole in mere seconds. I'm beginning to think he has a split personality. Jekyll and Hyde. It would make sense. I swallow. I knew coming in here was a lost cause, but I didn't think he would be so dismissive. My shoulders slump, fists balling when I see the satisfaction on his face at my resignation.

"Good girl. Now go pick out your dress. Sunday you will become Mrs. Marchetti."

***

"You look beautiful," Valentina whispers, with tears running down her cheeks.

"You really do," Allegra, who showed up around twenty minutes ago for the fitting, adds on a soft sigh. My gaze bounces to Mia and Theresa who are both nodding their agreement.

Glancing at the floor-length mirror, my heart rate picks up and my lips part. With my long blonde hair and piercing blue eyes, I really do look like bridal *Barbie*. I never really thought about my wedding day or the dress I would wear - there was no point because I knew everything would be picked out for me, just like my future husband – but the gown I have chosen is perfect and exactly what I would choose for myself.

The strapless, sweetheart neckline molds to my breasts perfectly. The simple but elegant lace bodice highlights my waist and the mermaid skirt. It is exquisite. My chest tightens, tears pooling in my eyes. For the first time in my life, I feel like I am good enough. Not only do I feel secure in my skin, but I finally feel confident enough to stand beside a man like Nico.

"So stunning." Valentina steps up beside me, a big grin on her face. Taking my hand in hers, she gives me a comforting squeeze. "I don't know anything about your mother but just know, I am sure she would be so proud of you right now."

Emotion tightens my throat. The tears I was trying so hard to hold in run down my cheeks. My mom. This is usually the type of thing a girl would do with her mother. Yet mine is absent. Had she stood up to my father, things would have been completely different, but she chose her path. Conspiring with my dad. Allowing him to beat me. A stronger woman would have protected her child, not allowed the abuse to continue.

Being a mom myself, I know with everything in me, I would protect Romeo with my life. Yet Catherine Caldwell decided to turn a blind eye to everything that happened to me. If that wasn't bad enough, she decided my dad's torment wasn't sufficient and mentally abused me herself. I didn't understand it at first, didn't know what she was doing. But being away from her for so long, I can see it clearly now. See that both my parents were narcissistic abusers, but that my mother, though not physical toward me, was worse. Bruises disappear. But the mind? It carries the hurtful words she spat at me every day, and for a long time I believed them to be true. Though her voice is still there, it is not as loud. It's a process, but it gets quieter and is more of a whisper when I am feeling insecure. With every day that passes I grow more confident in who I am, fighting her words of hatred off with a metaphorical shield.

Wiping the tears away with my free hand, I shake my head. "She wouldn't. But that's okay. I have a new, better, family now."

Chapter 32

Nico

Sighing, I lean back in my chair, happy that I have finally finalized the details of Ocean's wedding present. It took a lot of convincing on my part, but there is no doubt in my mind that she is going to love my gift. I have gone above and beyond to make it happen, but Ocean is worth it. I want to see her smile. See the way her ocean blue eyes light up in joy, hope and excitement, the way they always do when I do something nice for her. She tries to hide her emotions from me but fails every time. Though I pretend otherwise, I want to be the man she needs. I don't know if I can fully give that to her. But I'm going to try. That much I know.

My cellphone ringing has me glancing down to where it vibrates on my desk. Stilling, my head cocks when I see the name flashing across the screen. After the absolute shit show of our meeting last week, I didn't think Vadim would be calling me, so let's just say my interest is piqued.

Grabbing the phone, I swipe to answer. "I assumed everything we had to say to each other was said in our meeting."

"There is no need for such hostility, Nico. I was just calling to congratulate you." My hand tightens around the phone. I straighten in my chair, my body stiffening with his words. There is only one thing he would be congratulating me for, and how the fuck does he know about my impending wedding? My jaw clenches at the thought that I may have another fucking rat in my fold. Vadim chuckles, the sound making all the hair on the back of my neck stand on end, and I want nothing more than to wipe his existence from this earth. "You see, I knew there was something off last week. Your reaction to what I said about the girl was..." he trails off. "Was not how one would react to hearing about some whore they didn't give a fuck about. Imagine my surprise when not only were my assumptions correct, but that you're marrying her." He laughs, though I see no humor in this fucking conversation. "She is going to be your wife. And she is the mother of your *heir*." I freeze, my breathing turning ragged at the mention of my son. The air of superiority in his voice, the fact he knows every one of my secrets has me seeing red. He laughs again and the sound is like nails on a chalkboard. I grit my teeth. "Yes, I am also aware of the son you have kept hidden."

"You will fucking stay away from them. You know the rules, Vadim, no women or children." My voice is low but calm. I need to steer this conversation in the right direction. One that has me coming out on top. I need to stay composed, even though everything inside me is demanding I find Vadim and the fucking rat traitor and put a bullet in their heads.

He sighs, "I know. That's why I called you. The deal with her father and Anderson is off."

I pause, my brows jumping in surprise, and though his words give me hope, I know not to trust him.

"And why should I believe you?" I ask.

"Well, you shouldn't," he admits. And I know that no matter

what he says, there will never be a time when I let my guard down with this man. After all, he did order the execution of my papà. "But you have my word. Things are different with her being your wife. I won't touch the girl. Her father isn't aware of the information I have, nor will I give it to him. He won't stop looking for her though, Nico. Just remember that."

"I can handle him and Anderson if it ever comes down to it." My words are final. There is only one way for them if they ever come for Ocean. Death. He grunts his acknowledgment and without another word ends the call.

Dropping the phone to my desk, I lean back in my chair. I'm not stupid. The war with Vadim is far from over and, though I will never trust him, with that one call, the Russian boss has extended a truce of sorts. He knows as well as I do that there are rules in place. He can't touch Ocean once she becomes my wife. It's one of the reasons this marriage is happening – though I will never tell her that.

Exhaling, I feel some of the stress of the last few months drain from my body. Vadim coming after Ocean might be one less thing to worry about, but I still need to find out who the rat is. I thought I had that situation under control after showing my men what will happen if they go against me.

Seems that while I have been distracted with my family, someone got brave. Thought that I was so preoccupied with everything that they could fly under the radar with their traitorous behavior. That's okay though. They will soon learn. I have been hungry for blood for a while now. Craving that feeling of the kill. When I find the traitor – and I will - he can damn well be sure, I am going to make an example of him. The torture is going to be slow, painful. By the time I am done with him, he will regret ever opening his mouth and spilling my secrets.

***

After sitting down with Dante and filling him in on my conversation with Vadim, I make my way upstairs. It's late, so I know my little *Tesoro* will be sleeping. Exactly how I want her.

Pushing the door open, I grin when I find her just as I knew I would. With one leg kicked out of the comforter, she sleeps peacefully in our California King bed, unaware of the predator waiting to pounce.

Quietly, I shut the door and move to the crib to check on Romeo. Just like his mamma, he sleeps soundly, without a care in the world. My chest tightens. He has no idea of the kingdom that awaits him. The situations he will face in the future. The decisions he will have to make. The blood that will stain his hands. There's a part of me that wants to keep him away from this world but the other, bigger part of me, can't wait to teach him all about the *famiglia*. It's his birthright after all.

Leaning down, I drop a kiss to his forehead, whispering. "I love you, *mio figlio*."

Straightening, I turn, my eyes locking on my prey. Smirking, and without another thought, I stride over to her, removing my clothes in the process.

Climbing on the bed, I crawl up her prone body. Only then does she begin to stir. Her body tenses, eyes fluttering open. She blinks.

"Nico," she mumbles, her voice slightly slurred as she rouses.

"Shh," I rasp, pressing a finger to her mouth. "Go back to sleep." Her blue orbs widen as realization hits her. She knows what I want. To fuck her while she is asleep. "Do I need to give you something to help you relax?" She shakes her head, her blonde hair like a waterfall over the pillow. "Good girl," I praise, pulling the lace tank from her breasts. They bounce free. So supple and round my mouth waters for a taste.

Dropping down, I take her in my mouth, sucking at the little bud with vigor. Ocean gasps, her back arching. "Careful. They are sensitive," she moans.

My gaze shifts up, locking on her face. Her eyes are squeezed shut, her body becoming pliant as she gets lost in her pleasure. Releasing her nipple, I watch when her eyes pop open. I smirk at the look of sheer disappointment covering her features, but it doesn't last long. Never breaking eye contact, my tongue darts out and I suck her other nipple into my mouth.

She moans, the little noises like music to my ears. I lap at the beaded flesh, enjoying when she begins to rub up against me. Shoving the cover away, I position myself between her thighs. I'm rock hard, almost desperate to get inside her tight cunt. Raw primal possession shoots through my veins and I can't wait another minute.

Reaching down, I push my hand inside her little sleep shorts. My mouth waters at how wet I find her, my cock turning to steel. Satisfied, I rumble. "You are always so responsive to me, *Tesoro*. I barely have to touch you and you soak my hand."

"Nico," she gasps when I push two fingers inside her tight pussy.

"Hmm, so fucking wet. And mine. Who do you belong to baby?"

"Yo-you," she stutters her response without hesitation.

"Fuck," I growl, pulling my fingers from her cunt and ripping her shorts from her body. "That's right, baby. You are mine." I shift down her body until I'm eye level with her pussy. My tongue darts out, running from her slit, down to her asshole and then back up to her clit. She squirms, whimpering as I play with her. I lick at her cunt like a starving man who can only be sated by her. Ocean doesn't know it, but she consumes me. My obsession for her runs so deep, I feel her in every part of my body. In my soul. Consuming me. *Owning* me.

Deciding I can't wait any longer to get my cock inside her, I release her clit and push up to my knees. Palming my cock, I stare down at her with an intensity that sucks all the air from the room. Ocean smiles timidly, chewing that pouty bottom lip of hers. I growl. Jealous of her own teeth. Fuck, I am so far gone for this girl it would be embarrassing if anyone knew the extent of my obsession.

"I want to put another baby in you." All rationality has flown out the window and the need to get her pregnant again thrums in my veins. I missed it with Romeo. I want to be there every step of the way with our next child.

Ocean tenses slightly, and if I wasn't watching her so closely, I would have missed it. My eyes narrow and when she doesn't fight me on it, like is her usual default mode, I make a mental note to ask her about it later.

Right now, I want inside her, so everything else can wait. Lowering, I line my dick up with her entrance and with a snap of my hips, I am inside her.

"Fuckkkk," I grind out, her tightness enveloping me.

"Nico," she moans, her back arching, taking me deeper.

"Look at you, baby. Taking my cock so well. Such a good little *Tesoro* for me." I coo, dropping down and taking her lips with mine. I rock into her, slowly, enjoying as I feel every inch of her perfect cunt molding to my cock. She may not be asleep like I wanted but fucking her when she is awake is just as much of a life changing experience. Being with her, even just touching her, does things to me I can't explain. But isn't that why I have always felt this weird fascination toward her? Isn't this why she is the only woman on earth that I would want as my legitimate wife? Fuck, I am in so deep, it should scare me, but all it does is plunge me in that hole deeper.

"You are so fucking sexy, Ocean. Your pussy is swallowing my cock. Gripping me like you never want me to leave. And I won't. Not until I've knocked you up again."

"Nico," her voice is a hitched moan.

"That's right. It is *Nico*. Pray to me baby. Pray for mercy that I will never give you. I am your God, and this is your confessional. Tell me how it feels. Scream out my name. Let everyone know who owns you." I groan, slamming into her harder. She tightens around me, so close to the edge I know that if I play with her clit, it will push her over. Reaching down, I circle the little bundle of nerves. Her cunt clamps down around me, contracting as her orgasm hits and she milks my cock.

"Nico," she cries out, her pussy spasming as she soaks me with her juices.

"Good girl," I praise, thrusting into her harder. My balls tighten and the way she is gripping me, I can't hold back any longer. Gripping her hips, I push into her, as deep as I can go, and still. My dick pulses, eyes closing as pure bliss heats my veins and I release my seed inside her womb. Exactly where it belongs.

"Jesus Christ," I groan, my cock jerking my release into her.

A soft hand lands on my cheek. My eyes snap open to find Ocean's blue orbs scanning my face with a soft, contented look of her own. My chest tightens. I don't deserve this girl. But that doesn't mean, I'm not keeping her.

Pressing a kiss to her palm, I roll to the side so as not to squash her. Wrapping an arm around her waist, I pull her into me, all the while keeping her plugged with my dick so that my cum doesn't leak out. Can't have that.

"Nic–"

I cut her off. Not because I'm being an asshole but because I'm too tired for whatever she is about to say. "Sleep, *Tesoro*."

She huffs at my dismissal but snuggles into me all the same. I grin.

She can act like she hates me.

But I know different.

She may not have said the words since she has been home, but I know with certainty.

Ocean loves me.

Chapter 33

Ocean

Today is my wedding day.
 Though I knew this day would always come, it looks completely different to anything I ever expected. Even the groom. When I was sixteen, I was told that I would marry Xavier Anderson, a man I would never consider for myself had I been given a choice in the matter. I know Nico is a bad man and there is small part of me that feels like we are rushing into this. The other part, a much *bigger* part, wants to be tied to him in every way possible. I want to be his wife. And yes, I am aware of how messed up this is. Just like the marriage my father had arranged for me, my choice has also been taken away from me with this wedding, but somehow it feels different. I feel different. Despite the circumstances, I feel like I am exactly where I am supposed to be.

 A year ago, I ran from Nico after being told he was engaged to another woman.

 Two years ago, I ran away from my family for forcing me into a marriage with another man.

 With all that we have been through, we have managed to come full circle.

Though our relationship has been rocky to say the least, I know deep inside my heart that everything is exactly as it should be. I felt it in the way Nico made love to me the other night. I see it in his eyes, every time he looks at me. Not for the first time, hope blooms inside me with thoughts of what we can be… A proper family.

"You look stunning, *Mia Figlia*." Valentina's soft voice behind me startles me out of my reverie.

I smile, meeting her gaze in the mirror. In the time I have been living here, Valentina has become the mother I never had. She is graceful, kind, poised and exactly the kind of woman I can look up to.

"*Mia Figlia?*" I repeat.

She beams, her whole face lighting up as she takes my hand. "My daughter."

My breath hitches, lips parting in surprise. Tears pool in my eyes as emotion clogs my throat. "Daughter?" I whisper thickly.

She nods. "Yes, daughter. You're family. My daughter. Nico told me all about your parents. I'm sorry I mentioned your mother during the dress fitting. I know now it was the wrong thing to say. But know this, Ocean." Her eyes bore into mine. "*I am proud of you. All that you have been through and the woman you have become on the other side of that.*" The honesty in her voice has a tear leaking down my cheek. Valentina doesn't realize this, but it's exactly what I need to hear in this moment. She chuckles, gently wiping it away. "Don't cry. You will not only ruin your make up, but you will set me off, too. Then we will be in trouble."

I laugh, shaking my head. "Thank you. For everything."

She beams, taking my hand and gently squeezing. "You don't need to thank me, honey. In fact, I should be thanking you. You and Romeo were exactly what I needed to heal. I'm a great believer in everything happening for a reason, even if you don't know what that reason is yet. Though you might feel differently, Nico finding you again was fate. You were made for my son. I see that. He sees that. I just wish you would see it. Own it, Ocean. Believe in who you are and take what is yours with both hands. Go, stand by his side and be the queen that you were always meant to be."

My breathing picks up with each word taking root inside me, giving me strength and making me believe that I can be the woman she is describing. Her words are powerful, as is the conviction in her voice. It makes me believe that Valentina Marchetti was a motivational speaker in a previous life. Or if not, then she should definitely consider being one.

A knowing smile curves her lips. She squeezes my hand again, smirking.

"Come on. Let's go get you married."

***

My hands tremble around the bouquet of white roses as I wait for the harpist to start picking at her strings. Whatever she plays is the music I will walk down the aisle to. Or in my case, the stone path that leads to the backyard where our wedding will take place. Where Nico got a damn harpist from, last minute, I will never know, but it makes me feel all warm inside, that he has gone to such lengths.

I don't know what else I can expect from our wedding, nor do I have any idea how many people will be watching our union. I have had no input regarding our wedding, apart from my dress, and for some reason I'm okay with that. As far as I am aware, Valentina has taken care of everything and if she put as much effort into my wedding as she does her cooking, I'm sure it will be perfect.

Soft, melodic, instrumental music sounds, making my head

snap up. That's my cue. Exhaling a breath, I straighten. This is it. In less than fifteen minutes, I will be Nico's wife. Ocean Marchetti.

"Be the queen you were always meant to be."

Valentina's words from earlier echo in my mind. She is right. I'm not the same girl I was two years ago, a year ago, or even a couple months ago. I'm strong and worthy of standing beside Nico. I'm a fucking Queen and its time I own it.

With those thoughts in mind, I inhale a breath, then put one foot in front of the other, slowly making my way out of the sliding doors and to the man I love.

Love.

Because I do love Nico. I loved him before I ran away, and I will love him for the rest of my life. Our story hasn't been easy and I'm sure there will be more speed bumps along the way. At times I will probably hate him and vice versa. But he is worth it. Our family is *worth* it.

With slow steps, I move down the cobble path, anticipation heating my veins the closer I get. Rounding the corner, I come to a stop, my breath hitching in my throat when my gaze lands on Nico holding our son. My heart rate picks up to an unnatural speed. I stare at them, transfixed and full of so much emotion I feel like I can't breathe. They are my whole world. My everything.

Without thought or hesitation, I move toward Nico, not once acknowledging the people here to witness our nuptials. There could be no one, there could be hundreds of people, but my boys are all I see as I make my way down the short, rose petal covered, aisle.

Stepping up to my men, I gasp when I find that Romeo is wearing a custom made all in one suit that matches his father's. Tears prick my eyes, emotion tightening my throat. This is too much. A finger grips my chin, lifting until my gaze meets familiar blue orbs. Nico's lips curve knowingly, and I flash him a watery smile.

"You look beautiful, *Tesoro*," he murmurs, leaning down to drop a kiss to my cheek.

"So do you. And Romeo, look at his outfit. It matches yours," I whisper the obvious.

"It does." Nico nods, before his gaze shifts behind me.

Pulling my chin from his grip, I follow his line of sight to Valentina. She steps toward us, reaching out as Nico hands her Romeo. She smiles and the happiness on her face hits me right in the chest. Before I get the chance to see who else is here, I am pulled forward and into Nico's hard chest. His mouth drops to my ear.

"Time to become Mrs. Marchetti, *Tesoro*. There will be no escaping me now."

My stomach flips. I glance up at him, the man who has consumed my life and I see everything he hasn't said staring back at me.

Love.

Nico has never told me that he loves me, but I see it, clear as day.

Nico Marchetti loves me.

Even if he can't admit it yet.

My heart flutters, the truth hitting me right in the chest, and I roll my lips between my teeth to stop a big smile from breaking out on my face.

No matter what has happened between us or what is still to come. I know with certainty we will get through it.

Because I love Nico Marchetti and he loves me.

Chapter 34

Nico

"I now pronounce you husband and wife." Father Michaels announces, a wide smile plastered all over his face like this is an everyday wedding and I'm a normal man. It couldn't be further from the truth.

Shifting my gaze, I stare down at the woman who captured my attention from the moment I saw her. My *wife*. I smirk, satisfaction filling me. She is mine. Officially. Now there will be no doubt in hers or anyone's mind who Ocean Marchetti belongs to. Cupping her face, I press my lips to hers, sealing our fate and tying us together.

Applause breaks out, making Ocean jump in surprise. She blinks up at me and as if just realizing we have guests, she blushes. "I forgot we weren't the only ones here. I didn't see anyone when I walked down the aisle. Only you and Romeo," she breathes out.

I cock my head. It makes sense, considering she hasn't seen my gift yet. Even though I had hidden it well amongst our twenty or so witnesses, I had wondered why she hadn't reacted. Taking her hand, I turn her toward our audience. Observing her, I watch as her cheeks turn pink when her gaze sweeps over the people. I know the exact moment she spots my *gift*. She goes completely still, then blinks and blinks again as if trying to confirm what she is seeing is real. A cry bursts from her throat, eyes darting to me, incredulity shining in them. She slaps a palm over her luscious mouth, face creasing. Watery blue orbs bounce between mine, love and something else I can't decode flickering in them. I smirk down at her before removing her hand.

"Let's go and say hello, Mrs. Marchetti. I know you are dying to," I drawl.

Her chest heaves as she sucks air into her lungs. With parted lips, she stares at me like I am an alien or something. "Nico," her voice is a whisper, thick with emotion. My chest constricts at her happiness. Most women would have this reaction to expensive jewelry, but not my *Tesoro*. No. By giving her this small gift, something that didn't cost me anything but a plane ride, she looks like the happiest woman on earth. I should be jealous, considering she didn't look this happy when taking our vows, but I can't bring myself to ruin this moment, I can only bask in her joy.

Running a thumb across her bottom lip, I smile. "Go, before I change my mind and steal you away to our bedroom."

She chuckles, surprising me when she throws her arms around my neck and hugs me tightly to her body. "Thank you. Thank you. Thank you," she repeats like a mantra. Pulling back, her eyes lock on mine. My pulse kicks up erratically at what I see staring back at me. "I love you." The three words are a caress against my skin. My blood heats but my face remains impassive. A small part of me thinks she only said those three little words because of the gift, but I shake the thought away. Even though she hasn't told me that she loves me since she has been home, I know she feels that way. It was in her eyes, all over her face, when I made love to her the other night and as clear as day, it's staring back at me now. Dropping another kiss to her lips, I jerk my head to the teary-eyed woman surrounded by some of my men, Mamma and Allegra.

"Come on." Taking her hand, I lead her back down the aisle, to where my gift stands, looking like an emotional wreck.

"Patty," Ocean cries, pulling her hand from mine and throwing her arms around the woman. My jaw clenches and I try to push down my jealousy. It's irrational, but I hate that her attention is elsewhere.

"Look at you. You're stunning. I can't believe you are married." Her southern drawl is filled with sincerity, but still, she manages to shoot me a glare. Had it been anyone else, I would have removed their eyes. I will let it slip, this time, but only because she took my woman and son in when they needed help, giving them a safe place to live.

Ocean follows Patty's stare, her face a little pale when she looks from me to Patty. Tension fills her features and I know she is worried about what I might do. Since I'm in a generous mood, I put her at ease. "We are so happy you could make it, Patty. I trust your flight was okay?"

She nods, her chin lifting haughtily. "It was. Thank you for allowing me to witness this moment. Ocean and Romeo are my family. Home is not the same now they are gone." I hear the accusation loud and clear, biting back a smirk at the feisty woman, but my wife's eyes widen in horror.

"Patty, we are still family." Ocean placates the woman, trying to diffuse the tension, so that the situation doesn't escalate. *My* wife knows I'm not a patient man, which just makes Patty's scorn for me all the more amusing.

"We are." Patty agrees, taking my wife's hands in hers and smiling at her softly. "Now where is my boy? I haven't had the chance to hold him yet."

Mamma steps forward, handing Romeo over without argument. "Here you go, Patty. I need to go check that the caterers are ready to serve dinner." Taking my Ocean's hands in hers, she leans in, kissing both her cheeks. "Welcome to the family, *Mia Figlia*. I already told you before the ceremony, but I will say it again. You look beautiful. I am proud to call you my daughter."

My wife smiles wide, a range of emotions flickering across her exquisite face. "Thank you, Valentina. For everything."

Mamma nods once before her eyes come to me. Cupping my cheeks, she glances up at me with a look I can't quite decipher. "Nico. *Mio Figlio*. I am so proud of you and the man you are becoming. Though Ocean may not be the woman your papà chose for you, I know he would have been pleased with how things worked out."

I want to frown. Tell Mamma that no, Papà would not have been happy or allowed this marriage to happen had he been alive. But I don't want to burst her happiness, so instead, I lean down, pressing a kiss to her cheek. "Thank you, Mamma."

With one last smile in my direction, she turns and makes her way toward the house. I glance at my wife, to find her eyes already on me. A dreamy look covers her face. I both love and hate it. Though, I have shown her a softness I am not accustomed to these last couple days, Ocean can never forget the man I really am.

Grabbing her hand, I pull her into me possessively. "Come. Let's go and greet the rest of our guests."

***

Sipping my scotch, I watch with narrowed eyes as my wife talks with Patty – who is holding my son - my mamma and Allegra. Though it makes me a little green with envy, I think this is the happiest I have ever seen her look. Her blue eyes sparkle with life and vitality. She looks positively glowing. My gaze drops to her stomach. Hmm. Maybe she is pregnant? The thought alone makes my cock swell in my pants, and I shift to ease the ache a little.

Thirty minutes ago, the final course of dinner was served and though a handful of our guests are still eating their dessert, everyone else seems to be enjoying the soft music or engaging in conversation. It wasn't a large service and that was intentional. I wanted to keep it small with only my closest friends, family, a couple of my trusted capos and their wives. Maybe sometime in the future, when everything has settled down, we can have a bigger wedding, something that would be expected for a Don. But for now, today was perfect.

Movement out of the corner of my eye has my gaze shifting to Leo. Though he is sitting, talking with Mario and Giuseppe, his eyes are on my wife as he watches her ... wistfully?

My jaw clenches, eyes boring holes in the side of his head. He must sense me watching him, because in the next moment, his head snaps up, gaze locking on mine. He swallows nervously, a look of contemplation on his face before he makes his decision. Pushing out of his seat, he heads straight for me.

"Great wedding, Nico," he says, dropping down in the seat beside me.

Irritation slithering through me, I eyeball him. "It is. But if you don't take your eyes off my wife, it will end as a red wedding. With *your* blood."

He watches me cautiously, exhaling a sigh. "I meant no disrespect, Nico. It's just, I haven't seen Ocean since we brought her home. I wanted to apologize for everything that went down."

"There is nothing to apologize for. You were simply following the orders that I issued." I wave him off. Staring him down, I wait for him to challenge my words. Fortunately for him, he doesn't.

He nods, conceding. "You're right. Congratulations. You're a lucky man. She really is beautiful."

I stiffen, red hot possessiveness rushing through my veins. This fucker needs to learn his place. Cocking my head, I study him. The pulse that beats erratically just above the collar of his dress shirt. The sheen of sweat on his forehead. He is scared. As he should be. Lowering my voice, my tone turns deadly. "Motherfucker, I am the only man that is allowed to think that about *my* wife. Ocean is mine. If you so much as look at her in a way I don't like, I will remove your eyes, friend or not. Understand?"

"Of course," he rushes out, his easy acquiescence making me smile. But the asshole still needs to watch himself. I will follow through with my threat should he not heed my warning. He knows that.

"What did I miss?" Dante drops down in the chair at my other side, the humor in his voice easing the tension a little.

"Nothing. Leo here was just about to tell me how the refurbishment at the club is going."

Dante chuckles. "Sure, he was." He takes a sip of his whiskey, waving his hand. "As you were, Leo."

Chapter 35

Ocean

My heart beats erratically in my chest as Nico leads me to our bedroom.

Patty is looking after Romeo tonight, in the guest bedroom that has been assigned to her for the duration of her stay. Though we have had sex many times, the anticipation of what he is going to do to me, now that I am legally his wife, shoots pure liquid lust straight between my thighs.

Shoving the bedroom door open, he drags me inside before kicking it shut. Leaning against it, he watches me with so much heat in those pale blue orbs, my body burns with desire.

"Nico," I whisper breathlessly.

Pushing off the door, he takes a step toward me, his eyes sparking. My pulse kicks up, tongue darting out as I lick a trail across my suddenly dry lips.

"Wife," he drawls, closing the distance between us. Reaching out, he grabs a lock of my hair, twirling it around his finger. "You are *my* wife." It's not a question but a fact. The pure, undiluted, possession in his voice causes a shiver to wrack through my body.

Swallowing, I nod. "And you are my husband."

Satisfaction leaks into his eyes, a smirk curving his sinful lips. "I am. And now, I am going to do some very *husbandly* things to you." He pauses, his grin growing when he adds. "And some not so *husbandly* things. I'm going to use your body until you don't even know your own name. I'm going to take us both to new heights, ones we may never recover from. I'm going to fuck you until you can't take anymore, but I won't stop, not until I've had my fill. I'm going to pump your cunt so full of me, I will be leaking from your mouth." Gently, and so at odds with the animalistic way he is speaking, he pushes me onto the bed.

I gasp. My heart beating in my throat, my ears. A throb starts between my legs, my pussy clenching around nothing. Despite the slight fear licking up my spine, I want Nico. All of him. All the darkness and all the light he tries so carefully to hide. But I see it. It was in the way he surprised me by bringing Patty here to witness our wedding. The way he couldn't stop kissing and touching me.

Dropping to his knees, his eyes meet mine. He pushes the fabric of my dress up my body, the lace and satin material scratching up my already over-stimulated body. I squirm, the need to have him inside me so strong, it's palpable. I want him, now. Want to feel as he stretches me wide open. Want that stroke of pain before it turns into pleasure.

"Nico," I moan, when he runs his fingers up the crease of my thigh.

"You're so fucking soaked, *wife*. Your panties are sticking to *my cunt*." As if he can't help himself, he swipes his tongue up my lace covered sex. My hips lift, pleasure flooding me and pure carnal need taking over. Nico grips my thighs, pinning me to the bed and holding me in place. "Stay still, *Tesoro*. I want to enjoy every second of this moment. Possess every inch of you as I fuck you as my wife for the first time." His hands wrap around the band of my panties and before I can blink, he rips them from my body.

"I wanted to keep those," I protest, glaring down at him.

"I will buy you some more," he says dismissively, his eyes lasered in on my bare pussy. Licking his lips, he thumbs my folds apart, fully exposing me to him.

I squirm, suddenly feeling shy. I am laying here, on display and wide open for him while he is still fully dressed. "Nico. I–"

He cuts me off. "You will not hide from me, *wife*." The possession in that one word makes me shiver. "I want to see you. All of you. Look at this little pussy, that takes me so well. This cunt that is about to be filled with me. Maybe my seed will take root tonight, hmm. Maybe nine months from now we will have a sibling for Romeo." His gaze sparks, making me stiffen. Guilt hits me when I remember the secret that I am keeping from him. The birth control that Allegra sourced for me. I know it's not one hundred percent effective and there is still a chance he could get me pregnant, considering he refuses to wear condoms, but at least I am protected more than I was a couple weeks ago. His eyes narrow in suspicion as he scrutinizes my reaction, but I keep my face blank.

As if satisfied with whatever it is he is looking for, he smirks. "Now, I am going to fuck you in your pretty dress and then I'm going to fuck you out of it. I will not stop until we are both nearly dead from the pleasure, so I hope you're ready, baby. By the time I am done, I will be imprinted in every part of your body for the rest of your life."

He pushes off the bed, his gaze locked on mine as he removes his shoes, dress shirt, pants, boxer briefs and socks. His lips curve into a sensual smirk. He is so hot it should be illegal. Climbing back on the bed, he crawls up my body, settling between my legs. His hand comes up, wrapping around my throat. He squeezes gently, reminding me who is in charge here.

"You're so fucking sexy, *Tesoro*," he murmurs, his tongue darting out and licking across the seam of mine.

Knowing what he wants, I open up, giving him access. He wastes no time, his tongue slipping inside, tangling with mine. With one hand still wrapped around my throat, his free hand travels down the fabric of my dress, to the apex of my thighs. I shiver when he runs a finger from my clit down to my slit. He circles my hole teasingly for a couple of seconds, then pushes inside. My back arches. I moan. Moisture seeps from me, I'm so wet I should be embarrassed, but at this point I am past caring. Nico has seen every part of my body in all ways possible. He took my virginity and has fucked me in ways I never even imagined possible since.

Pumping into me with slow strokes, I moan as pleasure builds only to whine in protest when he pulls out. He chuckles. "I know what you need baby and that's my cock. You will only come on my dick tonight." He grunts, positioning himself between my spread thighs. Gripping his cock, he presses the thick head at my entrance. I suck in a breath, knowing what comes next. With one fast movement, his hips snap forward, and he thrusts inside me.

"Ah," I cry out at the intrusion.

"Shh," he presses his lips to mine in a gentle kiss. "You can take me, *Tesoro*. Every single inch. I was made for you, just like you were made for me." He groans, his hips meeting mine when he bottoms out inside me. Stilling, he allows me a moment to adjust to his size. I am grateful. I don't think I will ever get used to his monster cock, no matter how many times he takes me. Sighing, I let my muscles relax and open my legs a little more to accommodate him. It only takes a moment for the pain to subside, and pleasure to take over. My eyes roll shut as I lose myself to the feeling, but I should have known Nico wouldn't like me closing myself off to him.

"Eyes on me, *wife*. I want you to watch as I take what's mine," he growls.

My eyes snap open, landing on Nico. The look in his blue orbs has my chest warming. Though he has never said it, the look on his face says it all and, in this moment, I know my earlier suspicions were correct. He does love me. Lifting my arms, I wrap them around his neck, pulling him closer. The satisfaction flickering in his gaze tells me he likes the move.

"Make love to me," I whisper timidly.

He smirks, pressing a kiss to my lips. "Oh, baby. You know I don't do making love. But for you? I might just make an exception." As soon as the words leave his lips, he slams into me in one brutal thrust.

"Nico," I cry out, his name a prayer on my lips. I don't know whether I'm praying for mercy or for more of his ruthlessness. Clawing at his back, I hold on for dear life as he fucks me like his life depends on it. "This isn't making love," I choke out. I may be naïve when it comes to sex, but I know the difference between making love and fucking and this is definitely the latter.

His lips brush mine. I feel rather than see the smile on his face. "I know. First, I'm going to fuck you how I like, and then I will make sweet, gentle, love to you just how you like," he growls, his voice thick with desire. Pushing up onto his hands, he never misses a beat as he glances down at me. "You look so good impaled on my cock, *Tesoro*. Look how good you take me." His praise shoots straight to my sex. Even more wetness seeps from me, coating his cock with my juices. The satisfaction in his eyes tells me that he feels it. "You're soaking my cock baby. Just how I like it." The groan that rumbles in his chest has my stomach tightening. Nico smirks, the hand around my throat constricting. "That's it, *Tesoro,* come on my dick. Show me what only I can do to you."

His words are my undoing, pushing me over the edge. My orgasm takes hold, coming on demand just like he asked.

"Nico," I cry out, my body tensing, spasming with the force of my climax.

His mouth slams to mine in a bruising kiss. I slump back into the mattress, a contented moan on my lips. He swallows every sound that leaves my mouth, taking them as if they are his own. In a way they are. Nico does own me. Every inch of me. Heart, body and soul.

As if to prove my thoughts, he plunges into me, and with one last thrust, he stills, growling into my mouth as his cock swells and pulses his release. Warmth coats my insides, filling me up just like he promised.

"Fuck," the one word is a rough whisper, but he doesn't stop his ministrations. He moves in short, shallow thrusts and there is no doubt in my mind that he is making sure every piece of his essence stays inside me. Pushing up, he stares down at me. I hold back a gasp at the vulnerable look in his eyes. I have never seen Nico this way so openly before. I want to commit it memory, but I don't get the chance. He blinks it away as if it never existed and replacing it with his look of indifference. "Jesus Christ. I can't get enough of you."

Pushing aside my disappointment, I smile, reaching up and wrapping my arms around his neck. "I feel the same." Pausing, I look away as I say the next words. "I love you."

Gripping my chin, he brings my gaze back to him. A big smile curves his lips. He presses a kiss to my forehead. "I know you do," he states.

Careful not to slip out of me, he rolls to the side, taking me with him and tucking me into his side. Though I burrow into him, I can't help but feel a little disappointed that he didn't say the words back. I know he feels it too. I see it in the way he looks at me, feel it in his every touch. Sighing, I snuggle into the safety of his chest.

The words didn't come today, but I know they will. I just need to be patient.

Chapter 36

Nico

"I wish you didn't have to leave," my wife chokes out, hugging Patty harder. My jaw clenches but I force myself to stay put and not rip her away from the woman. It's irrational, sure, but I hate anyone touching my wife but me.

It's been two days since the wedding, and it's time for her to head back to Charleston. I am happy she is leaving, if only for the fact that I will finally have Ocean to myself. I have done my good deed for the decade, shown grace by inviting Patty and now it's time to send her packing.

"I will visit again soon my dear," Patty replies soothingly, her way of trying to pacify my wife. Patty's gaze shoots to me, before dropping to where I rock my son in my arms. "Nothing will keep me away from you or my boy." Her narrowed eyes snap back to me, a challenge in them that I refuse to acknowledge. She is trying to bait me and though it is taking everything in me not to respond, I know it's not worth my time. Arguing with this woman is beneath me. A smirk curves my lips. I could always kill her, and make it look like an accident, then I wouldn't have to deal with her rude self.

Ocean pulls back, her big blue eyes shining with tears. She swallows. "I will call you every day. I promise."

Patty cups her cheeks, pressing a kiss to one then the other. "I will look forward to that." She turns, arms extended as she looks at Romeo expectantly. "Can I have a cuddle with my boy?" She blinks innocently, but I see the disdain clearly written all over her face. I nearly snort. This woman knows exactly what she is doing. Kudos to her for trying to go toe to toe with me. However, she will never win. She knows that as well as I do and if she doesn't quit her shit, she will see just who she is dealing with.

"Sure. I need to go and make sure Christopher is ready to take you to the airport." I say, stepping forward and handing over my son. There is a reason that I booked her a commercial flight for the journey home, and that's because my pilot, Hansen, will be taking me and Ocean into the city for a... honeymoon of sorts. It won't be our main one, but it's something. I plan on taking my wife to an exotic private island, with sandy beaches and surrounded by clear blue water, when things have calmed down. Somewhere I can have her all to myself and we can relax. Glancing at Ocean, she watches me with a soft, grateful look in her eyes. Unable to resist, I pull her into my arms, my mouth dropping to her ear as I growl. "As soon as she is gone, you are mine." She shivers, making me smirk. My wife can't get enough of my cock, and I am here for it.

Releasing her, I grab Patty's luggage, wheeling it toward the door and outside. Christopher stares down at his cellphone as he waits beside the SUV. "All ready?" I ask, making his head snap up to me.

Slipping his cell into his pants pocket, he nods. "Yes sir. I will take Ms. Patty to JFK and then meet you in the city."

"Go straight to the Marchetti building. You can pick us up

from there and take us to the club. I have some business to take care of at The Executive Club before I can relax with my wife."

"Of course," Christopher replies without hesitation.

Footsteps on the marble tiles have me glancing over my shoulder. My wife, son, and Patty head down the steps toward me. Oceans talks animatedly with Patty, as the latter carries Romeo in her arms. Taking my son from Patty, I watch Ocean say her final goodbyes to the woman who became an important, integral part of her life. A woman that showed her kindness and love. A woman that gave her a home. All those things should ease my hostility toward Patty but for some reason… they don't.

"I better go," Patty sighs, pulling out of the tight grip my wife has on her.

Ocean smiles sadly. "Go. Call me so I know you got home safe."

"I will." Patty agrees, before turning her attention to Romeo. She cups his face, pressing a kiss to his cheek. "You look after my family." Her gaze bores into mine threateningly. I almost laugh. Almost.

"Always," I drawl, though I owe her nothing.

She nods, looking back to Ocean. "This isn't goodbye, but a see you later. I love you both. And I'm so proud of you." She chokes on her words, her eyes turning watery. As if she doesn't want Ocean to witness her emotion, she turns, rushing toward the SUV and where Christopher holds the back door open.

A sob from my right, has me looking at my wife. She looks so sad, I wrap an arm around her, pulling her into my body and dropping a kiss to her head. It's on the tip of my tongue to tell her that I love her, but I don't want those three little words to be overshadowed by her sadness of Patty leaving. So instead, I hold her close, whispering words of comfort in her ear as we watch the car disappear down the long drive.

***

"I'm excited to spend a couple days in the city." Ocean chirps, her sadness over Patty leaving now replaced by the excitement of leaving The Hamptons. "Maybe I could catch up with Serena while we are here?" Her big blue eyes are wide as she looks at me, almost begging me to say yes.

I pin her with a look. "Don't beg, *wife*. You're a queen. Act like it."

She blinks several times as if she didn't expect my response, then chews that full bottom lip of hers. A sly smirk curves her lips as she straightens her shoulders, looking like she is ready to take on the world. "I want to catch up with Serena while we are in the city. Is she still working at the club?"

I shake my head. Usually, I wouldn't know this information but, since I knew she was one of Ocean's only friends, I kept a close eye on the dancer. There was a time or two that I interrogated Serena to see if she knew anything about Ocean's whereabouts, but she was just as unaware as me. Her reaction alone told me all I needed to know. She was shocked at her friend's disappearance and didn't know shit. "Do you think Leo will know how to get ahold of her? I lost her number…" she swallows, then adds. "When I left."

Watching her, I run a palm across my mouth. Hmm. The tightness in my chest that I usually get at the memory of when she disappeared isn't there today. Maybe I have finally moved past it. "Leo should have her contact number on file from when she worked at the club," I confirm.

She smiles before it drops to a frown. "I feel so bad. I just left and only now have I asked about her. She was my only friend in New York. She should have been at the wedding," she finishes on a whisper.

Reaching over, I take her hand. "I am sure she will understand, *Tesoro*. And if she doesn't? Well, she wasn't a friend in the first place."

Ocean sighs, a smile pulling at her lips. "Always so direct."

I smirk, just as we pull up outside The Executive Club. "Always. Now come on. Let me take care of business and then I can take care of you when we get back to our penthouse."

Chapter 37

Ocean

Curled up on the couch in Nico's office, my body warms as memories of all of our moments together in here hit me. Looking back, I was naïve in thinking that he had no interest in me. It's clear to me now that everything he did, the possession, his asshole behavior, was his way of showing me that he wanted me.

A sigh of contentment leaves me, and I can't remember the last time I felt this way. My gaze flickers to my husband and I grin when I find that he is already watching me. His stare is intense, a living entity consuming my whole being as he talks to someone on his phone. I smile wider, my eyes bouncing from Nico to Dante who sits across from him. I watch as his fingers glide across his cellphone, a small grin tugging at his lips. I briefly wonder if he is messaging Allegra and when his smile widens, I know without a doubt that he is. Warmth trickles through me at the possibility that they can be together. From the small things that Allegra has said, it all comes down to Nico getting her out of the contract that their father entered her into. I glance back to my husband. With one look at him, there is no doubt in my mind that he will do everything in his power to help his sister out of the mess their father created.

"If the product is good, Carlos, then we will have a deal. I will talk to you when the shipment arrives to let you know my thoughts." Nico's deep voice slips into my thoughts bringing me to the now. Scrubbing a palm over his face, he drops his phone down on the desk. He opens his mouth, no doubt to say something, when a knock sounds at the door. Irritation flashes in his eyes at being interrupted, but he calls out. "Come in."

The door opens almost instantly, Leo stepping inside in the next second. His eyes come to mine briefly before snapping to Nico. I haven't spoken to him much since I've been back and not because I don't want to. I know he feels guilty for his involvement in what happened in Charleston, for the way things were handled, but he doesn't need to. What's done is done and though at the time I was angry, Nico finding me brought me to exactly where I am meant to be. I forgive my husband, Dante, Leo and anyone else that was involved in that night. Sometimes you have to let things go, to be able to move on from your past, and that's exactly what I am doing so that I can embrace my future.

"Giuseppe is here to see you."

My husband nods. "Send him in."

I was introduced to Giuseppe at my wedding. From what Nico told me, he is what you call a *consigliere*. First, he was an advisor to Lorenzo, Nico's father, and when he died, Nico decided to keep him on as his. I don't know what being a *consigliere* involves, and to be honest, I never bothered to ask, but I do know it is a high-ranking position. Though I should probably take more interest in my husband's business, I can't bring myself to get involved more than I already am. I decided that the less I know, the better, and that is how it will stay.

Leo leaves and a couple minutes later, the old man with greying hair and a rounded belly steps into the office. "Nico, my boy," he greets, closing the distance between them and taking his hand.

"Giuseppe." My husband replies with a slight frown, standing from his chair and shaking his hand. "I wasn't expecting you today."

The middle-aged man takes a seat, his eyes coming to me for a moment before shifting to Dante - who he says a quick hello to - then back to Nico. "I was in the city and just wanted to check in. I haven't had time to speak or catch up with you, since your wedding."

Nico searches his face and, if I didn't know any better, I would say there is a hint of suspicion flashing in his blue eyes. The same suspicion that I have seen directed at me, many times. "I've been..." he pauses, "A little busy. And anyway, nothing has changed since we last spoke. The Romanos are still pushing to go ahead with the wedding." I don't miss the way Dante tenses at that information. "And we are awaiting a shipment from Carlos Quintero."

"And the Russians?" Giuseppe asks, with accusation in his tone. I stiffen when he glances at me.

"Are not your problem, Giuseppe," my husband waves him off.

"I am the *consigliere,* Nico. Let me help," he snaps.

Nico's eyes narrow, but before he can speak, loud banging sounds. *Bang. Bang. Bang.* My heart lurches in my chest, eyes shooting to Nico. My husband darts out of his seat as do Dante and Giuseppe. My stomach drops, fear snaking through every inch of my body as the noise gets louder, more intense, more...Is that gunfire?

I fly off the couch toward Nico, who within two long strides is in front of me, with a gun in his hand. He cups my cheeks, pressing a kiss to my forehead. "Stay here, *Tesoro*. Giuseppe will keep you safe."

I shake my head, crying out. "No. Please don't leave me."

"Baby, listen to me. I will be back. Everything will be okay. Just stay here. It's a safe room, don't leave until I come back, you hear me?"

I glance up to find Dante, standing by the door, also holding a gun. My heart pounds in my chest erratically when I think about them both going out there, into the line of fire. I want to demand Nico stay with me, but I know there is no point. All it will do is waste time.

"Okay," I croak out with a small nod of my head.

He smiles, pressing a kiss to my lips and looking as relaxed as I have ever seen him. I swallow at the thought that he is used to stuff like this happening. "Stay here," he repeats before straightening. He turns his attention on Giuseppe. "Keep her safe."

"Of course, Nico. Go," the old man nods solemnly.

Without another word, my husband disappears through the door before it closes with a click of finality. I want to cry. I want to be back in the Hamptons, in my gilded cage, with my son, where we are safe. Anything but this nightmare.

On shaky legs, I move to the window that overlooks the club. I don't know if I will see anything, but it's worth a try. Palm on the glass, my breaths come out thick and fast as I watch for any sign of my husband. I don't see anything. Nothing. No one. Just darkness.

Tears prick my eyes and I'm aware of the presence at my back, but I take no notice of it. That is until a chemical smelling cloth covers my mouth. I claw at the arm, the hand. Kick back with all my strength but it's no use. The grip on me is too strong and the smell I inhale makes me drowsy. But I don't give up. I fight with everything in me. Fight for my husband. For our son.

My vision dots, turning blurry. My body turns weak with my fight, and I know I am losing strength. My muscles weaken, lungs burn. And then I hear it. Eleven sinister words before I black out.

"That's it, girl. Let's get you back to where you belong."

***

The sound of hushed voices and water dripping rouses me from my sleep. My throat feels dry, sore, eyes feel heavy. With all the energy I can muster, I crack my eyes open, blinking away the heaviness. Everything is blurred, unfocused. Ugh, why do I feel like this.

Reaching up, I still when I can't move my arms. My heart rate kicks up in my chest, fear taking ahold of me. Something's not right. And that's only confirmed further when I glance down, to find my arms and legs strapped to the chair with rope. I blink, searching the deepest parts of my mind for how I got here. And then it comes back to me. The club. Nico. The hand on my mouth. The...

"Ahh, the princess is awake." I freeze at the voice. It's familiar but at the same time, it's been so long since I've heard it, it sounds different. I swallow, lifting my head when I hear footsteps move closer. My heart beats so fast, I'm surprised when it doesn't fall out of my chest.

And it's all because I know what I'm going to find – or who in this case.

My gaze lifts, pulse turning to an unnatural speed. My whole world crumbles when it locks on the smug face in front of me. A face, I thought I would never see again. A face, I *hoped* I would never see again.

But who was I kidding. I knew he wouldn't stop or give up. Was stupid to think otherwise.

Because he found me.

My father, the monster in my nightmares and my reality, found me.

"Hello, *Emilee*."

Chapter 38

Nico

"**N**ico," Dante's voice sounds distant though he is right next to me. His arms lock around me as he drags me to my office, to safety. He knows what I want, *what I need,* and that is to get to my wife. Before Dante gets me through the door, I glance around at my club floor, transfixed as I watch the scene playing out in front of me. Some of my men fight back while others lay dead on the floor. I have no clue where Leo is, but I hope he makes it out of this alive. No matter what has happened between us regarding Ocean, he is still my friend, despite being a fucking asshole lately.

Gunfire bounces around the space, loud and determined and I know it's only a matter of time before the Feds show up. From their accents, I know it's the Russians ambushing us. Though I'm not even a little surprised he broke our truce, it somewhat confuses me. The last time I spoke with Vadim, I knew the asshole couldn't be trusted, but I didn't think he would retaliate so soon.

"Fuck," I growl as we enter my private elevator. I punch the button for the top floor, waiting with anticipation and a hint of anxiety for the cart to rise.

"What the fuck is happening?" Dante barks, punching the metal.

"I don't know. But there is no coming back from this attack. The Russians will die for this," I grind out.

"Agreed." My best friend responds as the elevator comes to a stop and the doors slide open.

We step outside and I frown when I see Leo rushing toward us. That answers the question of whether he is okay or not. His hands thread through his hair, and he tugs as if he is trying to ground himself. I don't like the look on his face, and I positively *loathe* the words that come out of his mouth. "Nico, it's Ocean. She isn't in your office."

My blood runs cold, heart stuttering in my chest as everything turns to white noise. I don't see or hear anything, just the rush of absolute anger coursing in my body. Pushing past him, I stride down the hall, knowing in my heart that what he is saying is true. Shoving my door open, a feeling I can't explain hits me right in the chest when I find no sign of my wife or *Consigliere*. I grit my teeth, adrenaline, and rage spiking in me further.

"Find my fucking wife." I scream and like a child that has lost his favorite toy, I swipe everything from my desk in one quick fury-filled move.

Fuck the club. I can rebuild.

Fuck the Russians. I will kill them all.

But Ocean? She is irreplaceable.

I cannot lose my wife. Not for a second time. And if the Russians have her like I suspect... I shake my head. Well, I don't even want to think about what they are doing to her. I need to stay calm and if I think about that, I am going to completely lose my shit.

Locking all my muscles in place, I take a deep breath trying to calm myself. My chest heaves, pulse spiking to an erratic rhythm that for the first time in my life I cannot control. Jesus, fuck. Everything turns black, my vision turning hazy. The need for revenge thrums in my veins but the need to find my wife is the only thing I can think about right now. She could be anywhere. She could already be... I shake my head, not allowing the thought to take root.

Then it hits me. I pause. The tracker. The god damn tracker I injected into her while she was sleeping. Isn't this the exact reason why I did it? Yes, it wasn't the main reason, because at the time I was blinded with the fear that she would try to run from me again. Joke's on me really, because right now, I would rather her be running from me than be in the hands of my enemies. Grabbing my cell from my pants pocket, I bring up the tracker app, ignoring the war that is going on around me.

"Nico?" Dante questions, his concerned voice filtering into my thoughts.

"The tracker. I inserted one when I brought her back," I mumble more to myself. I haven't told anyone this information. Not even Dante. I am not embarrassed by what I did, it's not an emotion I feel. I just never felt the need to tell anyone my business, because no one needs to know what I do when it comes to what belongs to me.

The gunfire comes to a stop, but I don't take any notice of what could be happening downstairs or whether the Russians have killed my men and are now on their way to do the same to me. All I care about is locating my wife. My body tightens and I wait with bated breath for the app to load. It takes mere seconds and I release a breath when the red dot settles in place. My head snaps up to Dante.

"She is in a warehouse down at Port Authority." My voice is frantic but I'm past caring that I am showing any emotion.

"Go. I will take care of this." His words leave no room for argument.

I pause. "You sure?"

"Yes. But Nico, take as many of our men as you can. You don't know what you're heading into."

I nod. "Take care of this shit and call me when you are done."

"Just go, Nico. Find your wife and bring her home." I hear the emotion in his tone. I briefly wonder if he is thinking about my sister right now and how he would feel if she was the one taken by Vadim.

Shaking my head, I focus on what I need to do. My gaze goes to Leo, gun in hand as he stands guard by the door. "Do whatever Dante needs you to." I issue the order and expect him to follow them.

He nods his head, bouncing on his feet with a feral look in his eyes. People think that Leo is the innocent one out of the three of us, because of his blonde hair and all-American good looks, but he is just as bad as me and Dante. Bloodthirsty and ready to go at any moment to drop bodies if I should ask him to. "We've got this, Nico."

With one last look at them both, I exit through the secret door, calling Christopher -who went to my penthouse to drop off our luggage - on my way to make sure he is waiting for me somewhere out of view from the Russians.

***

Within an hour, I have over a hundred of my men ready to storm the warehouse my wife is still being held in. No one was more surprised than me that they have kept her at the same location, but checking the tracker every couple of minutes, confirms it. I don't know whether it's a good or bad thing, but I'm trying to be positive. If I think about any bad that could be happening, I am going to lose my shit and burn down the whole fucking city with everyone in it. And that's simply not conducive to my plans.

I haven't heard from Dante, and I can only assume he is still dealing with whatever is going on at my club. Though I have checked in with my mamma, to make sure everything is okay at home, I haven't told her what is going down in the city. It will only panic both her and my sister and right now, I have enough shit to deal with.

Christopher speeds toward Port Authority. We have a convoy of SUVs behind and in front of us, all ready for what comes next. All ready for a war that we have no choice but to win. I don't know what I am going into, or what I am leading my men into, but they will follow my orders and do what they are trained to do. Lives will most likely be lost today, regardless of how prepared we are. It doesn't matter how many men or how much gun power we have, the Russians have clearly been planning this and right now they have the advantage because they hold one of the most precious things in my life in their hands.

Ocean.

Nonetheless, I will get my wife back.

And the people who dared take her from me will die today. I will make sure it is slow, and that they feel the soul crushing pain that I am feeling right now with the absence of my heart.

They may think they have won.

But this is only the beginning.

Vadim is as good as dead.

That's a promise.

Chapter 39

Ocean

Blood drips from the corner of my mouth where my father hit me. I would like to say I'm shocked by the easy way he attacked me, but then I would be a liar. Abuse comes second nature to him, is part of his identity. And he will never change. Once a monster, always a monster.

I don't want to show weakness in front of him, but I can't deny that I am terrified. I fear what he may do to me and how far he will go to punish me for running away. For ruining his plans for me. I would like to think he has limits, but at this point I don't think he has any. I can only be thankful that my son is far away from whatever is about to happen. There is no doubt in my mind that he would harm Romeo, just to punish me. The man is a monster in every way, one that won't stop until he gets what he feels he is owed.

Pure dread slithers through my veins, a shudder wracking my body just thinking about it. I glance around at my surroundings, at the room I'm being held in, and it only heightens my panic. I have no clue as to where I am, but the large space is empty apart from a small table in the corner. From looking at the interior of the building, it looks like I am in a commercial building of some sort. Maybe a warehouse? Where it is or how much time has passed since I was taken, I don't know. I just pray with everything in me that Nico got away from the club safely and is doing everything in his power to find me.

"Tsk, tsk, dear daughter. I hear that you have not only gone and fucked away your virginity - something that belonged to another man - but you also stupidly went and got yourself knocked up and *married*. Fucking married. You were supposed to be Xavier's wife by now. You ruined all my plans," he seethes, slapping me across the face. My head jerks to the side, pain exploding through my face, but I don't let him see it. Glancing up at him, I shrink into myself at the look of pure disdain and evil in his eyes.

It's funny, though really not humorous at all given my current predicament, but the fact I can go toe to toe with someone like Nico – the head of the damn Mafia - but wither in my own father's presence tells you exactly the kind of man he is.

"Fuck you," I spit, mustering every bit of strength I have into those two words. My insolence does as I thought it would and I am rewarded with another punch to the face. It's harder this time, a clear sign that he is going to lose his shit completely. My head snaps back, excruciating pain shooting through my whole head. Fuck, that hurt.

His chilling, wicked laugh seeps into my bones, turning my blood cold. "You won't be fucking *me*, dear daughter, but you will be fucking your new husband. Despite your insubordination and errant ways, the Andersons have agreed to still take you on. Though I can't promise Xavier will treat you well once he knows the extent of your betrayals, I have assured him that I will train you how I see fit. And that is with Mr. Mikhailov. He is going to mold you into the perfect trophy wife for Xavier. He will break you in every way possible, until you are a shell of yourself and the only word that you know and will come out of your dirty mouth is yes. He will teach you how to spread your legs for Xavier, how to fuck him like the good little whore you are and thank him for it. You will learn to smile when you are on his arm like the flawless *wallpaper* wife you were supposed to be. And you will not disappoint me this time, Emilee, or so help me God," he finishes.

"My *husband* will kill you," I mutter weakly, knowing full well that I am grasping at straws. At this point I don't know if Nico is even alive. My chest constricts, bile climbing in my throat and tears pricking my eyes at the thought. I refuse to live in a world where Nico doesn't exist.

My father cackles like a bad movie villain. "Oh, Emilee. Your husband, or should I say, ex-husband, is most likely dead. He cannot save you."

My fists ball, but before I can respond, the door is shoved open. My head snaps up, eyes locking on the three men that enter the room. The man that is two steps in front of the others is clearly the boss, though I have no idea who any of them are. My heart rate picks up when his intimidating gaze flicks to me. His lips curve into a smirk, eyes raking up and down my body in a way that makes me feel sick.

"I see you have had a little fun, Samuel." The statement is spoken in a thick accent; one I don't recognize but sounds Eastern European maybe.

My gaze shifts to my father who grins devilishly. "I did Vadim. Thank you for bringing my daughter back to me." Vadim? Who the hell is Vadim? Is this the Mr. Mikhailov he has assigned to break me? Fear like I have never felt ignites inside me. Please no.

"It was my pleasure." His eyes spark with something I can't decipher. I swallow, wondering what this man's intentions are. He focuses his attention back on my dad. "We need to move. The club is gone, but I do not know if Mr. Marchetti made it out or not. We can't risk him finding us if he is alive." A sob bursts from my throat at the mention of my husband. I pull at the rope, knowing it won't achieve anything but willing to try all the same. I freeze when the man I now know is called Vadim chuckles darkly. "Sweetheart, your effort to escape is impressive but there is no point. You will not get out of here." Humor laces his accented voice.

"Please. You don't know what you're doing. Whatever my father is paying you, my husband will pay more." I plead with him, hoping and praying with everything in me I can get through to this man.

"I am sure he would." The smile that twitches at his lips has me shrinking into myself. It is downright scary. "But there is no point in you begging. The deal is done. I am going to have fun with you, little girl," he says cryptically, but I know what he means. My heart stalls. Without saying it, he has confirmed he is Mr. Mikhailov.

"Please." I cry, past caring that I'm showing weakness.

Vadim merely flicks me a glance then looks back to my father. "We leave within the hour."

"Good. The sooner we get back to Seattle the better," he drawls, nonchalantly.

I pause at the mention of my home city. My heart pounds in my chest, pure panic taking over. Blood pumps in my ears, drowning out any more of their conversation and my pulse is so erratic, I turn lightheaded. I can't go back to Seattle. If I do, my life is as good as over. I would rather die than go anywhere with my father. I need to somehow get away. Get out of these restraints and run. How I am going to achieve that, I'm not sure, but I need to at least try. If not for me, for my son. For my husband. For my new family. Screaming, I pull at the restraints, my body jerking from side to side. I watch in horror as Vadim jerks his head at the other two men that entered the room and says in a cold, detached, tone. "Sedate her, then transfer her to my SUV. Mr. Caldwell's private jet is waiting at Teterboro for our arrival." He turns to my dad. "Correct?"

My father nods. "Yes. I will message my men to make sure everything is set." He pulls his cellphone out of his dress pants pocket and gets to work. I almost snort. Even when kidnapping me, he is impeccably dressed.

My gaze shifts to the other men to find they are all dressed in black pants and dress shirts, similar to my father and my... husband. Frowning, everything starts to click into place, like a puzzle and realization hits me. I gasp, my eyes snapping to Vadim. He is the Russian mafia. The Bratva as Nico called them, and my husband's enemy. I swallow.

I didn't think things could get any worse and yet, somehow, they have.

My heart pounds in my chest, breaths coming in thick and fast. No matter how much I want to fight, I know it's pointless, just like Vadim said. There is no getting out of this. Tears pool in eyes, only to fall over the rims of my lower lids and stream down my face when my family flash through my mind.

Romeo. My beautiful boy who I have not had nearly enough time with. His perfect face flickers in my head, so clear as if I am watching a movie reel, and I wonder if I will ever see him again. See the boy he grows into and the man he becomes.

Nico. My dark, handsome devil. The man I never wanted to get involved with but had no choice but to love. He steamrolled into my life, never giving me a chance to second guess anything. We were a given. And despite who he is and what I know he is capable of, I love him. Every flawed, imperfect inch of him. I love him so damn much, it's a living, breathing thing inside of me and I wouldn't change any part of him.

I let my mind drift to my boys, my happy place. I am past caring about the assholes in the room and the fact that they are currently witnessing my meltdown. But I let all my emotions out. I let the sobs stuck in my throat break free, piercing the silence in the space. I cry and I cry, for all that I have had, all that I may have lost and all that I am about to lose. I can feel their eyes on me, but I don't look at them.

Lifting my face, I stare at the ceiling and pray. I pray to a God, to everything holy, that this is all a nightmare, and I will see my boys again.

Because I would rather be dead than live in a world where they don't exist.

Chapter 40

Nico

"Surveillance is set up around the buildings and we have men in place. They are ready to take out anyone that is a threat. We are good to go." Gregorio, a hacker of mine, announces, looking up from his laptop.

I nod, adrenaline pumping through my veins as I prepare to walk my men into a potential war zone and retrieve my wife. I'm not a good man, I am very aware of this, but right now, I am the worst of the worst. Because I would walk them through hell and let every single one of them be killed if it means getting Ocean back safely.

My jaw clenches, raw anger pulsing in every inch of my body that we are even in this situation. Vadim took my wife, and not only had the audacity to take Ocean, but also my consigliere. Giuseppe, a man I have known since birth. My papà's right hand man and now the man that stands beside me, has been taken by the Russians and at this point I don't know whether he is dead or alive. I am not a particularly religious man, but I hope he is, if only to protect my wife.

I am aware how things work in our world, and Giuseppe

staying alive will come down to how much use he is to the Bratva. If Vadim thinks he can use Giuseppe against me, then he will keep him alive. If not, they will kill him. Despite my rage and thinking the worst when I first realized Ocean was gone, I know my wife is still alive. Once I put myself in Vadim's shoes, and thought over everything, I recognized that, if it was me that had taken his wife, then I would use her as insurance against him, therefore I would keep her alive. Ocean is Vadim's insurance. A way to bend me to his will and make me do whatever the hell he wants. He knows she is my weakness and will use her however he deems necessary. I will kill him before he can do that, but I know logically these are all reasons that make her his best advantage right now.

My gaze shifts around the warehouse we currently occupy. It's a couple blocks from where my wife is being held and a temporary holding area slash makeshift headquarters of sorts, while my men wait for further instruction. My heart pounds in my chest and I can almost taste the blood that will be spilt today.

"Surround the building and be prepared for retaliation. Anyone that gets in your way, shoot to kill, but be mindful that my wife and Giuseppe are somewhere in that building. If Ocean is harmed in any way, even if it is a hair on her head that is pushed out of place, I will kill you. Understand?" My words are cold, deadly, and leave no room for argument. If any one of my soldiers has a problem with my instructions, they can leave now. Their murmured agreement echoes through the building, confirming they are in, no matter what happens. I smirk. Time to get my wife back.

"There is movement on the tracker, Nico. I have a drone circling the warehouse and a convoy of vehicles are entering the compound. My guess is they are getting ready to move her,"

Gregorio informs me, his gaze fixed firmly on the laptop in front of him.

My body stiffens, everything inside me demanding that I fuck the risks and go to her now. But that would be a suicide mission and I would like us both to get out of this alive.

"Let's move out. My wife does not leave that warehouse." It's a warning, and they know their lives will be as good as over if she sets foot outside.

Moving to the exit, I make my way out onto the street, my men following behind me. Pausing, I inhale the salty sea air that comes with being so close to the docks, letting it wash away every thought in my brain but one. In this moment, I become who I was made to be. Who I need to be. The devil Ocean always thought me to be. The Don who will stop at nothing until vengeance is served. The husband that will kill anyone who stands in the way of him and his wife. Channeling all these thoughts, I let them consume my body until there is only one thing left. Ocean. I have always tried to keep the darkest part of me hidden from my *Tesoro,* and though she has seen a little of how twisted I can be, she definitely hasn't seen me at my worst. Today, she will see exactly who I am. See the lengths I will go to ensure she remains mine.

"Spread out. I want every potential exit covered." I instruct as we move toward the warehouse. Some of my men heed my command, only leaving around two dozen of my soldiers surrounding me in a protective stance. Not that I need protecting; but it's expected of them. It is programmed into them during their training and initiation when they become part of our organization. Protect your Don with your life. At all costs.

Moving as a team, we make our way to the side of the building. Glancing down at my cellphone, I make sure that my wife is still in the same spot as she was when I checked five minutes ago. She is. Something inside me settles and I wait for Gregorio to notify me that the cameras have been deactivated.

"Cameras are down. You are good to go." Gregorio drawls through the earpiece, me and several other of my men are wearing. I told them it's because I want to be able to keep in touch with everyone, and know what is happening, but really, I wanted to cover all bases and if any of my soldiers get to Ocean before me, I want to be informed immediately.

"You heard the man. Let's go." I instruct, more than ready to get my wife back.

One of my men steps up to the wire fence, metal cutters in hand. I watch as he cuts through the wire in what feels like minutes but is in fact mere seconds. Impatience runs through me and it's only when he steps back, after having made a big enough space for us to climb through, that I release a breath. It's go time.

Stepping through, I duck when the sound of gunfire hits my ears. I don't know whether it's the enemy firing shots or my men taking them out, but I hope it's the latter. Don't need my men dying this early into the mission.

Glancing around at my soldiers, I glare. "Keep alert and be prepared for anything."

Their grunts of agreement are the only response I need, and we move toward the warehouse in sync. As if I've had a shot of epinephrine, every nerve ending in my body sparks to life, blood pumping through my veins and pounding in my ears. It's from that reaction alone that I know I'm close to Ocean. I can almost taste her. Smell her.

Pushing those thoughts aside, I focus on the task at hand. Trudging forward, shouting, gunfire and an explosion is our soundtrack as we move toward the building. Ignoring all the chaos around me, I listen as Matteo, a capo of mine, barks into the earpiece.

"All the guards out front are dead and the vehicles are on fire. No one will be getting out of here unless it's on foot. That will literally be impossible, considering we have the area surrounded."

I smirk, then turn to my team. "Let's move inside."

With a nod, we all move as one to the door. Pulling it open, I aim my gun, ready to take out any potential threat but it's empty. I know one hundred percent that it's not by chance. Vadim and his men will be ready and waiting for us, somewhere inside this shithole place.

My soldiers step inside, armed and surrounding me. Stealthily we move down the dark, dank hallway. There are a couple doors on either side, but it's the one up ahead that calls to me. As if our souls are one, I know with everything in me that my wife is behind the dirty gray door at the end.

Quickening my strides, I shove off the hands that try to grab at me. I know they are only trying to protect me but fuck them. Ocean is behind that door.

Coming to a stop outside, I inhale, trying to steady my erratic pulse, but it's no use. The only time my heartbeat is ever steady is when my eyes are on Ocean.

Gun in the air, and without another thought, I lift my leg, kicking the door open. I didn't know what to expect when we came here, but whatever I imagined could not even begin to explain the gut-wrenching horror in front of me that turns my blood ice cold.

Because there sits my wife.

Guns pointed at her.

Clothes ripped.

Bloodied and bruised.

My pulse stutters, pure, raw rage heating my veins when my eyes flicker to the left of Ocean. To the man *I* trusted. The man my father trusted.

The man with a devilish smirk as he pulls a knife from his pants and holds it to the delicate skin of Ocean's throat.

Giuseppe.

In one second, everything clicks into place.

He is the fucking rat.

My jaw clenches as I stare him down, but he doesn't wither. My *consigliere* just watches me with a satisfied grin on his ugly face. I shift my gaze to a man I don't know, but one that I have seen in pictures.

Ocean's father.

Sick bastard will also die tonight.

My eyes slide to Vadim beside him, then to the twenty or so guards behind them, with their guns now trained on me.

"Nice of you to join us, Nico. Drop your weapon and tell your men to do the same. It would be an unfortunate turn of events if I had to kill your wife, but I will slice her throat without blinking, if you don't do as I say." Giuseppe's smug voice seeps into me, making my eye twitch. The rat bastard better make the most of today, because it will be his last one on this mortal coil.

"What the fuck are you doing, Giuseppe?" I grit out.

He tsks, his gaze shifting to the butcher knife in his hands. He runs a thumb down it, a faraway look in eyes. "You fucked up, son. I–"

"Don't call me that. I am not your fucking son," I hiss.

He chuckles, shaking his head. "Always so volatile. I told your papà countless times, to beat that attitude out of you, but he wouldn't listen." His eyes narrow. "He was too soft on you and look where it got him. Now drop your fucking weapons, otherwise I will slit her god damn throat." The bark in his voice tells me he isn't messing around.

My wife's soft whimper has my eyes dropping to hers. She looks so scared; it makes my chest crack. I've tried to avoid looking at her too much because I knew what I would see and all the emotions on her face would cause a tornado of fury inside me. If I want to get us out of here alive, I need to keep a level head. For both of our sakes.

Breaking eye contact, I turn to my men.

"Drop your weapons." I demand, ignoring the looks of concern on their faces. In doing this, we are at a disadvantage, and they know it. I know it. But I will not risk my wife's life. Facing Giuseppe, who was like a second father to me, I look for any sign of the man I have known my whole life but come up empty. All I see is a traitor. A fucking rat. "Why?" I force out, barely keeping a hold of myself.

Giuseppe shrugs. "Easy, really. Your papà told you about the future he envisioned for the *famiglia*. You refused it. When he died and you became Don, you took us is in a completely different direction. One that saw a loss in money for *me*. Vadim offered me..." he trails off as if searching for the right words. "A very lucrative deal. One I couldn't refuse. His visions for the future mirror mine. With you dead and me as Don, we can work alongside each other, making the *famiglia* and the Bratva the most powerful organizations in the world." He smiles sardonically. "Plus, he is paying me more money than I could ever spend in ten lifetimes, let alone this one. It's a win win." He pauses, pinning me with a glare. "I would have stood by your papà forever. But you? Your arrogance and morals. It will ruin the organization your grandfather and papà built. You're an embarrassment, Nico. Led by pussy. *Your* whore may as well have you on a leash. She leads you around by your cock, messing with your head. I see the way you look at her. How you are with her. She is the reason you have become soft, the reason you now have a *conscience*." He accuses with so much contempt in his tone, it would make most men wither. But not me. He doesn't know who he is fucking with.

Twisted In Obsession

Lead around by the cock, he said?
Soft, he said?
I will show the traitorous bastard just how *soft* I really am.

Chapter 41

Ocean

My heart races so fast in my chest, I feel like I'm going to pass out.

I stare at my husband, though he keeps his eyes trained on Giuseppe who is holding a knife to my throat.

Nico dropped his weapon.

Without hesitation, he put the gun on the floor and demanded his men do the same.

And now they are at risk.

Because of me.

I don't see how we are going to get out of this mess, and now I am the reason my son might lose both his parents.

I feel sick.

How did we even get here?

To this point.

It's surreal.

Like I am stuck in a never-ending nightmare, waiting to wake up.

This should not be my life... but it is. And though I am more scared than I have ever been before, I need to be strong. For my husband. For our son.

"Mr. Marchetti, I would say it's a pleasure, but I would be lying. I am Mr. Caldwell, and *Emilee* is my daughter. She was promised to another man, and I have every intention of delivering on that promise. Whatever claim you think you have on her, you don't. She will be Mrs. Anderson. And if I have to kill you to ensure that happens, then I will." My father's deep, vile, voice pierces the silence of the room, making the tension thicken. A hand wraps around my hair, pulling it with so much force my head snaps back. My eyes meet Samuel Caldwell's cold ones, and my skin crawls with disgust. "You have a duty, don't you dear daughter? One you ran away from." His finger caresses my cheek softly. It is so at odds with the threat of his tone, I want to be sick. I stare at him. Wondering how the hell I am related to this monster. I know he expects an answer, but I won't give him one. He can go fuck himself.

"Take your fucking hands off *my* wife." Nico's deathly low voice filters through the fog in my head, grounding me. Usually, the tone he is currently using would scare me, but right now it warms my insides and calms my erratic heartbeat. I draw strength from it. Hoping and praying with everything in me that we get out of this. That we get to see our son again. Get to be a real family.

Because I love my husband, and though I haven't said it, I love the life he has given me. It may not be everything I pictured for myself, but it's more. So much more and I refuse for our time to be cut short because of a man like my sperm donor.

"Nico," I whimper, only to be cut off when a palm is slapped over my mouth aggressively.

"Cleary you haven't educated her on how to behave. Taught her to speak only when she is told to. She is a disobedient little cunt, but I am sure Vadim and then her new husband will soon beat and fuck her into submission. It's the least she deserves," my father taunts. Jesus, he is even more crazy and delusional than I previously thought.

My husband's eye twitches, his jaw clenching. It's a clear sign he is about to lose his shit but without a weapon he is at a complete loss, and there is only one way this can end... unless Nico has something up his sleeve that he hasn't yet revealed, we are completely at their mercy.

"I strongly suggest you make the most of the hand that is currently covering *my* wife's mouth. Because by the time I am done with you, I will have removed it from your body, along with your other limbs, that I will throw away like the trash you are. But your hand? I will keep that as a memento of this moment. Of a time when you believed you were at an advantage. It will be displayed as a trophy of sorts. A warning, to anyone who dares touch what doesn't belong to them."

Boisterous, mocking chuckles hit my ears, but the thick accent of Vadim cuts through the laughter making me stiffen and confirming what I already knew. "Do not be stupid, Nico. You cannot win here."

Nico's eyes laser in on the Russian. A predator singling out its prey and ready for attack. A shiver runs down my spine when a vicious smirk tips his lips. Not because I fear Nico, but because there is something in the look currently on my husband's face, that makes me believe we may just get out of here. Or is that just wishful thinking? Is the dehydration and pain making me delirious? I hope not.

"And you," Nico seethes. "I will take great pleasure in killing you, Vadim. I should have done it when you killed my papà, but the wait will be worth it. I'm going to make your death slow. Enjoy every second of spilling your blood." His voice is low, but lethal, and if looks alone could kill – which right now I wish they could – Vadim would be dead.

Tilting my head as far as I can with my father's hand still

covering my mouth, I watch as Vadim barks out a laugh. The arrogance that shines in his dark eyes. The conceited tip of his chin. It tells me all I need to know. He thinks he has won.

"Strong words for a man who is clearly at a complete loss. You have no weapons. You are outnumbered. Is one pussy really worth all this?" His hand darts out and he pushes my father away. I suck in a breath, flinching back when Vadim runs a finger down my face. My eyes snap to Nico's, but he doesn't see me. His gaze follows the trail of Vadim's digit as it caresses my cheek. "Maybe I will work out another deal with Mr. Caldwell and keep your whore for myself. I'm sure you have broken her in well. I have heard the rumors of your…" he trails off, his eyes sparking. "Proclivities. And let's just say, we have very similar tastes," he smirks sinisterly. "Though mine are probably a little darker. But she will get used to it and even learn to like it."

My heart stutters, then kicks up to an unnatural speed. It thumps against my ribcage in harsh beats. Bile fills my throat. The sound of blood whooshes in my ears. Fear turning my veins to ice. "No," I whisper, shaking my head. I would rather have my father take me to Xavier Anderson then be handed over to a man like Vadim. Both are a fate worse than death, but I would sooner take my chances with Xavier over the Russian.

Nico smirks, but it's not a nice look. He straightens. A king amongst men with not an ounce of fear on his face. "That's good to hear Vadim. You won't mind when I remove the finger you have on my wife's face and plug your ass with it then."

Vadim squats down. His face is so close to mine I feel when his hot breath tickles my cheek. He brings his free hand to my yoga pant covered leg, running it up my thigh. "Hmm, I think I'm going to enjoy breaking this cunt." He leans in as if he is preparing to kiss me. Grimacing, I shrink away from him. His mouth opens, but it's the vile grin, curving his lips, that has my stomach dropping.

"You–" he starts, but is cut off by the sound of gunfire.

A body drops on the concrete floor beside me, blood dripping from his forehead. I scream, all the air leaving my lungs when I am knocked to the floor by a big body. Pain shoots through me, my head snapping back at the force of my fall as the wooden chair shatters.

"Fuck," I groan, black spots marring my vision and turning it blurry. Loud voices and gunshots are the only thing I hear through the pounding of blood in my ears. It sounds far away, but that can't be right.

My eyes flutter shut, a weird sensation slithering into my body. I smile as images of my son and Nico flicker in my mind, like a reel. Sighing, I feel like I'm floating on air. Having an out of body experience even with the weight pressing down on me. My eyes blink open but the heaviness of my lids, the dull pain and fuzzy vision, has me squeezing them shut. Everything hurts, the images of my boys now replaced by something darker.

A small white light pulls me toward it, but it seems too far away. I can't reach it, no matter how hard I try. The dark surpasses the light, begging me to succumb.

Before I can make sense of what is happening around me, I allow the darkness to pull me under.

I surrender to it.

Embrace it.

My son and husband, standing at the altar in their matching tuxedos is the last image to flash in my mind.

Then everything goes black.

Chapter 42
Nico

"Get my wife out of here," I scream at no one in particular, but expect them to follow my instruction, nonetheless. I hate that another man will touch her, carry her out of here, comfort her. But her safety comes first and right now, with her blacked out on the floor, amidst the ruins of the chair she was bound to, she is a hindrance to our survival.

Vadim thought he had won. Little did he know that I had an army behind me, ready to go when Gregorio gave them the signal. You see, I have a little pin on my suit jacket, one that is recording everything. My hacker knew the Russians were about to kill us and signaled my men surrounding the building to fire. Hearing his voice in my ear, I threw myself at my wife, protecting her with my body so she didn't get hit by a stray bullet.

Pushing off Ocean's small body, I lift her into my arms before cradling her face in one hand. Her eyes are closed but the steady rise and fall of her chest tells me she is breathing. I press a kiss to her bruised lips.

"I'm going to get us out of here, baby." My chest tightens

with every word out of my mouth, but I mean them. Enzo crouches down in front of us, lips in a tight line, awaiting my next order. I mostly ignore the fight going on around us, more concerned with getting my wife to safety and hoping my men will keep me protected.

"Take her to where Christopher is waiting in the SUV. You know the location. I will get there when I can." He nods, circling his arms around Ocean's body, ready to take her from me. I grit my teeth, my hands flexing with the need to punch him in his damn face, but I hold back the urge. "You keep my wife safe. You hear me?"

"I've got her, Nico." He raises his voice, so I can hear him over the noise filling the warehouse.

Glancing around, I see dead bodies on the floor and looking a little closer I find it's mainly Vadim's men. But I don't see Vadim, Giuseppe, or Ocean's father which can only mean one thing. They fled. My soldiers are surrounding the building, so they shouldn't get far. They know not to kill Vadim. Know he is mine. And I am going to enjoy every second of his death just like I told him I would. It's been a long time coming after all.

"Aldo. Santino." I bark through the chaos. Despite the commotion, they hear me, their focused gazes locking on mine. Carefully, stealthily and managing to avoid any bullets, they make their way over to me. "Cover Enzo. Get my wife out of here." They nod in unison, eager to fulfil my orders. With one last glance at the fight around us and noticing we have the upper hand. I figure this is probably going to be the best opportunity to get Ocean out of here. Emotion tightens my throat when I look down at her small, beaten, limp body, in Enzo's arms. I want to rip him away from her, but I know this is for the best. I have to finish this war once and for all. "Get out of here," I order, making sure to cover them as they leave the room.

Watching them, I release a breath when I watch them exit

the room. They still have to get Ocean to the SUV, and I can only hope they get there without issue. Deep down, I know my men will take good care of her, otherwise I would never let this happen.

A hard body slamming into me shoves any thought from me, knocking me back down to the cold, dirty floor. "Get down, Nico." I recognize the voice as one of my men's, but which one I'm not sure. "Fuck," he groans, rolling to the concrete beside me. Looking over, I find Adamo, holding his side. Blood covers his hand as he holds the wound, trying to stem the heavy bleeding.

"Christ. Stay still and keep your hand where it is. One of the others will get you to safety." He nods, not looking the least bit concerned that he is bleeding out.

Glancing around, I exhale when the gunfire finally stops, and I find at least twelve of my soldiers still standing which means the opposition has been taken out. A buzz sounds in my ears, the aftereffects of being around such loud noise. Trying to shake the irritation away, I look up to find my men now standing around me as they wait for my next orders. I bark them out, knowing I need to get out of here. One, to find Vadim and two - which is the most important reason - to make sure my wife made it to the vehicle safely. Once I have everyone in place, some carrying the injured and the rest following me, we move as a unit toward the door that Vadim and Samuel Caldwell must have escaped through. I don't even make it through the door, before I hear growly voices and find the assholes being held by my men.

Smirking, I lower my weapon, sauntering toward Vadim and Samuel. Both will die today. I know it. They know it.

"And here you thought you had the advantage." I tsk, shaking my head on a grin.

Vadim's mouth is bloody as he struggles against my soldier

holding him. He spits blood, narrowly missing my black loafers. "You are making a mistake, Nico. My men will avenge me. Mark my words, you are a dead man walking if you kill me."

A dark smile curves my lips. I get right in his face. "No, Vadim. I warned you, but you didn't listen. Now, because of the choices you made, and the fact you dared to touch my wife, you will die. It won't be a fast death. It will be slow, and I will enjoy every second of it." I turn my head, glancing at the man who shares DNA with the woman who owns my heart. The woman I love. I pause. Love. Such a simple word but holding so much meaning. It's not the first time I have acknowledged my feelings for my wife, but it's the first time I've used the word love and in front of these two assholes, no less.

Still, it's true. I do love Ocean - she will never be Emilee to me – and when I get her back in my arms, I am going to tell her the words she has been waiting desperately to hear. I will also show her with my actions, every day for the rest of my life, how much I mean them.

"And I will take great pleasure in killing the man who tormented *my* wife for all those years." I cock my head. "I hate what you did to *Ocean*, the abuse you inflicted on her, but at the end of the day, what you did, it brought her to me. It led her to the life she was always meant to live. She is a queen. *My* queen and I will forever make sure she knows that." I finish, my face and tone full of disdain for this man. With one last look of disgust in the monster's direction, I turn, my gaze drifting over my men. "Load them up in the van and take them to the meat warehouse." I command and without a word, they get to work, doing as I ask. I glance around, frowning when I don't see Giuseppe. "Where is the traitor?"

"We don't know, Nico. Men are still surrounding the perimeter, so he won't get far." It's Luca that answers me.

I nod, pushing my frustration aside. My men will get him. We didn't come this far to let him get away.

Releasing a weary breath, I grab my cellphone out of my pocket, pulling up Christopher's name. Hitting the green button, I listen as it rings out. My jaw clenches the longer he doesn't pick up, and my pulse kicks up in fear.

The ring tone cuts off, the sound of his voice replacing it and making some of the tension leave my body.

"Boss?"

***

My footsteps speed up when I spot the black SUV outside the chain link fence. Adrenaline rushes through me the closer I get, and I can't wait to wrap her in the safety of my arms. Before I reach the door, it's flung open, the soft voice I feel like I have been waiting a lifetime to hear, hitting my ears.

"Nico." My battered and bruised wife cries out, jumping into my arms.

A calm washes over me as I cradle her in my arms, my mouth buried in her neck as I breathe her in, and I realize with utter clarity that she is without a doubt the other half of my soul.

A sob breaks free from her mouth, her hot breath tickling my neck with every bit of her emotion. I hold her tighter, never wanting to let her go. I want to look at her face, study every inch of it. But I have a sneaky suspicion that if I focus on her injuries too much, I am going to make her father's and Vadim's deaths one thousand times worse than what I already have planned for them.

"I've got you, *Tesoro*," I soothe, holding her so tight I'm surprised I don't break one of her delicate ribs. Pulling back, I finally look at her. My jaw tics when I see the black and blue bruises marring her perfect face and I suck in a calming breath, trying to steady my rising temper, before I speak. "Do you need to see a doctor? I have a couple on call. Here in the city and in the Hamptons. We can go home, to the estate, if you feel more comfortable." I tell her, trying to keep my voice even.

She nods, hiccupping with her tears. "I want to be with Romeo."

I press a kiss to her forehead. She winces, gently grabbing her head and rubbing. Red hot rage slithers into my veins, my eye is twitching with my anger.

"Does is hurt?" I softly run my forefinger over the knot on the side of her head.

"Yeah," she admits, her blue orbs glistening with her tears.

Placing a kiss on the tip of her nose, I force a smile. "Come on. Let's get you home and seen by the doctor. Once I know that you're okay, I need to come back to the city and take care of some business."

She eyes me warily, her throat bobbing when she swallows. "My father." It's not a question but a statement, one she doesn't need an answer to. I won't fill her head with the nightmares that frequent mine.

"Come." I say, ignoring her. With her safely in my arms, I climb into the back of the vehicle, settling her down on the seat next to me and buckling her in. "Take me to Marchetti towers. And call Hansen on the way. I want to be back in the Hamptons within the next couple of hours." I instruct my driver, Christopher, sitting back in the seat and getting as comfortable as I can with the anger burning inside me.

My mind goes to Dante and the fact that I still haven't heard from him. It's definitely concerning, and I make a mental note to call him to find out what is happening at my damn club. But that can wait for right now. Ocean needs me and I have no intention of doing anything or leaving her until I know she is okay.

Staring at my wife, I marvel at her strength. Despite everything she has been through, she is still standing strong. She amazes me more with every day that passes and I know, without a doubt, that I will do everything in my power to protect her.

To keep her safe.

For as long as I live, and maybe even when I am burning in hell, I will make sure she is protected.

My throat tightens, and I know it's the right time, to say the words that I should have spoken weeks ago. Words that are true and have been true for longer than I care to admit.

Without another thought, I murmur, "I love you."

Her head snaps up, wide blue eyes locking on mine. Her lips part in shock. I bite back a smile. She has never said it, but I knew she had resigned herself to the fact that she may never hear those three little words from me.

Today I have given her what she wanted but was always too afraid to ask for, and I mean every single word of it.

Despite all that has happened today, the biggest grin I have ever seen lights up her stunning face. It's beautiful, contagious, and I can't help but get caught up in it.

"And I love you, Nico Marchetti. My husband. My world."

Chapter 43
Ocean

Rocking my son gently in my arms, I stare absently as Nico's family doctor cleans my face up with saline soaked gauze.

Nico was insistent that I had every part of my body x-rayed to make sure I had no broken bones or internal injuries. I thought it was overkill but there was no arguing with him about it, so I humored him and let the doctor check me over thoroughly like he was being paid to do.

Turns out there were no broken bones or internal trauma, but I am littered with bruises and very tender. The right side of my body, from where I was slammed to the ground, is the worst. But I now know they are the result of Nico protecting me, so I can't even bring myself to be mad about the black and blue markings all down my body. My facial wounds on the other hand... the dark bruises may fade, and the split lip will heal, but they will forever be a reminder of what happened today. I knew the man I refuse to call father to be a monster, but today I saw an even worst part of him. One I hope to never see again. And if Nico keeps his promise of killing Samuel Caldwell, then after today I never will have to look at his ugly face ever again.

My thoughts briefly shift to my mother and how she will cope without her husband. A pang of guilt hits me that I am wishing death on the man who helped bring me into this world, but then I remember all he has done to me. The physical abuse he bestowed upon me, when I was just a young girl without the strength to fight back. He is a weak man, and he deserves everything that is coming to him, to die in the most heinous of ways. My mom will be okay. She always is. She is a chameleon, one that will fit and thrive in whatever environment she finds herself in. My mother, complicit and just as guilty as my father, does not deserve another second of thought or anything else from me and neither does my brother. As far as I'm concerned, they no longer exist.

My husband's deep growl snaps me from my thoughts, bringing my gaze to him. He watches me through narrowed eyes with a look I can't decipher. His cellphone is to his ear as he tries to call Dante for what feels like the hundredth time. He still hasn't answered his calls and, though Nico won't say it, I can tell he is worried about his best friend.

After Nico met me at the SUV, Christopher took us to the Marchetti building. The helipad on the top of the skyscraper was where Hansen was waiting for us with the chopper. We were back on the estate within the hour, and I have never been so happy to see my gilded cage as when it came into view. I never thought I would feel that way, but when I think back to the moment Nico first brought me here, how I was highly against staying here, I now see it was the best thing to happen to me. I was glad to be back but, more than anything, I wanted to hold Romeo in my arms, see with my own eyes that he was okay. Valentina had confirmed it on a phone call to Nico and by the confusion in her voice had no idea what was happening in the city or why we were coming back so soon. I have no doubt he will tell his mother and sister everything, but my guess is he is holding off until he has spoken with Dante. That doesn't mean I don't feel sick with guilt every time I look at them and see the concern and questions in their eyes.

"Right, all done. I will prescribe you some pain medication for the bruised ribs. Get rest and drink plenty of water. You will be fine, Ocean. You just need to take it easy for a couple of weeks." The doctor pushes his glasses up his nose, a soft, sympathetic smile on his face. His gaze shifts to my husband who nods at him.

"Thank you, Doc. Mamma can you escort Emilio out?" Nico mutters.

Valentina stands, forcing a smile. "Of course."

They leave the room and it's only seconds before Allegra speaks. Her voice is small, worry evident in her tone. Even though it is clear she is trying to be strong, her lip wobbles as she chokes out three words.

"Where is Dante?"

Nico's gaze shifts from me to his sister. He sighs, running a hand through his thick dark hair. "He is dealing with shit at the club. I will know more when I talk to him."

A tear leaks down her cheek but she brushes it away. Clearing her throat, she pushes to her feet, her gaze turning pleading. "You are hiding something, Nico. I can see it in your eyes. Is he okay at least?"

My husband's jaw clenches in frustration, and I can see how much this is all taking a toll on him, but he doesn't shy away from her question.

"Honestly? I don't have a fucking clue, Allegra. I have been trying to call him and Leo for over an hour now. I am sure they are fine, but I will feel much better once I have it confirmed." He clears his throat, his gaze shifting to me. "Now that I know my wife is okay, I am going to head back to the city and see for myself what is going on. Until then, unless he finally calls me, I don't know anything," he admits.

A broken sob bursts from Allegra's mouth and she collapses onto the couch. With my free hand I rub soothing circles on her back, trying to help in any way. "Please bring him back to me," she chants over and over. To herself or Nico, I'm not sure. It's a prayer. One I hope God answers, too. I see the way they look at each other, the love between them and if Dante is gone because of me...

I will never forgive myself.

***

I am watching Romeo sleep when I hear my bedroom door being pushed open. Glancing over my shoulder, I see Valentina and Allegra step inside, their small smiles unable to hide the worry and fear in their eyes.

"Is he asleep?" Valentina asks quietly.

I nod, turning to face them. "Yeah."

"Would you like to join us for dinner? I made lasagna," she says, her eyes darting to her daughter. "It's Allegra's favorite. I thought with everything going on..." she trails off, but the insinuation is clear.

"Have you heard from Nico?" I murmur, closing the distance between us.

"No." It's Allegra that answers, her voice strangled as tears spring to her eyes, and she visibly shakes with that one word.

Valentina takes her daughter in her arms, stroking her hand down her dark hair. "Now, now. Everything will be okay," she soothes, but I witness the pain in her blue eyes. "Come on. Let's go eat, while we wait for news," she murmurs, dropping a kiss to Allegra's forehead.

I force a smile, taking one last look at my son and grabbing the monitor. As three we make our way down to the kitchen in heavy silence. The smell of fresh basil, garlic and oregano hit my nostrils, making my mouth water. I wasn't particularly hungry, what with everything going on, but nonetheless my stomach growls in protest, begging me to feed it something.

And that is what I do.

Dinner is peaceful. We all stare at nothing, our worry tangible and thick enough to choke on. But we ignore it because Valentina made lasagna, so we sit and eat, trapped in our own nightmares, while we wait for news from Nico that never comes.

Chapter 44

Nico

"I'm sorry, Nico. I thought Dante was following me to safety. It was only when I got outside that I realized he wasn't with me. The building went up like a damn firework before I could get back inside. I..." Leo trails off, pain flickering in his eyes as he swallows. "I tried to save him. But it was too late."

I stare at what used to be my club and is now a pile of ash in disbelief. How the hell am I going to tell my sister that Dante perished in the fire? My throat tightens with so much emotion it almost chokes me. I pull at the collar of my shirt as if that will ease it, but of course it doesn't. Nothing will. Not now. Not ever.

Police and the fire department surround us, but all I can focus on is that my best friend is gone.

Dante Vitale, the man who has been by my side since we were children, is dead.

Pain explodes in my chest, flowing to every part of my body and making it feel heavy. Tears prick the backs of my eyes, but I don't let them fall. No matter how much I want to scream and lose my shit, I hold them in. On the outside, I look as I always do. A picture of calm and collected. On the inside, I'm dying.

Clearing my throat, I turn to face Leo. "Deal with the Feds. I have somewhere I need to be." I run a hand down my tie and without saying another word to him or anyone else, I stride to where Christopher is waiting in my SUV. My legs are sluggish, every step weighted down by the grief that is consuming my body. My heart pounds in my chest. Sweat drips down my spine. Fuck. I feel like I can't breathe.

Sucking in some air, I move faster, just wanting to be in the car where I can hide away from the world. My papà always taught me that crying was for the weak, therefore it was beaten out of me when I was a little boy. Every time I fell, or hurt myself, I would have to hold in the tears that threatened for fear of being hit. But right here, right now, with Papà gone, I have no one to tell me that it's wrong to show emotion. To cry for your best friend. Being who I am, it's a hard thing to admit to having so much emotion, but at this point, with the death of my best friend, I am past caring.

Finally reaching the SUV, I grab the handle, pulling the door open. Once inside, I instruct Christopher to take me straight to the warehouse where Vadim and Samuel Caldwell are being held. If I was going to make their deaths painful and slow before, now that I know they are responsible for the death of Dante, I am going to make it a million times worse for them. For every second my right-hand man suffered, I am going to make them suffer tenfold.

Sucking in a breath, my head falls back onto the buttery leather headrest. My eyes close and I allow the pain of loss to seep into every inch of my body. The need for revenge takes over, adrenaline sparking in my body with the need to kill the men responsible for making me feel like this. I need this. Need to release the ticking time bomb that is about to explode inside of me, before I head home to my family and break the news about Dante.

I squeeze my eyes closed, letting the grief rip through me. My mamma is going to be devastated but Allegra... she is going to be... I shake my head. I can't even think about my sister and how this is going to affect her. She loves Dante. He loved her. My breathing comes in thick and fast, and I feel like I'm drowning. I scrub a palm down my face. They were supposed to get their happily ever after once I had dealt with the Romano shit. And now, for reasons that don't make sense, it's been taken away from them in the cruelest way possible.

I exhale a weary breath, knowing with everything inside me that I will never recover from Dante's death.

And even worse than that.

Neither will my sister.

***

The sound of flesh hitting flesh is the only noise in the cold warehouse.

I pound my fists into Vadim's bruised and bloodied face, trying to relieve this empty feeling inside me. It's not working and, at this point, I doubt anything will. But I won't stop until he is praying for death. This man is responsible for Dante's demise, and he will pay for it.

Stepping back, I halt my assault and let him believe he is getting a reprieve from the brutality I am bestowing upon him. Vadim slumps back in his seat, sucking in much needed breaths. I chuckle sadistically, lifting my foot and kicking him in the leg. A whimper sounds from the left. I smirk when my gaze meets my wife's sperm donor's fearful blue eyes. The fear he is not even trying to conceal fuels the monster inside me. He knows his time on this earth is almost over. It's just a case of when he will meet his maker.

The sound of liquid hitting the concrete floor has my eyes shifting to his pants. My nose scrunches up in disdain when I see the blatant wet patches. Asshole pissed himself. I sigh. It's always the way. The begging. Pleading. The resignation crossing their features when they realize it's no use, that I will show them no mercy. Then comes the stone-cold fear. The pissing and shitting themselves. No matter how many times I've been through the same process, I can't help the contempt that fills me. He got himself into this mess when he got into bed with Vadim and tried to take my wife. Now he has to face the consequences. Both him and Vadim.

They should face it like a fucking man and own their shit. They knew what they were getting themselves into when they decided to cross me, so when it's time to pay the fucking piper – me in this case – they could at least look me in the eye. Be the men they believed they were when they decided it would be a good idea to go against me. Not the whimpering, soiling messes they have become.

The door opening, followed by heavy footsteps, has me twisting my head. A dark smile curves my lips when I see two of my men dragging a sobbing Giuseppe toward me. I thought the coward managed to get away from Vadim's warehouse during the gunfight. I should have known better, really. There is no escaping the Marchetti *famiglia*.

"We found the rat trying to escape, boss. Thought you would want us to bring him to you," Maximo grunts.

I tsk. "Did you really think you could get away, Giuseppe?" It's a question, but I don't expect an answer, so I continue. "You will pay for your sins against me and my organization, like the rat bastard you are." I reach out, cupping his chin as my lips go to his ear. Lowering my voice, I whisper. "You will die today.

You will join my disgusting piece of shit papà in hell just like you deserve." Pulling back, I glance at my soldiers. "String him up."

"Nico, please. I beg of you. Think of Giulia. My family."

I chuckle, but it's humorless. "You should have thought of them before you decided to betray me. Don't worry though, I will make sure they know exactly what you are. A deceitful, greedy, traitorous, asshole."

He screams, shouts, begs, pleads. I tune him out, my gaze shifting back to Vadim, who looks at me with a manic gleam in his swollen eyes. Spitting blood to the floor, he grins. "You think by killing me, this will be over? You are wrong, Nico," he hisses, the venom in his voice clear. "I have a successor and he will come for you. Mark my words, he will come for you all. He will kill your whole family, make your wife his whore, and you won't even see it coming." His chilling laugh fills the warehouse, echoing off the walls like a haunting whisper.

I quirk a deadly smile, pushing away his words. There will always be an enemy, it comes with the territory of being who I am. Stepping toward Vadim, I bend, getting in his face. "Let him. He will only end up the same way as his predecessor. Dead. At my hands."

He shakes his head. "You can't beat us, Nico. The war is bigger than you know. You think Giuseppe is the only one to come to me? You're wrong. And soon you will see just how wrong you are. You have enemies buried deep inside your organization, but they present themselves as your allies. They are ready and waiting for the moment to take you down. To kill you. They will strike and when they do? The Marchetti name will no longer exist."

A chill runs down my spine with every word out of his dirty mouth, but I don't show him any sign that he is affecting me. Instead, I pull my knife from my pants pocket, running it down the side of his face. He winces when I pierce his skin but shows no other sign of fear. I watch as blood trickles down his face with a sadistic smirk. Adrenaline pumps in my veins and it's time for these motherfuckers to die.

Leaning in, my voice turns deadly as I grit my next words.

"Let them all come. I will be ready."

Chapter 45

Ocean

Nico didn't come home last night.
 Me, Allegra, Valentina, and Romeo stayed in the den the whole night. I didn't sleep though, too worried about where Nico was, if he was okay and whether he had found Dante. The questions played on a loop in my mind, begging to be asked, but I kept them locked up tightly inside, not wanting to fuel Allegra's apprehension or Valentina's anxiety, which she is trying hard to keep hidden from her daughter.

It was the longest night of my life. We were all scared, the unknown making us on edge, but not one of us voiced our concerns. Instead, we held each other in silent support, praying for the best but ready for the worst. It was pure torture – even worse than enduring those hours with my father and Vadim – the not knowing. The waiting...

The sound of a helicopter has my ears straining. Pushing out of the Chesterfield chair, I carry Romeo to the window, my heart lurching when I see it landing on the helipad located on the Marchetti estate grounds.

Nico.

Spinning, I keep my son cradled in my arms as I hurry out of the bedroom and down the stairs. Allegra and Valentina are already in the big foyer, with the door pulled open, ready and waiting for my husband. My heart pounds in my chest, the only sound in the spacious entrance is our collective heavy breathing, as if we know this is the moment that is going to change our lives forever.

Within minutes, Nico appears, two men and Christopher behind him. My pulse spikes, tears pricking my eyes when I meet his gaze. It tells me everything and is not the outcome I had hoped for. I know Allegra witnesses the look, too, when a choked sob rips from her mouth and she collapses to the floor. Valentina lowers herself beside her, tears streaming down her face, in silent grief as she tries to comfort her daughter.

"No. No. No. No. No," she repeats brokenly, her face now buried in her mamma's neck. I want to go to her, console her in any way I can, but I stay rooted to the spot, breaking a little more with every *no* out of her mouth.

"Nico?" I whisper, when he closes the distance between us.

He shakes his head dismissively, his silent way of telling me he is not ready for any questions right now. He presses a kiss to my head, then Romeo's, breathing him in as if he is drawing strength from our son, before he goes to Allegra. Blowing out a breath, he drops to his haunches, bundling his sister into his arms.

"I'm so sorry, Allegra. So, so, sorry," he murmurs, carrying her limp body down the hall and in the direction of the media room.

Holding my son in one arm, I reach down with my free hand and help Valentina to her feet. She sobs freely now that her daughter is out of sight.

"I can't believe it. Dante..." she cries, trailing off before sucking in a breath. "He was like a son to me. I have known him since he was just a little baby. Allegra, she loved him. He can't be dead." She shakes her head in disbelief. "She won't survive this. Like you are to Nico, Dante was her other half. Her soulmate." Her whispered words are haunted, almost as if she didn't want me to hear them.

"Come on. Allegra needs us." My voice is strong, despite me feeling otherwise. Squeezing her hand, I lead Valentina toward the media room. We all need to be there for Allegra in any and every way possible. Try to help her through this, though I'm not certain anything will make this better. Something tells me this is only the beginning. That harder times are ahead, and things will never be the same. But as Nico's wife, I will be strong. Be the woman he expects me to be. I will be a pillar of strength and comfort, a shoulder to cry on, because they need me, all three of them. Even if my husband won't admit it.

Despite the things I kept hidden and the way I came to be part of their family, both Valentina and Allegra have been there for me since the moment I set foot in this place. And now I intend to be there for all of them, helping in any way I can.

***

Instead of staying in the den, tonight we stay in the media room.

Romeo sleeps in his travel crib again, which Nico had one of the staff bring over from the den. It's clear he wants his whole family together and after everything that's happened, I can't deny him that. My husband looks tired, grief stricken, and I can tell he is only just holding it together. If only to be strong for his sister and mother.

Allegra cries, the tears falling from her eyes like a waterfall as she stares off at nothing. My heart aches for her. For the love she has lost and the one she never really got a chance to explore. Her grief is a living, breathing thing, sucking all the air from the room and so heartbreaking I can't stop my own tears from falling. This is all my fault. I don't voice my thoughts but deep down I know it's because of me that Allegra has lost her soul mate and Nico his best friend. I swallow, stifling the guilty sob that wants to break free. This isn't about me. It's about my grieving family.

Just before 7.30 a.m. Romeo stirs, breaking the silence in the room. Jumping off the couch, I lift him from his crib and turn to my husband whose eyes are already on us.

"I'm going to feed and change him, then I will make everyone coffee and something to eat."

Nico scrubs a palm down his weary face, nodding. "Thank you, baby."

With a smile, I leave the room. Heading up the stairs, my legs feel like they are full of lead with each step heavier than the one before. Only when I'm in our bedroom do I let the sorrow take over and the tears fall.

I cry for my husband.

I cry for Allegra.

I cry for Valentina.

I cry for Dante.

And I cry for me.

For the trouble I brought to this family, now ripped apart because of my monster father. I don't know how long I sob for, but it's only when Romeo lets out a hungry cry that I wipe the tears away and move to the plush chair near the window to feed him.

I didn't get a chance to express my milk so have no bottles made up. Releasing my breast, Romeo latches on easily and I watch as he feeds. My boy, so innocent, with no idea of the chaos that is happening around him or the world he lives in. I'm not naïve enough to think he won't take over his father's empire one day, because he will. Romeo is Nico's heir and no matter my apprehension or disapproval about letting him be part of this organization, I know I will have no choice. It's his birthright, just as it was my husband's.

I run a finger down his soft, contented, cheek as more tears blur my vision.

I wish I could change his fate but that means not having Nico.

And that's a life I will never imagine.

Nico is mine and I am his. I know that like I know the sky is blue and the grass is green.

Even with fears for my son's future, I know deep down that everything is exactly as it should be, so I inhale a calming breath and shake away all my negative thoughts. I refuse to let them drown me. I am Nico's queen, and I will be resilient because I have no other choice but to be.

Romeo will be strong, just like Nico, and the heir he is meant to be.

And with his father's influence he will be everything that Nico is and more. Because like me, he has no choice.

As a unit, a family, my boys will rule this world exactly as they were born to do.

And I will be the proud queen beside them every step of the way.

Epilogue

Ocean
One month later...

As I suspected, things since Dante's death have been difficult, to say the least.

Though Nico puts on a brave face, I feel and see the anguish he holds tightly inside him. It's why he has distanced himself from me. Though he showers both me and Romeo with love and affection, I know he has put space between us. He is trying to save face. Like I will think he is less of a man if he shows me his pain. It's frustrating, but it's a process and one we will get through.

As for Allegra... she wears her pain, sorrow, and grief like a badge of honor. She is a shell of herself, spending most of her time locked away in her room and only allowing Valentina and Nico to visit. It hurts that she is pushing me away, but I know it's not about me. It's her way of dealing with everything that happened and I would never deny her that. One day she will let me in, and I will be there with open arms to support her.

Valentina, bless that woman, has been a godsend. She really is the backbone of the Marchetti family with her selfless ways and her strength. She is everything good in this world and I can only be thankful that she is my family.

As for my own mother? From what Nico told me, she had my father's disappearance investigated only days after Nico killed him. Yes, I knew my father would find death at Nico's hands, and my husband told me that the night he didn't come home was the night he exacted the revenge both Dante and I deserved.

Though he spared me the gruesome details, I couldn't help but feel relief that the man who had inflicted so much pain on me was now dead and could no longer hurt me. Nico was questioned about my father's disappearance, due to my mother informing the police that he had come to New York to retrieve his daughter from Nico Marchetti, but nothing came from it. As far as the agents were concerned, Samuel Caldwell was involved with some bad people, Vadim Mikhailov in this case, and their deaths were put down to a deal gone wrong between them. The case was closed and thankfully we could all move on from it.

I officially changed my name to Ocean. Like shedding my skin, I shed my birth name and am now formally Ocean Marchetti. Emilee Ocean Caldwell died the day I ran from my parents and though I have a couple of fond memories of growing up, the bad ones outweigh the good and she doesn't deserve my forgiveness. Therefore, I will never speak to my mother again and she will never meet her grandson. She has no business being here in my new life, so she can stay in Seattle where she belongs.

As for the secret birth control I was keeping from my

husband, it was no longer an issue. Allegra had provided me with a month's worth of pills and once I finished them, I couldn't bring myself to ask her for more considering everything else that was going on. She was grieving her lost love, and it would be selfish of me to even consider asking her, so I let it be, resigning myself to the fact that I would most likely be pregnant again very soon. Not that Nico has had his usual high sex drive, but we are still making love and I'm not naïve enough to think that it won't happen. It did before and I'm sure it will again.

I'm not mad about it anymore. To be honest, I think it's exactly what our family needs after Dante's death. It will give my husband something else to focus on. Valentina another grandchild to nurture and love. And Allegra… well I don't know what me having another child will do, but maybe, just maybe, it will help her in some way. I just want her to be okay. I know it will take time, but we have a lot of it. I didn't know Dante well, but I know he wouldn't want this for her. He would want her to thrive. Live her life and be happy. And one day she will be. I know it.

"*Tesoro*," my husband calls.

"In the bathroom."

In mere seconds, Nico is standing over the bath I am currently soaking in. He smiles and my chest tightens with that all-consuming love I have for him.

Dropping to his knees, he reaches up and runs a finger down my cheek. "Hmm, I was going to suggest fucking you in the shower, but I see that's off the table now."

"You can join me in here?" I say hopefully.

He smirks. "I think I will. You can sit on my lap and ride my cock."

My pussy clenches with need at his dirty words, needing to feel him inside me, more than I need air right now.

"Okay," I breathe.

He grins, standing to his full height and stripping out of his designer suit. Desire tightens my stomach and I have a feeling this is going to turn into some hot, much needed, sex.

Fortunately, I just put Romeo down to bed, so we don't need to worry about waking him. Nico jerks his head, silently asking me to move forward. I do, allowing him to get in the tub behind me. Wrapping his arm around my waist, he pulls me in close and I shiver when his hard length slides up my back. Hot breath hits my ear and when his tongue caresses my pulse point, I nearly come on the spot.

"Does my little *Tesoro* want my cock?" I nod, licking my lips as pure desire thrums in my veins. He lifts me with one hand, positioning his cock at my entrance with the other. And then he is lowering me slowly onto him. My eyes roll shut when he fills me completely. I don't think I will ever get used to the feeling of him inside me. I assume for many people it would be considered a once in a lifetime experience, but for me, I get to keep Nico forever. When he is fully seated inside me, his chest rumbles with a satisfied groan. He nibbles my ear lobe, his voice thick when he speaks. "Such a good girl, taking my cock in *my* tight little pussy. Now ride my dick until I come. I have two days' worth of my seed ready and waiting to fill you."

Sighing, I smile, leaning back against his hard chest.

"As you wish, *husband*."

He shivers against me, and I feel rather than see his smile. Though he would never admit it, he loves it when I call him husband. "I love you, *wife*."

My breath hitches in my throat. I will never get used to him saying those words to me.

"And I love you, Nico."

Epilogue

Three months after that....
Nico

I stare at the white marble stone in our private family crypt, my fingers tracing over the name.
Dante Enzo Vitale.
A week after I delivered the news to my sister, and without a body, we held a funeral for my best friend in a private ceremony. It was the hardest thing I have ever had to do. Not only was my grief all consuming, but my sister's devastation also broke me a little more. From a young age, I protected her, and it killed me that I couldn't shield her from this.

Dante was our family, the man Allegra loved, a huge part of our lives and now he is just... gone. I don't know how to wrap my head around his death and I'm man enough to admit that I will never get over the loss of him.

"He was my everything," a soft voice whispers behind me.

Glancing over my shoulder, I watch Allegra making her way

toward me. "I'm sorry." I say, my shoulders slumping. Though I know his death was not my fault, I can't help but feel responsible in some way. If only I had made him come with me that day, he would still be alive.

A tear runs down her cheek, a shuddered breath leaving her as she steps up to me. Her blue gaze locks on his name, tracing every curve and line engraved in the stone. Her face falls, the sorrow she shows me every day marring every inch of her.

"It wasn't your fault. We both know the risks of this life. I just miss him so much, Nic. We were planning our lives together. Marriage. A family." Her breath hitches, a sob breaking free, and I pull her into my arms, pressing a kiss to her temple. Her body shakes with the force of her cries, my chest cracking a little more with every sound that leaves her mouth.

I don't know how long we stay like that, me holding my sister while she mourns a love that never even had a chance to begin. A love that my papà would never have allowed, but one that Dante risked his life for anyway. The fact he was willing to risk my papà's wrath proved how much he loved my sister. Showed me that he is exactly the kind of man I would want for Allegra. I blow out a weary breath, frowning when my sister pulls out of my arms.

Wiping the wet from under her eyes, she sucks in a breath as if preparing herself for her next words. Turning to me, she pins me with watery blue orbs. I frown, knowing whatever she says next is going to change everything.

"Nic," she starts, her gaze darting to Dante's headstone before coming back to me. My pulse kicks up when I see determination staring back at me. "I don't want you to get me out of the marriage arrangement with Riccardo–" I open my mouth, ready to cut her off and tell her that I will absolutely be getting her out of this contract if it's the last thing I do. If not for her, then for Dante's memory, but she holds up a hand, stopping me.

"The love of my life is gone. If I can't have Dante," she whispers his name. "Then I don't want anyone. But I also know what it will cost you if you succeed in ending the contract. You, Mamma, Ocean, Romeo, and your future baby are all that I have left," she continues, reminding me that my wife is pregnant again. That in less than five months we will have another baby. "And I won't risk your lives if I don't need to. Tell the Romanos the marriage will go ahead."

I shake my head, grabbing her forearms and imploring her with my eyes. "Allegra, you don't understand. I've heard the rumors about Riccardo, and so have you. I don't want you anywhere near that. I will not let it go ahead. I will not risk you."

More tears fall from her eyes, a small smile gracing her lips. "Listen to me, Nic. You don't trust the Romanos but I'm strong. Dante made me *strong*." She enunciates each word. "Let me do this. Let me be on the inside, to see if I can find out what they are planning. You know as well as me that they are plotting something, and we need to find out what before it comes to fruition. Before they can hurt us."

"But he will hurt you," I grit out.

She smiles, like she has it all figured out. "That is why you will insist on some conditions. That if they want the marriage to go ahead, then they will have to accept a new agreement. That will include me taking two of your men as my personal bodyguards. You will also make sure that I am allowed a cellphone to speak with you whenever I like. And that I can visit you at least twice a week. That way, you can make sure he isn't abusing me."

I mull her words over, my jaw clenching when I realize what she will have to do if I allow this. "You will have to fuck him. He will expect you to produce an heir." I growl, my lips turning down in disgust at the thought.

She shrugs as if it's no big deal. "I will have our family doctor put me on double birth control. I will get the shot and implant. I want to be sure I am covered and there is no chance of me getting pregnant." I grimace at her words, but it makes sense. She smiles weakly. "Let's do this. And when you get the evidence you need, you can pull me out of there."

My jaw clenches, but the more I think about it, the more it makes sense. Ever since those cryptic words Vadim spewed, I've been wondering whether the Romanos are the ones involved with the Russians. I don't particularly want to put my sister in the line of fire, but it's the only way to have someone on the inside, and if I can get them to agree to the conditions she mentioned, then at least I know he won't attempt to abuse her... physically at least. I shake my head again. "No. I won't put you through that."

Her spine snaps straight. She glares at me. "You can and you will. I will go to them myself if I must. But it will be easier with your help and support."

My jaw flexes, nostrils flare. I exhale, shoving a hand in my hair and pulling at the strands. My gaze flickers to Dante's stone. Fuck.

What do I do, brother?

Tell me what to do.

I close my eyes. Dante would never allow this to happen, but I also know my sister well enough to know that she will go through with this plan, whether I like it or not. I can't win in this situation unless I lock her up like a prisoner, and after everything she has been through, she does not deserve that.

My gaze locks on my sister's. Her blue eyes are filled with a plea. She wants to do this. But what scares me more than that is I can see the emptiness in her, the resignation, bleakness and recklessness since Dante died. She is willing to go into the lion's den, willing to put herself at risk because she doesn't care what happens to her. I should say no for that reason alone, but it will only push her further away.

The only way I will ever consider this madness is if the Romanos accept the new conditions of the agreement, and if they don't, the whole thing is off no matter what my sister wants.

With gritted teeth and a whole lot of reluctance, I give her my answer.

"We have to get them to agree to the terms first."

The End.

For now...

**Allegra's story coming this year. Preorder here:
https://books2read.com/u/mer01r
For a sneak peek, sign up to my newsletter.**

https://authorkellykelsey.myflodesk.com/wp2aquzed8

※※※

Quick Note from The Author

Wow, what a ride Nico and Ocean have been. Thank you so much for reading, your support means so much to me!
I have loved every minute of their journey and I hope you loved them too. If you did, it would mean so much to me, if you could leave a review.
I want to thank Gabriella, Kalie and my pa Kerri, all of whom have been superstars. A big thank you to Andrea for all your help with getting the correct Italian words and phrases. And last but definitely not least, you my readers. Without you all, I couldn't do any of this, so I thank you.

To keep up to date with all things Kelly Kelsey, you can follow me on social media.

Facebook Readers Group - Kelly Kelsey Readers Group
Instagram – Authorkellykelsey
Goodreads – KellyKelsey
Tiktok – Kellykelseyauthor

kelly Kelsey

Newsletter – https://authorkellykelsey.myflodesk.com/wp2aquzed8

About the Author

Kelly Kelsey is a UK-based author who started her writing journey during the pandemic when her career in events came to a complete stop. The more she read the more she wanted to try her hand at writing and eventually self-published her debut novel in July 2021. She now has nine books published and has been involved in several anthologies.

Books

Student/Teacher Standalones
Sweet Temptation
Sweet Possession
Sweet Addiction

The Maxwell Family
Jump Series – Thalia and Theo
Elimination
Checkmate
Unconditional
Inevitable – Aria and Bishop

Beautiful Beaumont
The Secrets We Keep

Novellas
Wrong Desires
Jingle All the Way

Marchetti *Famiglia*
Dancing in Sin – Nico and Ocean.
Twisted in Obsession – Nico and Ocean.
TBD – Allegra Marchetti and ? – Pre order: **https://books2read.com/u/mer01r**
https://authorkellykelsey.myflodesk.com/wp2aquzed8

The Jump Series
Elimination

Thalia Maxwell has it all. Daughter of one of the richest men in the world and a movie star mother. Except all she dreamed of is for the chance to make a career in showjumping. Thalia manages to convince her father to send her to train with world number one showjumper Theodore Rhodes after she finishes school.

Arriving in Wellington Thalia expects hard work and dedication. What she doesn't expect is the tension, the push and pull between a man she should never have. A man that is in a relationship. A man that could ruin her. As they get to know each other and feelings develop, will she be able to stay away from him or will she jump in headfirst?

Theodore Rhodes is at the top of his sport. His results and reputation in the world of show jumping are yet to be beaten. When he gets asked to train Thalia Maxwell, he jumps at the chance. Not because he wants to but having a big name like hers will bring him even more into the spotlight than he already is.

But when Thalia arrives, he expects a spoiled little princess that wants to play my little pony. What he doesn't expect is a girl so determined and beautiful he can't help but be drawn to her. The more time they spend together the further he falls. Will he risk everything for the one girl he should never have?

ELIMINATION is a new series and book 1 in the series with a cliff-hanger. It does contain tropes that some may find triggering such as cheating. However, the series will end in a happily ever after... eventually!

Thalia

Excitement courses through me as I spot the imposing sign on the brick wall.
Rhodes Farms.

The place I have wanted to train ever since I watched Mr. Theodore Rhodes, himself, compete at the Global tour in New York a few years back. I was mesmerized by him. The way he rode. The way he was at one with his horse. His riding was an art form. He won the whole competition, and I knew then I wanted to be just like him.

Theodore Rhodes is the number one show jumper in the world and the one person who can help me achieve my show jumping dreams. He won individual and team gold at the last Olympics - his third time competing for Team USA.

After much discussion—and begging on my behalf—my parents agreed to let me train with him, with the stipulation that I finish high school first. Of course, I agreed, and I graduated from St. Constantine's private all-girls school a couple weeks ago. Now my journey can really start. I will be a showjumper. I will prove to my parents that this is what I want.

We pull through the wrought iron gates. I scan the area

through the blacked-out SUV windows, taking in the lush green grass and palm tree lined drive before the barn comes into view. I smile knowing I am going to see my horses in just a couple more minutes.

Zeus and Lolly.

I have had them for a couple years now, competing on the East Coast whenever I had the chance between modelling, filming, and school. I want to take the next step now and that can only happen if I get the right trainer.

Coming to a stop, I open the door before the driver gets the chance to do it for me and hop out. I hear my father's stern voice but that doesn't stop me as I race toward the stalls. I have never gone this long without seeing my horses, so the excitement is real. Spotting a woman, I come to a halt.

"Hey, do you know where my horses are? Zeus and Lolly?" Her eyes widen before she composes herself.

"You're Thalia Maxwell?" I nod in confirmation. It's only when her mouth gapes that I remember what my name means.

Thalia Maxwell, daughter to the owner of the world's biggest diamond and jewelry corporation, Christian Maxwell III, and America's sweetheart, movie star, Elena Maxwell. She straightens, clears her throat. I frown. I don't want to be treated any differently from anyone else here.

"Uhh, yeah. Follow me." She spins on her heel, and I follow her lead. "I'm Tessa by the way. Barn manager at Rhodes Farms."

"Hey," I reply. She glances over her shoulder with a small smile then carries on to my horses' stalls. She comes to a stop at a door. I peek over, smiling when I see Zeus. He is gray in color and around 16.2 hands, big compared to my five-foot six height. Spotting me, he neighs. I open the door, strolling in and wrapping my arms around his neck.

"Hey boy. Did you miss me?" I ask even though he can't reply.

"Zeus and Lolly have been very well looked after," Tessa says. I glance over at her and smile.

"Thank you. This is the longest I have gone without seeing them," I tell her. Both my horses were transported from New York to Florida over a month ago. I know it sounds cliché, but I have been lost without them.

"Lolly is next door," Tessa adds. I release Zeus and make my way to Lolly. I grin at my girl. She is around 16 hands and brown in color with a black mane and tail. She is beautiful. Opening the stall door, I walk in and wrap my arms around her just the same as I did with Zeus. I breathe her in, breathe in the smell of horses.

It feels like home.

I hear footsteps approach and I know it is my father. My mom couldn't make it today, as she is on location for a new movie she is filming.

"Thalia?" I release Lolly, stepping out of the stall to find my father with his cell in hand and a frown marring his face.

"Here, Daddy." He glances up at me with a smile.

"Come. Mr. Rhodes is in his office." I swallow down my nerves as I follow my father. I have never met Theodore Rhodes in person, but I have seen pictures. He is known as the hottest guy in show jumping and it is not hard to see why. With his dark hair, striking blue eyes, and chiseled features, he is a god. Beautiful. I have been around good-looking men, worked with them on several modelling campaigns, but Theodore Rhodes beats them all. Unfortunately for all women that covet him, he isn't single. He has been with his girlfriend for six years and as far as I know, there has never been any rumors of him being unfaithful. Not like you would be if you were dating British socialite,

Melody Whitworth. With her blond hair and brown eyes, she is gorgeous and together, they look like the picture-perfect couple.

Coming to a stop at a big oak door, my father knocks. A few seconds later a deep male voice responds, sending a shiver down my spine.

"Come in." My father pushes the door open before stepping through. I follow behind him only to come to a stop when I spot the man behind the desk. My breath hitches. I swallow.

Hard.

Jesus. Pictures do not do this man justice. In person, he is even more god-like. Noticing my stare, he clears his throat and holds out his hand for me to take. "You must be Thalia?" My cheeks heat in embarrassment at being caught ogling him. I take his hand.

"Yes," I breathe. He smirks. A smirk I feel right down to my…pussy? I frown, stunned by my reaction. This never happens to me. I have never been interested in men, choosing to focus on my horses, yet for some reason, this stranger has my stomach in knots with lust.

This is bad. Really bad.

The guy is not only in a long-term relationship but is twelve years older than me. I glance at my father who would, for sure, have me back on our jet and back to the East Coast if he heard my thoughts right now. Being the baby of the family, I am my father's little princess. The good girl. Never had a boyfriend and I am sure he would like to keep it that way. My father takes a seat, dragging me out of my thoughts.

"Nice to meet you, Thalia. I'm Theo, but I am sure you already knew that," He says smugly, releasing my hand. The instant loss leaves me cold. I shake my head trying to compose myself.

"Nice to meet you, Theo," I say in a voice I don't quite

recognize. I need to get it together before my dad realizes something is wrong. And anyway, Theo is way out of my league. A grown man with a girlfriend who I am sure has no interest in me other than training. I am a paying trainee. He is my trainer. I chant the words silently to myself, reminding myself to keep my head in the game and off this glorious specimen in front of me. He smiles once more before rounding his desk and taking a seat.

"So, Mr. Maxwell—" My father holds his hand up to stop him.

"Please, call me Christian." He nods before carrying on.

"Christian, I know we spoke in detail before about Thalia's ambitions and what she is looking to achieve from training with me. We discussed her accomplishments so far and that she is now looking to step up a level, move up the ranks." Theo's gaze moves to me. I blush at the intensity in his blue eyes. "Is that correct Thalia?"

Clearing my throat, I nod. "Yes. I have followed your career for a long time now, Mr. Rhode's..." I trail off at the look on Theo's face.

"Please call me Theo. If you are going to be training with me, I would rather we be informal with each other. Mr. Rhodes is far too formal when we will be working closely."

I nod. "Like I was saying, I have been following your career for a long time now, Theo. Your performance at the Beijing Olympics was extraordinary. It is what inspired me to want to do more. To be better. I have wanted to train with you for a long time, but I needed to finish school."

Theo's eyes light up at my hero worship and my tummy flutters with excitement that I have pleased him. "I want to compete at a higher level. Do the tours in Europe. Maybe make the nations cup teams. I understand I have a long way to go but I am willing to do what it takes." I feel my father's stare at my speech, but my eyes stay locked on Theo's. My gaze drops to his lips when I see them twitch.

"You are passionate, Thalia; I will give you that. But I need you to understand the work that will go into getting you to that level. It does not and will not happen overnight. Show jumping is one of the toughest sports." I frown at his words, but he continues. "But with your parents' backing, I think you have as good a chance as any. Show jumping is also a money sport, you have that. Your father has already informed me that you will have your parents full support in whatever we need to do to get you to where you want to be."

"Whatever it takes," my father cuts in. Theo nods.

"I have schooled both your horses and studied videos of you competing. While they are both nice horses, they are average at best. They need to be exceptional to compete at the level you want to." My jaw clenches, fists ball at the audacity of this man. How dare he speak about my horses this way. Before I can stop myself, the words tumble out of me.

"My horses are just fine. They may not be competing at top level yet, but they can," I hiss. I feel my dad's eyes on me, but I don't move my gaze from Theo. Something flashes in his eyes, his lips curving into a smirk.

"Thalia," my father warns. Being childish, I shoot Theo an indignant look before he carries on like the arrogant asshole he apparently is.

"As I was saying. While they are both nice animals, I feel that to compete at top level, you need a top-level horse. Fortunately for you, I do have one in mind and although the owners aren't desperate to sell, I have it on good authority from the current rider that they are willing to allow you the chance to view and purchase him. We will need to be discreet, but I think it will be the perfect horse for what you are looking to do." Theo glances at my father then back to me.

"You know my position, Theo; I am willing to spend the money to get my princess," I cringe at my dad calling me that in front of this man, "to where she wants to be. What sort of figures are we looking at?"

Theo clears his throat. "I have been told he is going to be in the high six figure numbers. That being said, it will be worth it if it gets Thalia the results and exposure she wants. He is competing at top level in Europe and is on all the Dutch Nation Cup teams with very good results. I think it would be the perfect fit." I frown at his words. Although it would be exciting to have a new horse, I don't want to sell my current ones.

"I don't want to sell Zeus or Lolly. I won't." I look at my dad, shaking my head as if to drive the point home. My father's eyes soften.

"Princess, we won't be selling them. I just think that if you want this as much as you say you do, you are going to have to take Theo's advice. He knows what he is talking about and if that means buying a better horse then that is what we will do." I smile before my gaze moves to Theo. Something passes in his eyes that I can't quite decipher before he speaks.

"I think this is the right move, Thalia. Of course, we will spend a couple of weeks getting to know one another, so I can see the level you are at with both horses. But ultimately, I think buying a horse or even a couple of horses that have good records competing at top level is the best way forward."

I nod, feeling my anger at his earlier words dissipate. "Of course. I want this and I trust your advice. I wouldn't be here otherwise." He eyes me for a long beat before he nods.

"Good. I am glad we cleared that up. Now onto the next thing. You will have two assigned grooms and one stable hand which are included in the price of your monthly fees. I will introduce you to them later today. You will also meet my whole team. I have three other students here training with me and they all live on site, as do the staff. Your father mentioned you will be living off-site in a condo purchased for you." My father cuts in.

"Yes, that is correct. It is around ten minutes from here and Thalia has a vehicle to travel back and forth."

"Good. I also understand you will be taking college courses online so I will take this into account when working out your schedule."

"This is important," my father says in a tone that leaves no room for argument. "Thalia knows that it is part of the condition of being here, so she knows to take her studying seriously." My father shoots me a stern look to remind me that I promised to continue my studies. The fact I can study online is a bonus. I don't want to go to a classroom.

"I am sure we can come up with something that suits us all. With two horses, Thalia will only need lessons four or five times a week. The rest will be trail rides, flatwork, or the horse exerciser." The way Theo says my name has my core clenching. I didn't know my name could sound so sexy on someone's tongue.

"That is what I want to hear. Studying is important and although I know Thalia is determined to make a career in show jumping, I still want her to continue her studies. She is a very bright girl." My father beams at me while my eyes slide to Theo to find him watching me intently. Something in his stare makes goosebumps break out all over my body and wetness seeps between my thighs. What the hell? That's new. I squirm and as if he knows what he is doing to me, Theo grins before his eyes move back to my father.

"Theo, I would also like to discuss the NDA. As you know, my wife is a very high-profile actress. But not only that, Maxwell is one of the biggest names in the US and while I trust you to be discreet during Thalia's training with you, it is something I insist on being signed by yourself and the people who will be working closely with my daughter." Annoyance flashes in Theo's eyes before he schools his features.

"That won't be a problem, Christian. Consider it done." I don't miss the bite in his tone. I grimace that he is having to do this, but it comes with the territory. When you are the daughter of a world-famous actress and one of the richest men in the world, it is something that must happen.

"Good. Now that the formalities are over, I would like to take Thalia to her condo and then tomorrow, she is all yours." My father pushes to a stand, holding his hand out for Theo to shake. "It was nice to meet you in person, Theo. I trust you will make sure my daughter gets settled once I leave." It's not a question. My father expects Theo to take care of his 'princess'.

"Of course, Christian. I will make sure she feels at home here at Rhodes Farms." Theo's eyes slide to me before going back to my father. I push out of my chair, my gaze on Theo as I flash him a small smile. He smiles back causing my stomach to twist. Ignoring it, I rush out of his office and back to the waiting car that will take me to my condo.

Sweet Addiction

Knox: Being the star quarterback of the NFL, I had it all. Women, money and a life most could only dream of. I thought I was invincible. Then I made a mistake, then another and it all came crashing down. I was suspended from the NFL and forced into a relationship and job I didn't want. But then i met her—my fiancee's sweet innocent daughter. She stirs something inside of me that I never knew existed. I know I should stay away. I know it's reckless to want to touch her, to want to make her mine. But I am Knox McCabe and living life on the edge is what I do best. So why change now?

Madison: Being Madison Devereux, people think I have it all. Popular. Rich. Beautiful. What more could I want, right? Wrong. All I want is to be able to follow my dreams but doing that means hurting my mother. Then suddenly she gets engaged to NFL bad boy Knox McCabe. He is mysterious, gorgeous and the new coach at my school. What starts out as a game of lust and desire soon turns into something neither of us can stop. It's reckless, wrong but it feels so right. I should walk away. Stop the madness. But Knox has other plans, ones that include me. Everything I have ever wanted is within reach, will I risk it all for a man that belongs to the one person I never want to hurt?

Knox

"You have got to be shitting me?" I glare at my agent before my gaze moves to my publicist Clarissa. The latter's mouth forms a tight line, and she shakes her head.

"I'm afraid not. You really messed up this time. There are online petitions calling for you to be removed from the NFL permanently." She sighs, rubbing her temples as if trying to find the strength to deal with me. "Listen to me Knox and listen good. I know this all seems far-fetched but it's the only strategy we have come up with that we think will make you look human and not like the above-the-law god you seem to think yourself to be. Scarlett Grisham is a fading actress. She needs the publicity as much as you do. She is a good choice for this—"

I hold my hand up to stop her. "Scarlett is one of your clients, isn't she Clarissa?" It's not a question but she answers anyway.

"Yes," she admits although I knew what her response would be. "But that is not why I am doing this. We need to transform your image. Right now, you are seen as a playboy, the bad boy of the NFL. I will arrange for you and Scarlett to meet to get to know each other. If all goes well—and I think it will—we can move on to the next stage in your *fauxationship*." I pin her with a look that says, I have no idea what that is. "Like a relationship but fake," she explains before continuing. "You will be pictured out at restaurants, doing the grocery shopping, and other normal couply shit. You will be in the tabloids, seen in loving embraces, kissing, cuddling, and in a couple of months we will announce your engagement. I know it's not what you want, and I am not asking you to marry Scarlett, but you will be engaged. The world will think that the twenty-nine-year-old lothario Knox McCabe has finally settled down and become a one-woman man. When the dust has settled, we can slowly start the breakup rumors if that's what you want. You never know. You might fall for her for real." Clarissa smirks.

I shake my head. I know of Scarlett Grisham. Yes, she is a beautiful woman, but there is also talk that she is crazy. At seventeen she seduced and became pregnant by the director of her hit show, Girl Talk. Peter Devereux was ten years her senior and a married man at the time. The press went wild over the news and still to this day—eighteen years later—they talk about it. The only reason Peter never went to prison was because they were living in New York City and the age of consent for sex is seventeen. There was also the fact that Scarlett publicly admitted to seducing him. After taking a few years out to raise her daughter and only accepting small roles, she finally got back into the world of showbiz and became a huge star. You would have thought the opposite after going after another woman's man and being very open with not caring about his poor wife but no, both of their careers hit superstardom. He was a director in demand, and she was the actress offered role after role. Until now. At thirty-six, her career has all but dried up. I guess that's where I come in.

"Scarlett Grisham is hardly the right choice. She has as many skeletons in her closet as I do mine," I point out.

"That may well be. But at the height of her fame, she was the golden girl of Hollywood. People saw her as the sweetheart single mother, doing her charity work and keeping her nose clean. She has had no bad articles written about her in the last fifteen years. Yes, there will forever be the reminder of her less-than-good deeds—her teenage daughter is proof of that, but I can control it to fit a good narrative. Let me do it for you. Just think about the headlines. The bad boy NFL player and the ex-darling of Hollywood. People will go wild for it. And more than anything it will make you look good." She sighs in exasperation. "Look Knox. Do it. Don't do it. But I am going to be frank with you. It's the only way I can save your reputation. It's not bad enough that you were caught driving while you had a goddamn Victoria's Secret model sucking your dick, but then you proceeded to tell the female officer to join you and the male one to fuck off. You now have public indecency on your record. Plus, the whole bullshit with that quarterback you fucked up in your last game. People don't like you right now. Even your loyal fans are questioning their devotion to you. Let's kill two birds with one stone. Over the next few months, we will present you as remorseful for your actions. To the world you will be the devoted boyfriend and then fiancé to Scarlett Grisham. You will live together and act like a model citizen and while you are doing that you will also complete your community service."

I stare at her, waiting for whatever bullshit she is going to tell me now. I knew I had to do it. It was part of my agreement when I went to court. But I was never involved in what that service would be. "Which is?" I prompt.

Clarissa keeps a straight face, but I see the amusement in her eyes. "You will be teaching physical education at Scarlett's daughter's private school. For a year," she adds.

My head swivels to my agent, who has stayed quiet this whole time. Now I know why. He knew what Clarissa would offer me, knew about the teaching. "What the fuck? I am not a PE teacher," I spit, pinning accusing eyes on Brett. "Get me out of it," I demand.

Brett shakes his head. "Can't. Your lawyer negotiated to get you the best deal. That was it. It's better than picking up litter off the side of the road and the only reason the judge agreed to it is because she didn't want a circus of paparazzi following you while doing it." He exhales. "This is the best option for you right now, Knox. My advice? Take it. You don't even have to fuck Scarlett, just live with her and take her out for the occasional dinner for all we care. But it needs to be for a year. By then the negative stories should have all died down. The Rams have suspended you and will only talk to me about contracts if you can prove yourself over the next year. Take the teaching position. Be the doting boyfriend. This will be good for you Knox. It will give you time to grow the hell up and be a better person. I don't want to hear one bad thing about you in the press. If I do, I will have no choice but to think about ending our working relationship. I don't want to do that, man. I've been with you since the beginning, but I can't be seen supporting someone who self-sabotages and is constantly making bad headlines. I have already had two clients drop me because I am sticking by you. Don't make me regret standing by you Knox."

I scrub a palm down my face. I didn't realize my bad choices were affecting other people. People I care about. And I do care about Brett. He took a chance on me when I was just a college kid with a dream. I owe him this. I owe him to be better.

Mind made up, I look from Brett to Clarissa. "Fine. Set up a meeting."

Madison

Two months later...

"**W**hat the fuck?" I mutter to myself as I flick through the article on my cell. My mom, engaged? To someone she supposedly only started dating two months ago. I only spoke to her a couple days ago and she never mentioned it. When I ask her about her relationship, she always brushes it off which makes me think that all is not as it seems.

Her dating NFL bad boy Knox McCabe came out of the blue, the timing was also very convenient. He was on the front of every tabloid and for all the wrong reasons. Then suddenly, he is the doting boyfriend with only eyes for my mother? Yeah. No. I don't buy it.

Call me a skeptic but there is also the fact that I know my mom. She never dates younger men—daddy issues or something—and Knox is seven years her junior. I could be wrong about all this, they could be hopelessly in love, but something tells me that my instincts are right.

I haven't met Knox in person yet. I am on summer break and decided to spend it in New York with my father and his wife. It's been perfect and given me the chance to pursue what I want most in life—to become a wildlife photographer. My dad's wife is the editor in chief for the most successful nature magazine in the world—Wildlife World. Vanessa Devereaux not only bought me my first camera, but she encourages me to chase my dreams. Much to my mother's disgust. Mom wants me to follow in her footsteps, to be an actress. I can think of nothing worse.

Growing up she was your typical stage mom and at eight years old she started pushing me to audition for different roles in acting and modeling. After a few years of playing parts I thought I wanted, I realized I wasn't doing it for me but to make my mother happy. I hated acting. I hated modeling. When I told her all this she was horrified. The daughter of actress Scarlett Grisham hating the very industry that she loved. Unacceptable.

She continued to push me but the more she pressed the more I refused. Not wanting me to embarrass her she agreed to let me live a normal childhood but only if I did acting and modeling when I finished school. I accepted her terms—emotional guilt will do that to you—but I have no intention of being an actress. I want to be a photographer. I just need to find a way of telling my mother that.

Flicking to my call log, I press down on my mother's number and bring my phone to my ear. The call rings out and I don't think she is going to answer but then her voice sounds down the line. "Hey sweetie. How's my baby?"

I grit my teeth at her nonchalant attitude. She knows damn well I would have seen the article. "Don't 'hey sweetie' me, Mom. What the hell. You're engaged?"

She sighs and I know without seeing her that she is rolling

her eyes so hard right now. "Don't be so dramatic Madi." She chuckles. "Although it will come in handy when we get you back into acting."

I pinch the bridge of my nose, praying for patience I don't feel. At eighteen, I sometimes feel like the adult in our relationship. Which is no surprise. Mom got pregnant and had me when she was only seventeen. It was a whole scandal at the time and not only because my mother was a teenager but because my father, the director of the series she starred in, was a married man and ten years her senior. Case in point. Scarlett Grisham loves and has always dated older men. As much as she would never admit to it, she is still hopelessly in love with my father. He is the love of her life while she is probably his biggest mistake. Don't get me wrong, my dad loves me, but I think deep down he wishes he had never gotten involved with my mother.

"Mom, what is going on? Is this for real or is it just another PR stunt?" I ask, wanting to know what the hell is happening and why she is messing around with someone like Knox McCabe.

"Jesus Christ Madison. Don't sugarcoat it," she barks. "I will discuss this with you when you get back, which is in two days right?"

She is evading the question which means my suspicions might just be right. "Yeah." I exhale already feeling drained at the thought of going back to LA. "I will send you my flight details."

She squeals like a best friend rather than a mother. But I guess that describes our relationship perfectly. Since the moment I was old enough to understand things, Mom always treated me like more of a friend than a daughter. I remember when I was fourteen and she was drunk. I spent four hours with her while she rambled on about my father, how much she loved him, and how *he* lost the best thing that ever happened to him by letting her go. The sad thing is she genuinely believes that. But the truth is, Dad never loved Mom. It was a fling that turned into me. I know that no matter how much time passes, no matter that he is married to Vanessa—the real love of his life—Mom will never get over Peter Devereux. She loves him. Always has. Always will.

"Perfect. I can't wait to see you, baby. You will love Knox. He is the best."

I roll my eyes at her over enthusiasm. "Okay Mom. I will talk to you later."

"Bye sweetie," she sings before hanging up.

Dropping my cell on the bed, I shake my head. What the hell has my mother gotten herself into now? Before I can think about it further a knock sounds at my bedroom door. My head snaps up just as Vanessa appears. She smiles. "Hi honey, do you have a few minutes? I wanted to talk to you about something."

"Of course. What's up?" I pat the empty space beside me silently asking her to sit.

Moving further into the room, she drops down next to me and takes my hand. Her eyes meet mine, so kind, so full of love. "We will miss you when you head back to LA," she says thickly, the emotion in her voice clear.

"I will miss the both of you too. I always feel more settled here in New York," I admit.

Vanessa nods. "You know you are always welcome here Madison." She sighs. "Look, I know that you are still deciding what you want to do after school and although I don't want what I say next to sway your decision, I want to put it on the table. Wildlife World would like to offer you an internship."

My eyes widen in shock, and I gasp. "W-what? Are you serious?"

She smiles. "I am. I discussed it with your father and again, he doesn't want you to feel pressured into it or like we are pushing you to do this. We both want you to be happy and do whatever it is you love. However, after our discussions over the years, we both know that photography is a passion of yours, especially nature and wildlife. If you want the internship, it's yours. If you decide to do something else..." She shrugs. "Well, we will support you in whatever you do."

My heart constricts. I hit the jackpot when it came to a stepparent. Throwing my arms around her, I say, "Thank you, Vanessa. I would love to intern at your magazine."

She chuckles. "Take some time to think about it, honey. The offer stands for as long as you need."

I open my mouth to tell her I have already decided when my dad's voice sounds. "There you both are." My gaze shifts to him and he frowns before smiling. "So, you told her about the internship?"

"I did," Vanessa replies before climbing off the bed. "I hope you don't mind?"

He shakes his head. "Of course not." He smiles down at her, kissing her temple quickly before his eyes shift back to me. "I know it's what you want baby but take some time to think about it. I know your mother has plans for you and I know how much you hate to let her down."

I frown. He's right, I do but that doesn't mean I am going to give up an opportunity like this. "I don't need to think about it. And don't worry about Mom; I will talk to her when I get back to LA."

He nods. "Okay then. Dinner's ready. Let's go and eat before it gets cold."

Climbing off the bed, I follow them down to the dining room feeling more excited than I ever have in my life. All my dreams of becoming a photographer can come true.

I just need to have a talk with my mom.

Sweet Possession

Asher: They say everything happens for a reason even if you don't know that reason at the time. Being screwed over by the two people closest to me, I thought I lost everything. I thought that statement was the truth until I saw my angel and at that moment, I knew she was my reason. I can't take my eyes off her and I will do anything to make her mine. Even stalk and manipulate situations if I need to. Everything starts to fall into place but things out of my control want to interfere and try to change my plan. They can try all they like but they don't know how far I will go to keep my Angel in my sights.

Remi: They say everything happens for a reason even if you don't know that reason at the time. What a load of rubbish that statement is. Life seems to want to break me at every turn. But I won't let it. I've been through hell and won't be beaten. Everything I want is within reach and then I meet him. A mysterious, gorgeous man. He wants to turn my world upside down and it's tempting... but then secrets are revealed, and people want to break us apart. How far will they go to succeed? How far will Asher go to keep me as his?

Asher

The smell of sweat and cheap liquor permeates the air, making me want to gag. I stare at the stage but focus on nothing.

This run-down shithole of a strip club is not the type of establishment I would normally frequent, but it's been a rough day.

A bad two weeks, for that matter.

I laugh at the memory of that day, but it's humorless. Walking in on your fiancée fucking your best friend since first grade is not funny.

The devastation of that day plays in my head like a movie, hitting me right in the chest. I don't know which is worse, losing Calista or Brody.

All I know is that it hurts so bad, I feel the pain in my now dead heart.

It's what brought me to this seedy place on the wrong side of town. I needed to get away. Needed to forget.

If only for one night.

Taking a sip of my bourbon, my head snaps up when catcalls break out all around me, and my gaze lands on the stage.

A woman walks out in a lacy black bra and thong; not unusual in a strip club, but there is something about her. The way her head is held high, and although she screams confidence, I can see the vulnerability in her eyes.

I stare at her and, in that moment, something strange happens. Something that hasn't happened since that day two weeks ago. My cock hardens in my pants. Shifting in my seat, my eyes trace every inch of her body from head to toe. Shiny, chocolate-brown hair that reaches her small waist. Chocolate eyes. Perfect, pert tits that bounce with every sway of her hips. Long, tan legs that would look so good wrapped around me. Flawless skin. Heart-shaped face with plump lips and a button nose.

Jesus.

No wonder the crowd perked up. The girl is fucking gorgeous.

I watch as she dances to a song, though I'm not sure what it is. My gaze is fixed on the stage in front of me, captivated by the woman moving her body like a temptress. Taking my eyes from her, I glance around, and sure enough, all eyes are fixated on her, like I knew they would be. A sliver of possessiveness and a whole lot of jealousy course through me. I pause. What the fuck? I never once felt like that towards Calista, so why am I feeling these emotions right now?

The song comes to an end, and the girl drops down, grabbing at all the bills on the stage. Its only then that I notice she didn't strip. No. The angel is still in her underwear, yet she is by far the most popular girl that has danced so far. With a handful of money, she pushes up, straightens her spine, turns, and sashays away, only to stop when a drunk asshole grabs at her leg. I growl in anger as she slightly stumbles. It takes everything in me to stay in my seat, to not beat the living shit out of the fucker.

But I don't need to. Security is there in a second, pulling the man away and out the door.

The beauty on stage stares after him, her lips slightly parted. It's then I see the innocence in her eyes, on her face. She looks young. Fresh faced compared to the other dancers. Blinking, she snaps out of wherever she just went and continues off the stage and through the curtain so I can no longer see her.

I watch the space she disappeared into long after she has gone and briefly wonder if she's coming back out. This incessant need takes over me. The need to go back there, find her, and make her tell me everything about her. But I don't. I stay seated, my eyes never leaving that black drape that has hidden the angel from my view. I sit there until the last girl comes on stage, until the lights come on, signaling the bar is closing.

I never see my angel again.

But that doesn't mean I won't be back.

I need to know her.

And I have every intention of doing just that.

The next evening, I find myself pulling up to Legs Eleven, the rundown strip club where I saw my angel last night. A woman like her should be nowhere near a place like this, let alone on the stage in her underwear while creepy dudes salivate over her. That may be hypocritical of me to say, being as I was one of those men last night, but I am not some weirdo. I just happened to be in the right place at the right time.

Hopping out of my car, I make my way to the entrance, pay the cover charge, and then find a free table near the stage. Not a minute later, a topless waitress appears, her eyes lighting up as her gaze rakes over my body.

"Hey sugar, what can I get you to drink?" she purrs, her

finger darting out and running down my arm. I grab her hand, pushing her away. She frowns like she can't quite believe I'm not interested.

"A water is fine," I say coolly, my eyes back on the stage. She huffs, spins on her stripper heels, and makes her way to what I assume is the bar to get my drink. I watch as a naked girl wraps herself around the pole. She isn't half bad. Just not my type, with her surgically enhanced breasts and cheap, dyed, bleach-blonde hair.

A half hour passes, and there is still no sign of my angel *or* my water. I am just about to turn to signal a waitress when the music starts. The lights dim even more, and the girl who I am here to see walks onto the stage. I watch as she takes a harsh breath, then looks up to the ceiling as if she is praying to someone who won't answer her. Then, like she remembers where she is – as if you could ever forget – she starts moving her body in such a sensual way, my cock hardens in my pants.

Fuck me.

That has never happened before. Not until yesterday, at least.

If she can make me hard by just moving her body side to side, then I'm pretty sure that most of the men in here are in the same state. Anger courses through me at the thought. I glance around, and it's the wrong thing to do because I suddenly want to rip every eye out of every socket in here. I want to get on that stage and cover her with my body so no one else can look at her.

"Here's your water." A feminine purr startles me out of my thoughts as she slams it down in front of me. As she turns to leave, without apologizing for taking so fucking long, I grab her wrist. She yelps, then scowls down at me. "Let go of me. No touching the ladies," she hisses.

I jerk my head to the stage. "Who is that?"

She looks to the stage and back to me, a look of jealousy and disgust crossing her face. "Oh, that's Crystal. I wouldn't bother with her though. She's a frigid, moody bitch. Thinks she is too good for this place, yet here she is, doing exactly what we all are. Stripping." She yanks her arm out of my grip and sashays away.

The song comes to an end, and, just like last night, the angel grabs up the bills and walks away without entertaining any of the catcalls being thrown her way. I am up and out of my chair, making my way to the small booth in the corner. It has a flashing neon sign saying *Book a Private Dance*. I push my way in front of the two men in the queue, ignoring their disgruntled words.

"I want a private with Crystal," I say impatiently, grabbing some notes out of my pants.

The lady, who must be pushing fifty, if not more, stares at me, her lips pursed. "Back of the line, asshole. You cut in."

Slapping the bills on the counter, I make her jump. "I want a private with Crystal. Now how much will it cost me to have that?" I grit.

Her eyes narrow before her lips curve into a grin that screams that she's about to make me pay extra. "One hundred dollars for the dance." I start to count it out, stopping when she speaks again. "And a hundred for me. Just because you're a jerk." She flashes a look that dares me to argue. I won't. I just want to get the angel to myself.

And I don't care what it costs me.

Remi

"Crystal, you're up. Room twelve," Jason, the owner, shouts at me as I stuff money in my duffle. Slamming my locker closed, I look at him. He knows that I hate private dances. That I hate to be touched, even if he doesn't know the reasoning behind it. As long as he's earning his fifty-percent cut, he doesn't care. It's not like I can say no; it was a condition of working here, and there is no way he'll give me special treatment. Even if I am his highest-earning girl.

I glance around the room and remind myself why the hell I am doing this, dancing in some shitty bar when it makes my skin crawl.

I'm all alone.

And I need the money since my mom left me alone with all the bills to pay. Plus, I now have school to pay for after taking a year off from my old one to work. I even got lucky, for once, and managed to win a scholarship at a prestigious school. And that shit does not come cheap. There is no way I'll give it up after all the work I put in to win it, and if that means strutting myself on stage in front of a bunch of pervy old men or in the private rooms, then I'll do it. I just need to keep my wits about me. Any sign that they are going to touch me or cause trouble, I'm out. No person would like a stranger touching them, but mine stems from something much more sinister. Men my mother would bring home with no regard for me. A couple of them touched me in ways they shouldn't have. I was fortunate it didn't go further, it could have been so much worse, but I still have the mental scars. No young girl should have to worry about grown men touching them inappropriately.

Sighing, I check my makeup in the mirror then stride out the door to the private rooms, all the while ignoring the bitchy stares from the other girls. They don't like me, and they've made that clear. I am the youngest - not that they know how old I really am - and I make the most money. It's made me a target for all their vile insults. I don't care though. I'm here to earn money, to pay my bills, to be able to afford to eat. Nothing more, nothing less. If they have a problem with that, then that's on them.

Stepping up outside the back entrance to room twelve, I take a breath. I can do this. Get in. Earn money. Get out. Pushing the door open, I stride in with a confidence I don't feel, only to falter when I see the man waiting for me. My jaw slacks, eyes widen.

He is gorgeous. A god. The kind of man you see on the cover of GQ magazine with his dirty blonde hair and piercing blue eyes. He looks like a better-looking, leaner Chris Hemsworth.

I swallow. What the hell does he want with me? Why is a guy like him in a place like this?

Instead of speaking, or even moving, he sits there in his chair like a king as he runs a thumb across his bottom lip. I shuffle on my feet, nervously.

"Hey," I greet but he doesn't respond, just watches me. "What would you like?"

He cocks his head, his hungry eyes raking down my lingerie-covered body. I shiver under his intense gaze. I mean, I know I look hot. It's how I got this job and why I am the top earner in this place. But with the way this man is staring at me, it makes me feel... powerful.

"Dance for me." The rasp of his voice goes straight between my legs, making my pussy clench with need. Jesus. If I have that reaction from just the sound of him, I hate to think what he could do if he touched me.

Nodding, I move to the corner of the room where an iPod sits in a docking station. Settling on one of my favorites, Little Bird by Annie Lennox, I hit play and make my way to the raised platform with a pole in the middle. Never taking my eyes from him, I let the music consume me as I move around the pole, my hips swaying and moving sensually to the music. His gaze never leaves me as he leans back in his chair, relaxing like this is an everyday occurrence for him. Maybe it is. I frown. This place doesn't suit him.

When the song comes to an end, I drop to my knees, my back to him as I arch it up. My long, dark hair hits my feet as I lean back and get a look at him from this angle. His eyes narrow in on me, and I scramble to my feet when he pushes out of his chair and moves towards me.

"Wh-what are you doing?" I stutter as he steps up in front of me. Again, he doesn't respond, he just reaches out and runs a finger down my cheek. I pull away. "No touching the girls," I hiss, ignoring the shiver of arousal he elicits from me.

He smirks. "I think you like me touching you."

I step away from him and scowl. "I don't think so." Spinning, I make my way to the dancer's entrance and grab the handle to pull the door open, but I'm stopped in my tracks when he speaks again.

"What's your name?"

I glance over my shoulder at him. His hands are shoved in his pants pockets, and I have never seen such a good-looking man in my whole life. He really is stunning. My eyes drop of their own accord as I take in his body. I can't see him fully with his clothes on, but by the way his shirt clings to his abs, I can tell he is the whole package. Hot and a good body. The kind of man women would drop to their knees for without him even asking.

My eyes snap to his when he chuckles, and an arrogant grin curves his lips. I roll my eyes. "Crystal. The name's Crystal." With that, I step outside and slam the door behind me.

The next night goes pretty much the same way. I do my set, grab my money, and head backstage to get ready to leave, only to be stopped when Jason shouts out my name.

"Crystal, room twelve. You're in there for an hour tonight," he barks out, leaving no room for argument. Excitement and a sliver of fear courses through me at the thought of it being the same man from last night. And if it is, why is someone like him, someone who could surely have anyone he wants, paying to watch me dance for an hour?

Unless he wants something else. I shake my head to myself. No matter how hot I think he is, he is not having that. If the other girls want to earn extra by having sex with clients, that's fine. But it's not for me. I may be a stripper, but I am not selling my body. I draw the line at that.

Quickly checking that my makeup is in place, I straighten my spine and make my way to room twelve. I feel a sense of déjà vu as anticipation runs through me at who I might find behind the door. On the one hand, I hope it's the guy from last night, but on the other, I hope it's not. Because that means I've caught his attention. And I don't need anyone's attention on me right now.

Pushing through the door, I step through, only to stop when I find him sitting in the same position, thumb running across his bottom lip, eyes on me. I shudder at the intensity he exudes and almost run back the way I came. But then I remember I need this job and being in here for an hour means extra money.

"Hey," I chirp confidently as I make my way inside the dimly lit room. When he doesn't reply, I shake my head and move to the corner where the music sits. I go to hit play, guessing he wants the same as last night. But then he speaks.

"Don't." The command in his tone makes me pause.

Spinning, I face him, and suddenly I feel very insecure under his attention. I'm wearing lingerie, but I may as well be naked with the way his hungry eyes devour me.

"What do you want tonight?" I ask, confused.

He stares at me for a long beat before pushing out of his chair. My eyes widen as he stalks towards me, and panic takes hold. My eyes dart to the cameras in the room, praying that whoever is in security sees this and rescues me. "Stop," I blurt. "You can't touch me. It's not allowed. I don't do extra."

He pauses a step away from me and frowns. His head cocks to the side as his eyes drill into me. Letting out an amused breath, he says. "I'm not going to hurt you, angel. I just don't want you to dance tonight."

It's my turn to frown. "Then what do you want with me?"

He smirks. "I just want to talk."

Shaking my head, I shuffle sideways towards the door. No man ever just wants to talk. There is always an ulterior motive, and I'm not about to wait around to find out what his is. No matter how gorgeous he is.

My eyes snap to his, and I stop when his deep drawl shatters the silence. "Please. I don't beg Crystal, but I'm willing to beg you. Just give me an hour of your time. I paid good money for that hour, and I will pay more if that's what it takes to get you to stay." The plea in his tone gives me pause.

"Why do you want to talk to me? You don't even know me," I murmur.

He smiles. "Exactly. I want to get to know you."

My brows furrow in confusion. It doesn't make sense. "Look, you seem like a nice guy and not some weird, hot serial killer." He smirks, no doubt at the fact I called him hot. "I just don't understand why someone that looks like you," I wave my hand at him as if to prove a point. "Is paying *me* to talk to them. You probably have women throwing themselves at you, so why are you here wasting money on me?"

He steps closer, his hand comes up and a finger runs down my cheek, making me flinch. He frowns, softly stroking me. I shiver at his touch, my body coming alive at just that small contact. He knows it, too, if his smug grin is anything to go by. "You're right, women do throw themselves at me. But it's you that I am captivated by. One look at you on that stage last night, and I knew I had to know you."

I suck in a breath. What the hell? Is this for real? The words are out before I can stop myself. "Why me?"

He shrugs. "Why not you?"

I chew my bottom lip in contemplation, but I know my mind is made up. "Okay," I blurt.

His lips curve into a triumphant smile. He steps away from me, his hand dropping from my cheek. The loss of contact makes me feel empty. With that thought, I know I should walk away, I don't need any distractions. Especially not the male kind. Before I have the chance to change my mind, his hand connects with my lower back, and he pushes me towards the sofa that sits to the right of the stage.

Dropping down, I shift until I am against the arm, making

sure to put space between us. He notices but doesn't make any move to close the distance. Instead, he reaches to the ice bucket beside him and pulls out two bottles of water, handing one to me.

"Thank you," I mumble.

Nodding, he leans back to get comfortable, those piercing eyes never leaving me. I twist the cap on the bottle and take a long sip, trying to wet my now dry throat. The atmosphere in here is almost stifling, suffocating me as I wait for him to speak.

"What's your name?" he repeats his question from last night, but I won't give in and tell him. Rule number one: don't reveal your identity. I don't need anyone finding out who I really am.

"Crystal." I give him the same answer as before.

With a shake of his head, he smiles. "Your *real* name."

"No," I snap, my eyes narrowing in on him, daring him to argue.

"Fine, I will leave that question for now, *Crystal,* but mark my words, you will tell me. Now, how old are you?"

I scoff at his arrogance. "None of your damn business. What is this? An interrogation?"

He growls, making my spine stiffen. As if sensing that I've tensed, he softens his features. "I just want to know you." His voice is soft, making me relax some.

"Twenty-one." The lie rolls from my mouth easily.

He nods. "Now, what is a girl like you doing in a place like this?"

I groan as I rub at my tired eyes. I've had this question asked a couple of times. People don't seem to understand that when you're desperate, you will do almost anything. "I need to eat, pay my bills. It pays better than working in a diner or a grocery store."

He seems to mull over my words for a long beat before speaking again. "Did you not go to school?"

My heart pounds in my chest as my whole body turns rigid with his question. It's a basic question, sure, but one I could easily trip up on if I don't think carefully. "Of course, I did. I just didn't have the money to go to college. That's why I'm here. I applied for community college and figured I could make good money here while studying."

His thumb runs across his full bottom lip, drawing my attention. I lick my lips at the thought of him kissing me, of those lips running over my body, and I shiver. "Mmm," he hums, and I bring my eyes back to his. My cheeks heat as he smirks, and I drop my eyes to the couch. We sit in silence for a while which makes me anxious. Is this all he really wants? To talk? It seems weird to me, if so.

"What are you going to study at college?" he asks, breaking the quiet.

I shrug. "I'm not sure. Maybe something like business or accounting."

"But that's not what you want to do, right?" Jesus this man is intuitive. "I mean it seems such a boring, mundane choice for a girl that could have anything she wants."

I snort. Does he really believe that? I am not a girl that can have anything she wants. I'm a girl struggling to make ends meet. A girl that would love nothing more than to be a professional artist but knows, deep down, it's a pipe dream, and I'm better off sticking with the *boring* and *mundane,* as he put it. "What's your name? And what do you do?" I ask, ignoring what he said. The question reminds me that I know nothing about this man and that maybe I should have asked his name when he was pushing to know mine.

He smiles like he was waiting for me to ask. "I'm a teacher... amongst other things. And my name is Asher."

The name somehow suits him, but as for being a teacher, I can't see that. He's just too hot. I briefly wonder what school he teaches at but push that aside for now. "Asher?" I repeat his name in a whisper, tasting it on my tongue.

His eyes squeeze shut, and I swear he groans a little before they snap open. "Now, what's your name?"

I push off the couch with a smile, and stride to the door, pulling it open in the next second. "Crystal," I say before I walk out.

Sweet Temptation

Eden: They say a moment can change your life.

I shouldn't want him. But I do.
I should stay away. But I can't.
He's off-limits.
But that won't stop me.
After all, rules are meant to be broken.

Nate: They say a moment can change your life.

I shouldn't want her. But I do.
I should stay away. But I can't.
She's forbidden. Off-limits.
A sweet temptation, one I should never have.
But that won't stop me.
After all, rules are meant to be broken.

Prologue

Eden – Age 14

I shove the key in my front door, wondering what state I will find my mom in today. Yesterday was a bad day when I got home....... I found her passed out on the kitchen floor surrounded by empty liquor bottles and Xanax.

Please be okay today, Momma, please, I chant over and over in my head. I take a deep breath and push the door open, stepping in I call out to her, "Mom?" No reply. "Mom?" I call again while still chanting a silent prayer in my head.

I check the kitchen first, there is no sign of her. I head back toward the entryway calling out for her. "Mom!" I call again, the worry in my voice evident. Still, I get no reply. My pulse picks up as I start to panic, my heart beats against my ribs as I make my way to the living room. I freeze just inside the door, scrunching my nose up in disgust. The smell hits me first... vomit.

Tears prick my eyes as my gaze lands on my mom, laid out

on the couch, an empty vodka bottle beside her. I rush to her prone form - avoiding the puddle of vomit by the couch - relaxing a little when I see her chest rising and falling. At least she isn't dead—this time. I think to myself bitterly. Grabbing her hand, I gently shake her.

"Mom. Mom. Mom." I repeat. She doesn't respond, too passed out from the liquor and God knows whatever else she took. I shake my head.

I shouldn't have to deal with this at fourteen years old, but I do. Living with an addict for a parent, I've had to grow up quickly. To be there for my mom. When I look at other kids my age, I see the difference between me and them. But scenes like this have become a regular occurrence over the last few years.

Ever since my *father* left, I have had to step up. I hate *him*. I hate that he just left us. Left me. He gave up on us for a younger woman, moved to another state. I resent *him* for leaving me to clear up the mess he created. I resent my mom for not being stronger. For constantly putting me through this. I resent her for losing her nursing job due to addiction. Leaving us to depend on the monthly maintenance *checks he* sends. Fortunately, our two-bedroom house on the outskirts of Seattle is paid off, otherwise that would have been another thing to worry about. Although it's small, it suits us just fine and is in a nice neighborhood.

Mom stirs, dragging me out of my thoughts.

"Honey is that you?" she croaks, her voice barely audible, weak like the person she's become. I hate that she has made me feel so bitter towards her. I shouldn't blame her. She was so in love with my dad. That all-consuming type love. He was her life. Then one day he decided he didn't love her anymore, Leaving mom heartbroken.

Anger courses through me at the thought, I take a deep breath to calm myself. "Yeah, Mom, it's me. Let's get you a shower, then into bed." She mumbles something unintelligible, as I help her sit up. It takes her a few seconds to steady her swaying body as I hold her. She opens her eyes, tears fall from them, down her face, my chest tightens at the sight.

"I'm sorry for being this way, baby." she sobs, and it breaks another little piece of me, making me feel guilty for my earlier thoughts. I rub her back in a soothing motion, trying to calm her.

"Ssshhh, it's okay, Momma. Everything will be okay." But even as I say the words, I know I am lying to myself. Things have not been okay for a long time now and I cannot see that changing.

My cell vibrates in my pocket. Pulling my hand from my mom's back, I fish it out. My best friend Piper's name flashes on the screen—she is the only person who knows what I am going through with my mom. The only person who knows everything and I have for support. I don't think I would have been able to cope if it weren't for her. I decline the call, dropping my cell on the coffee table and make a mental note to call her later.

"Come on, let's get you cleaned up." I pull her to a stand, holding her fragile, unstable body as if she is going to break. Tears prick my eyes thinking about who my mom once was. She was beautiful - still is in a broken way.

Back when she was eighteen, she became Miss California, had everything going for her. But ever *since he* left....... Well let's just say, there is barely anything left of her, thanks to the alcohol and pills. Her appearance is haggard, skin sallow, hair brittle and unkempt.

I clench my jaw in frustration. I wish she would get better; wish she would realize that *he* is not worth all this. More than anything I wish she could be there for me in the way she is supposed to. Glancing at my broken mom, I instantly hate my selfish thoughts. But then I remember it's my truth and sometimes the truth is ugly.

A few minutes later, I manage to get her up the stairs and in the bathroom. I'm not a big girl by any means, but mom is now pretty much skin and bones, so I don't struggle to much getting her up the stairs. I strip her out of her clothes while she drunkenly mumbles - bits I hear, bits I miss- but what I do hear has my blood boiling.

"I will get better, honey. It's just hard right now with your dad leaving," she slurs the same thing she tells me every time this happens. I resist shouting at her, but all I want to do is scream *that he* has been gone for two years, and she is worse. Not better. It wouldn't do me any good though, so I leave it.

Twenty minutes later, I have her showered, changed and in her bed. She passes out as soon as I lay her down. I sigh as I leave her room, exhausted and hungry. Heading downstairs, I tidy up the mess my mother left behind. If I didn't, it would be left, and I refuse to live in a shit hole.

After I finish the cleaning, I search through the cupboards, finding some ramen noodles for my dinner, which I quickly prepare and eat. I will need to go shopping tomorrow, get some decent food in but for now these will have to do.

When I'm done, I make my way to my room. Hopping on my bed, I lay down and stare at the ceiling. Thoughts race through my mind. How did we get here? Why did he leave? Were we not good enough? It's a vicious cycle. One that's left me with an addict mother who cannot let go of a man who no longer wants her.

My thoughts drift to *him*. He was a good father up until he left. We were a family. A happy one at that. I was a bit of a daddy's girl. Mom worked shifts at the hospital, so my time was spent with my father. When I told him I wanted to dance, *He* was the one who found me a dance school and took me to classes. When I knew I loved cupcakes, *He* would make sure we had them every Friday.

And now? Now, I cannot remember the last *time he* called

to check in on me. *He* thinks sending a monthly check is enough, thinks by doing that it makes him a father. I wonder *how he* would feel if he knew how things had turned out, knew I was failing school. Would he come back and help?

I snort bitterly. He can't even call because he is too busy, so I doubt he gives a second thought about me or my life. *He* is too caught up in his trophy girlfriend, his new life in California.

A stray tear rolls down my cheek. I swipe at it furiously. *He* doesn't deserve my tears. Closing my eyes, I pray.

Pray for the day things change, for mom to get better and for that day to come sooner rather than later.

Eden – Age 18

So much for praying for things to get better.

To say things got worse would be an understatement. And now I am alone in a bar, doing the one thing I swore I wouldn't do. Getting drunk. I sit glaring at my drink as anger from the whole situation threatens to consume me. A laugh bubbles out of me, but its humorless. I pick up my drink, necking the entire thing just to help me forget.

I glance around taking in my surroundings. The bar is chic, it overlooks the pretty California beaches and Pacific Ocean. Any other time, I would appreciate the beauty of this spot, but as I sit here, underage with my fake ID, I can't help but hate the place. Hate Orange County and that I was forced to come here.

I don't usually drink. Have never been drunk. But I was now on my third vodka cranberry, and I didn't even care. Today I need it. Need to forget all the shit, the life I left behind and everything I have known for the last eighteen years. There is a silver lining though, one that makes it a bit easier to relocate. My best friend Piper accepted into Beaumont College, and would be living only an hour away.

My mom was a good mom, once upon a time. Before my

father left and everything went to shit, at least. Ironically, he is no longer with the women he left mom for. Traded her in for an *even* younger model. I would laugh at what a living, breathing cliché the man is if he hadn't turned my world upside down.

He decided to come visit me for the first time in six years. Visit is a little farfetched. What *he* came for was to announce his engagement to a woman he had been dating for the last eight months. I say woman, but she is closer to my age than his.

During his visit, he found out I wouldn't be graduating high school. He wasn't happy.

You see, dear old Dad is the Dean of a prestigious private high school in California. The embarrassment of people finding out his only daughter would not be getting her high school diploma is something he didn't want to suffer. It took him all of a few hours to realize something was up and a few minutes to start throwing his weight around. I frown as I replay his words from that day in my head.

"*Jesus, Eden, why didn't you tell me it had gotten this bad? She is not capable of looking after herself, let alone you,*" he had boomed. "*And to let you miss so much school. What about college? It won't be an option without a high school diploma? I'm so angry. It is preposterous. Humiliating.*" I had let out a humorless laugh at his audacity and then let loose.

"*If you actually checked in more than once every couple of years, then maybe I would have been able to talk to you. You left us. We are fine without you. I can take care of the both of us just fine.*" I screamed back at him.

"*Like hell you can.*" was his response.

After calming down, we all talked. For the first time in six years, all of us sat down and spoke. He wanted mom to attend rehab and would pay for it on the condition I would agree to attend his school to repeat my senior year. I laughed at his ulterior motive. Daddy dearest would never do anything out of the goodness of his heart. Even for his daughter. My traitorous mother was quick to agree to this, much to my annoyance.

Now mom is in a rehab facility in Arizona, to complete a three-month treatment program. And me? I'm in sunny Orange County living with *daddy* and his real-life real housewife, about to repeat my senior year at Regis Saints Academy.

I have done my research on the place. From what I can tell, it is a place for trust-fund brats. Spoiled kids who thought they were special with their designer outfits and latest gadgets that had probably never known hardship. Maybe I was being judgmental, and these kids would be different, but I am bitter and angry about my whole situation. I just need to focus on why I am doing this. Mom is finally getting the help she needs. I can do this. For her. It can't be that hard, can it?

I am basically living the real OC life. With the big mansion, the step ford looking wives and the rich men. Declan earns good money as the Dean of Regis Saints, but it's not what made him rich. No. That is the app he designed and developed for use in schools and sold for millions.

Honestly, as much as it pains me to admit this, I have seen it and even used it. Its good. I asked him why he continued his work at Regis Saints when he obviously didn't have to. His response?

"*Work is in our blood, Eden, whether I have ten-thousand dollars, or ten-million dollars, it doesn't matter, I will still work.*"

I didn't know what to say to that, so I said nothing. His young, gold-digging fiancée doesn't work. Eyeroll. So, I guess she does enough *not working* for both of them. I am only going off what I have seen but it is obvious why she is with him, he isn't a bad looking man by any means, but he must be twenty years older than her.

A deep, sexy, masculine voice pulls me from my thoughts, sending a shiver up my spine.

"You look like you could use another drink?"

My head whips round, eyes connecting with his face, they widen before all the air leaves my lungs. I have never seen such a beautiful looking man in my life. I blink to make sure he is real and not an apparition I have conjured up in my drunk mind. Yep, still there. As if he can read my thoughts, he flashes me a smirk. A smirk so sexy, I swallow just to wet my dry mouth. My eyes rake over his face shamelessly, drinking in every inch of him. He looks like a god. Face chiseled and defined. Sparkling emerald, green eyes full of mischief. Tousled dark hair that is begging to have my hands run through it. My gaze drops down his body, mouthwatering at what I find. He wears a simple black t-shirt that showcases every bit of muscle, although they are covered, I can see the outline of his abs. I count them in my head. One, two, three, four.... is that an eight pack? I think it is.

My eyes drop further south of their own volition. He wears navy khakis which showcases the prominent bulge. His cock. I gulp. I may not have much experience with men but even through his pants I can tell he is big. My gaze snaps up when a throat clears. When I find the sexy strangers' eyes on me, my cheeks heat in embarrassment. His lips curve, eyes sparkle with amusement. I glare before turning my gaze on my empty glass. Bastard knows I was checking him out. His arm brushes mine as he takes a seat on the stool beside me. My eyes flick back to him, he raises an expectant brow and I realize I haven't yet spoken.

"What makes you say that?"

He smiles knowingly. "Because you look how I feel." He signals the bartender with a wave of his hand. Do I look that bad?

I know I'm attractive and that's not me being conceited; I have been told enough times. I was even model scouted last year at my local mall in Seattle but never pursued it. With my dancer's legs, long blond hair, and blue eyes. I can easily be mistake for your typical Californian girl. I got mom's looks and *his* eyes. For a long time, I hated looking in the mirror and seeing *him* staring back at me.

My eyes dart to the mirror behind the bar where I slyly check myself out. I internally scold myself at the sight that stares back at me. Messy hair, face free of make-up. As for my outfit? I glance down at my ripped denim shorts, black tank top, and Chucks. I never usually care what I look like but right now I do, especially when I look at the man beside me. All attractive, nicely dressed, and put together.

"So, what can I get you to drink?" he asks, flashing his perfect white teeth.

I turn my whole body to face him, ready to decline his offer.

"Look, I'm sure you are a really nice guy. But I am not really in the mood to be hit on, and I am not a one-night type of girl... so you can leave." I turn back to face my empty glass, hoping he will get the message. As hot as he is, I don't need any distractions. I just need to finish my senior year and get the hell out of Orange County.

"Tell me," He drawls so sexy it makes my core clench. That's new. I turn to face him again, this time with a cocked brow urging him to speak. "How is a woman who looks like you......" he trails off, his lips twisting as if he is searching for the right words. He clears his throat. "I mean, you are exquisitely beautiful, but I'm sure you know that." He pauses waiting for my reaction. I don't give him one. "Anyway, why are you on your own? Looking like the world has ended? A girl as pretty as you should never be without a smile." My heart flutters at his compliment, but I still don't give in. Like I said, I don't need the distraction, no matter how hot he is.

"Look, you can probably have any woman in this place. Probably most of the men too," I add, with a wave of my arms. "Why don't you go and hit on someone you actually have a chance with? An easy fuck which is more than likely what you are looking for. I'm not that girl, you are wasting your time. I just want to sit and drink in peace." His eyes narrow before his lips tip up in breathtaking smile, that leaves me momentarily stunned. There are no words to explain how attractive this man is.

"Beautiful and funny...just my type," He smirks, leaning in so close his hot breath fans my face. My breath hitches at his close proximity. "You're right. I could probably have any woman in here. It's not like I didn't notice the come fuck me eyes when I walked in. I don't do desperate. I can smell their desperation from here," A snort bursts from me on its own volition. Jesus, he may be gorgeous, but he's an arrogant bastard. "But you? You didn't so much as look at me until I approached you. Even then you barely spared me a glance," His emerald eyes bore into me making me squirm in my seat. Noticing he smirks. "I do like a challenge. I think I will take my chances and join you." He finishes, leaning back in his stool getting comfortable, he shoots me a wink. I roll my eyes, acting nonchalant even though I can feel my arousal in my panties. They are embarrassingly wet; I was sure by the time I leave here my shorts will be too. Not that I will ever admit it...something tells me this man doesn't need anything else to inflate his already oversized ego.

I eye him. Feeling confident, I cock my head with a smirk. "Beautiful, huh? Quite the charmer, aren't you?" He flashes an arrogant smirk not deterred by my words. "Maybe if I were a few more drinks in, I would have fallen for what I am sure is normally a bulletproof way to get a woman into bed. Unfortunately for you, I'm not. And I definitely will not fall for a little line like calling me beautiful." I shoot him condescending wink. He eyes me a beat before his head falls back on a laugh. I stare at him as he chuckles. If I wasn't so angry right now, I would probably enjoy his attention.

His eyes meet mine as his tongue traces his full bottom lip. My eyes dart to the movement, watching as he wets the perfect plump flesh. "Pessimism doesn't suit such a beautiful face." I groan as the bartender hands us our drinks – the green-eyed stranger sliding him some bills across the bar in return. He turns with a sigh. "Look, we obviously got off on the wrong foot. You probably get hit all the time and by the look on your face, it is the last thing you want. So, let's cut the shit and start over. I'm Nate." He thrusts his hand out for me to take. "I can leave you be, if that's what you really want? I just don't want to sit alone. And as much as you probably don't think you want it; something tells me you could use the company. What's your name, Blondie?"

A smile tugs at my lips. He is right. I was used to being hit on. Half the male population at my school in Seattle had hit on me to no avail. The boys I went to school with, they were immature, their sole purpose in life was to see how many girls they could sleep with by graduation. I wasn't going to be another notch on some boy's bedpost, so I steered clear, earning me the nickname 'Pruden'—a mix of prudish and Eden. They thought they were clever. I didn't care. When they eventually realized they wouldn't get anywhere with me they stayed away.

I take a sip of my drink before taking Nate's hand with a smile. "Eden. I apologize for being a bitch. It's been a bad day." He grins with a nod of his head.

"I know that feeling," His jaw ticks, a dark look in his eyes. "I just found out my ex of six years is engaged to the guy she cheated on me with." My mouth gapes in disbelief that anyone would want to cheat on him, before I let out a low whistle

"And I thought I was having a bad day. You definitely win."

He shrugs, waving me off. "Yeah, it was a shock for sure. But they are welcome to each other." He dismisses it like it isn't a big deal, but I don't miss the anger flashing in his eyes. "So, what happened to you? Boyfriend? Ex-boyfriend?" He licks his lips as his eyes rake over me, his gaze scorching my skin in ways I didn't know could happen. "Nah, not an ex. I can't imagine any guy lucky enough to have you would ever leave you. And if he did, he is an idiot." A laugh bubbles out of me and I shake my head in amusement.

"You can't help yourself, can you?"

He chuckles. "Not when there is a gorgeous lady involved. Sorry." He smiles sheepishly. "So, what is it, then? What is so bad?"

I eye him, debating what to tell this man. I can't say too much about my situation because it will give away my age. And since I am underage...with a fake ID...drinking in a bar, I don't need trouble, so I keep it simple. "It's just family stuff. Asshole fathers." I grumble.

Nate searches my face, over the top of his beer. Obviously noticing a shift in my mood, the tension in my body, he smiles. "How about we leave the deep stuff?"

I chuckle, feeling my body relax. "That's the best thing you have said since you walked in here."

He shifts his whole body to face me, caging me in with his muscular legs. His green eyes lock onto my blues as he leans into me. My pulse speeds up, breath hitching at his nearness. His throat bobs as he swallows his beer, my eyes track the movement. I want to run my tongue up and down his strong throat, taste him. As if sensing my thoughts, he smirks knowingly. I give my head an almost imperceptible shake, needing to gain some self-control.

"Tell me about yourself Eden? What do you do? How old are you?" he asks.

Again, I need to keep the answer simple, I will never see this guy again; he doesn't need to know I am repeating my senior year at high school, that I am only eighteen, in here with a fake ID. "I graduated in June. Twenty-one. What about you?"

An emotion flashes in his eyes, but before I get a chance to decipher it, he smiles, but this time it doesn't quite reach his eyes. "Twenty-eight and I'm an app and software developer." I freeze, not at his age but his job. What are the chances? He is in the same line of work as Declan. I'm not about to talk about *him though* so instead, I blurt.

"You are way too hot to be a techy guy."

He laughs, heartily before gently nudging my shoulder. "Now look who's flirting."

I shrug. "I doubt you are unaware of how attractive you are. Your ego is so big, I'm surprised you could get through the entrance." I jerk my head towards said entrance.

He chuckles harder. "I like you, Eden. Straight to the point, real, don't apologize for who you are. It's rare in people nowadays. Especially for people in Orange County." I bite my bottom lip; his eyes narrow in on the movement. Warmth spreads through my body, my stomach swirling in excitement. This reaction is foreign to me. I have never felt like this with a guy before. Ever.

Nate shifts his stool closer. I take a deep breath, his masculine scent invading all my senses, making me feel dizzy. "Do you live round here, Eden?"

"I do. For now," I croak out. He moves in closer - leaving hardly anything between us -his big body dwarfing mine. His hand drops to my bare thigh, my skin prickles when he draws small circles on my skin.

"Are you cold, Eden?" He asks huskily, his hot, minty breath fanning across my face. I swallow, shaking my head. He smiles. "You know. I've never done this sort of thing before," My brows furrow in confusion. "Never hit on a woman, I mean. I've never had too. I know I sound egotistical but it's the truth. They usually come to me," He shrugs, "But you? There is something about you, you're different."

I roll my eyes, even though his words are doing things to me. Mainly soaking my panties. "Another one of your pickup lines, Nate?"

"Nope. Just the truth. You can't tell me you don't feel this connection between us? Its electric." I search his face, only finding truth in his words. My gaze drops to my lap. He is right, there is a pull between us. I startle when his thick fingers grip my chin, lifting till I meet his eyes. The intensity in his has my breath hitching. "I want to see your gorgeous face." He slowly moves closer, so close his lips ghost mine. "I know you don't know me, and I don't know you. But I think you're really fucking sexy. I have never wanted to kiss anyone as bad as I want to kiss you. And as much as you think you don't want this..." His hand on my thigh moves higher, "I can tell you do. Your body gives you away. I can smell your arousal from here." He growls.

I pull my chin out of his grip, as my eyes widen in embarrassment. Can he smell my wet panties? Jesus, right now I wish I hadn't been a Pruden. I wish I were more experienced to deal with a guy like him. He raises a brow, daring me to deny what we both know to be the truth. He is turning me on. He knows it. I know it. I stare at him, neither confirming nor denying his accusation so he continues. "I can tell by your erratic breathing. The way goosebumps coat your soft skin. You're not cold, Eden. Your turned on," He winks smugly. "I have a talent for reading women." I clench my thighs at his words, my panties getting even wetter. I don't even want to think about the puddle I will be leaving on this stool.

I have kissed boys before, but they were just that. Boys. Nate is all man. I'm not experienced like other girls my age. I am still a virgin at eighteen. But somehow, I have gone from not wanting him to hit on me to wanting to do very naughty things with him. A stranger. I want his hand to travel higher, I want him to feel my wet panties. Hell, at this point I am about ready to let him take my virginity on this bar. I inwardly chuckle at the situation. Maybe I should do something for me. To be irresponsible. To fuck someone, I have only just met.

My tongue darts out to wet my dry lips. Nate's eyes follow the movement. I lean in, my lips resting against his. I can taste the beer. Taste the man. "And maybe I have a talent for reading assholes." I pull back, smirking with a wink.

He barks out a laugh, the sound going straight between my legs, "Touché, Eden. But don't kid yourself, you could cut the sexual tension with a knife right now." I snicker. He is right, you can. It would be so easy to lose myself in him right now. Maybe I should? I do want to forget, after all and something tells me Nate could make me forget everything.

My cell buzzes breaking me from my thoughts. I snatch it off the bar, groaning at the name on the screen. A message from Declan, demanding I get home now. I furiously type a message back before pulling up my Uber app.

"Everything okay?" Nate asks. I click on my ride and push my cell into my shorts pocket before turning to Nate.

"Yeah, I gotta get back. Family stuff." I shrug. Pushing to a stand, I get ready to make my exit. "Thanks for the drink Nate." I don't give him a chance to respond, turning on my heel, I make my way to the door. Just as I step outside, a big hand wraps around my elbow. I turn, jaw clenched - ready to shout at whoever dared to touch me - when my eyes lock with emerald ones that have somehow become familiar.

"At least let me wait with you. It's getting dark, you don't know what weirdos are about," Nate rasps.

I cock a brow. "You mean apart from you?"

He chuckles, shaking his head as he leads me to the sidewalk. After a long beat of silence, Nate speaks. "I know I said I wouldn't hit on you, but can I at least get your number?" I look up at him with a smirk.

"Your tenacity is admirable Nate."

He smiles, something that looks a lot like determination flashes in his eyes. Grabbing my hand, he pulls me towards the alley at the side of the building. I should be afraid. Should scream for help. But I don't do any of that as excitement course through me. "Where are we going?" He doesn't answer but flashes me a smile. Coming to an abrupt stop, he backs me up until my back hits the wall, his big arms caging me in.

"Tell me to stop if you don't want me to kiss you?" he whispers, searching my face. My head spins, this is all happening so fast. But as I look at him, I know I don't want him to stop. I want him to kiss me.

Before I can stop myself; I wrap my arms around his neck, yanking his head down to me. His lips crash on mine, taking my breath away. In this moment, with his mouth on mine, my whole-body sparks alive in a way it has never before. Nothing has ever felt so freeing as his mouth on mine. I never want it to stop. Nate devours my mouth like a starved man, finally having a meal. His tongue darts out, seeking entrance to my mouth. I give it him, moaning when his hot tongue meets mine. His hands move down my legs, wrapping round my thighs as he lifts me like I weigh nothing.

My eyes fly open as I feel his dick harden. It only takes seconds before I am grinding against the hard length, losing all my inhibitions. Who am I right now? This isn't me. I moan, at the feel of him and briefly wonder how he would feel inside me. I internally roll my eyes; I might be acting completely different to usual but it's not like I'm actually going to fuck him against this wall. He groans as his hand snakes between us. Through the fabric of my denim shorts he rubs my swollen clit. The feel of his hand there and the material rubbing against me has me gasping. Shit, if he keeps this up maybe I am going to fuck him against this wall.

Shaking the thoughts away. I push into his hand, chasing the friction I desperately need. He chuckles against my mouth, the sound vibrating through my body, shooting straight to my pussy. My orgasm builds, taking me higher and higher only to disappear when Nate pulls his hand and lips away. Frustration courses through me as I pant, trying to catch my breath, He smirks before his lips move to my neck, kissing and nibbling the sensitive flesh.

"You are so fucking sexy, Eden," he murmurs thickly, causing me to shiver. His hand comes up, unhooking my arms. Never breaking eye contact, he guides my hand down to the hardness in his pants. "Look what you have done to me. I'm so fucking hard for you." My eyes widen, he isn't lying. He is rock hard, and big. Very fucking big.

Dropping my hand, I slide down his body, a moan escapes as I graze his hard cock. I clear my throat. "My ride will be here," I chew on my lip, realization setting in at what I have just done. His eyes search mine.

"At least let me get your number?" he rasps; his tone almost pleading.

I smile, I shouldn't give it to him, but I want to. "Sure, why not?"

He grins, pulling his cell out of his pocket. He hands it to me, my thumbs race across the screen as I input my number before handing it back. Seconds later my cell buzzes in my pocket. I fish it out, frowning when a number a don't recognize flashes on the screen. I look to Nate who smirks back at me.

"Just making sure you didn't give me a random number." I roll my eyes before starting back to the main sidewalk. Feeling confident, I spin.

"I would never do that to someone who kisses as good as you." I wink.

An arrogant smirk spreads across his face, "If you think that was good, just you wait till I get you in my bed." The confidence in his voice has my cheeks heating. I have no doubt this man, knows how to please a woman. "Don't worry, Eden. I assure you will enjoy every second of it." I shake my head before spinning on my heel and rushing to my Uber which is now waiting. Jumping in the back seat, I pull the door only to find it won't move. My gaze snaps up to find Nate holding it. He crouches so he is eye level with me. My pulse races up as he moves in and kisses my cheek. I squeeze my eyes shut as my skin tingles from his touch.

"'Night, Eden." he whispers seductively.

"Night, Nate." I croak in a voice I don't recognize. His eyes flash triumphantly. Like he knows something I don't. Pushing to a stand, he gently closes the door. The car peels away, I fall against the seat, releasing a harsh breath. I know full well nothing good can come from seeing him again. I lied to him. About my age. About college. I should block his number. But even as the thought passes, I know I won't. I want him. And I have never wanted a man.

I don't need the distraction, but if I am going to have one, Nate will be the perfect one.

Printed in Great Britain
by Amazon